Slinger Sanchez
Running Gun

A NOVEL BY
BRUCE GLIKIN

AMBER FIELDS PUBLISHING COMPANY

HOUSTON, TEXAS

With the exception of those names that are easily recognizable in running circles, all the characters in this book are real in the mind of the author only.

Copyright© Bruce Glikin

Library of Congress Number : 98-071234

ISBN Number: 0-9663458 - 0 - 0

Amber Fields Publishing website address:
www.amberfields.com

Printed in the United States of America on acid-free paper.

FIRST EDITION

Acknowledgements

The most difficult task in the preparation of 'Slinger' was neither in the word-smithing, nor the formatting. The dilemma was in composing a list of names to thank. People whose generosity both past and present, would take an entire book to describe. These are the people that my forgetful mind has remembered. Forgive me for those I've forgotten:

Stewart and Shirley Alexander, Eric Andell, Bill Anthony, Don Baxter, Sister Mary Brendan, Paul and Madeline Bunch, Amby Burfoot, Clyde Burleson, Justin and Stacy Chaston, David and Kate Chester, Marshall Cohen, Joe Doggett, Joe Fleming, Glenn and Susie Good, Robert Gray, Laura Greenbaum, Leonard Hilton, Paula Hitchcock, Rabbi Robert Kahn, Al Lawrence, Hersh and Molly Levitt, George and Disa Lyon, Samantha Mackenzie, Carol McLatchie, Susan Middleton, Juan Palomo, Sherry Peterson, Tom McBrayer, Jerry Parker, Lance Phegley, Scott Phegley, Bill Rodgers, Lori Schaffer and Bob Pierce, Mark Scheid, Deborah Shetlar, Don Slocomb, Chuck Stein, Bill and Debbie Smith, Sean and Anne Smith, Mack Stewart, Cheryl Wacher, Sean Wade, Jon Warren, Jeff Wells, Dave and Anne Wittman , Blair Zimmerman.

Special thanks to Mary Jo Gillaspy for her artistic input.

And a very special acknowledgment to Jim McLatchie, a man whose passion for runners is unmatched.

And finally, thanks to my mother and father, angels possessing a sweetness that cannot be put into words. Cherubs at ages 80 and 90, with a clarity of thought and judgment that I am envious.

"If I had to describe 'Slinger' in one word, I'd have to say riveting. I couldn't put it down. Bruce Glikin understands what it's really like in the world of top-level running—the work, the pressures, the satisfactions, the camaraderie. As I followed Jesse into his major meets, I felt the nervous sensation I used to get before big races. 'Slinger' is packed with excitement, heartache, pathos, drama, and surprise. I loved it!"— *Jeff Wells, Former American record holder in the Marathon, winner of six major marathons, and four-time All-American*

"Athletes' stories have never appealed to me, but by the time I finished reading the account of Slinger's first race, I found myself with a lump in my throat and tears in my eyes. This is powerful writing." — *Juan R. Palomo (The Salt Journal, USA TODAY)*

"If you love running, you'll love 'Slinger Sanchez Running Gun'. I read it straight through. It's simply the best running novel ever written." — *Sean Wade (2:10 marathoner, New Zealand Olympian)*

"The realistic unique characters and the riveting sequences will engross both the runner and non-runner alike. And somewhere along the way, the reader is reminded of what track, and specifically sports in general, were meant to be." — *Jon Warren, Men's Distance Coach, Rice University; U.S. Olympic Trials participant, steeplechase, marathon*

"An accurate character portrayal of a world class middle distance runner, 'Slinger' Sanchez is the kind of runner that every runner dreams about being on long runs." — *Dave Wittman, 1996 U.S. Olympics Trials participant, Men's 1500 meters*

BRUCE GLIKIN

Slinger Sanchez
Running Gun

Bruce Glikin was born in Englewood, New
Jersey in 1949 but moved to Houston, Texas
at the age of four. He graduated from high
school in 1967, and enrolled in the University
of Arizona where he received a Bachelor's of
Arts Degree in 1971 with a major in Journal-
ism. He has been running for over 30 years,
his strong suit the marathon. Seven of his
twelve marathons were in the 2:40 range, his
personal best time of 2:39:11. He was also a
National Age Group Silver Medalist in the
two-mile and the steeplechase. He is a member of the Houston Harriers, and currently
classifies himself as a recreational jogger.

Chapter 1

"First call for the men's 800 meter final."

Jesse Sanchez jogged slowly toward the entrance of Hayward Stadium as the announcer's words boomed over the public address system. His stomach roiled and he covered his mouth. It heaved again as he fought the urge to vomit. A roar from the crowd inside the stadium followed. The noise jolted him, his runaway heart kicking frantically. It seemed to be banging in his chest like a big rock, fighting to break out.

From the corner of his eye he saw a streak. A towheaded kid on a dirt bike was zooming straight at him. Sanchez cut left. The youngster did the same. Jesse could feel the boy's elbow graze him as they missed crashing by inches. The youngster powered forward without missing a beat, over the sidewalk and on to the street.

"Watch it, kid!"

The youngster raised his right arm and extended his middle finger. "Fuck you." He grinned. It was a nasty sneer. The smirk remained etched on his face as he pedaled across the campus, hand held high.

Little son of a bitch, Jesse thought. That was all he needed. Some snot-nosed kid trashing the most important night of his life. In less than fifteen minutes he was scheduled to run in the finals of the 2000 United States Olympic Trials. The men's eight hundred meters. Sanchez's black eyes shot daggers. He gritted his teeth. He was nervous, nauseous and pissed. His brain was addled.

He continued jogging around the stadium. At the athlete's entrance he was waved through by an official. As he entered the stadium the starter's gun cracked. A roar from the crowd erupted as eight black sprinters powered their way out of the blocks. Jesse glanced at the packed stands. He nervously ran his hand through his long black hair, tethered in the back by a white cloth band. The ponytail swung when he ran, like a horse's silky tail. Both his mother and his coach had given him a wrath of grief about the long hair. But he'd be damned if he would cut it. Same thing about the tiny diamond stud earring in his right ear, and the red-fisted tattoo below his hip. The tattoo was visible where his shorts split. A defiant symbol that he'd had inscribed when he was twelve years old. It was right after his old man had left for good. The night the drunken asshole had beaten his mother to a bloody pulp. He remembered the futility of trying to defend his mother. And the feeling of getting smashed in the jaw by the back of his father's hand. His old man had big hands, just like Jesse did. The blow had knocked him into a sheet rock wall. When he hit the floor his mouth was bleeding and he was unconscious. When he came-to he saw his father storming out the door. That was the last image he had of him.

As Jesse jogged, his fists were clenched his knuckles protruding like white stones.

Fists. Jesse understood them. The red one tattooed below his hip was inspired by stories of Che Guevara. He had heard stories about him when he was a little boy. The Communism stuff didn't mean anything to him at the time. He just liked the fact that the Latino was a rebel, afraid of nobody. An outlaw with boulder-sized cojones who laid his life on the line for the poor. He was a defiant bastard. Jesse felt an immediate kinship to him when he heard the stories.

Like Guevara, his life had been a fight, as was all this Olympic Trials hoopla. This wasn't a celebration of athletics, he thought. This was war. The trials had been misery. The most agonizing torture he had ever been through. Even worse than the times with his old man. And the past day had been the

2

worst. His mind clicked into reverse as he replayed its events. It started early that morning.

A series of high pitch staccato howls shattered the calm of a quiet night. Following the sixth screech, he reached across his chest. With the tip of his right forefinger he probed the watch crystal. He felt a flat button at the crystal's base and pushed. On the seventh screech the screaming stopped.

He remained on his back, eyes open, the cramped dorm room as dark as a pocket. His breathing was steady, but several beats quicker than his normal resting rate of 36. Sometimes his pulse dipped into the low 30's, on days when he was well rested and under little stress.

But the previous night had been a sleepless one. He was consumed with anxiety. The culprit was a foot race, a contest to be staged that evening. It was a run that would be the defining moment of his career, not to mention his life. It was a moment he had secretly dreamt of since adolescence, a time that was neither fulfilling nor happy.

The race was 800 meters, a two-lap tour of a 400-meter oval. A distance that was a few feet shy of a half mile. It was the men's finals of the U.S. Olympic Trials 800, a contest to determine the country's three slots in the upcoming Olympic Games.

The metric half-mile was two revolutions of merciless burning, a war of sinew and nerves. It would be a frantic over-distance sprint of flying elbows and gnashing spikes. It was a race where runners never caught their breath, a battle where intuition and reaction devoured planning and intellect.

One couldn't really plan an 800. Too many things that could go wrong. Yet it was a race that demanded planning. Even the slightest of tactical errors would prove fatal.

Sanchez lay still for a lengthy period of time before reaching to his right. He fingered the switch of a table lamp and turned it. The peanut-shaped bulb threw off a fulvous glow under the mottled white shade. He sat up, rubbed his eyes, lifted back the sheets, and stepped down. The tile floor felt cold to his bare feet. He walked gingerly to a hard-backed metal chair where he'd dropped his sweats. He dressed quickly. Then he sat on the chair, and began lacing up his Nike Air Max's. The trainers were battered and worn. Close out shoes that he'd picked up at a running expo for half price. Jesse had put over two thousand miles on them, the uppers shredding, the soles worn. The mileage was more than four times what the shoe companies recommended before replacement. But at a hundred and fifty dollars a pair, that was not an option.

Jesse ran high mileage, sometimes up to a hundred and forty miles a week during his buildup phase. By the company's guidelines, he should be replacing shoes at least once a month. But he helped support his mother and brother. At the end of each month, when bills came due, there was rarely money left over.

With the 'right' coach, Sanchez would have had all the shoes he needed. The athletic companies did that. Supplying the 'right' coaches with equipment for their elite runners. But his coach was Kevin McClanahan. And 'Right' and 'McClanahan' were never confused as synonyms.

The athletic companies viewed McClanahan as a pariah. He was intractable, contentious, outspoken, and foul-mouthed. His words cut right to the bone. Corporate executives labeled him a loose cannon. He had opinions on everything. From marketing and promotional tactics, to disbursement of athletic funds. And he trumpeted his thoughts in public forums on his Internet site. His web page garnered thousands of hits. During big meets his 'in-box' was flooded with e-mails.

The athletic companies despised the Scotsman. But that paled to the rancor of track and field powers. McClanahan had gone straight for the jugular. He cursed both the North American Track Federation (NATF) and the International Track Federation (ITF), for their failure to promote track and field. For

4

their abuse of funds. And most vocally for their selective drug enforcement. Public confrontations with NATF President Joseph Nixon, and ITF President Primo Magiano, had gotten nasty. McClanahan minced no words as he blasted them at public meetings and press forums. The track czars had responded by setting their public relations jackals on McClanahan. They painted him as a self-serving, foul-mouthed, contentious hypocrite. The worst offender of the very sins he linked to others. Rumors were rife that both Magiano and Nixon were initiating legal action against McClanahan. Just waiting to pounce. McClanahan was undaunted. He pressed on. His acerbic words were read by a growing legion of dedicated athletes and followers on his Internet-site. Close sources kept him privy to behind the scenes-action. Movements that evolved with shocking predictability. The pattern was always the same. Both U.S. and international officials turned their heads when bankable 'stars' tested positive. With like consistency, they came down on, and punished, 'undesirables.'

Jesse Sanchez's dilemma was straightforward. He ran for Kevin McClanahan. It was a catch-22 that meant no shoes, no shorts, no singlets. Nor anything else from the running shoe companies. But Jesse felt no bitterness toward the Scotsman. His difficult youth had matured him beyond his years. He understood that with every gift came a price, one that was often not worth paying. Besides, leading up to the trials, he'd done nothing to justify receiving free merchandise. Jesse Sanchez was a runner without portfolio.

Coming into the trials he was unknown. He was a mystery runner, an enigmatic 800-meter specialist who had qualified on the latest possible date.

The qualifying effort came on a Friday night all-comers meet in Houston, Texas, on the Rice University Track. It was an unlikely time and place for an Olympic hopeful to make a bid. But the license to participate was even less shocking than what he'd done at the trials. Going into the evening's 800 meter final, he was undefeated. He'd won all his heats running from the front, his 1:43.2 the fastest qualifying time.

His efforts set the rumor mill churning, and his avoidance of the press stoked the flames of suspicion even hotter. Mystery men didn't just show up to the trials, and do what he had done. No one knew him. The mavens of track and field were whispering. And with Kevin McClanahan his coach, the whispers had grown louder.

But Sanchez was unaware of the controversy swirling around him. He had intentionally isolated himself, avoiding the press. His days were spent in his dorm room reading books and listening to music. He hadn't read a newspaper, listened to a radio, or watched television since coming to Eugene. He wanted it that way. It was crucial not to get caught up in the media circus surrounding the trials. He was focused on his running and nothing else. It was essential not to lose focus.

He was going to compete at 7:00 p.m. that coming night in Hayward Field. And in front of over fourteen thousand screaming track and field fans, the most knowledgeable track and field fans in the United States, he would run the race that would define his life.

He'd done the work and he had the speed. He had turned a 200-meter sprint in 21.1, and 400 meters in 43.9. It was blazing quickness for a half-miler. Sprinting talent that was unheard of outside of the Juantorena's, Coes, Ovetts, Aouitas, Morcellis and Kipketer's. An exclusive fraternity of the greatest middle distance runners in history.

His fast twitch fibers were probably inherited from his biological father. He was a big white dude of Irish descent, a guy who had played high school football and ran the hundred. But Jesse had a lot more than raw speed. He had endurance and strength, the ability to run long distances at an unrelenting pace.

The distance gift probably came from his mother, a woman whose ancestors had lived at altitude. They came from a small village just outside of Cuernavaca, Mexico. Jesse was also born at altitude, in Taos, New Mexico. His mother always remembered him running. Sometimes when she took him and his brother Jose to the ski basin, he would run at heights approaching 12,000 feet. She had no idea it was laying the foundation for a world class cardiovascular system.

A decade later Jesse Sanchez was a complete package. A hungry runner who had made it to the 800- meter finals of the 2000 U.S. Olympic Trials. It was time to remove the wrapper.

Chapter 2

As the sprinters finished their race, Jesse walked to the warmup track. As he reached the smaller track he dropped his athletic bag, and sat on the rubberized surface. He lay on his back and lifted both legs straight up. As he stretched he shut his eyes, hoping to calm his nervousness and nausea. He tried to focus on his upcoming race, but his mind was spinning. With the din of the crowd ringing in his ears, his thoughts returned to that morning.

When he stepped outside his dorm, a gentle breeze filtered his silky hair. He reckoned the temperature was somewhere in the 50's, a welcome change from the sultry climate he'd left behind just days earlier. The summers in Houston weren't tough to train in. They were hell.

Typically the temperature was in the 90's, from the beginning of June until the end of September. With matching humidity, it made Bayou City a festering steam bath, a place where runners slogged through workouts drenched in sweat.

As Sanchez walked from the dorm toward the street, thoughts turned to his childhood. He remembered boarding a bus from Taos to Houston and the ensuing ride across mountains and prairie. The move was followed by the desertion of Jesse's biological father, who had also fathered his brother Jose. He never married Carmen Sanchez. She never took his name. Sometimes when Jesse was on runs by himself, recovery efforts that were supposed to be easy, he thought of his father. The rage would build, and he'd start running faster. The anger would often propel him to race-pace running. It was a self-defeating exercise that sometimes led to physical breakdown. When that demon drove him, he would fantasize taking on his father now. As an adult, he imagined how he would have defended his mother against his father. Sometimes he imagined killing the cabron, beating him to death with his bare hands. The gutless drunk rarely struck his younger brother Jose, Jesse remembered. Probably because Jose was retarded and never talked back. When his father started beating up on his mother and Jesse, Jose would run into the bedroom he shared with Jesse. He would bury his head under the pillows, and weep like a baby. His whole body would shake. When the beatings ended, Jesse would climb into bed with Jose and hold him. Though bruised and bleeding, he'd whisper to his younger brother not to worry. He would take care of him.

But even worse than the beatings, Jesse carried the scars of his father's wounding words. He had constantly taunted Jesse. He told him he would never amount to anything. It was the same message he got from his classmates. In school they labeled him 'medio-pelo' or 'half breed'. He was neither white nor Hispanic, a tall, painfully thin boy, with copper-colored skin, dark eyes, and Anglo features.

Carmen Sanchez would have been content to stay in Taos, New Mexico. But a single mother, with two young boys to take care of, has few options. Houston had an abundance of work, unlike Taos where it was largely seasonal.

Remaining in Taos would have been a blessing for Jesse in his development as a runner. But how was Carmen Sanchez to have known that her son had that kind of ability? And even if she knew, how would she have fed him and her younger son Jose? A boy whose mental capacity would preclude him from ever holding a job on his own.

So the Houston summers, never ending days of heat and humidity, which began in April and lasted until October, was a torture that Jesse Sanchez quietly endured. He accepted the steamy tropics with a stoic complacency, never griping about the conditions he despised. Jesse rarely complained about anything. His mother's burden had made him that way. He understood what real hardship meant.

Carmen Sanchez assumed that Jesse ran as a form of escape, a quiet boy whom she knew was filled with anger. She never realized Jesse's secret ambitions. Until she met McClanahan, she never knew he had talent.

The Scotsman had discovered Jesse as a fluke. It was less than two weeks after Sanchez arrived in Houston. The gangly fourteen-year-old was running along Hillcroft, near the Southwest Freeway. McClanahan watched from his battered MG as Jesse ran. His trained eye was quickly mesmerized by the ease of movement and fluid motion that drove the long-legged, spindly youngster along. In that gentle stride he saw an untapped potential of wealth, a once in a lifetime possibility.

He watched the boy run for almost two months, before approaching him one afternoon on a run of his own. The Scotsman ran along side Jesse, the two matching each other stride for stride. They flew over pavement at a six minute per mile pace. McClanahan was even more impressed that the boy wasn't even breathing hard. He was running next to a gifted youngster.

The two bonded quickly, and McClanahan arranged a meeting with Carmen Sanchez. He told Jesse's mother that he trained a group of runners, some national and world class, at the Rice Track on Mondays and Wednesdays. He offered to provide Jesse with transportation and free coaching. His only requirement was that Sanchez worked hard.

Carmen Sanchez was initially suspicious of the Scotsman, as she was of all men. It was not an epiphany that changed her mind, but the passage of time. After Jesse began working with the Scot, it took her almost a year before she came to trust him. Witnessing the love and devotion that he displayed for his own wife sealed her acceptance. Soon her trust became implicit.

She came to understand that beneath the gruff Scotsman's gnarly exterior, beat a heart. Kevin McClanahan became, for all practical purposes, Jesse Sanchez's surrogate father.

Sanchez had been working with McClanahan for almost eight years. In that time he had developed a trust in the Scotsman that was implicit. No matter how challenging the workouts he ran them. He had come to learn that running had no shortcuts. That consistent work was the only answer to success. That to run on a world class level meant being able to push through pain. Both psychological and physical. He understood that was the real reason the Africans runners were so great. Accustomed to hardship and difficult lives, they trained in a manner that Americans never attempted. They accepted the fact that injury was a by-product of high level training and was unavoidable. When one occurred they dealt with it. A process that every great runner went through. Jesse was determined to become that type of runner. Like a Kenyan, but even better. He felt that McClanahan had provided him the tools. But he understood his responsibility. At the moment of truth, it would be only him.

Sanchez had observed runners whose coaches were nothing like McClanahn. They were quick to ease pressure when their athletes suffered stress. When their runners were fatigued, had a niggling injury, or were experiencing difficulty in their personal lives, they were quick to console them with soothing words. And then scale back their workloads. Jesse had even witnessed coaches who encouraged their runners to skip workouts, when things didn't 'feel' right. But he had come to learn that, that type of 'kindness' was disingenuous. A brutal disservice to the runners receiving it. The motive was often in the coach's self- interest. A thinly veiled attempt to maintain clients. Those were the men who often charged the highest monthly coaching fees.

Jesse had witnessed his share of runners victimized by the kindness trap. The failures that followed were inevitable. In times of extreme stress, which was what racing was all about,

Sanchez learned that runners repeat their workout behavior. The ones with the proper preparation adapt to race stress. Those who have been coddled, crumble.

Jesse had also learned, that equally devastating to the competitive runner, was the mixing of programs. Those who tried to pull from more than one coach were rarely successful. Like a kitchen full of chefs contributing to the same dish.

The feast that was Jesse Sanchez had been carefully prepared. Now it was time to sample the fare. Subjective pallets would not be permitted. The judge would be a clock, a magistrate of unparalleled fairness.

"Jesse, can you speak for a moment?" The female voice was gravelly.

Jesse opened his eyes. He sat up. Staring at him on the other side of the warmup track was a dumpy, closely shorn, raven-haired woman. She had a dusky mole on her left cheek. A single, long dark hair grew out of it. She was clutching a tape recorder in her right hand. The woman was wearing frumpy looking baggy jeans, mud-brown hiking boots that were scuffed, and a man's denim work shirt. She was a tough looking, tough sounding woman, Jesse thought. She had been bugging him since the early rounds for an interview.

"No. Not now."

"Just give me a minute, Sanchez. I just want to….."

"Please leave me alone. I've got a race."

"I just want to know…."

"No. Not now, damnit!"

The woman smirked. Then she shut off her tape recorder. She turned and walked away slowly, the sardonic grin still pasted on her doughy face. She wondered if Sanchez had a clue. Did he know the buzz? What the press and the athletes were saying about him behind his back? As she headed toward the grandstands, Jesse lay back on the warmup track and shut his eyes. A myriad of nightmarish snippets from his past went through his head. Then his thoughts returned to that morning.

He was jogging from his dorm across the campus, aware of his ease of breath as he ran. The air was fresh and sweet, bathed by the perfumed scent of lush flora. Eugene was resplendent with roses the size of plates, and majestic trees which shimmered in the breeze. Shockingly green carpets of thick grass blanketed the fertile Willamette Valley. It was part of another world. A magical oasis, light years removed from the swampland he'd left behind. It was a distance runner's dream. As his plane had hovered over Eugene, he was stunned by the lushness of the Willamette Valley below. It was how he'd envisioned Ireland, the land of his biological father's ancestors, a place whose rich blood mixed his open veins.

He wondered if Eugene held luck for him. It was the track and field mecca of North America. It was a place where the most knowledgeable track fans on the continent would congregate on a moment's notice, to witness a time trial or a workout. Steve Prefontaine, Mary Decker Slaney, and Alberto Salazar had all called it home, along with a host of other American distance greats.

If Eugene was a distance runner's dream, then Houston was the nightmare. The nation's fourth largest city was the tropics, an urban sprawl of tar and cement. It was a landscape cut by snaking waterways. The rivulets were labeled bayous, repositories that were nothing but open sewers. The fetid waterways were pocked with sewage treatment plants. Foul smelling wastewater facilities that overlooked the effluence in its channel-bound path. Along the banks of the bayous twisted miles of asphalt hike and bike trails, less than idyllic training grounds for serious runners.

Eugene was a Mecca for distance runners. And it revered them. Houston didn't. Bayou City idolized size. So it only stood to reason that muscular sprinters, with their sculpted torsos and bulging quadriceps, were the runners of choice. Jesse Sanchez, at 6'2", 148 pounds, hardly fit the mold. Untrained eyes did not see, or understand, a body that was almost all muscle. One that possessed the cardiovascular system of a gazelle. All they saw was a loser. The skinny guy in the comic book ad that gets sand kicked in his face.

As Sanchez jogged he felt tight, not unlike all his early morning runs. The tightness was a combination of his preliminary races, and past years of running. Though a young man, he'd racked up thousands of miles of running. The pounding had begun to take its toll on his joints, tendons, and muscles. A regular stretching routine may have benefited him. But like most distance runners, Jesse hated to stretch. Sanchez would rather run ten miles than stretch ten minutes.

As his jog slowly accelerated into a run he broke a sweat. Soon all his body parts were behaving properly. As he ran he reflected on the races he'd run leading up to the final. The 800-meter prelims had gone smoothly. The customary nagging of his left Achilles was still there. And a tad of soreness in the same side hamstring, a place where the tendon inserts just beneath the buttock. But besides that, his body felt good.

Pain was something Sanchez had learned to embrace, not run from. Every runner has aches and pains, he reasoned. The trick was to recognize the difference between normal discomfort and acute pain. The type that signals an existing or developing injury.

He had come to understand that all seasoned distance runners are extraordinarily in touch with their bodies. Like fine tuned machines they know when something's not right. The problem is, they're often lax in addressing their afflictions. Sanchez was like that. Often times he'd try to run through acute pain. He feared the consequences of a missed workout, even more than the repercussions of an impending injury.

Less than thirty minutes into his run, as Sanchez moved toward Hayward Field, daylight softly lit the Hayward Field Track. He jogged along the sidewalk leading into the track stadium, turned at an open gate, and continued to the track. It was a world class facility left open to the public twenty- four hours a day. It said a lot to Sanchez about the mentality of the community, a place that encouraged runners of all levels.

In Houston it wasn't like that. Houston Tech had two excellent facilities, an outdoor track and an indoor facility. But both were off limits to the public. It was a curious circumstance at a public university, one that was frequented by some of the finest sprinters and field men in track history.

Rice University was a private institution that also forbade the public. But the small university, which had produced some of America's greatest marathon runners, —Jeff Wells, John Lodwick, Marty Froehlich, and Sean Wade—usually looked the other way. Remindful of its past, it seldom cracked down on the harmless interlopers who cruised its private tartan.

The only other facilities readily available to unaffiliated runners were public school tracks, and an asphalt oval in Memorial Park. But they were hardly the types of places where serious runners sought to train. They were patchwork venues of rutted cinder or cracked-asphalt. Spots where debilitating injuries were mishaps just waiting to happen.

As Sanchez stepped on to the track he ran clockwise, against the normal flow of traffic that races were run. Though early in the morning, there were already a number of runners on the rubberized surface. In the outside lanes where he jogged were runners in warm-ups and tights. They were businessmen, homemakers and students. People who lived in Eugene and liked to begin their day with a run.

On the inside lanes were the more serious runners, immersed in intense interval sessions. Runners of all ages and both genders were participating in the intervals, some talented, others not.

They were hammering out a series of pre-determined distances, with pre-determined breaks, referred to as intervals.

Technically the break, whether timed or not, was the real interval. But the term was a catchall phrase, usually including the running part or 'effort.'

The timed repeats are usually run in groups. They separate joggers from racers. Intervals are bursts of hell followed by heavy breathing. Runners who can tolerate them usually progress. Those who don't, never reach their potential.

As Sanchez moved past the grandstand, he envisioned the coming evening. He felt a queasy feeling in his stomach and his legs were heavy. A myriad of negative thoughts bombarded his mind. He continued off the track, and out the stadium, as he headed back toward his dorm. The worst part of a race was the time leading up to it. When sleep was coveted but seldom came. Sanchez hadn't slept a wink the previous night. His mind played over and over the coming race.

As Sanchez approached his dorm his run slowed from a jog to a walk. He shuffled the final half-block leading to the building. His legs felt like stone as he moved and he was exhausted. He would take a shower, go out for breakfast, and try and force down food for which he had no appetite. Then he'd return to his dorm, crawl back into bed, and try to sleep.

But Sanchez had no illusions. He was wired with anxiety and fear, conditions that would make sleep difficult if not impossible. It was almost twelve hours leading up to his race, a time frame that would seem like twelve years. The day would culminate in a bloody battle. A war in which eight men would fight and three survive.

Chapter 3

"Gonna' run again from the front, Sanchez?"

The words stopped Jesse's daydream. He opened his eyes and sat up. He turned in the direction of the voice and stared. On the outside of the chain link fence separating the warmup track from the fans, was a goofy looking, freckled-faced kid, with a bulbous nose. He was clad in knee length plaid shorts, and black high-top sneakers bound with pink laces. His T-shirt read, "KILL GOD, KILL YOUR PARENTS, KILL YOURSELF."A Dodgers cap was pulled backwards on his egg-shaped head. Jesse didn't answer. He picked up his athletic bag and moved to the other side of the track.

"You're gonna' get the shit kicked out of you, if you run like that."

Jesse glared defiantly and pointed his finger. The young-ster, recognizing the madness in Sanchez's eyes, turned and ran.

Nothing had gone well the past day and night, Jesse thought. Almost nothing. Except one thing. He grinned. Perfect white teeth flashed like pearls.

It had been just few minutes before five p.m. that evening when three loud raps on his door was followed by silence.

"Yeah?"

"Are ya' gonna' open the fuckin' door, or am I gonna' have to kick it down?"

The voice had a deep timbre, masculine and direct. The accent was Scottish, thick enough to be cut with a knife.

"Kick it down. Because I'm too tired to get out of bed."

"If yer' too tired to get yer' ass out of bed, then ya' better not run tonight. I didn't fly across the fuckin' country to watch ya' run like a donkey."

Sanchez got up, moved toward the door, and opened it. Standing in the hallway was a tall, lean, middle age-male, all angles and planes. He was about Sanchez's height and build, mid-fifties, but with the carriage of a man much younger. A snow-white beard blanketed sunken cheeks, setting off an unblemished, but time-weathered visage. The features were chiseled and sturdy, lighted by liquid brown eyes. They possessed a clarity that spoke of unwavering character. They were firm eyes that shone with honesty, but whose twinkle spoke of devilment and misbehavior.

"I thought you weren't coming."

"Surprise." McClanahan gently cuffed Sanchez's cheek with an open hand. Then he stepped inside the dorm room and Sanchez shut the door behind him. The Scot continued to the hard-backed chair by Sanchez's bed, sat, and propped his feet up on the bed.

"Where did you get the money to fly here?"

"Hit the trifecta last night."

"You're kidding?"

"Noooo. I wouldn't shit ya'. Picked 'em one, two, three. Third bugger in the first race nosed out the fourth by a pubic hair. Paid $650 bucks."

"Whoa!"

Sanchez knew McClanahan was leveling. The Scotsman had a penchant for betting races. Dogs, horses, cockroaches, and humans. Any species that ran without battery or motor.

"I guess you got the results of my prelims?"

"Yup. Picked 'em up on the net. Motherfuckers must have been dawdling. Don't expect that in the finals. They'll be puttin' down the hammer."

"I know that. They're holding back."

McClanahan stroked his beard. "Ya look like shit, Slinger."

18

"Thanks. Coming from you, that's a compliment."

"What's buggin' ya? That time of the month?"

Sanchez gazed down at the floor. He shuffled his feet. He fingered his earring. "I don't know. I guess I'm nervous...Maybe a little scared."

"Afraid of getting' yer ass kicked?"

"Probably."

"Then don't run. That'll get ya' back to Houston unde-feated. How many assholes can say they went undefeated in the trials?"

A thin smile curled on Sanchez's lips. He sat on the bed and slumped back against the frame. He gazed at McClanahan.

"How do I run this thing?"

"First put one foot down. And then the other. And then keep movin' them buggers back and forth, as fast as ya' can, until ya've made it around that circle twice."

"Seriously. How do you want me to run this thing?"

"How do I want ya' to run this thing? How do yooo want to run the motherfucker? I can't get out there and do it for ya.'"

"Don't be a pendejo. This is the biggest race of my life. You're my coach, and I need your help."

"Ya' don't need shit. Yer ready."

"So why did you come in here?"

"To let ya' know yer buying me dinner tonight."

"I'm broke."

"Better think of somethin''.

McClanahan got up and walked to the door. He opened it. The he turned around slowly and faced Sanchez. "Run from the front. Ya' don't want to get boxed."

Sanchez felt a chill go down his spine. McClanahan had read his mind. It was exactly the type of race that he'd envi-sioned running, but was fearful of attempting. He'd run from the front in the prelims. But this was the final. And the prelims and the final were light years apart.

Running from the front had its distinct advantages. It minimized the chances of being tripped or boxed in, horrors, which plagued all middle and long distance track runners.

In the mile, 5,000 meters and 10,000, a runner in a bad position, 'boxed in' early by his competitors, could generally work his way back into a better position. He would move up in the pack as openings occurred, as the race progressed. But the half was different. Sitters weren't given that cushion. Getting boxed in an 800 had fatal consequences, even in the race's early stages.

The half had evolved into a two-lap sprint, a grueling test of speed and endurance. It was a race where world class runners hummed right from the get-go. Those who waited to make a move in the second lap were often too late. It was critical to be in an unencumbered position, preferably at the front, when the bell for the final 400 meters sounded.

The metric half-mile, like all middle and long distance track races, is a race where the least distance covered holds the greatest advantage. A metal rail runs the circumference of the track adumbrating the inside lane. So the runner who stays closest to the rail covers the shortest distance. The wider a runner strays, the more distance he must run. So the front runner, who jealously guards the inside rail, covers the least distance around the track. And he also minimizes his chances of being boxed in, tripped, or spiked.

But the front runner puts himself in an extremely vulnerable position. It's a spot where back biting sharks often draw blood. As the pack of predators hone in on him, drafting in his slipstream as he pulls along the field, they gnash with flashing jaws at the first signs of weakness.

As they strike, they blaze by the leader's right shoulder, passing in a frenzy of flying elbows and flashing spikes. The rabbit is stew, his legs and arms stone. Rigormortis has set in, once graceful movements reduced to desperate, spastic thrashings.

The front-runner is a target for his competitors, quivering bait begging to be eviscerated. But if he's good enough, he can steal his race. He finishes unscathed, his vanquished competitors bruised and bloodied, following.

Front running is a tactic reserved for the elite, the runner clearly superior to his competition. It's a situation that is extremely rare, especially in a sport where winners and losers are often determined by hundredths of seconds.

McClanahan's cryptic dictate, 'run from the front,' was a clear message. He was telling Sanchez, that he was the best runner in the 800 field. Clearly superior to his competitors. And that no one would threaten him. If he took it out hard, and ran the type of race he was capable of, he would win.

Sanchez studied the Scotsman's dour face. The visage belied any signs of insincerity. McClanahan's honest brown eyes didn't waver. McClanahan wasn't a bullshitter, Sanchez thought. He made mistakes, but he'd never bullshit you.

"Okay. I'll take it out."

McClanahan just nodded. "See ya' later."

Chapter 4

McClanahan, Jesse thought as he stretched on the warmup track. It was the only good thing that had happened since he'd gotten out of bed. As soon as the Scotsman had left his dorm room, his angst had intensified. All his insecurities resurfaced. And when Jesse walked out of his dorm and began his trek toward Hayward Field, nothing felt right, his stomach tightening.

It was a clear, mild evening as he jogged toward the stadium. He was clad in black Lycra tights and a white nylon windbreaker. On his back was a small canvas pack. It held his racing spikes, singlet, and a fresh towel.

As he jogged he could hear the distant echo of the public address system, and the din of the crowd. This is it, he thought. A lifetime of hopes and dreams reduced to two laps of a 400-meter oval. He could feel his stomach churning as he moved. Stage fright, he thought to himself as he ran. "Bullshit", he corrected himself in a whisper. This wasn't stage fright. He was petrified.

This was nut-cutting time. When the Olympic creed of 'Not the Winning, But the Taking Part,' was nothing but a rotten lie. Three runners would make it out of the 800 finals and go to the games in Sydney. The rest of the field would stay home. When it came to track and field, Americans knew the Olympics and nothing else. They defined a runner's career. It was unlike Europe, where sophisticated track and field fans understood the significance of other events: the European Championships, the Commonwealth Games Championships, the World Championships of Track and Field.

In their eyes, a United States middle or long distance runner without an Olympic gold medal, was an also-ran. Billy

Mills, with his storybook run in Tokyo, had taken the gold. So had Frank Shorter and Dave Wottle in Munich, Joan Benoit Samuelson in Los Angeles. But for every Mills, Shorter, Wottle and Samuelson, there were scores of scenarios that had not ended as well.

There was Jim Ryun of Kansas, whom the American public remembered, for his 'failure' at Mexico City. And Mary Decker Slaney of Eugene, Oregon, for her ill-fated collision with Zola Budd in Los Angeles. Never mind that Ryun and Slaney were arguably the greatest male and female milers that the United States had ever produced. That didn't enter the equation. In the American public's mind, both let their country down when it came to the big one. As did Steve Prefontaine, the James Dean of American distance running. The Coos Bay, Oregon native son who had become a legend among track and field aficionados. Pre finished fourth at Munich, the victim of his gutsy front running tactics. It was a suicidal, fearless approach that meant gold or nothing.

And then there were those who never made it to the show. Like Bill Rodgers, the great marathoner that was at the top of his game in 1980, only to have his Olympic dream shattered by politics.

Jesse understood that every American 'failure' was a runner who was often more appreciated overseas than in his own country. Track savvy foreigners realized the significance of the Olympics. But they understood they were not the end-all, be-all, to which Americans had elevated them.

As Jesse approached the stadium, he could feel the heaviness of past Olympic ghosts. They were spirits that had never been fulfilled. It was an eerie feeling, surreal yet genuine.

He heard the crack of a starter's pistol fire as he approached Hayward Field. A roar from the crowd followed. His stomach roiled. He felt lightheaded. It was a time to remain calm. He silently muttered the same. But the admonition meant nothing. He felt like a live wire, his nerve endings raw.

"Second call for the men's 800 meter final." Jesse sat up on the warmup track. He reached for his backpack and pulled it toward him. Then he reached inside and pulled out a pair of Adidas Adi Star MD's, silver and purple distance spikes with orange stripes. He lay them next to the pack, unlaced his training shoes, and stuffed them into the backpack. Then he stood up and wriggled out of his tights. The action revealed a pair of navy blue splits. He bent over and fitted the tights into the backpack. The action exposed the red-fisted tattoo below his right hip. He sat back down, and took his time as he smoothed the thin, white, cotton running socks covering his feet. He felt for lumps and misplaced seams, anything that could cause a problem during his race. Satisfied that the socks were smooth, he reached for his spikes. He worked deliberately as he slipped on the snug fitting racing shoes. The spikes embedded in the sole, though much shorter than those worn by sprinters, provided traction. They were critical proponents for speed on rubberized surfaces. Road racers wore flats. Track runners wore spikes. Neither was interchangeable.

The shoe was feather light, about 7.5 ounces, nylon body with synthetic leather trim. It had a thin, EVA heel wedged on its upper, with a nylon forefoot spike plate containing seven spikes, and rubber heel outside. The shoes were built for speed, stability, and shock absorption. It was footgear far removed from heavier trainers. They were the equivalent of a track runner's ballet slipper. A feather-light cover made for flight.

To Jesse, equipment weight, like body weight, was critical. Every additional ounce of shoe, or clothing mass, equated to pounds of additional burden over the course of an 800-meter race. He would be taking about four hundred and forty foot strikes in his two-lap race. Just one additional ounce equated to twenty-seven pounds.

24

The first time Jesse Sanchez slipped into spikes, he was hooked for life. As he strode lightly down the track, the spikes flashing beneath his toes, he felt fluid, light, and powerful. He felt a freedom of movement and force, like a graceful gazelle, bounding across a sun drenched savanna.

It was a feeling that always returned, every time he slipped into spikes. They gave him a sense of empowerment, like a gunslinger sporting pearl handle revolvers. Leonard Hilton, the-ex-mile great, and a close friend of McClanahan's, had given Jesse his first pair. As Jesse circled the track, Hilton had studied Sanchez. The Scotsman nudged Hilton with his elbow. "If ya' didn't see the face, kid looks just like you did when you was a young fucker, Slinger."

Hilton had just nodded. The resurrected nickname stuck to Jesse, and Houston's new young gun was a work in progress.

As Jesse stood, he could sense the quickness of the surface beneath him. It was the same type of covering he would be racing on. The Hayward Field Track, like all world class facilities, is made of a synthetic tartan material. It is about 7/8" in diameter, laid on top of a concrete and asphalt base. It's a surface made for spikes.

An adept distance runner, one who can race up on the balls of his feet, gains a huge advantage wearing them. With every flashing foot strike the runner is propelled forward, a minimum of wobble and slippage on the lightning fast tartan surface. McClanahan likened spikes to vaginas. "Look like hell, but feel great once yer inside 'em."

But like all pleasurable things, spikes come boxed with an unwritten warning label: PROLONGED USAGE CAN LEAD TO ADDICTION AND INJURY. Plantar fascitis, chronic heel pain, and Achilles tendinitis are among the snares.

Jesse's affliction was the last on the list. His Achilles tendon sometimes acted up after tough track sessions or races. Knots along the tendon were already sensitive to his touch.

They were lumps of gnarled scar tissue, precursors of future problems. His Achilles was always stiff in the early morning.

The Achilles tendon has two major functions during running. The calf muscles lower the forefoot to the ground after heel strike, and raise the heel while "toeing off". A force on the tendon greater than its' inherent strength causes Achilles tendinitis. The tendon can be strained, or suffer a minor tear, at or close to its point of insertion on the heel. Or the bursa between the tendon and the upper part of the bone may be inflamed. Often the tendon may become sore, thickened, and tender to the touch. Some of its fibers may be torn or degenerated, while the tendon's covering becomes thickened.

Sanchez knew that Achilles tendinitis seldom went completely away. Sometimes it could be managed with ice and stretching. Other times surgery was the only fix. Multiple surgeries were not uncommon. And the list of world class middle and long distance runners who had gone under the knife, read like a 'who's who' of the world's best.

As Jesse walked slowly onto the third lane, he stopped momentarily. His eyes focused straight ahead. Then he pushed off on his left foot. He moved in measured strides, gradually accelerating until he was sprinting near full gait. He came to rest about a hundred and fifty meters from where he began.

As he stopped he could feel his heart thumping madly. He felt winded as he walked back across the infield to his starting spot, his legs like stone. A wave of panic washed over him as he tried to calm his labored breathing. "You're a chickenshit," he muttered in a whisper. "Cut the crap."

He did four more strides. Each successive effort felt progressively worse than the previous one.

"Third call for the men's 800," he heard on the P.A.

He gathered up his gear. Then he jogged toward the infield of the Hayward Field Track. The 800-meter competitors were congregating. As he moved he was overcome by a wave of nausea. He continued past the grandstands, and out to a grassy field in the back.

He came to a halt, away from everyone, as his head and stomach spun out of control. He bent over and heaved. A spray of vomit fulminated from his mouth. He continued heaving until there was no more. As he righted himself the announcer called "This is the final call for the men's 800. All runners report to the infield immediately."

Jesse was shaking as he jogged back toward the field, his mouth filled with the acid taste of vomit. His competitors would see the fear in his face, he thought. He was toast. His race was over.

As Sanchez checked in, Chip Martin and Mickey Landis sat perched in a press box, cameras running as they prepared to call the race for television.

"Mickey, this is probably the strongest 800 meter trials final we've ever had. The U.S. has definitely gotten its act back together on a world level. In the field we've got eight runners, six who are seasoned veterans, men who have all run under 1:45. But more importantly, these are men who know how to run an 800-meter race under intense pressure. They're veterans of four seasons on the European circuit since the '96 games in Atlanta."

"That's right, Chip. And that's an intangible that can't be underestimated when it comes down to a big race. And this is a big one. For when you're running in Europe against the best 800-meter runners in the world—and I'm talking the Moroccans, the Kenyans, and all the other Africans. Along with the Brits, and the rest of the Europeans. I mean, that's where you learn how to run under pressure. And what tough running is all about. You get shoved, slugged, kicked, and spiked. But after a few seasons of that, you get callused in a way you just can't, running in meets in this country. European track is where you develop as a world class competitor. And that's what we've got in this field. Six guys who are veterans of that circuit, and have been through those wars."

"Absolutely. And of those six we're talking Larry Edwards of Lawrenceville, Kansas; Dan Skiles of Mackinaw, Michigan; Barry Phillips of Gainesville, Florida; John Crandall of Rochester, New York; hometown favorite Mark Pratt of Eugene, Oregon, and Danny Schumacher of Phoenix, Arizona. I think you'll see the team of three come from these six men."

"That's definitely where the smart money would go," Landis said. "But let's not forget that this is the Olympic Trials. And things don't always go according to form."

"In the prelims the fastest time was run by a mystery man, a young runner from Houston, Texas named Jesse Sanchez," Martin said. "He blitzed through the semis in 1:43.2 running from the front. We really know little about him. Other than the fact he qualified at a last minute meet in Houston, Texas, at an all comers meet at Rice Stadium. That, and he's coached by Kevin McClanahan, the controversial Scotsman. A man whose not exactly a favorite among the shoe companies, and track and field hierarchies."

Landis laughed. "One thing about Kevin McClanahan is you never have to worry about him having a hidden agenda. He'll tell you right up front what he thinks. And that's made him a highly controversial figure in the world of track and field. But McClanahan knows his craft. And some of the finest middle and long distance runners around the world consult with him regularly. Though it's ironic that his hometown, Houston, Texas is not exactly a bastion of middle distance greats. There was Leonard 'Slinger' Hilton in the 70's, who gave me my share of grief when I raced against him. 'Slinger,' at one time, held the record for most sub four minute miles run in competition. But other than Hilton, I'd be hard pressed to come up with another great middle distance runner from Houston. When you think of Houston, you think of The Carl Lewis', the Leroy Burrells, and the Floyd Heards. Men who were coached by Tom Tellez. In short you think of sprinters."

"That's right. Houston's a sprint Mecca. But in Jesse Sanchez you've got a young runner who obviously has some talent. But the question is how far can that talent take him in an Olympic Trials 800-meter final? This isn't the type of venue where you'd expect an unknown to just show up out of the blue, and make the team. Jesse Sanchez is an unknown. His semifinal time raised a lot of eyebrows. We'll just have to see how he reacts to the pressure of a trials final."

"It's often the downfall of the inexperienced runner to go too hard in the early rounds," Landis said. "If you've run too hard in the prelims, it can spell for a disastrous final. If you've expended too much energy, you may find that the well's dry when it's time to reach down deep. That's why I have to go with the veterans for making this team. They've been through this process. They know what it takes. And you can bet your money that there's still a lot left in their tanks for the finals. It should be an interesting race. I look for it to be a tactical race, and that's the kind of race that can end up in a lot of problems. Whenever you have a group of national and world-class 800-meter runners lined up in a race of this magnitude, the chances of a slow, tactical race are always present. And tactical races can spell disaster. I'm talking pushing, shoving, elbowing, spiking, and in the worst case scenario, a fall."

"That's the ultimate nightmare. A group of kickers bunched together, moving at a pedestrian pace. That's when a fall is inevitable."

As Martin and Landis spoke, the announcer called Jesse's name. He stepped forward, and acknowledged the crowd. But it was as if he were somewhere else. He was aware of the din in the stadium. But he felt lightheaded. The largeness of the track was a daunting vista. As the last runner was introduced the starter said, "I will give one command, 'Runners -

29

Set'. Then I'll fire the gun. At one hundred meters you may break for the inside lane."

As he spoke the runners were lined up behind their lane markers, extending from lanes one to eight. The furthest runner, in lane eight, started the greatest distance down the track. But the apparent visual advantage would be lost once he reached the one hundred-meter mark, and broke across the track toward the first lane. Every runner, regardless of lane assignment, would cover the same running distance before converging in the first lane.

Jesse felt numb as he stood. "Runners Set...."

Chapter 5

Jesse leaned forward in lane four. The starter's right hand came straight up clutching a pistol. A loud crack was followed by a puff of white smoke and he leaped forward. He sprinted out at a destructive pace, bolting down the track around the first curve. At the hundred-meter mark he broke for the inside lane.

McClanahan gazed at his watch. Twelve flat. His focus returned on the field as Sanchez smoked toward 200 meters, leading the field.

"Jesse Sanchez is out very fast," Martin said. "Unofficially we have his two hundred split under 24 seconds. That's a kamikaze pace for an 800, especially a race of this magnitude. He already has a good five yards on the field and he's not giving any indication of slowing down."

"Suicidal pace," Landis said. "Obviously Jesse Sanchez doesn't want to get involved in a kicker's race. This field is loaded with tremendous kickers. So you have to believe that his strategy is to take the sting away from the kickers and make them suffer early. So when it comes to that final straight away, they won't have anything left."

"That's what it appears," Martin said. "Although we don't have any idea what kind of kick Sanchez has, if any. Because this is exactly the kind of tactic he used in his prelims. He ran from the front, very reminiscent of a runner who always did that here at Hayward Field. And of course I'm talking about the late, great, Steve Prefontaine. But you have to remember that Pre was not a half-miler. And he certainly never took off as quickly as Jesse Sanchez is moving this evening."

As Jesse passed through two hundred meters, he had no idea what type of time he was running. All he knew was that he was moving quickly. And from the sounds of smacking feet and heavy breathing behind him, he felt as if all seven runners were right on his right shoulder. The thought panicked him. He pushed on. As he passed the three hundred meter mark McClanahan gazed at his stopwatch. 36. McClanahan made a fist and pumped it.

"Jesse Sanchez has just run a 48 second first quarter and he has a good ten meters on this field! His pace is absolute madness! There's no way that he can maintain that!"

"This is youth and inexperience at work," Landis said. "This kid's running a fearless race, and you just have to hope, for his sake, that when the field does start to come back at him, that he's got something left. I give him a lot of credit. If he can steal this thing, more power to him."

Jesse passed the 400- meter mark. Over the deafening din of the crowd he heard, "Go bugger!!! Hammer!!!!"

Sanchez was oblivious to the digital clock as he responded to McClanahan's yell. His legs felt light. He made a conscious effort to relax his arms and shoulders as he circled the curve. At 500 meters, McClanahan checked his watch again. Sixty seconds. Another 12 second 100. Sanchez had separated further from the field.

The screams in the stands had grown deafening. "Jesse Sanchez continues to airmail the American field in the men's 800 finals," Martin said. "Trailing behind in a tight pack is hometown favorite Mark Pratt of Eugene, Oregon, Barry Phillips, and Jim Marshall. And they're followed by Larry Edwards, Danny Schumacher, John Crandall, and Dan Skiles."

"Jesse Sanchez has just gone through 600 meters in one minute and twelve seconds! This is absolute madness! If he can hold on he has a chance to shatter not only the Trials and American records, but also the world 800 mark of 1:41. If he can just run a pedestrian 200 meter time of 28 seconds, he'll have a world record!"

"This is unbelievable!" Martin howled. "Jesse Sanchez has all but obliterated this field. Unless he completely craters, we'll have a new, world record!"

As he spoke, Jesse pumped his arms. He was driving for the final two hundred meters home. The roar of the crowd was deafening, but he never heard it. It was the sound of footsteps that initiated a chill of fear. They were catching up with him. He could hear them and feel them.

As he powered his way around the curve he could sense his calves burning and his shoulders tightening. He was slowing down. They were going to catch him, he thought. It was just a question of where.

He had no idea of what pace he was running. But the darkness of his error struck him like a brick to the back of the skull. He'd gone out too fast, and now he was paying. A big brown bear had jumped on his back, and dug in its claws. He had two hundred meters to go. The beast was on top of him, going along for the ride. Every muscle in his body was screaming. He was 'rigging up', the dreaded track term for rigormortis.

"You'll never amount to anything, you worthless little son of a bitch." His father's words rang loudly in his head, as his body slowed. Jesse felt his eyes get hot, and knew there were tears. At that moment he felt the back of his father's leather hand as it smacked his face. He saw his mother being struck. Lying on the floor. Her dark eyes wide with fear. Blood streaming from her nose. Her man standing menacingly over her, poised to strike her again.

Jesse's body was shutting down, the demons of his past crippling his shattered mind. As he approached the track's final curve, he could sense the field's breath, hot on his shoulder. An eternity seemed to pass before he approached the final 100. The crowd was on its feet screaming. McClanahan glanced at his stopwatch as Jesse pulled to within a hundred meters of the finish.

"Jesse Sanchez is struggling!" Landis shouted. "Mark Pratt has unleashed his kick and is making up huge chunks of ground on Jesse Sanchez!"

As Jesse approached the hundred-meter mark, an echo reverberated in his brain. "Ain't a middle distance runner in the world who can kick with you for a hundred meters." They were McClanahan's words. They had an eerie closeness. As if the Scotsman was right with him.

The words were followed by a myriad of past images. The grueling workouts in the heat. The long runs. The interval workouts that had tested the fiber of his being. He had a choice, he thought. To succumb to the pain. To avoid the dreaded prospect of success. Or to accept it. And the consequences that came attached.

As Jesse crossed the final one hundred meters, McClanahan focused on Sanchez's face. He saw madness in his young runner's eyes. It was the same derangement that he'd witnessed when Jesse was a teenager. It happened in a pool hall. McClanahan had pulled the kid off a man who outweighed him by fifty pounds. And was fifteen years his senior. He had taunted Jesse and thrown the first punch. When McClanahan finally managed to restrain Jesse, his victim's nose was smashed like a corkscrew, his face bruised and bleeding. It was a killer's madness that McClanahan saw in his young runner's eyes that day. A madness that every great athlete has burning inside.

As Jesse rose on his toes, his surroundings became a blur. He was locked in a zone, a vacuum of his own device. He was in a trance as he made his desperate bid for home. The roar of the crowd was deafening, but Jesse Sanchez never heard it. His concentration was total, every step a choreographed movement from his past, the memory of his muscles taking over. Pratt sprinted madly as Jesse moved.

Every muscle in Sanchez's body screamed for mercy. But he powered on, oblivious to the screams, understanding that the mind always quits before the body.

As he pumped his arms toward the finish, the thunder from the stands was deafening. Jesse still heard nothing. But reality had set in. His body had betrayed him. He was turning to stone. He sensed a runner just on his outside shoulder ready to pass. He saw what he thought was the finish line. In a blind leap of faith, he lunged forward. He struck the track hard, the jolt of his palms to the tartan sending a shock wave to his shoulders and back. He was down on the track, doubled over on all fours, pounding hooves thundering past him.

McClanahan glanced at his stopwatch. The screaming from the fourteen thousand fans was still frantic as Jesse palmed the tartan. His heart kicked at over two hundred beats a minute. As he fought for oxygen he felt confused, as if in a state of shock, unsure of what had happened.

As he pawed the ground his head came up. He watched the runners ahead of him, supporting and cradling each other. Some had their arms wrapped around each other's necks. But Jesse wasn't with them. He was down on the ground, alone. Like road kill on a lonely highway.

A wave of panic consumed him. And the desperate sense of crushing failure became reality. He had lunged and gone down. But it had been too soon. He had seen the finish line, but it had been an illusion.

He had disgraced himself, his mother, and McClanahan. His biological father had beaten him again. Jesse was still the loser. He was still the same 'medio-pelo' half-breed, the worthless piece of refuse, that had been beaten and taunted. Nothing had changed. He slumped back down on the tartan and shut his eyes. Then he covered the back of his head with his hands. He wished that death would come right there. He had endured enough pain and suffering for one lifetime. He wanted no more.

"Unbelievable!!!!" Landis screamed. "This is unbelievable!!!!" What a stunning ending!!!! Jesse Sanchez has just won the U.S. Olympic Trials 800 meter finals in the world record time of 1:40.5!!!! There's a new sheriff in town, folks. Jesse 'Slinger' Sanchez."

"This is the most amazing race I've ever witnessed!!!!" Martin screamed. "Jesse Sanchez of Houston, Texas has demolished this field with a world record 1:40.5, after apparently having rigged up with less than two hundred meters to go!!! I can't believe this!!!! This is truly unbelievable!!!!"

Jesse felt a hand on his shoulder. A man's voice asked, "Are you alright?"

"I'm okay."

A squat, bald figure, wearing a NATF shirt, helped him to his feet. Jesse asked softly, "Who won?"

"Are you kidding, son?"

Jesse shook his head. "No."

The official looked at Jesse with wide eyes. He realized the tall youngster was serious.

"You won. You ran 1:40.5 A new world- record."

Jesse remained frozen. He lifted his right leg and scraped the spikes along his left calf. He could feel the sting. He wasn't dreaming.

He gazed at the stands, and saw fourteen thousand fans on their feet, clapping and screaming madly. His body trembled as reality set in. His eyes watered, and a flood of tears followed. As hot tears of joy poured down his cheeks, Mark Pratt and Barry Phillips, the men who had finished second and third, more than four seconds behind him, came up and embraced him. He continued crying effusively, the thunder in the stands still reverberating. Pratt and Phillips pushed Jesse out on the track. They urged him to take a victory lap.

Jesse managed only a few steps before stopping. A sheepish smile was followed by a self-conscious wave. He felt both overcome with joy and fright as fans clapped and screamed. He turned his head and spotted McClanahan, who was on the infield walking toward him. A rush of adrenaline followed. He sprinted toward the Scotsman as the track fans roared. Jesse smothered his mentor in a bear hug. As the two embraced, Jesse sobbed.

When they separated, McClanahan eyed Jesse with a dour look. "What fuckin' happened between 600 and the final straight?"

"You serious?"

"Fuckin' 'A' right I'm serious. Ya' ran a 28 second two hundred to finish. Yooo were turnin' to shit."

"I won. Isn't that enough?"

"Nooo. Not if ya' want to do anything at Sydney. Ya slow down like that at the Olympics, and they'll eat yer ass."

"I just ran a damn world record."

"So what? You can go faster."

"That's all you've got to say?"

"That, and ya' owe me dinner. And since ya' ran a record, I reckon ya' owe me a Guinness, too."

Jesse just shook his head. But he couldn't hide his grin.

As reporters approached Jesse said, "I don't have anything to say to them. I just want to get out of here."

"Just tell 'em ya' have to take a piss test. After ya've done that, I'll get yer ass out of here."

"Good."

Jesse acknowledged the crowd once again before giving a terse statement to reporters, and jogging toward the drug testing area.

The Olympics were only eight weeks away. World records came and went, but an Olympic medal was forever. He knew that McClanahan was right. There was still work to be done.

Jesse went into the Olympic drug testing area. He consumed over a liter of water before he was able to urinate. After completing the drug test, McClanahan was waiting for Sanchez outside. He shepherded him out of the stadium, trying for a quick getaway. But as the two walked toward McClanahan's rent car, reporters swarmed them.

Media reps fired questions at Jesse and McClanahan as they moved. As the two reached McClanahan's rent car, a white Ford Escort, the female reporter with the shortly cropped raven hair who had confronted Jesse earlier, stood in McClanahan's path. She blocked the driver's side door. She pushed the 'record' button on her tape machine as McClanahan approached.

"Why all the secrecy?" she asked McClanahan.

"No secrets."

"Why are you in such a hurry?" another reporter shouted.

"We're hungry and thirsty. We just want to get us some dinner and drink a few beers."

"Jesse Sanchez is an unknown," the raven-haired reporter said. "How does an unknown run a world record?"

"Unknown? I know him."

"What are you hiding?" another reporter snapped. "No one comes out of the wood work and runs a world record."

McClanahan smiled. He pointed at Jesse. "He did."

"How do you feel about running a world record?" he asked Jesse.

"Good."

"That's it?"

"Isn't that enough?"

"Where have you been the last four years?"

"In Houston."

"You've never run in any major meets," a willowy blonde-haired reporter asked. "How come?"

"My focus was to be ready for today. That's all I was concerned about. Keeping my focus on today."

The female reporter with the short raven hair said to McClanahan "There's rumors that your runners are taking drugs. What do you have to say about that?"

"I'd say they're true," McClanahan answered without skipping a beat. "Everyone of em's on the juice."

A hush followed his statement. "Which drug?"

"Some brand new shit. They don't even have a test for it yet."

That was followed by more silence as McClanahan held his ground. Jesse stood, with a quizzical look on his face.

"What's the drug called?"

"W-O-R-K." McClanahan spelled out slowly.

Nervous laughter from the other reporters followed. "Mr. McClanahan, you've accused both the North American and International Track Federations of selectively enforcing their drug testing procedures. What's your current stance?" the blonde-haired male reporter asked.

"Same thing."

"Which is?"

"They're a pack of sleazy motherfuckers. Can't be trusted."

"Are you referring to North American Track Federation President Joseph Nixon and International Track Federation President Primo Magiano?" the raven-haired reporter with the tape recorder asked.

"Them's the assholes."

"There have been rumors that both men and federations may be in the process of filing lawsuits against you because of your remarks and accusations."

McClanahan grinned. "Ever try and get blood from a stone?"

"So you're not planning on attempting to reconcile with them?"

"Reconcile?" McClanahan said drawing out the word. "I wouldn't piss on them motherfuckers' teeth if their mouths was on fire. Now if yooo'd please step aside ma'am, me and Jesse are gonna' go get us some dinner and drink some beers."

The woman moved, and as McClanahan and Jesse got into the rent car, reporters' questions continued, popping outside. McClanahan started the engine and put the car in gear. As they drove from the stadium Jesse said, "You believe that crap?"

"Yup."

"You know how I feel about drugs. I don't even take aspirin."

"I know that."

McClanahan was well familiar with drugs and their devastating impact on track and field. He had seen the ravaging after effects of athletes who had used steroids in the 60's and 70's. They were men and women who were facing organ transplants. Others consumed with cancer. And others who had been reduced to cripples. He'd seen shot-put specialists, men who had once weighed three hundred pounds of solid muscle, now stripped down to specters, hobbling around on canes. Drug usage was rife in almost every sport. But for some reason, track and field took the worst rap in the press.

Blood doping was often linked to world class distance runners. A number of world class cyclists had died from the procedure. It is a process whereby an athlete's own blood is removed, most commonly after a period of altitude training. The oxygen rich blood is refrigerated and kept in storage until the opportune time, about a week before the planned competition. The blood is then re-infused into the athlete's body, the massive dosage of enriched blood providing the athlete a boost.

But the danger comes in the composition of the enriched blood. If the re-infused blood is too thick, complications can occur, and in the worst case, death. That's what had happened with the ill-fated cyclists.

Blood doping was illegal. And so were a number of over the counter medications and solutions. Even the seemingly innocuous substance of caffeine. Combined with No Doz, it could give a sprinter or middle distance runner a boost out of the gate. There were a host of others, including DHEA, an over the counter preparation which seemed to give a spike to older athletes. But the most insidious, and the most difficult to test for of all drug preparations, was anabolic steroids. Scientists had perfected water-based steroids to the point that they would be virtually undetectable in a urine test. As close as twenty four hours before competition.

McClanahan had heard from numerous closely trusted sources of steroid 'doctors' in his own city, trained physicians and kitchen chemists, who had mastered the technique of administering steroids. They knew exactly how, and when, to administer the forbidden substances so they would never show up in an athlete's urine test. It was a nasty game of money and politics that had gone on for years. The athletes with the money, and access to the best chemists, could stay on the "juice" for the prescribed cycle. They would train at high levels, their recovery process speeded up. And get off it at the last moment, just prior to competition. The best-connected athletes would be tipped off, when track and field officials made so-called "unexpected" stops, for random tests. McClanahan had been at the 1988 U.S. Olympic Trials in Indianapolis. Reliable sources had told him that fifteen United States athletes had tested positive. Included in that group were eight who had made the Olympic squad. They were told they had six weeks to clean up their acts, before being tested again.

He'd heard the story time and again. Of how some of the world's best known sprinters, men who vehemently denied and castigated drug usage, were the worst steroid offenders. In

McClanahan's eye the result of their steroid usage was as plain as day. He'd seen sprinters add on huge amounts of muscle mass in short time frames. They cited weight lifting programs for their gains, claims that McClanahan knew were sheer folly.

But even more evident to him than the sprinter's added muscles was a change that was even less subtle. He'd seen numerous sprinters wearing retainers and braces, under the guise of having their teeth fixed. But the truth was far removed from their contrived ruse. Prolonged steroid usage causes the jaw to thicken and take on a whole different shape. The simple act of chewing can become difficult, as the 'new' jaw, or steroid jaw, is out of line.

In McClanahan's eye there was only one way to clean up the sport from the cheaters. Test the blood and not the urine. Cycling had gone to that system, and the cheaters had been virtually eliminated. But track and field had not taken that step. They had taken the position that the drawing of blood was a religious infringement.

McClanahan didn't give a damn for that type of reasoning. Blood tests were required in all types of civil jobs, just like they were in insurance exams. If the sport wanted to clean up its act and cut the hypocrisy, it could, over night. McClanahan despised drugs, as did Jesse. Both men had the utmost respect for the Kenyans, 'hungry' athletes who relied on tough training techniques to take them to levels that others could only dream about. The Kenyans trained in the toughest conditions. And they did workouts that their western counterparts could only fantasize. They were athletes in the truest sense, the type of competitor that Jesse Sanchez had become.

McClanahan had been railing for years against track and field officials for their highly selective, and hypocritical, testing methods. What it boiled down to was simple. The athletes who were out of disfavor were busted, while track and field officials turned their heads for the sacred cows. Mary Slaney had been wrongfully taken down before being reinstated. But the penalty had cost her precious time, tenure that was of essence to a woman who was in the twilight of her career.

McClanahan's attacks on authority had not gone unnoticed. His web site was closely monitored. Rumors were rife that his athletes were too.

The two men drove without talking as they headed toward the coast to escape the press and have some dinner. Almost twenty minutes later, as a service station loomed ahead on the right side of the road, Jesse said, "I want to call my mom."

McClanahan nodded. He put on his right hand turn signal. He pulled in the lot and stopped the car near the gas pumps. Jesse got out. McClanahan watched as Sanchez walked toward the convenience center to get change for the pay telephone.

Tough bugger, McClanahan thought, as he watched the tall, slender young man move. Balls right up to his chin.

Chapter 6

The next Wednesday, Jesse, British Steeplechase champion Justin Chalmers, New Zealander Sean Waitts, a 2:10 marathoner, and Americans Dave Winston and John Warner, both sub four minute milers, warmed up for a mile breakdown on the Rice Track. McClanahan, who would clock their intervals, was finishing a workout of his own. The Scotsman was 55, and his workout partner, Mac Stevens, 60. McClanahan could still scare five minutes in the mile, while Stevens at age 60, had set a national age group record of 2:13 for the half. He had missed a world record by hundredths of a second, a mark he would go for later that summer. It was a stunning record, a sixty year-old man running a time that men one third his age could only dream of. Stevens had run and trained with the Scotsman for over twenty years. He showed no signs of weakening.

Jesse's tenure with the Scot had been a little more than eight years. Watching McClanahan and Stevens had been an inspiration to him. The tough old birds knew how to push through pain and injury. Injuries were an unavoidable part of high caliber running, and older runners were highly susceptible. Jesse had watched McClanahan quietly endure his share, including a knee surgery, a procedure that would have ended the career of most runners. But Sanchez had come to learn that McClanahan was all guts, and his competitive juices still flowed. The Scotsman understood that pain was a constant companion, a clarion that trumpeted loudly that the body still possessed life. That attitude, and a work ethic that far surpassed his native talent, had shaped his career.

A former Scottish mile champ, McClanahan fell short on a world level. But, in Jesse Sanchez, he saw the prototype of a world class runner. A youngster as tough as a steel boot who

worked like a mule, and possessed raw talent of epic propor-
tion. He was a coach's dream, a once in a lifetime opportunity.
He knew that in running, as in any other sport, the elements
that form a great athlete aren't enough. Chemistry is of essence.
An interaction between athlete and coach that spurs the athlete
to new heights. And McClanahan understood that he and Jesse
had that spark from the get-go. Sanchez's affinity for the old
bird continued to deepen as he matured. He never diminished
his mentor's role in the continuing process of his development.

He came to understand that the Scot was unique, very
different from other running coaches whom he had observed
through the years. McClanahan was driven by love, a passion
for the sport and its athletes who were willing to pay the price.
It was a price that seldom yielded money for runner or coach.
But money was never a driving factor for McClanahan.

He clung to his blue-collar roots, a coal-mining town in
Scotland, a place where a man's worth was measured not by his
balance sheet, but his word. It was a mentality that had shaped
the fiber of his being, and would never change. McClanahan
charged a monthly pittance for his coaching fees, and to those
whose who were unable to pay, he charged nothing. Convinced
that what goes around comes around, he was content to let
fairness seek its own dividend yield.

But whether wealthy or poor, the Scotsman treated all
his runners the same. His words were few, narrative that was
brutally honest and to the point. Praise rarely came from his
lips. But when it did, his runners knew they had earned it.

His training philosophy was cryptically simple, a system
based on trial and error. He kept what worked and dispensed
what didn't. It was a method predicated on forty years of
carefully documented workouts. Results from runners of varying abilities, a dynamic formula that was constantly refined and
modified. It was a practical process, far superior to the hypo-

thetical models devised by exercise physiologists. It was based on real life, a teacher whose efficacy had no rival.

Jesse had learned by observing McClanahan, Stevens, and the older runners who trained in the Scotsman's group, that youth and old age were largely a state of mind. He had witnessed first hand how running seemed to turn back the hands of time. It convinced him that the activity cleansed both mind and body, the closest thing available to a fountain of youth. Sanchez had trained with vibrant and healthy runners who had logged over a hundred thousand miles. A time when most cars have been junked.

In recent years Jesse had seen running take its share of bad raps from the press. The death of Jim Fixx, a jogger who hid his pre-existing heart disease from everyone, fueled the first wave of anti-running finger pointers. Kenneth Cooper, messiah of the aerobic church, kindled the second. Cooper was the Holy Father, but had recently deserted his flock.

His latest tome had refuted many of his previous theories. A rapidly graying culture, one that often followed the latest fad, listened carefully as Cooper postulated that too much running could kill, by making runners more susceptible to infection and cancer. Jesse didn't buy the physician's latest warnings. He wondered about the sincerity of the findings. Were they accurate, or had the desire to sell a new wave of books influenced them?

In Jesse's mind there was no comparison to the older runners whom he trained with and the general public. It was the difference between highly trained athletes and couch potatoes. Graying runners were physically stronger than their counterparts, he observed. Their muscles, joints and ligaments worked better. They ate and slept better. They took fewer medications and spent less time in their physician's offices than their non-running peers. Their bodies looked better. And their skin had a healthier glow than their sedentary peers.

Any niggling injury incurred due to their running was usually negligible. Especially when compared to the host of afflictions consuming their sedentary equals. But the most noticeable difference to Jesse was the older runner's zest for life. They had an attitude for living that far separated them from their 'elderly', sedentary, peers.

As McClanahan and Stevens finished their workout, Jesse and his group lined up on the track for theirs. It was a typical Houston summer day, with temperature in the 90's and humidity to match. There was a stony silence among the runners as they viewed the workout sheet. None had anticipated the series of efforts that confronted them. McClanahan's summer track workouts, which were held on Mondays and Wednesdays, were typically short and quick. The one laid before them was not. The long efforts would be grueling in the brutal conditions.

Jesse grew with McClanahan's program. Every year his maturing body accepted the added stress of more demanding work-loads. The Scotsman's system was seasonally based. It encouraged group work as opposed to isolation. In the early fall, the beginning of his cycle, speed work was limited to a hill session each week. And a series of timed efforts on the trails or roads. As the fall progressed, one track workout was added to the hills, a second as the weather cooled further. In late fall and early winter, his runners were hammering long interval workouts on Mondays. Sometimes up to six miles in duration. On Wednesdays, faster pace efforts, generally about half the distance of Monday's work, were normal.

The relentless strength phase continued until spring, followed by a gradual reduction in track mileage as speeds became faster. McClanahan believed the middle and long distance runners that reached the top were those possessing the most strength. Of course speed was critical, but a speed-trained runner without a proper base was like a building with a faulty foundation. He could run an occasional great race. But when a series of races were run within a matter of days, like the trials or Olympics, his structure would crumble.

Summer, or track season, McClanahan's interval sessions were short and intense. It was the time of year that Jesse liked best, a period when he could run efforts at rapid speed, nearly all out. It suited his temperament as a track runner, when he could display his full talents. Serious track running was a far cry from road racing, a sport that attracted the masses. But even in road racing, it was the runners with track backgrounds who ruled. It was only logical that the most talented, and best-trained runners, would come out on top, regardless of venue.

Jesse and his group began their workout without conversation, understanding the severity of the task before them. They turned their mile in 4:15, and were breathing rapidly, sweating freely, as their minute recovery evaporated.

They ran 3:06 for the three quarter, and two minutes flat for the half. That was followed by a fifty-six second quarter, and a finishing two hundred of just under twenty-five. McClanahan's eyes focused on Jesse as the pack ran. It was apparent to him that Sanchez was struggling, a condition that he anticipated just five days after the trials.

McClanahan clicked his chronograph as Jesse's group finished its' two hundred. The Scotsman turned to a man who was a head shorter than he was. He was light complected, with a thick head of shocking red hair. "Let's go," McClanahan said. The two jogged out of the stadium. They ran along a grassy path of the Rice campus, toward a tall hedge of thick green bushes lining Main Street. Majestic oaks towered over the hedge, shading the campus and far out into the street. They provided a verdant backdrop to the Medical Center and Main Street to the east.

"Tough night, huh Murray?"

Danny Murray nodded his head. "So what else is new?"

"Older I get, the harder the fuckin' summers get."

"I've known you for over twenty years. You say the same thing every summer."

"I don't know how much longer I can keep doin' this."

"Until they shovel dirt in your face. You're obsessive compulsive."

"Where'd that come from? Ya seein' a shrink?"

"I should be. Then I wouldn't be here in this God awful hell hole, listening to you."

"Now yer trying to make me feel guilty. Ya' know it ain't easy havin' a Papist friend."

Murray extended his middle finger up at McClanahan. "This doesn't mean you're number one. And who said I was your friend?"

McClanahan stroked his beard and grinned. "Ya' know you love me, Murray."

" Right. Just like I love that last woman, the law defined as my wife."

"That's yer trouble. Ya' been single too long."

"Wasn't single long enough. When cancer took Eileen, I never should have remarried. I was blessed with one woman who loved me. I guess to have asked for two, was too much. "

"Didn't kill ya'."

"Left me broke. No more of that marriage stuff."

"Yar sour."

"Maybe. But I'm finished marrying. I've managed to squirrel away a few bucks. And when I retire I'll move back to Ireland. I'm not going to die a pauper."

"I don't have to worry about that. I got nothing. Margaret divorces me, there ain't nuthin' to argue over. Maybe a few cases of home brew. And the cat. Fuck the cat. She can have it."

Murray shook his head. "It's amazing that Margaret's stuck with you as long as she has. She deserves a Nobel Peace Prize nomination."

"Nooo. Margaret's a shit disturber. And she's surly. That's why we get along so well."

"You have no saving graces. And you end up with a woman who'd jump off a cliff for you. You're living proof that there's no reward for being a nice guy."

McClanahan grinned. He reached down and tousled Murray's hair. "Yer meaner than me, ya little shite."

"Bullshit. No way."

"I remember way back when, Murray. When ya' didn't take any shit from no one. I've seen ya' in action. Yer a mean little bugger."

"Those days are gone. All I want now is a little peace and quiet."

As they crossed the soccer field McClanahan asked, "Watch Sanchez tonight?"

"Yup. He looked beat."

"He was buggered. I didn't figure he'd be able to run the way he did. Just five fuckin' days after the trials."

"So why'd you run him so hard tonight?"

"Eight weeks to the Olympics. I'm gonna' bust his ass for the next six, then start to back him off. He's got more speed than any half-miler in the world. But when he gets over there in Sydney against them motherfuckers from Africa and Europe, he's gonna' need strength. It's too early right now to start backin' off."

"How about sending him to Europe?"

"Nooo. He don't need it. Motherfucker ran a world record training right here. Less they know about Jesse, better off he is."

Murray nodded his head. "You told me he had a world record 800 in him. I believed you. I just didn't think it would come this soon."

"There's more to come. He's just scratchin' the surface."

"Are you eventually going to move him up in distance?"

McClanahan made eye contact with Murray. His look was dead serious. "He'll have every record from 800 to five thousand in four years."

Murray just nodded. He had no reason to doubt McClanahan. The Scotsman had told him over eight years ago that Jesse Sanchez was special. As Murray watched the youngster develop under McClanahan's tutelage, that became apparent. McClanahan had told Murray that if things went right, Jesse could run an 800 record at the trials. When it happened, Murray was not shocked. Sanchez had done the type of work that no American middle distance runners would consider. And that only a handful of long distance runners would attempt.

'   McClanahan had witnessed America's middle and long distance running since he immigrated to the states in the early 60's. He saw it steadily decline. From its heyday in the 70's and early eighties, to its present day mediocrity. The demise followed the slide of a 'victim' based culture. One where standards continued dropping in every conceivable form. It was only logical that running had followed, he reasoned.

McClanahan had stated it bluntly, time and again to Murray. "Motherfuckers just won't put in the work any more." McClanahan remembered when Peter Snell, the great New Zealand half miler and miler, would routinely train as a marathoner, for the months leading up to the track season. It was a Lydiard based program, a seasonal approach where Snell routinely ran hundred mile plus weeks in the buildup along with a weekly training run of twenty plus miles. It was the type of work that was unheard of for middle distance men. But when racing season came, and Snell's mileage was cut back, he was as strong as a bull. He took a gold medal in the 800 meters at the 1960 Rome Olympics. And then he came back four years later to capture both the 800 and 1500 at Tokyo. It was a feat that was unheard of. Snell's strength carried him through countless grueling prelims and finals. And he ran them at a level that none of his competitors could match. The Lydiard system rang true with McClanahan. He employed it, and modified it, as years of trial and error made him one of the world's most savvy coaches.

Like Snell, McClanahan's runners who did the work ran to the top. The system had produced a host of national and world-class competitors. But the 90's and the new millenium had spawned a new breed of American runner. Those who were frequently looking for a shortcut. But Jesse never did. And that's why McClanahan had such a strong affinity for him. He did the work. The kind that most American kids coming up would never attempt.

Jesse felt that the Africans still possessed the work ethic that McClanahan embraced. And that's why they were virtually untouchable in international competition. Jesse Sanchez trained that way. It gave him confidence. That he would give quarter to no one. Kenyans included.

Murray and McClanahan continued running without speaking. It was like that with the two. Sometimes they ran for miles without talking. When you knew someone that well, there were times when words just got in the way.

Chapter 7

When Jesse pulled up to his garden apartment in Southwest Houston, he saw a black Jaguar convertible parked parallel to his entrance. Sitting in the car was a man in his mid 50's, short and squat. He was wearing a mud brown toupee that looked like a rug. His bleached sideburns had a henna cast. His pinkish skin was like leather, hardened and cracked by the sun. Wrinkled hoods framed beady brown eyes.

"Jesse Sanchez?"

"Yeah?"

The man smiled broadly, showing a lot of gum. A smile that had all the sincerity of an aroused snake. "You know, you're not an easy man to track down."

He got out of his Jaguar and walked toward Jesse, the smile still pasted on his fleshy face. He was wearing a black silk Nehru shirt with the top button closed. Dove-gray pleated slacks of a fine, lightweight worsted wool. Black alligator Italian slip-ons with no socks. And a matching belt. On his left wrist was a wafer-thin gold watch, with a black velvet band.

As he approached, Jesse caught the overpowering scent of toxic cologne. He smelled as if he had bathed in it.

"Sid Hatcher." He extended a chubby paw with short, stubby fingers. Out of courtesy Jesse returned the gesture. Immediately Jesse's right hand was covered by a second. He felt queasy, his hand enveloped like a slab of sandwich meat between Hatcher's mitts. Sanchez wrested it free. "So, Jesse! Congratulations on your world record! Let me tell you, that was some performance!" The effusiveness of Hatcher's words was benign, compared to the gushing zeal of his tone.

"Thanks. What can I do for you?"

"What can you do for me?" Hatcher smiled broadly again and chuckled. He playfully slapped Jesse's shoulder with an open palm. "The question is, what can I do for you?"

"Are you selling something?"

Hatcher guffawed loudly. "Do you know who I am, Jesse?"

"No."

"Well, I guess you don't read the sports pages or watch ESPN."

"I don't have cable. And I don't have time to read sports. I work days and take night classes at community college."

"Good man! I like that! I like that! Trying to improve your self. Not many athletes think that way."

"Listen. I just got through with a track workout. And I'm hot and tired. I'm going to take a shower and get something to eat. If you can tell me what you want, maybe I can help you."

Hatcher held up his palms. "Sorry, Jesse! Excuse me for my ignorance. I understand that you're a busy man." Then he reached into his back pocket and pulled out a thin, black leather case. From it he lifted a card and handed it to Jesse. The card read:

SID HATCHER
Athlete's Representative

"You an agent?"

"I like to think of myself as a representative and advisor. Some of my clients are among the best known celebrities in sports." Hatcher furtively picked his nose with his pinky.

"I'm not interested in an agent. Not now."

Hatcher threw up his open palms again. "Hey, Jesse! No problem! I understand! All I'd like is the opportunity to talk to you. How about you get cleaned up? And the two of us go get some dinner. My treat!"

"No thanks. I'm not interested in an agent right now. Not until after the games. It wouldn't be fair for me to lead you on and have you buy me dinner.

"You're a very considerate young man! And honest! I like that! Wonderful traits! Beautiful! You'll go far."

"Great. See you later."

"Let's forget business, Jesse. I'd like to take you to dinner. It would be my honor."

"I don't know. I've got some...."

"I insist. I won't take no for an answer. Go ahead and shower. We'll get some dinner, and I'll get you back home early. I promise. I've got reservations at a great place."

Jesse fingered his earring. His teeth clenched. "Alright. But I need to get back early. I've got to study and get up early tomorrow morning."

"No problem, Jesse! I understand."

"Okay. Give me a few minutes. I'll grab a quick shower."

As he walked toward his apartment he felt uneasy. He knew if McClanahan had been there, he would have told Hatcher to go fuck off, and that would have been it.

Jesse was overcome by the smell of Hatcher's cologne as he rode in the open Jaguar convertible. He was thankful the top was down, certain that he would have gagged if the car had been closed.

Hatcher got up on the 59 loop heading north, and exited on Kirby. He pulled into the valet parking lot of Carrabas. As the two walked inside the restaurant Jesse's eyes widened. It was an upscale restaurant and bar, a trendy place that he had never been. A shoestring budget limited Sanchez's restaurant choices to cheap buffets and fast food chains.

As they were seated, Hatcher spoke to their waitress, an attractive young woman with lush strawberry blonde hair. "This is Jesse, Darlene. Bring him whatever he wants."

The waitress smiled at Jesse. "Can I get you something from the bar?"

"You have beer on draft?"

"Sure do. What kind?"

"Miller?"

"Absolutely." She turned her head . "The usual for you, Mr. Hatcher?"

"Right, Darlene. Perrier with a twist of lime."

"Very good. I'll be right back with your drinks."

"Thanks Darlene... Darlene, before you go, I'll bet you don't know whom this good-looking young man with me, is. Do you?"

Jesse's cheeks flushed. The waitress stared at him. "Sorry, Mr. Hatcher. But I can't place his face."

"Well Darlene, this is my new friend Jesse Sanchez. And Jesse Sanchez just happens to be the greatest middle distance runner in the world. Last week he broke the world record in the half mile. And next month he'll be going to Sydney to bring back a gold medal to the United States from the Olympic Games."

Darlene eyed Jesse. Crimson painted cupid lips turned up in a big grin. "I should have guessed you were a runner. You look like a runner...So are you going to run the marathon?"

"No. My event's the 800."

"800?"

"Half mile."

"Oh." The smile left her face. "I have some friends who run the Houston Marathon."

"Not my distance." Jesse fingered his earring. Then he smoothed his long hair. He felt uneasy.

"Don't give up. Maybe someday you can run one too."

"Maybe so."

"I'll be right back with your drink orders."

As she walked out of earshot Hatcher said, "Doesn't that bug you, Jesse? You run a world record at 800 meters, and people want to know if you can run a marathon?"

"No big deal."

"It is a big deal, Jesse! A young man like you deserves better than that!"

"When it comes to running, most people in this country think of either sprinters, or the marathon. That's just the way it is. I'm not going to get bent out of shape over that."

"Exactly! That is how things are. But I'm going to change that. I'm going to make Jesse Sanchez a household name that will be every bit as familiar as Carl Lewis and Michael Johnson. All I'm asking for is a chance."

Jesse squirmed in his chair.

"Jesse, right now you're a very hot commodity. I mean with potential shoe contracts, endorsements, and appearance fees, we're talking seven figures. And fast. The trick is to strike while the iron is hot. And to use your head."

To emphasize the head part, Hatcher planted his stubby index finger deep into his temple. As he spoke the waitress came with the drinks. She placed the Perrier in front of Hatcher, the beer in front of Jesse. "Would you like to order now? Or do you need some time?"

"Give us a few moments, Darlene."

"Sure Mr. Hatcher. Just signal me when you're ready." She turned and headed back across the dining room toward the bar.

Commodity. The word had a nasty ring in Jesse's head. Hatcher had just reduced him to chattel. A nameless and faceless thing. Like an asset of fluctuating intrinsic value, determined by current market conditions.

"I told you before we came to dinner that I'm not interested in an agent right now. Not until after the Olympics."

Hatcher smiled again. He picked his nose with his pinky. He tried to be discreet as he wiped it on the inside of the table-cloth. He took a long sip of Perrier before placing the glass on the table. "So you work as a roofer? And you attend college at night?"

Jesse nodded.

"I also understand that you give your mother most of your earnings."

"My mother worked like a dog at two jobs to support my brother and me when I was growing up. I'm not giving her anything. We help each other. She's my mother."

Hatcher held up his palms outward in a defensive manner. "Jesse! The last thing in the world that I'd want to do is offend you! If I have, my apologies! That's the problem with this culture of ours. No one has any sense of family any more. I have a mother too, Jesse. And believe me, I understand where you're coming from."

Jesse just nodded. He felt his stomach tightening. He sipped his beer. Then he fingered his earring.

"If you could make life easier for your mother, and your brother, wouldn't you?"

"I intend to."

"Good!" His nostrils flared as he gushed. "That means we're both on the same page."

As Jesse studied Hatcher, he wondered about Hatcher's past. Sports agents were rarely men who had succeeded in athletics. Or who could be trusted. Jesse had heard his share of horror stories of runners who had been screwed by unscrupulous agents. It was a strange profession, sometimes attracting some of the lowest scum around. And their tentacles had reached to the far corners of the globe. Even the Africans were not immune.

Jesse had learned through fellow runners that the Kenyans, the world's largest source of distance running talent, had been overrun by agents. And the Africans were being taken. He had read an excerpt from a track and field journal that quoted Nairobi's daily newspaper. "Reality seems to be dawning, albeit belatedly to Kenyan athletes, that foreign agents are foes, only too eager to make hay while the sun shines."

The journal went on to quote former 5K-world champion Yobes Ondieki. Speaking of the many foreign agents who are trying to promote Kenyan talent, he said "They are vultures who eat the meat and leave the bones where there is no more to be eaten from the athlete."

The article went on to note that no longer did Kenyan runners simply go to universities. Instead, many are whisked to all corners of the globe to race. "Be careful with some 'shadow' coaches who work with foreigners to exploit you through organizing foreign races," Ondieki concluded. Jesse understood that Ondieki's words were true. And from them, and the words of other runners, his deep-seated mistrust for agents had intensified.

"I'm going to be completely honest with you Jesse. Okay? Because if I'm not completely honest, I know I'll never get from you the kind of trust that I bend over backwards to extend to all my clients. Does that make sense to you?"

"I hear you."

"Good! Now that I know we're on the same page, I'm going to straight shoot with you and cut to the chase." As he spoke Jesse heard the unmistakable sound. The smell of Hatcher's cologne was masked by a bullfrog fart. Jesse moved back his chair.

"Jesse, we live in a world where windows of opportunity are very small. They open and shut on a moment's notice. You're a young man. And you're full of hope and desire. And you've just accomplished something unbelievable. You've broken a world record. And may I add one of the most impressive world records in track and field."

"Where's this going?"

Hatcher picked his nose again. Then he turned the clustered diamond on the stubby pinky of his left hand. "Records can be broken, Jesse. And like I say, windows of opportunity shut just as rapidly as they open."

Hatcher rocked his Perrier in his hand. He took a sip. His forehead had beaded with sweat and his ferret eyes had narrowed further. "I can make you a very wealthy young man. Right now. Within the next few months you'll have enough money to be set for life. And so will your mother. Neither one of you will ever have to want for anything. You'll never have to worry about making a rent payment, a car payment, or anything else. You just give me a chance to help you, and you and your family will be set for life."

"What are you suggesting?"

"Jesse, in the last few days I've spoken with some very important people. Very important people, Jesse. I'm talking about the executives who run the biggest shoe companies and athletic firms in the world. The players, Jesse. The men who run things and make things happen."

"And?"

"These men like you."

"How can they like me? They don't even know me."

"They like what you've done. And what you stand for."

"How do they know what I stand for? They don't know me."

"They know these things, Jesse. Trust me. And they're willing to offer us very substantial sums of money to endorse their product and become a part of their team. That's what this business is all about, Jesse. Teamwork."

"I'm not interested."

"Just hear me out. If you become a part of that team and win an Olympic medal. Something that you and I both know is practically a done deal. Then there's even more waiting for you."

"You haven't listened to a word I've said. I'm not interested." Jesse's fists had tightened.

"Be smart, Jesse. There's more than just product endorsements to make you a very wealthy young man. I have contacts at every major track venue in Europe and Asia. And they're willing to pay us very large sums of money just for your appearance at their meets. In fact, all it will take is a few phone calls, and I'll have meets lined up for you between now and the Olympics, that will guarantee you a very nice sum of money in appearance fees alone! Not to mention the added bonus of prize money.

"Maybe later. After the Olympics."

"Jesse, what I'm telling you, is you can fix your whole life. Right now. At this dinner table tonight. Just become a member of my team, Jesse. Let's become partners and it'll be you and me, Jesse, against the world."

"Partners?"

"Right, Jesse. Partners. But probably not the kind of partnership you're thinking. This isn't the kind of partnership where I take half, and you get half. No way, Jesse. Not that kind of partnership." Hatcher passed gas again.

Jesse moved his chair further back and covered his mouth and nose with his napkin. "Sorry. Bad stomach." Hatcher leaned forward as Jesse pressed against the back of his chair. He couldn't go back any further. There was a woman in a chair at a table behind him. He was almost touching her.

"Hey, you're probably wondering what I take. Aren't you? Well it's a pittance, Jesse. All I get is fifteen per cent. And that's it! Not a cent more! No hidden fees or costs. Nothing else. Fifteen per cent slam-dunk. And hey, Jesse. That includes me taking care of all your financial records and investments too.

You won't have to worry about anything, Jesse. All you'll have to do is run, and I'll take care of everything else."

"You make it sound easy."

"Easy? It's simple! You and I become partners, and I do all the dirty work. All you have to do is run."

"That's it?"

"That's it. Just one minor concession and we'll be ready to go."

"Concession? I don't understand."

"A concession's a compromise Jesse. In other words, you give a little to get a lot."

"I understand the meaning of concession. You may think I'm a dumb Mexican, but you're mistaken."

"Jesse!!! God forbid if I offended you!! I just..."

"Cut the bullshit. What type of concession are you talking about?"

The words took the smile right off Hatcher's face. He picked his nose again. This time he wiped his pinky on his pants leg. Jesse felt his stomach roiling.

"There's a lot of people in the business of track and field who would like to see you make it Jesse. Especially me. You're a nice young man. And you'd be a credit to the sport. And since you've been so direct with me in your question, I'll be equally direct with you in my answer. The fact that your father was Anglo, and your mother brown, makes you an even hotter commodity.

"What does that have to do with anything?"

" You're a bridge between cultures, Jesse. Like a Tiger Woods. And frankly, I think the public will eat you up. And everyone that I've spoken with. I'm talking about the big boys Jesse. The men who really count. They feel the same way as me."

"I don't want to be compared to Tiger Woods. I'm my own man."

"Of course you are. And you'll be your own very rich man. But Jesse, we've got a little problem. Not an unsolvable problem. But there is a problem. You see Jesse, the men who can make you over night can break you just as quickly."

Hatcher cracked his knuckles.

"What are you talking about?"

"In a nutshell Jesse, the men who pull the strings have told me they don't like your coach. Actually Jesse, that's not what they really said. They said they hate him. Despise him. You see Jesse, Kevin McClanahan, has a very bad name in this field. The shoe companies hate him, for reasons I know you understand. And every major track and field organization hates him too. Jesse, the man is even hated in his own town. Who in the Houston running community likes him?"

"The people who really know him. Who gives a damn about what assholes who don't know him think?"

"I understand, Jesse! I understand! I know how you must feel about the man. And I can understand your sense of loyalty. And I appreciate that, Jesse. I darn appreciate that. But you've got your whole life ahead of you to think about."

"I've given it thought. And I've made my decision."

"Sure you have. But consider this. If you make the wrong decision, that open window we talked about can slam shut in a New York minute. Suppose you have a bad Olympics, Jesse? Or suppose even worse than that, that you get injured? What do you think you'd be worth in endorsements then? Or what do you think track meet promoters would be willing to shell out for you in appearance money?"

"That's a risk I'll have to take."

"I can answer that question, Jesse. Not one red cent. You stay with your coach, and you'll never go to the pay window. I guarantee it. They'll find ways to keep you from ever earning a dime from track and field. That's a slam dunk."

Jesse's dark eyes narrowed. "What did your father do for a living?"

"He was a lawyer."

"So he made good money?"

"He did alright."

"And he stayed with your mother?"

"Yeah."

"How did he treat her?"

"Okay."

"Then you and your mother were lucky."

"Sure babe. Sure." He flicked the tip of his pinky in and out of his nose again.

"My old man was no good. He knocked up my mother twice and never married her. Got her pregnant when she was sixteen. He was a drunk. And he beat the crap out of her. I'd try and stop him. But I was too small. Just a little kid."

"Sorry for you babe. My heart goes out."

"He'd beat the shit out of her. Blacken her eyes. Bloody her nose. Knock out teeth. Kick her. I'm sure he hurt her inside. But she never reported him. She never even went to the hospital or saw a doctor. She was too scared."

"What a crying shame, babe. You know I......"

"Afraid that he'd kill me and my brother. You have any idea what it's like having a father like that?"

"Must have been rough, babe."

"Rough? I'll tell you rough. How about a woman with a grade school education, trying to raise two kids on her own? Rough? Shit. You ever see a woman in a grocery store put things back at the check out line, because she didn't have enough money to pay for them?"

"I'm telling you I...."

"Rough? How do you think she must have felt coming in late at night, exhausted, after her second job, a job of scrubbing someone else's floors and toilets to pay the rent? Rough?

Let me ask you another question. Do you have any idea what it's like being a kid, and watching your mother, a young woman, turn into an old lady over night?"

"J-e-s-s-e-e. I can understand exactly where you're coming from. And that's exactly the cycle that I want to end for you and your mother. Right now! Over night! I'm giving you the opportunity to bury that past forever."

"No. You don't understand fuck all. You don't even have a clue as to what I'm talking about."

Hatcher's face reddened.

"Enlighten me, Jesse. Enlighten me."

"I never had a father. Just a drunken son of a bitch. When we moved to Houston that changed. Kevin McClanahan became the father I never had. He gave me the shirt off his back. I'm not even going to start to tell you all the things he's done for me. Because I know where you're coming from."

"Listen, I just want…."

"I know what you want. And I'll stop wasting your time and mine. There's not enough money on the face of this earth to get me to sell out for Kevin."

"I'm not asking you to sell out. I'm just asking…"

"To turn my back on the only man who ever really loved me. "

"I'm trying to protect your future."

"No you're not. All you care about is fattening your wallet. I can't be bought."

"Listen, Jesse. This isn't a decision you have to make right at this moment. But I wouldn't wait too long. I'm telling you. You've got to strike while the iron is hot."

"You can take that hot iron and shove it straight up your fat ass. Because my answer won't be any different ten minutes from now than it will in ten years. I'll never turn my back on the people who love me. No, man. Not enough money on the face of this earth to get me to do that."

Jesse got up from his seat at the table and lay down his napkin. He turned his back and walked across the dining room and out to the parking lot.

As Sanchez walked down Kirby, the long trek back toward his apartment, Hatcher spoke on his cell phone. "No Bernie. Didn't go well." He passed gas and patted his belly. Then he munched on a breadstick. "No Bernie. Not a chance.....At this point I don't care. Fuck him."

Hatcher clicked off his phone. He signaled the waitress. Small fish, Hatcher thought as the waitress approached. He had baseball and basketball clients who were pulling in five million dollars a year. Why waste his time fucking around with some dumb Spic like Jesse Sanchez?

Chapter 8

When Kevin McClanahan wasn't working at his city job, he was training runners, talking to runners, or reading about runners. Every aspect of physiology and psychology that related to runners intrigued him. He had witnessed indigenous people of altitude turn out a profusion of the greatest distance runners the world has ever known. His dilemma was to produce that kind of runner at sea level.

In recent years he'd watched the Kenyans dominate the world scene, the bone-thin mountain dwellers possessing cardiovascular systems that were clearly superior to their flat land rivals. Their advanced oxygen processing capabilities developed naturally, a process that had not yet been replicated at sea level.

He'd witnessed Olympic champion Kipchoge Keino, and later world record holder Henry Rono, pave the way for the horde of Kenyan greats who would dominate the sport from the 80's into the new millenium. Members of the Nandi tribe, men who are easily recognizable by the absence of their two front teeth, they lived and trained at elevations approaching eight thousand feet.

The two legends opened the floodgate for the horde of countrymen who would follow. McClanahan knew that like Keino and Rono, Kenyan children begin their distance training early and naturally. That they run back and forth to school each day, sometimes as much as eight miles each way, padding along gracefully on the forgiving red clay roads. And that the climate they train in is good also. But he knew also that the rarefied mountain air makes breathing difficult. And it is that labor that converts to a distinct advantage, when the Kenyans come down from altitude and run at sea level.

Like all runners, he knew the Kenyans' maximal oxygen capacity, or VO2 max, increased with physical maturity. Unlike runners in western countries, they frequently attained world class capabilities by their late teens. Their ability to dispatch enormous volumes of oxygen to their muscles during their runs, made them clear cut favorites over their flat land rivals. In almost every distance competition they entered.

McClanahan had come to rate VO2 max as the most significant factor in predicting a distance runner's potential. More significant than the runner's ability to process lactates, a waste product that builds up in the muscles during hard runs and racing, or the runner's form and efficiency of movement, is his VO2 max. He felt the runner with the highest VO2 max, or the 'biggest engine', had the best chance of winning any distance race he entered. He knew that an average 'normal' runner, processes about 46 milliliters per kilogram of oxygen per minute. While most world class runners convert about 77, he knew of Kenyans who had tested above 80.

The Scotsman was also aware that only a handful of U.S. runners had ever tested above 77. Steve Prefontaine, the immortal distance legend from Coos Bay, Oregon, recorded an 84.4 at the Aerobics lab in Dallas. It was the highest level ever documented for an American runner.

In a secret session that McClanahan had arranged for Sanchez just two weeks before the trials, Jesse, hammering on a treadmill, his body hooked up with tubes and wires, recorded an 86.7.

When he collapsed with exhaustion at the test's conclusion, McClanahan and the Australian exercise physiologist conducting the test stared at each other with wide eyes. Sanchez had reached a level of fitness that was unheard of. He was on the threshold of a world class performance.

Barring injury, sickness, or a psychological meltdown, both men knew that all the elements were in place for Jesse to crank out a superb 800. He had the speed and endurance for a big race, and for many races to come. His distance base would carry him right into the Olympic Trials and far beyond.

Sanchez had put in months of heavy mileage, doing the kind of buildup that was normally reserved for marathoners. In the midst of his buildup phase, when his two-a-day workouts were cranking out up to a hundred and forty miles a week, he was in a constant state of fatigue. With no taper, just loping along in training shoes, tights, and a windbreaker, with New Zealand Olympian Sean Waitts, he went through the halfway point of the Houston Marathon in 1:03.

The effort had taken place that January. It was a time that was never officially recorded. It was clocked by McClanahan as Sanchez and the New Zealander dropped out according to plan, even though they were leading the race.

And in his track training, Jesse was just as daunting. He ran series of 800 meter repeats in 1:55 with one-minute rests. And mile breakdowns, where he went through the mile in four flat, going progressively quicker for each shorter distance. But his decided advantage over the Africans was his throw down speed. None of them had his sprinting ability. His 21.2 two hundred, and 46.5 quarter, had been clocked just two weeks prior to the trials, as he blistered through an incredible speed session on the Rice Track.

The sprints were run early in the morning, with only McClanahan and Sanchez present. The Scotsman wanted it that way, keeping Sanchez under wraps for his own good. The clandestine training had paid off. Jesse's performance in the trials had vindicated McClanahan's strategy.

But since the trials, the rumors concerning Jesse Sanchez's incredible 800 meter record had intensified to fever pitch. Few believed that an unknown could have accomplished his feat. Only the handful who knew Jesse intimately. They were people who understood why he had never run high school or collegiate track, friends who knew his complete story.

Following her common law husband's desertion, Carmen Sanchez moved Jesse and his brother Jose to Houston. Sanchez went out for track his sophomore year in high school. When it became apparent to him that his track coach had no clues about running, he never went back. It was a decision he never regretted. If he'd run in high school, Texas rules would have forbade him from training under McClanahan.

His collegiate track hopes were dashed with equal swiftness. Carmen Sanchez depended on Jesse's financial support to help her and her retarded son Jose. So leaving Houston was never an option for Jesse. The only two Houston schools that offered track and field scholarships were Rice University and Houston Tech.

Rice, a school with Ivy League standards was out of Jesse's reach. So with Houston Tech as his only viable option, he visited the school's distance coach, Arnie Thick. Sanchez requested a trial, a plea that Thick quickly dismissed. He told Jesse that all his distance scholarships had already been promised. The lie had nothing to do with Jesse's potential. It was directed at Kevin McClanahan. Thick both despised and envied him. He had witnessed distance runners throughout the world come to McClanahan for coaching and advice. The Scotsman had helped produce a bevy of national and world-class competitors. A byproduct foreign to Thick's efforts.

At first the rejection angered Sanchez. But it quickly melted. It took Jesse little time to understand the caliber of man who had denied him. Thick spoke like an excited Brooklyn cab driver with a mouthful of marbles. The speech patterns provided little cover for a room temperature i.q. After speaking with the distance coach for just a few minutes, it became apparent to Jesse that it would be difficult to run for such a man. The incident left a bad taste in Jesse's mouth. A track scholarship would have opened many doors and provided him the financial means of earning a degree from a four-year university.

Intent on continuing his studies, Sanchez enrolled at Houston Community College. Each semester he took classes at night, working days as a roofer. It was a process that was taking him beyond four years to complete his college degree. But with financial pressures, and his burning desire to become a great runner, it was his only viable option. Now it appeared his choice had been a good one.

The next Thursday morning, Sanchez ran an easy thirty minutes, followed by an easy hour run that evening. Friday morning he jogged for a half-hour, followed by a relaxed two mile in a Rice All-Comers meet that night. His time was 8:55, and he felt as if he were cruising.

Saturday morning he ran an easy ten-miler, and in the afternoon did a weight workout. Sunday morning he ran two loops of the Allen Parkway, throwing in a series of hills up and down the banks of the Buffalo Bayou, for a total of about thirteen miles.

Monday evening, McClanahan belted Sanchez with his toughest workout since the trials. He gave him two sets of five times a thousand meters, two minutes between the intervals, ten minutes between sets. The thousands were run in the low two twenties, as Jesse went through 800 meters in 1:55.

He was sore the next morning as he jogged, better by his evening run, and by Wednesday morning almost back to normal. That evening he warmed up with steeplechasers Justin Chalmers and Noyes Langston, the three carrying on a relaxed conversation as they jogged along the three-mile cinder trail outlining the perimeter of Rice University.

They jogged into the track stadium and under the stands to a water fountain. After drinking, they continued to the track. A group of runners were congregated around a stand housing the evening's workout sheet. As Jesse headed toward it, he recognized three of the women distance runners whom McClanahan coached. They were moving toward him in the outside lanes along with a fourth woman who was a stranger to the running group. They were sprinting, finishing their last hundred-meter stride, the warm-up before their workout.

Jesse's gaze locked on the stranger, a slender but shapely woman. She had the most gorgeous legs he had ever seen. As she moved closer he focused on her face. Her features were delicate, her clear skin a light shade of creamy chocolate. Her dark eyes were liquid and large. They possessed a shocking honesty that flashed of sensuality and strength.

For a brief moment she made eye contact with Jesse. In that moment she drank him in. He was her counterpart, tall, slender, and hard. Though his muscles were not overly developed, they were defined and cut. His skin was unlined, a coffee au-lait cast as smooth as silk. Though the skin and coal black eyes spoke of an exotic mix, the face appeared Anglo. A symmetrical high cheek-boned visage with chiseled features. His hair was jet black, silky, and long. It tumbled down his back in a ponytail that was held fast by a rubber band. There was a small diamond stud earring in his right ear. And where his shorts split on the same side, was a discreet tattoo, a raised red fist. As her eyes photographed him, her spikes got caught in the tartan. She stumbled. But she managed to regain her balance without falling down. As she righted herself, she grinned sheepishly at Jesse. Her teeth were pearly white and straight. The smile lit a flawless face. Jesse was certain that he'd seen it before, on a magazine cover or in an ad. It was the type of face he wouldn't forget. A model or an actress. The kind of woman he'd sometimes fantasize, but knew he would never touch.

His eyes followed the contoured lined of her athletic body, lean but shapely. She was wearing cream-colored shorts and a matching jog bra. As she put her hands on her hips, her diaphragm rising and falling rapidly from the effort, Jesse felt a stirring. A long, but graceful neck was like an elegant column supporting her smooth shoulders. The tropical heat and humidity had brought her flesh to a rich sheen, the sweat having made her light-colored garments nearly diaphanous. Her breasts were well formed and full, dusky-colored dark spots peeking out like big eyes. She smiled at him again before the group of women jogged back down the track to begin another stride.

Jesse's muddled brain was still on the woman as he gazed at the workout sheet. The workout was six times a 600-200, with a thirty-second rest following the 600, two minutes after the 200. The 600's called for 1:24, the 200's in 27 seconds. They were quick times, a workout that demanded fresh legs. As Jesse gazed at the workout sheet, McClanahan entered the track stadium with Stevens and Murray, the trio having completed their warm-up jog. "Legs comin' back?" McClanahan asked as he jogged up to Jesse.

"A lot better tonight than Monday."

"Good. How 'bout the Achilles?"

"No problem."

"Just run pace. Don't go no quicker."

"Okay."

Jesse moved to a strip of concrete along the infield that was covered with tartan. Runners were sitting and stretching on the strip, some slipping into racing-flats, others into spikes. As Sanchez sat down to slip into his spikes, his eye fixed on the dark-eyed woman. She was standing with her group in lane one, about to start her first effort. Jesse was watching her from behind, her weight pressed gently forward on her left foot, her right forefinger on the start button of her chronograph. The back of her leg was smooth and taut, supporting a peach like rear, firm and high. She was perfect, Sanchez thought. From head to toe. She was the type of woman that was way out of his class.

Chapter 9

"Piece of work, isn't she Sanchez?"

Jesse's dark eyes didn't move as they focused on the gorgeous woman. Danny Murray sat down beside Sanchez as she pressed her stopwatch and moved forward.

"Stunning. Who is she?"

"Shauna Arnold."

"Doesn't ring a bell."

"Finished third in the Marathon trials. Helluva cross country runner. Princeton grad. Fulbright Scholar. And she's headed to Harvard Medical School. She's a professional model, too. Magazine shoots. Commercials. Music videos. You've probably seen her. She's hot."

"Oh. I knew I'd recognized her face from somewhere."

"Why the sour tone? What's the problem?" Murray leaned forward as he spoke, stretching out his hamstrings.

"The obvious. She's incredible."

"I don't get it. Why is that making you pissy?"

"It's a no-brainer, man. She's way out of my league."

"Don't sell yourself short."

"Get real. I can't compete with the kind of guys who travel in her circles. I'm a roofer who goes to night school."

"That, and you're ugly."

Jesse grinned. "It's the one thing I like about you Murray. Your soothing words."

"Listen fart brain. Just because she's a super achiever doesn't mean she wouldn't like you. Lots of smart women fall for dummies."

"You speaking from personal experience?"

"If you're interested in her you've got to risk rejection. Roll the dice, Sanchez. Maybe she'll dig your b.s."

"Right." Jesse stood up, his spikes laced. "And maybe you'll kick my ass in the 800."

"Show some respect, squirrel. I could turn a pretty good half when I was your age."

"Murray, why do you want me to make an ass of myself? You know that women like her aren't looking for guys like me."

"You know what? You're absolutely right." Murray stood up. "Why even bother with her? For that matter, why even go to the Olympics? Can you imagine how screwed up your life would be with a gold medal, and her arm crooked to your elbow to boot? Hell. All that baggage could weigh you down."

"Enough Murray. I...."

"Hell. With all that fame and fortune, you'd probably have to retire from roofing. What kind of a life would that be? Is there meaning to a life without lunch pails, refried beans, and Porta Cans?"

"Okay, man. You've made your point."

"I'll tell you one thing, Sanchez. When you find the right one, you go for it. I know about that. I had a good one. They don't come around often."

Jesse made a fist. He playfully tapped Murray. "I hear you, man. But when she turns me down, I'm going to make you pay. I make a fool of myself, and I'll get even with you."

"I don't care."

"How's that new car, Murray?"

Murray's face turned red.

"Stay away from the Explorer, Sanchez. That vehicle's the first major purchase I've been able to afford since the divorce."

"Food for thought. Sometimes a little sugar in a gas tank sweetens an engine."

Murray pointed his finger at Jesse. "You stay away from my Explorer, Sanchez. Or I'll whip your skinny ass."

Jesse just grinned.

Sanchez jogged to the end of the track. He ran a quick 100-meter stride. Within the first few strides he sensed that his legs were light.

The workout went easily for him that evening, his legs feeling fresh as he flew through his intervals. They were lightning quick times, efforts that only a handful of the world's greatest half milers could emulate. Three times during his workout he passed Shauna Arnold and her group, and each time he sensed her eyes glued to him.

As Sanchez finished his last effort, he walked over to his gear. He sat on the tartan step in the infield, slipped out of his spikes, and back into his training shoes. Then he joined a group of six runners that jogged out of the stadium. They continued out to Main Street, running at a relaxed pace on a cinder running trail that circled the university. The temperature under the shade of the giant oaks outlining the campus was a good fifteen degrees less than the track.

As Sanchez and his group cruised the three-mile loop for their cool down, McClanahan, Stevens and Murray walked across the tartan Rice track. They jogged out of the stadium and onto a grass soccer field. Shauna Arnold caught up to them from behind. As she pulled even with McClanahan she looked up at him and said, "Can I join you guys?"

"We're old fuckers. We go slow."

"That's okay. My legs are tired."

"Any objections?" McClanahan cocked his head toward Stevens and Murray. Both men sported moon size grins. Neither answered.

"I guess ya' can. But neither one of 'em like women much. So I wouldn't run too close to 'em."

"Speak for yourself," Murray snapped. "Just because you have an affinity for sheep."

Arnold giggled. "Are you guys always like this?"

"Nooo. When we're alone we're a lot more pissy. I been takin' sensitivity training, and I'm teaching these old farts everything I learn."

"Yeah," Murray said. "His group leader's Hannibal Lecter. He and McClanahan hit it off right from the get go. They've got matching philosophies."

"Which is?" Arnold asked in a lilting tone.

"Cruelty's a synonym for kindness."

Arnold giggled as Murray and McClanahan traded barbs, the soft-spoken Stevens an out of place gentleman.

On the second loop Murray asked Arnold "So how's your running been going since the trials?"

"Until just recently it was a disaster. I made a big mistake hitting it too hard right after the trials."

"Went to fuckin' Africa," McClanahan said.

"Really?" Murray asked.

"Yes. Two days after the trials I flew over to Kenya. For four weeks all I did was eat, sleep, and run. I was running three times a day, and no matter how much I was sleeping, I couldn't get enough. I was really exhausted and my runs were getting worse and worse." She looked up at McClanahan. "You know what happened when I got back to the States?"

McClanahan just nodded.

"What happened?" Murray asked.

"If it hadn't been for this guy," Arnold said as she jabbed McClanahan, "I'd still be in deep trouble. When I got back to the states I was so exhausted I thought I had mono. I couldn't do the simplest of workouts, and I was having an unbelievably hard time breathing. I went to every specialist in the Boston area that you can imagine, and not one of them could figure out what was going on with me."

"Buncha' over-educated dumb-fucks." McClanahan tried to hurdle a puddle as he spoke. He came up short and his shoe came down in water and mud. "Aw fuck!"

"They tested me for mono. Leukemia. Barr Epstein. Allergies. Liver problems. Female problems. One idiot even suggested that the problem could be psychosomatic."

"How ya' like that fuckin' term? Why not just say she was fuckin' crazy."

"He suggested that I'd had some type of a mental let-down after running the trials. I'll tell you, I felt so worn out at that point, and was so unsure of what was going on, that I was ready to go see a head shrinker. I was getting desperate."

"Shoulda' seen you Murray. You coulda' straightened her out."

Murray's face blushed, his skin turning the color of his red hair.

"Nothing was working and my running was getting worse and worse. Finally, this guy" she said pointing to McClanahan, "found out that I'd been having problems, and he e-mailed me."

"Hate fuckin e-mails. I gotta work for a livin.' Runnin' don't pay the bills."

"He asked me what my symptoms were and I e-mailed him back. Then he e-mailed me a one line message. 'Get a ferritin test and send me the results.' I did, and he called me. He said that I was anemic and needed to get my iron stores built back up. I started eating red meat and taking an iron supplement. And the results were immediate. I started feeling like a different person. When I went out for a run I didn't have trouble breathing. And soon the fatigue left too. Now I'm pretty close to back to where I was right before the trials."

"Kevin got the bulk of his medical training as a kid in Scotland when he worked in the coal mines." Murray's blush was still noticeable as he spoke to Arnold. "He always took a Physician's Desk Reference down with him. He studied it during breaks."

"You worked in the coal mines?" Arnold looked up at McClanahan, her dark eyes as large as saucers.

"Yup."

"He learned all kinds of marketable skills in Scotland," Murray said. "Among other things, the guy's a world class fisherman."

"You fly fish, Kevin?"

"No. He's not quite that sporting," Murray broke in. "Kevin's idea of idyllic fishing is a little different from the poets."

"What do you, fuckin' know 'bout poetry, Murray?"

"He likes to find a piece of private property where the owner's not around and sneak in. Ever seen a guy drag a thirty-foot net across a forty-foot tank? It's a Zen act of sorts."

"Now he's a fuckin' philosopher too. Why you read all that shit, Murray?"

" I wouldn't know how to label it," Murray said. "Cosmic poaching, maybe? I guess if you peel away enough layers there's some underlying beauty."

"Murray's just jealous. He never catches nuthin'. Fish or women."

"McClanahan confuses bludgeoning with catching. The only thing he's ever caught is a cold."

The barbs flew back and forth until the foursome finished their second loop of the soccer field and continued back to the track. They stopped by their running gear, which was scattered on a tartan strip in the infield. Arnold was sitting next to McClanahan as Jesse and his group entered the stadium. McClanahan watched her eyes as they fixed on Sanchez.

"You undressin' him, Arnold?"

"You're subtle."

"Ya' like him? Don't ya'?"

"I don't know him."

"But ya' like the way he looks?"

"He's gorgeous." She answered in a whisper. "Is he seeing somebody?"

"Nooo."

"How come?"

"He's focused on his runnin'."

"And I'll bet if he did get involved with somebody, it would take the smile right off your face."

McClanahan stroked his beard. His eyes narrowed. Arnold felt them peering into her brain. "There's less than eight weeks left until the Olympics. Now's no time for either one of you to start nuthin'. You've both put in too much work to fuck it all up now."

"So he's off limits?"

McClanahan sat for what seemed like forever to Arnold, just staring her down. She turned her head. His stare was too intense for her. "I coached a guy in the 70's that was the most talented marathon runner I ever worked with. Started with him in grade school, and coached him all the way up until he was 25. The motherfucker had the fastest American time in the marathon going into the '76 trials. Three months before the trials he meets this broad. Over night he's completely fucked. I warned him. Told him it wasn't no time to start nuthin'. But the motherfucker didn't listen. He was so damn pecker blind, he couldn't see nuthin' but her. She ruined him. He got married right after he met her, and he went to the trials and ran the worst fuckin' race of his life. Afterwards he was too embarrassed to even talk to me. He and his wife left town and never came back. He hasn't talked to me since. And this was a guy who practically lived with me and Margaret for almost fourteen years."

"You don't trust women?"

"That's bullshit. I've sent more fuckin' women to the U.S. Olympic marathon trials than any coach in this country. I coached Margaret, too. Whole career. You know what she did."

Arnold nodded. She knew that Margaret had been one of the U.S. all time greats on the open and master's running circuits.

"I don't have no trouble with women. I've just been around this game too long and seen too much. I know what happens when runners start screwin' around right before a big meet. It fucks up everything."

Arnold didn't answer. She knew what McClanahan was saying was true. That the relationship between a coach and his runner, eliminating the sexual element, was in many ways a more intimate relationship than most spouses experienced in the course of a marriage. She realized that savvy coaches knew their runners better than the runners knew themselves. And that what amounted to minutiae to some, were vital clues to the coach-detective. She understood that a top coach knew the mundane things about his runners. Their diet, medications, past illnesses, and orthopedic problems. And their running histories. Their times at various distances, their ability to shoulder work loads, their racing strengths and weaknesses. Most of all he knew about their personal lives. What made them tick. He was aware of everything from their childhood traumas, to their current work and relationship problems. It was an intimacy of the highest level. The type of closeness where a savvy coach became so attuned to his athletes, that he could tell by the tone of their voices, their body language, and the expressions on their faces, how things were going for them.

Arnold knew that. And she envied McClanahan's athletes for that. She longed for the one-on-one relationship of being in the same city with her coach. Arnold had a falling out with her own coach a year before the trials. Since that time

McClanahan had coached her by way of e-mail and telephone. She had no reservations about McClanahan's coaching abilities. But she felt a sense of loss. She longed for the frequent contact that McClanahan had with his runners.

She had considered moving to Houston, but her modeling and acting career would have quickly come to an end. She was within driving distance of Manhattan. And the Boston area where she kept her apartment was just minutes away from Harvard Medical School where she would be attending the coming fall.

Running was important to her, but not her entire world. Besides, she had doubts as to her ability. It was one thing to be good on an American level, another entirely to be world class. A silent voice kept telling her that she had been too thinly spread in the years leading up to the Olympics. The three women who medalled in the Olympic Marathon, would be the three women who had devoted the most time to their craft. It was non-stop training, consecutive years of running where everything else took a back seat. It was a life that was neither glamorous nor exciting. It was unrelenting hard work and focus, an existence dedicated to a pursuit that seldom yielded tangible rewards.

Arnold's Olympic competition would come from female runners who were tougher that ninety-nine percent of the professional male athletes throughout the world who made millions in other sports. They were men who thought of themselves as tough, but had no idea of what real work was. The best female distance runners were women who dedicated their lives to their sport. America had produced its share. They were singularly focused, but even with their dedication and focus, knew their chances of capturing an Olympic medal were remote. Arnold understood that her chances of medalling at the Games were not realistic. She had trained hard, and had remained reasonably focused, but not like the world's elite. Women from Africa, Asia, Europe, and Australia, who ate drank and slept running. Knowledge of that truth was the source of her lack of confidence.

"I'll stay away from Jesse."

"I can't tell ya' what to do. You're an adult."

"What do you want, Kevin?"

"Just don't sleep with him until after the Olympics."

"No one's ever accused you of being indirect. Have they Kevin?"

"Yooo asked. I told."

Arnold turned her head away from McClanahan and stared out into space. "Okay. You've got a deal. But just until the Olympics."

McClanahan just nodded.

As the workout ended Arnold went back to her hotel and showered, while McClanahan, Margaret, and Jesse drove to Double Dave's, a pizza parlor in Shepherd Square just off the 59 loop.

The trio took a table in the back. They were joined by the men and women McClanahan coached, their boyfriends, girl-friends, husbands, and wives. The five dollar all you can eat pizza and salad buffet included the first draft beer, with fill-ups 75 cents. Mounted wall televisions were showing baseball and the X-games. As McClanahan drank beer from a plastic cup, eyeing the television, Jesse spotted Shauna Arnold as she walked into the restaurant. She walked past the pool tables toward the upper deck where they were sitting. He felt his heart beat faster.

She was wearing a white peasant blouse and tight blue jeans. Her hair was pulled back in a twist held fast by a tortoise shell clip. Her lips had a light flesh-colored gloss. Other than that, no makeup. She was stunning. Pencilled-in eyebrows, mascara clotted eyes, and ruby-painted lips that he saw so often were useless to her. Houston was resplendent with beautiful women. But this was the most exotic woman he had ever seen.

As she moved across the room toward him, Jesse could see a fluttering under her blouse. He felt his palms moisten.

As she approached them McClanahan said, "Tell them at the register you're with Jesse. Saves ya' a buck when yer with a date."

Jesse felt his neck heat with embarrassment. Arnold smiled. As she eyed Jesse she asked, "Have you already paid for yours?"

Jesse was tongue-tied. All that came out was a nod.

He remained mum as Arnold ate and drank, feeling inadequate and foolish. When McClanahan left the table and went down below to shoot pool, Arnold turned to Sanchez and said softly, "That was some performance at the trials."

Her tone was honest, and the sincerity of her words put him at ease.

"Thanks. I hear you had a pretty good run yourself."

"Light years away from yours. I barely got third on the U.S. marathon team. You shattered a world record."

"Everything fell into place. I guess it was my day."

"You don't just go out and set world records because it was your day," Arnold said. "I know a little bit more about running than that."

"I've got a great coach and a lot of support."

"And incredible talent."

Jesse fingered his earring. He had trouble with compliments.

"I'm not so sure how much of it's talent. We've just put in a lot of work."

Arnold pecked at her salad. He seemed sensitive, she thought. She wondered if he was easily hurt by women.

"So Kevin tells me you're working as a roofer to put yourself through school."

"That's right."

"That must be tough...I mean working in that heat,

84

running, and going to school."

"I don't have a lot of other stuff going on. The work and the school keep me out of trouble. If all I did was run, I'd probably end up in jail."

"I doubt that. You don't seem like the type."

Jesse grinned. "You don't know me. I've got a temper."

"I don't know a great athlete who doesn't have something burning inside."

"How about you?" Jesse made eye contact with Arnold as he spoke. He was stunning, she thought. His skin was so smooth and soft. And his long, silky, jet black hair. And those big dark eyes and long lashes. She longed to touch him. And have him touch her.

"I'm not a great athlete, Jesse."

"Come on. You're no slouch. You finished third at the marathon trials. What's burning inside you?"

Arnold lay her hand on Jesse's knee. "Is there any place quiet we can go talk? Maybe just take a walk?"

Jesse felt a stirring. "Sure. I know a place."

Arnold followed Jesse out the door and they got into his pickup truck. He drove down Shepherd and picked up 59 South, and at the 610 interchange went north. He drove past the Galleria area and exited on Woodway-Memorial. Then east on Woodway before turning left into Memorial Park. He continued down the asphalt road leading into the golf course, and parked beside the three-mile cinder-jogging trail.

Night had fallen but the trail was well lit by bright lamps. The amber glow softly lit the emerald oasis, a unique refuge in a city short of public park space. Majestic pines towered over lush carpets of freshly mowed grass and a rare summer breeze scented the fragrant clippings. "What a beautiful place," Arnold said. She shut the passenger door. Scattered joggers and walkers worked their way around the loop as she spoke.

Jesse nodded. "It is. A lady whose father was governor of Texas donated the park to the city."

"It's beautiful."

"Yeah. But I don't think she ever envisioned what's happened. From what I've read, this place was filled with wildlife, not that long ago. They say it wasn't unusual to see deer running through the woods. That's all gone now."

"It's still an oasis, though."

"Yeah, but it's wall to wall cars and people if you come out here in the evening. The jogging trail's like a subway platform jammed with walkers and joggers. It's so crowded you can barely move."

The two walked for almost half a mile without talking before Jesse broke the silence. "Want to tell me what you were talking about at the pizza parlor? About every great athlete having something burning inside them?"

Arnold stopped. She lightly touched Jesse's face with her fingertips. He felt a burning inside. "This is something that I've only shared with a handful of people. But I feel comfortable with you. I know I can trust you. My father was white, and my mother was black. Big deal. Right? "

Jesse shrugged his shoulders.

"This is the new age," she continued. "Am I another victim? No. I'm not looking for any sympathy. And I've dealt with who I am. But it still bugs me. I'm not big on labels. But everybody thinks of himself or herself as something. What am I? Black? White? Mulatto?" she laughed. "When's the last time you heard that term?"

"Hadn't."

"The fact of the matter is, I'm still not sure what I am. Does that make any sense?"

"Of course it does."

"I mean, we're supposed to be living in times when race doesn't mean anything. But it does. Anybody who thinks that race no longer has any relevance is just deluding himself. And when you're like me, you aren't accepted by whites or blacks. That's the hard truth. But that's not what really pisses me off. This isn't easy for me."

"Take your time." Jesse lay his hand on her shoulder for a brief moment. She felt like satin.

"My father left my mother when I was five. My mother raised my sister and me. Maybe that's why I've got this unresolved crisis. I guess that's what's burning inside me."

Jesse chuckled.

"You think that's funny?" Arnold's eyes ignited with rage as she spoke.

"No. I'm just laughing, thinking of myself. What you've gone through isn't that different from me."

"What are you talking about?"

"Your childhood and mine. My mom is Hispanic. And my old man was a white dude. He left us when I was 12."

"I'm sorry."

"I'm not. I wish I had never known him. He was a worthless piece of crap."

"Drink?"

"Yes.

"Abusive?"

Jesse nodded.

"My dad too. We've got a lot in common."

"Except I ended up at Houston Community College, and you ended up at Harvard Medical School."

"You ended up with a world record in the 800 meters."

"Would you trade?"

"I'm not sure. I'd have to give that some thought. Ask me that about twenty years from now."

"Think we'll know each other in twenty years?"

"Hope so." Arnold took Jesse's hand. She led him off the trail. Under a towering pine tree she stopped, got up on her toes, and pulled his head down toward her. As he tasted her moist lips he felt drunk with ecstasy. As the kiss ended she said, "I made McClanahan a promise."

"What was that?"

"We wouldn't be lovers until after the Olympics."

The directness of her words unnerved him. It was like a fantasy coming true.

"Do you always keep your promises?"

"What do you think?"

They kissed again, oblivious to their surroundings as they drank each other in. As they came apart Jesse's heart was pounding and his body was hot. "When are you going back to Boston?"

"In the morning." She took his hand again and led him toward the golf course. They walked in silence before reaching a manicured green, far away from the trail, out of view. It was pitch black, the moon providing textured light. "We don't have much time," she whispered. The moonlight reflected in her dark eyes like quicksilver as she unzipped her jeans and lowered them.   Later, as the two drove back to Arnold's car, Sanchez wondered if he could maintain his composure for another eight weeks. The turn around in his life had come so rapidly that it had caught him unprepared. One moment he was nobody, a half-breed Mexican laborer who slapped roofs on tract homes. And now he was Olympic bound, a world record under his belt, with the near certain prospect of becoming wealthy within a matter of weeks. That and he had a lover, a gorgeous and intelligent young woman. The type of lady who just weeks before he could only dream about. The incredible shift in fortune made Jesse nervous and anxious. Things like that weren't supposed to happen to him. Everything was going down too quickly.

Chapter 10

Jesse Sanchez never looked forward to the relentless July that baked the Bayou City. Each day brought scorching temperatures in the mid-to-upper 90's, with stifling humidity to match. It was a steam bath of jungle roots, a sweltering inferno that reduced strong men to flaccid puddles of sweat. It was the worst possible setting for a middle or long distance runner to train. But the miserable conditions had not dragged Jesse down. The dramatic turn around in his life had breathed fresh air into his oxygen starved vista.

The Houston summers had been a rude change for Jesse, a youth who had spent his formative summers in Taos, New Mexico. Even in the middle of summer, the early mornings and late evenings were never oppressively hot in the mountains.

As a kid Jesse had heard the words of Arthur Lydiard, the famous New Zealand running coach, who had opinions on most things and frequently shared them. He had preached to runners that humidity made running in heat more tolerable. He said that the sultry conditions made it safer for distance runners in the heat, as humidity promoted sweat, and sweat promoted cooling. Sanchez understood, even as an adolescent, that Lydiard's theory was based on theory, not experience. He was certain that if the renowned New Zealand coach had ever trained in a Houston summer, he wouldn't have promulgated such ill-conceived dogma.

Sanchez remembered reading those words as an adolescent, when he'd come in drained after a summer run. And the futility of trying to sleep after a hard workout. When his heart was racing madly, his body unable to cool. His home was not air-conditioned. It was a luxury which Carmen Sanchez, a woman who fed and clothed two children, could not afford. She cleaned homes and office buildings to make ends meet, and when bills were paid, there was seldom money left over. Even the floor fan near Jesse's bed was a luxury.

Running coaches all had their theories, Jesse reasoned. And he had read and listened to his share. There were a handful of great ones in his mind. And a few others whom he'd classify as good. But most were mediocre or poor. He had witnessed his share of self-promoters, men and women who were cashing in on the 'personal fitness—trainer-coach' boom. Those with the largest followings were the ones with the most convincing patter. Though they generally produced nothing but also-rans. A lot of people were like dogs, Jesse reasoned. Speak to them in a soothing tone and they'd follow, even if the words made no sense. Flatter them, and they'd come back forever. Jesse despised flattery. He viewed it as the lowest form of deceit. Like honey sprinkled with arsenic.

Praise from McClanahan was rare, the Scotsman's bluntness chasing off the weak of heart. But Sanchez loved him for that. He saw right through the 'touchy feely' smoke screen of the phonies, 'caring' men who in his eyes were nothing more than brown-nosed bullshit artists. Sanchez understood them for who they were. They were opportunists in it for the money. They promulgated 'innovative' training techniques, systems which were nothing more than the same hackneyed drivel that had been vomited up a million times before.

Sanchez believed none of their originality claims. He reasoned that foot races began well before recorded history, probably not long after the species got upright. And that training systems developed commensurate with evolution. Skin replaced fur, and sneakers bare feet. Jesse reckoned that the art of running and racing was a process as natural as creation itself. It was a method that defined his life. A procedure that would give him everything he had ever dreamt of.

All his dreams were now at his fingertips for the taking. He was on the verge of striking a golden note. He would be making a living at the craft he loved. He would become wealthy doing it. And he would have the woman of his dreams to share it. The prospects had lightened his load. And even in the blistering heat and humidity, his training had soared to new levels.

McClanahan never told Jesse what he was witnessing. He never hinted to his young runner that he would be untouchable in the Olympics. Barring injury or sickness the gold medal would be Jesse Sanchez's to take. The gold medal would be all his along with a new world record. A time that would put future 800 meter records out of reach for years to come.

McClanahan had kept close tabs on the world's best 800-meter runners. As their results filtered over the Internet—results from Europe, Africa and Asia—it became apparent to McClanahan what he had suspected for a long time. That he was training the most talented runner in the world. And that no other runner was even in Jesse's league. His young gun would cut the competition to shreds. Slinger Sanchez would take no prisoners.

It was a Saturday morning and Jesse's alarm went off at a few minutes before six a.m. He got up, washed and dressed, and walked into the kitchen. He downed two large glasses of water before walking out the door. Less than fifteen minutes later he was running down an asphalt hike and bike trail that followed the snaking waters of Braes Bayou. He ran east, heading toward the Medical Center, only the gentle whirring of tree perched cicadas disturbing the early morning quiet.

It was hardly an idyllic run, the bayou pocked with sewage treatment plants. The stench that emanated from them was often overpowering, magnified intensely on hot and steamy, languorous summer days. It was a fetor that not even the most severely damaged olfactory nerves ever became accustomed.

Jesse had witnessed Houston's second great economic boom. After the oil bust in the early eighties, it had come roaring back strong. But the burgeoning prairie, lined with freeways, and pocked by skyscrapers, and endless look-alike suburbs, was also a land of traffic jams and anger. Sanchez had witnessed his share of violence in and near his apartment in Southwest Houston. He'd also seen the aftermath of murder. Through the building trade he had learned that Houston had no zoning, and a paucity of planning. That both ideas had been anathema to its growth-at-all-cost mentality. He'd heard many describe the city as an overgrown horizontal village. A place void of beginning, middle, or end. A town that was driven by petroleum and fashioned by deal makers. He had read that it was once a swamp, an urban jungle that had sprouted like a virus in a petri dish and was still spreading. Easterners that Jesse had worked for viewed it as a hick town carved from a mud swamp, a bog whose metamorphosis had somehow produced the nation's fourth largest city. But it was a great city, and he loved it. A place he called home.

As Jesse ran, he was unaware of the black Ford Ranger shadowing him on his right. As he approached Gessner, the Ranger turned quickly off Braeswood. Sanchez continued off the jogging trail and into the street. The Ranger roared toward the crosswalk. Before he could react, the vehicle's driver's side door opened. He saw the grinning face of the driver, a white man in his early 20's, whose head had been shaved. On his arm was a blue-green swastika with a message that Jesse couldn't read. The open door struck him like a ton of bricks, the force of the blow lifting him off his feet. He heard male voices laughing as he struck the pavement. The gunning of the truck's motor followed that, and from the corner of Jesse's eye he saw the pickup as it roared east toward the loop.

Sanchez rolled as he hit the pavement, quickly righting himself as he bolted to the other side of the street. It was a reflexive reaction, the type that could only be expected of a highly trained athlete.

As he stood along the banks of the bayou, his pulse beating rapidly, he took stock of his injuries. His hips were painful to the touch, and his knees, elbows, and palms were scraped and bleeding. "Sons of bitches," he hissed. Then he ran in the direction of the truck, a seething anger raging inside. It was the type of anger that had always led to trouble.

It was almost an hour later when Jesse spotted the black Ford Ranger at a convenience store off San Jacinto. As the driver of the vehicle filled his tank with gasoline, the skinhead in the passenger seat glanced at his side, rearview mirror. He spotted a tall, lanky figure, running toward them.

"Fuck," he muttered, as he recognized Sanchez. They'd put almost ten miles on the asshole since they'd hit him, he thought. No way the jerk-off, could have made it here this quickly running. Someone must have given him a ride.

"Hey dip shit. Look who's coming."

The driver looked up. The swastika on his arm was in plain view, as was the message under it. WHITE POWER. As Jesse viewed the message, he saw red. He sprinted across the parking lot and caught the driver flush in the jaw with a hard right. The force of the blow knocked loose the gas hose. As the skinhead fell back and struck the pavement, the other one moved toward Jesse.

Jesse gripped the gas hose in both fists and swung. The metal nozzle struck the second victim in the nose, and a gusher of blood followed. He went down, writhing in pain on the pavement, holding his nose. Jesse flailed away, and then he jumped on top of his screaming victim. He reared back, and got all his shoulder behind a hard right. A cracking sound followed. Sanchez threw a barrage of punches. His knuckles were throbbing when the man went limp.

As Jesse turned his head, the first victim was righting himself. He stumbled toward the pickup truck. As he opened the door, Jesse lunged and caught him from behind. He turned the skinhead around. "You like messing with runners?" He caught him squarely in the solar plexus with a left jab. As the skinhead doubled over, Sanchez slammed the cab door on him. His victim crumpled to the pavement. "You're not so brave now, are you?" Sanchez hissed.

Jesse spotted a sheathed knife attached to the back of the skinhead's belt. Sanchez bent over and unsheathed the knife. With his free hand he grabbed the man's ear, and yanked his head.

As the skinhead stared into Sanchez's crazed face, crying like a baby, Jesse pressed the knife to his victim's throat. "Now you're going to die, you stinking piece of crap."

"Please don't kill me." The man's sobbing voice was thick with tears.

Jesse's eyes were bulging, as he pressed the knife. As he held the blade, his victim cried and shook. What seemed like an eternity to the skinhead ended as Jesse flung the knife into the street.

"Next time I kill you." With his open palm, Jesse slapped the side of the skinhead's face. It made a loud popping sound. The man covered his face with both hands and wept.

Sanchez got up and reached into the cab of the truck. He removed the keys from the ignition, turned, and began running. He ran west on San Jacinto, toward the Medical Center and southwest Houston.

When he got back to his apartment late that morning, he was still seething. He climbed into the shower and turned on the hot water. As the hissing spray pelted his open wounds, he winced with pain. He cleansed the wounds. Then he turned his back to the showerhead. As hot water struck his neck and back, he felt his bruised muscles relax. The force of the truck door striking him and the subsequent spill on the pavement had taken its toll. His knees had swollen. And his hips were sore to the touch.

Jesse sat down in the tub, back to the showerhead. As cascading hot water soothed his aching body, he recalled the morning's events.

He was lucky to be alive. Lucky that the impact of the truck hadn't maimed or killed him. Lucky the bastards whom he chased down hadn't pulled out a gun and shot him. As he sat he realized that what he'd done had been stupid. The odds of him finding those two sons of bitches at that convenience store were a billion to one, he thought. But as he ran toward town in the direction of that Ranger, he was blind with rage. All he could see was the grinning face of the skinhead, and the blue-green swastika on his arm. It was fate that had led him back to his attackers, he thought. It was fate he was still alive. Now he wondered if his body had been damaged. If the aftermath of having been hit by a truck would affect his training.

He stayed in the shower for almost fifteen minutes. It was difficult getting back on his feet. His back and hips were stiff. As he dressed his wounded elbows and knees, he heard the sounds of his mother and brother in the kitchen. The two had returned from mass.

Jesse opened the washroom door. He could smell the fragrance scent of frying onions and peppers. He went to his bedroom and dressed. Then he returned to the kitchen. Jose was sitting at the table watching television. His mother was behind the counter cooking. Jesse ruffled his brother's thick black hair, and playfully massaged the back of his neck. His mother had her back to him.

He approached her from behind, wrapped his arms around her, and lightly bussed her cheek. She was frying Migas in a big iron skillet. A dish of fried eggs, cheese, tortillas, toma-toes, onions and peppers. The aromatic scent was intoxicating. "You've spoiled me, mamma. How will I ever find me a girl who can cook like you?"

Carmen Sanchez smiled broadly. "I'll have to send you back to your grandmother in Cuernavaca when you're ready for a wife. She'll find you a good Mexican girl."

"Won't do no good mama. As soon as I brought her back to the United States, she'd become Americanized. Within a couple of weeks she'd be telling me to cook for myself. Or demanding that we go out to restaurants."

"So you better make a lot of money."

"Why get married? It's easier to just stay at home. Where else can I have my own personal cook and cleaning lady?"

As Jesse reached into a basket beside his mother for a tortilla, Carmen Sanchez gently slapped his hand. "Wait until I serve you."

Jose laughed as he watched his older brother being scolded.

"How come you're always in such a bad mood after mass? I don't think you should go back to that place. You always come back angry."

Carmen Sanchez turned around. She shook the spatula at Jesse. "Go sit down before I lose my temper."

"You're so pretty when you're angry, mamma."

"I'm warning you." She was still waving the spatula.

"Okay, mamma. Okay." He turned and winked at Jose, and his younger brother laughed loudly.

As Carmen Sanchez served her sons, she spotted Jesse's elbows, and then his knees.

"What happened, Jesse?"

"Mamma, I don't understand it. How can you continue to outdo yourself? This is the most delicious breakfast you've ever made." He shoveled food into his mouth, a futile attempt to avoid the questioning that was sure to follow.

"Jes—see. Answer your mother. What happened to you?"

"It was nothing, mamma. Just a little accident. I fell when I was running." Jesse fingered his earring.

As Jesse ate, Carmen Sanchez's eyes focused on Jesse's right hand. She could see his knuckles, which were bruised and swollen.

"Did you fall on the knuckles of your right hand?"

"It was a bad fall. I guess I tried to brace myself when I went down."

"Do you think your mother is stupid?"

"God strike me dead for such a thought ever entering my head."

"Don't you make fun of your mother." She shook her finger at Jesse. "What happened to you?"

"Mamma, why do you always worry? Everything is okay."

"You've been fighting again. Haven't you, Jesse?"

"These eggs need a little hot sauce." As Jesse spoke he reached for a bottle of Tabasco. Carmen Sanchez grabbed his hand and he winced with pain. "What happened?"

"I told you mamma. I fell when I was running. That's all."

Carmen Sanchez let go of his hand. "Jesse, you're no longer a boy. You have your whole life ahead of you. Why would you be getting in fights right before the Olympics? You have to start thinking, Jesse. I can't do your thinking for you."

"It was nothing mamma." Jose got up from the table and disappeared into his bedroom.

As Jesse ate, Carmen Sanchez walked to the telephone on the counter. She picked it up, dialed and paused. "Kevin? This is Carmen Sanchez."

"Mama!"

"I'm okay. But that hot-headed idiot you coach is not.....I'm not sure what's wrong with him. Other than a screw being loose in his thick skull.....I'm not sure what happened. Except his elbows and knees are scraped, and the knuckles on his right hand look broken. I'm sure he's been fighting. But he won't tell me what happened.....Okay. I'll put him on....Jesse, Kevin wants to speak to you."

"I don't want to talk to him."

"You pick up the phone!" She picked up the spatula and shook it at Jesse. "Don't you make your mother lose her temper!"

"Ayyyaaah. Okay, mamma. Chill out. I'll speak to him."

Carmen Sanchez remained silent as Jesse spoke with McClanahan. She listened quietly as her son retold the story of the events that had transpired earlier that morning. Secretly, she felt proud that her son was not a coward. But the fighting frightened her. She knew that with a temper like his, he could easily one day get killed. Her son had never looked for fights. But he'd never backed off from them either. Carmen Sanchez understood the source of Jesse's rage. She knew the anger that was boiling inside him. She felt guilty about her son's fury, a wrath from a troubled childhood. Ferocity born from the wounding words and leather hands of a drunken bastard.

That evening as McClanahan read through his e-mails, he received an attached file from an address titled (bigwing@aol.com)

McClanahan:
Do you think you and Sanchez have won? Better not celebrate too early. The walls have ears. Stay tuned for more fun and games, and don't book your tickets for Sydney yet. (Not unless they're refundable.) You, and you're so-called world record holder, haven't gotten away with anything. The shit has yet to hit the fan.

McClanahan got off line, powered down, and walked to his refrigerator. He grabbed himself a home brew and walked out into the backyard. He loosened a hose from its coil, turned on the water, and sat sipping his beer as spray washed his garden. McClanahan loved to garden. He made his own compost, and grew vegetables and herbs most of the year round. To him, the taste of his homegrown produce, and the produce at the local market, were light years apart. The store bought vegetables he and Margaret purchased, besides having been soaked in pesticides, were often coated with wax. They were tasteless offerings, benign produce with the delectability of cardboard.

But even more significant than the pleasure of dining on sumptuous produce, McClanahan loved gardening for its simplicity. It was a means of escape, a quiet time to leave behind a world driven by avarice and greed.

As he mused over his garden, thoughts turned to childhood. He remembered himself, a tall gangly youngster, chasing across the Scottish countryside after hares. He would run the hares down until they were exhausted, and return home with the rabbits, a vital source of protein for a family unable to afford the exorbitant price of meat.

Scotland was a rugged land, McClanahan thought. A place where working place stiffs lived on potatoes. A monotonous diet that he got so sick of, that at times he felt like spuds were coming out of his ears. Scotland's rocky vistas didn't yield produce like the rich tropical soils of the Texas Gulf Coast. Nor were fish and game as abundant. His was a harsh land, a place that bred honest, no-nonsense people.

McClanahan portrayed himself as a tough guy, but his wife Margaret knew better. She understood that her husband was extraordinarily sensitive. One who shielded his sensitivities from all but a handful of friends and family who really knew him. His passion was running and runners. Nothing could brighten his heart or break it quicker. He'd confided to Margaret, and a few close friends, that he was nothing but a running bum. A city employee who worked to pay the bills but lived and breathed for his runners.

To McClanahan, running was a renewable life source. Nothing, in his mind, compared to the working with young runners. It was impossible to put a value on the satisfaction he received, as he watched them develop and mature through his firm but loving hand. It was their youth that kept him young, an extended family with far branching roots.

In a lifetime of running and coaching, he'd never realized the type of satisfaction that he'd reaped from Jesse Sanchez. In 'Slinger' he'd nurtured a young runner, who was now realizing the ambitions of his dreams. The two were born thousands of miles apart. Their backgrounds couldn't have been further removed. But they shared a common spirit, both fighters, each possessing an unwavering sense of ethics and loyalty.

McClanahan drained a long swig of his home brew and felt a buzz. No one was going to stop Jesse Sanchez, he thought. No one.

Chapter 11

Monday morning Jesse Sanchez waited impatiently in a white-walled examining room for Dr. Dan Bassler. It had been McClanahan's idea to visit the orthopod, not Jesse's. Bassler was McClanahan's close friend, an orthopedic surgeon whose prowess was world renown. He was a physician who had treated a disproportionate number of the world's finest athletes.

Like McClanahan, Bassler was a controversial figure. He was well known in the running community, having as many detractors as promoters. He was at the pinnacle of his craft, a perch where jealous competitors were quick to spread rumors. Though Bassler's surgical calendar was booked far in advance, he took in more than his share of charity cases. It was a fact that was not trumpeted. Jesse knew that Bassler had a special affinity for runners. Youngsters in particular. He remembered when a friend of his, a teenage girl from a Hispanic family, required extensive reconstructive foot and ankle surgery due to an automobile accident. The sixteen-year-old was a promising distance runner, who without insurance was facing the prospect of a life as a cripple. Bassler performed a series of extensive surgeries on her. And he arranged for all her hospital expenses to be absorbed by his practice. It was big bucks. A figure that would have drained her family and put them into debt. It was one of many charity cases the physician had taken on. So it angered Sanchez whenever he heard one of Bassler's detractors belittling him. It was the same anger that roiled in his gut whenever McClanahan's name was dragged through the dirt.

Bassler still carried the remnants of his small town Georgia upbringing. His speech patterns and mannerisms suggested an uneducated southern hick. But Jesse realized the affectations were little more than camouflage. False clues that hid the real man. Jesse had come to learn that Bassler was an over-achiever. A physician whose thirst for knowledge was insatiable. His quest for the refinement of his craft knew no bounds. His surgical techniques were constantly evolving. Endowed with a childlike sense of curiosity, the orthopod was never content to accept dogma as truth. The inquisitiveness had made him a leader in his field.

The former Rhodes scholar had literally rewritten Gray's Anatomy. He found a misplaced nerve in the heels of cadavers, and developed a revolutionary technique that redefined heel surgery.

Bassler returned to Jesse's examination room about five minutes later. The technician had posted the x-rays on a lighted board. Sanchez watched as Bassler studied the films. The orthopod was an impressive figure, about six feet six inches, two hundred and forty pounds. He was bald on top, a salt and pepper mustache blanketing a thin upper lip. He viewed each picture carefully before sitting. Then he studied Jesse's face, rubbed his chin, and grinned. It was a toothy, unbridled face-splitter, a no-holds-barred smile that likened him to a goofy, overgrown kid. He was a middle-aged man. But the shining eyes were those of a youngster. His physical stature was imposing, but there was nothing intimidating about the face. As he sat grinning, he looked like a big kid who had just cleaned out a candy store and gotten away with it.

"What do the other guys look like, Jesse?" Then he giggled, a mouse like tee-hee that didn't fit his body.

"Not too good."

"I'll bet they'll never mess with a runner again. Not from what McClanahan told me." Then he slapped his knees and laughed until his eyes ran with tears. Jesse was hurting, but he couldn't help but laugh himself.

"What did you find, Doc?"

"Other than some knuckles, nothing's broken. Both your knees took pretty good shots. And so did your hips. But no fractures, and there doesn't appear to be any cartilage damage."

"Good. Then I can go." Jesse got up.

"I'd take it easy for awhile before I got back into any speed work. You took a pretty good shot. When you start running again, you'll want to ice your knees and hips afterwards. As far as your knuckles go, I could send you to a hand specialist."

"No thanks. There's only a month to go until Sydney. I'll just deal with it."

"You want an anti-inflammatory?"

"No. I hate medicine."

Bassler stroked his chin.

"Listen, I appreciate everything, Doc. One of these days I'm going to pay you back for all the times you've taken care of me."

"Don't worry about it. Just bring back a medal from Sydney. You give me a signed picture, and I'll stick it on my wall."

"You got it. I just want you to know how much I appreciate everything you've done for me."

Bassler grinned. "Just don't get in any more fights between now and Sydney."

Jesse nodded. "I won't."

As Sanchez left, Bassler envisioned the scenario that Jesse had encountered the previous day. He imagined the two skinheads in their Bronco. And what must have been the look of disbelief on their faces when they saw Jesse approaching.

The skinheads were almost ten miles past the spot where they had struck Sanchez almost an hour earlier. They must have shit a brick when they spotted him, Bassler thought. Then he began to giggle as he visualized the scene. Soon the giggle turned into unbridled laughter. He'd have paid anything to witness the ass kicking, he thought.

McClanahan had told him repeatedly that Jesse Sanchez was a tough son of a bitch. Tough was an understatement, Bassler thought. McClanahan's young runner redefined the term.

Chapter 12

That evening on the Rice University Track, Sanchez was suffering. McClanahan watched intently as Slinger struggled through a series of 4x800 meters, followed by a mile. It was obvious that Jesse's movements were labored. The discomfort most pronounced when he jogged between sets. The slower movements accentuated his pain, the jackknifed muscles punctuating his normal silky stride.

The next few weeks would be hell for the kid, McClanahan thought. Sanchez would run in pain as his bruised body mended. But the mending process would be speedy. The type of healing that only came by way of youth. It was the gift of possessing a 22-year-old body. One that could snap back from illness and injury with lightning quickness.

After the evening workout, Jesse drove back to South-west Houston. He stopped at a supermarket two blocks from his home and purchased groceries. Less than ten minutes later he pulled into the back lot of his apartment complex. He walked up two flights of stairs. As he entered his unit the fragrant scent of frying fajitas filled his nostrils. He shut the glass patio door behind him. Then he walked toward his brother Jose who was sprawled out on the living room floor. As the television blared, Jesse playfully ruffled Jose's hair.

Through open wood shutters leading into the kitchen, he saw his mother. She was standing in front of her stove, tending to a frying pan on the right front burner. Jesse moved toward her, and later placed the sack of groceries on a Formica counter to her right. Carmen Sanchez said, "How are you, Jesse?"

"Fine mama." He leaned over and kissed her cheek. Chicken strips and onions sizzled in the frying oil.

"A registered letter came for you from Indianapolis, Jesse. And you also got a long distance call from a young lady in Boston. She seemed very nice. You didn't tell me you had a girlfriend in Boston."

"I'm not sure you could call her my girlfriend. We just met. You know women. One day they're interested in you, the next day they're history."

"She sounded very interested. If I were you, I wouldn't waste any time. I'd call her right back."

"Where's the letter from Indianapolis, mama?"

"I put it on your dresser."

"Thanks."

He walked back to the bedroom he shared with Jose. Resting on top of a blonde pine dresser was an envelope. Jesse picked it up and gazed at the return address. The letter had been sent from the NATF. Affixed to the envelope was a registration form, and return receipt with his mother's signature.

Jesse picked up the letter, sat on his bed, and opened it.

Mr. Jesse Sanchez:

The NATF regrets to inform you that results of your drug test, administered subsequent to the U.S. Olympic Trials 800 meter finals, indicates that your testosterone levels have measured significantly above the acceptable testosterone/ epitestosterone ratio of 6 to 1, established for NATF and Olympic athletes.

Pending a hearing scheduled August 6, 1997, 9:00 a.m. at our home office in Indianapolis, you are prohibited from participating in any event, sanctioned by either the NATF or the ITF. Failure to heed this sanction will result in subsequent punitive actions.

Though the NATF does not serve as a legal advisory board, we urge you to keep the results of our findings confidential. This is for your protection.

You are both entitled and encouraged to bring counsel with you to your hearing, along with any supporting documents and evidence, that may strengthen your case.

The NATF will not pass judgment on your case until all facts have been brought forward and weighed. However, because the results of your urine test indicate unacceptable levels of testosterone, it is your burden of proof to demonstrate to our committee, that our findings were spurious.

We retain for legal counsel the firm of:

Janicke & Hartwick

117 State Street

Indianapolis, Indiana 10076

Please advise your counsel to contact Janicke and Hartwick for all matters concerning your case.

It is our sincere desire to speedily rectify this matter.

Respectfully,

Joseph Nixon

NATF Director

Jesse's mouth went dry as he finished the letter. He placed the letter on his bed and stared emptily into space. Then he picked it up and read it again. Then again, and again, before walking out of the bedroom.

"Save some dinner for me, mamma. It's important," Jesse called to his mother as he headed to the front door.

"Where are you going?"

"To McClanahan's."

"Is something wrong?"

"Yes."

"What is it?"

"I'll tell you later, mama. I don't have time to talk right now."

"How about the girl? Aren't you going to call her?"

"Later, mama."

Less than five minute later Jesse pulled up to McClanahan's driveway. He parked behind Margaret's ancient blue pickup and McClanahan's battered MG.

He rang the doorbell and waited. Footsteps followed. The door opened, Margaret holding it. "Jesse? What's going on?

You look like somebody died. What's wrong?" As Jesse walked inisde Margaret shut the door behind him.

"Everything!"

He reached into his warm-up pants, took out the letter from the NATF, and handed it to Margaret. "Let me get my glasses."

Jesse followed Margaret into the kitchen. He stood as she picked up a pair of reading glasses resting on the kitchen table. She read slowly, peering through wire-framed glasses purchased at Target. Jesse watched her face. Her skin turned a pallid shade of paste. "Shit." She took off the glasses, lay the letter on the table, and looked up at Jesse. "Muh—ther—fuck—er."

"You believe that crap? Where's Kevin?"

"Showering. Just got finished running. He was in a surly mood, bitching about the heat. This will really set him off."

Margaret disappeared into the foyer leading to the master bedroom. Several minutes later McClanahan ambled into the kitchen. He was wearing plaid shorts, a Hawaiian shirt, black socks, and tire-tread sandals. Jesse had seen guys living out of shopping carts who dressed better.

"What the fuck's goin' on?"

Jesse handed him the letter.

McClanahan took it and read slowly. Like Margaret, his face turned sickly. As he read, he realized what had happened. It had come back at him, he thought, like a ton of fucking bricks. It was payback. The shoe companies and the track and field federations were getting even. They had nailed him by taking down the kid. As McClanahan visualized Joseph Nixon's face, his fists tightened.

"What are we going to do?"

"We've got to get a fuckin' attorney."

"I don't have money for lawyers."

"Don't worry 'bout that. I know one."

"How can they get away with this?"

"'Cause they got the power."

"How could they have come up with a positive drug test? I've never taken any drugs. How could my testosterone levels be above the legal limit, unless I was on steroids? You know I'd never touch that stuff. Besides, even if I wanted to, where would I have gotten the dough to purchase that crap?"

"I ain't gonna' bullshit ya'. The way this stuff works is simple. Yer guilty until ya can prove yer ass innocent. I don't know how them shits came up with those test results. But it don't take a rocket scientist to figure it out. Somehow they altered the sons of bitches. Now we've got to prove that ya' weren't on the juice."

"What happens if we lose?"

"Then we're fucked. Means kissing off the Olympics, and everything else. They'll ban yer ass from track and field."

"I can't believe this."

"My fault. Payback."

"So what do we do now?"

"Get yer ass an attorney." He reached for the telephone. Margaret and Jesse remained silent as he dialed.

That night McClanahan lay awake deep into the night before falling into a fitful sleep. Scenes flashed back to 1997 in New Orleans, Louisiana. The setting was a public forum on track and field. A venue where both NATF and ITF Presidents Joseph Nixon and Primo Magiano were panel members on a discussion of 'How to Promote and Grow the Sport of Track and Field in the United States.' A series of benign questions and answers followed. Then McClanahan stood up.

"I got some questions for ya'. First of all, yooo', Magiano." McClanahan pointed his finger at the Italian. "Yooo say yooo care so much about this sport. I don't think yooo care fuck all about this sport." Gasps of disbelief from the stiff-collared audience followed. "How much could ya' care about the fuckin' sport after the kind of shit ya' just pulled in Italy? Ya' wanted the World Cross Country Championships in yar back-yard. And since they ain't got no hills in yar bloody town, ya bring in a fuckin' team of engineers and build yar own fuckin' course. Twelve million fuckin' dollars to build a fuckin' cross country course right in yar own fuckin' backyard, just so ya' can be entertained. How many fuckin' kids coulda' been helped get started in this sport with that kind of dough?"

"And yooo." McClanahan pointed his finger at Nixon. "Every dumb ass in the world that's followed track and field knows the kind of shit ya've pulled. Ya've spent a lifetime stealin' millions from the NATF. And how much fuckin' dough ya' got stuffed in safe deposit boxes and numbered accounts from corporate kickbacks? Ya' dirty motherfucker."

As McClanahan spoke, two refrigerator-sized security men came up from behind and grabbed him. As they dragged him out of the packed room, the eyes of the audience focused like lasers on the Scotsman. McClanahan continued bellowing. "Ya' talk about drugs, ya' lyin' motherfuckers. Ya' wanna' stop drugs? Then why don't ya' go to blood testin'? I'll tell ya' why", he thundered as he was led toward the exit. "It's cause ya' don't want to stop nuthin'. Ya' know fuckin' well right that if ya' clean up the sport, the records stop, and the crowds do too. Money. That's all ya' care about, ya motherfuckers. Money!"

McClanahan woke up, his heart pounding as he recalled the scene. He had ripped authority, and now it was payback time. But the authority figures had punished him in a way that was much deeper than any personal attack they could have launched on him. They had attacked Jesse. And that was a hurt he wasn't prepared for.

Chapter 13

The next morning Jesse took off from work. He and McClanahan drove to the law offices of Aronstein and Frost. They were in Post Oak Park, on the 26th floor of a high rise, just off the 610 South Loop.

James Frost, whose son had been coached by McClanahan, listened as Jesse and the Scotsman told their story. His face reddened with anger as the saga unfolded. Frost knew about McClanahan's character by way of his own son Josh, a moderately talented middle distance runner who was attending Duke Law School. From the boy he'd learned that McClanahan was honest to a fault. And the story he was hearing had a ring of truth that was so strong, it left no doubt in his mind of its veracity. Sanchez had been framed. The question was by whom. That enigma was not worth pursuing, the attorney thought. To uncover the layers of deceptions spawned by the track federation would be futile. Besides, time was of essence. His agenda was to present a case. One that was strong enough to convince the Track Federation to drop their charges against Sanchez.

When the meeting ended, Frost wrote a letter to the Track Federation. The terse note stated he would be representing Sanchez. It further maintained his client's innocence. In strong language it castigated the NATF for their ill-conceived findings. He stressed that any leakage of their spurious test results would further damage his client's reputation. And materially affect future remedy.

Next Frost contacted a private investigator, a former FBI agent that his firm employed. He instructed the investigator to track down a steroid 'guru'. One of the many shady characters who supplied illegal steroids to athletes and bodybuilders around town. He specifically sought a chemist who had worked with track and field athletes.

Late that evening Frost received a telephone call at his Memorial home. The investigator had located a source that fit Frost's requirements. He was willing to talk for a price. His name was Donny Pesko, 'roid guru', a self-taught chemist. He had worked, and was currently working, with a number of national and world-class sprinters. He employed a lab that was located just minutes from his Southwest Houston home. The investigator arranged for Frost to meet with Pesko Wednesday night.

Frost entered Pesko's home that night, an unassuming ranch style house in the Meyerland area. He made no objections as Pesko searched him for hidden listening devices. Once Pesko was satisfied that Frost was clean, the two went into the den. Frost sat in a tan leather couch fronting a glass-topped coffee table. Pesko sat across from him in a reclining chair covered like the couch.

Donny Pesko was short and pudgy. He was balding, with a dark, brush-like mustache. He was wearing black pants and black wing tips. A wrinkled white dress shirt dappled with coffee stains completed his outfit.

"Okay counselor. Your nickel. Go for it."

"Cut to the chase. I know what you do. You know why I'm here. My client is innocent. I need proof."

"Why me?"

"I need a quick education so I can present a defense. I've only got a few weeks."

"Lots of source material out there. A lot cheaper than what you're paying me."

"When I prepare for a case, I seek firsthand knowledge. If possible, I go straight to the source."

"I'm impressed. Not too many big time attorneys leave their offices for discovery."

"I don't usually. This is personal."

"What makes you think your boy's innocent?"

"Gut."

"I can buy that." Pesko reached into his breast pocket and pulled out a package of Juicy Fruit. He took his time as he stripped down a half dozen pieces of gum, before shoving them through his guppied lips into his oily face. As he masticated gum he said, "If your boy's innocent, he's as rare as rocking-horse shit."

"Oh?"

"You heard me right counselor. Scarce."

"What are you telling me? That most track and field athletes use steroids?"

"Track and field? How about almost every major sport you can think of. Have you taken a look at athletes lately, counselor?" As Pesko spoke his chewing quickened. He leaned back in his chair and cracked his knuckles.

"I watch sports."

"Right. But how close?"

"What do you mean?"

"See the size of the guys playing football today, counselor? Hell, you've got college teams that are averaging three hundred pounds a kid on the line. Back in our day, two forty was a pretty good size for a pro lineman."

Frost nodded.

"And look at the basketball players. See how big those suckers under the boards are getting? And I'm not talking height. Look at the arms and shoulders on those suckers. You think that comes from just pumping iron?" Pesko laughed as he chewed, rocking back and forth in his chair. "Baseball players. Look at the size of those mothers. You see some of the home runs those babies hit? We're talking t-shots. Think that's just from state of the art weight training?" Pesko stuck his pinky in his ear and drilled.

"I'd never given it that much thought."

"Not many people do. You'd heard the swimming rumors. What supposedly went on with the East Germans. Well, that truth has surfaced. And it's ugly. The East German coaches were feeding those kids steroids like it was candy. Told them they were giving them vitamin supplements."

"Let's talk about track and field, Mr. Pesko."

"Excellent. My specialty. You know how many sprinters I've got as clients? Hey, I don't want to bust your bubble. But if I started naming names, you'd probably have a cat." He paused, cracked his knuckles, and belched. "You know counselor, even guys like me have likes and dislikes. And you know who I hate the worst? I hate the goodie-two shoes that can do no wrong. The assholes who come out publicly and blast steroids, while they're main-lining the juice. Just like Goddamn junkies."

"I think I know who you're referring to."

"Fucking 'A' right." Pesko smiled exposing brownish yellow teeth. "And the public believes these guys when they look in the camera, and you see the whites of their eyes. And they start crusading against drugs." Pesko laughed again. "Bullshit. I hate those Goddamn hypocrites. The worst. You know it's one thing to be on the shit. And mind you, I don't have any trouble with that concept. Because as far as I'm concerned, what you put in your body is your own business."

"I feel the same way."

"But when the sons of bitches who live on the juice, have the balls to start getting sanctimonious, pointing the finger at everybody else, and then they tell you that they'd never touch the shit. That's when I get pissed. You know what I mean?"

Frost nodded.

"There's been guys like that I wanted to take down. Self-righteous assholes who should have had the whistle blown on them. Sometimes I've fantasized doing that. But then good sense got in the way of ethics, and I rationalized that business is business. So I kept my mouth shut."

"Think Ben Johnson was a bad guy, counselor? Let me tell you something. The only thing that Ben Johnson did that was different from most of the other assholes he competed against was that he got caught."

"Why?"

"He was dumb. That's all. If I'd have been his man, he'd have never gotten caught. No one who's been under Donny Pesko's care has ever been caught. Johnson must have had a fucking moron taking care of him."

"The drug testing labs were that bad?"

"Neanderthal."

"But they've advanced?"

"Some. But they haven't even come anywhere near to keeping up with us. We're so far ahead of them, it's a joke."

"How do you mask the steroids in a drug test?"

"A lot of ways. But with my method, there's usually not much masking to worry about."

"Why's that?"

"Because my product is primo. I've got water-soluble juice. Stuff that's undetectable within twenty-four hours of taking. No traces in the system. Zippo."

"So you're telling me it's highly unlikely, that an athlete under supervised intake, from a state of the art chemist, could get caught?"

"They could. But not the way they're testing in track and field."

"What do you mean? Am I missing something here? Are you implying there's a better way to test?"

Pesko grinned again broadly as he chewed. "Bet your sweet ass there is."

"How's that?"

"Simple. Blood testing."

"What's the difference?"

"Big difference. Your boy runs a race. He finishes. Then he pisses in a container. Right?"

"That's what I understand."

"Yeah. And they even have somebody watching him. Just to make sure it's his piss."

"How could it be anybody else's?"

"Suppose there's no one there to watch him? All he has to do is bring in a bottle of somebody else's urine."

"So if an official is present when the athlete urinates, that pretty much seals it?"

"Not necessarily. There's other ways."

"How?"

"I know athletes, men and women both, who have shoved catheters up their urethras. Then they use a baster to squeeze someone else's urine in their bladder."

"Amazing."

"No big deal. But the big thing isn't resorting to stuff like that. It's what shows up in urine. And if you know a little chemistry, it's easy to mask urine. Even when the track federations tell you how they're improving testing methods. We're always ten steps ahead of them. By the time their new testing procedures come out, we've already come up with ways of beating them. But they know that. And they don't care."

"And blood testing is different?"

"It's tough to screw with. Professional cycling went to it, and it pretty much cleaned the sport up overnight."

"Why hasn't track and field gone to it?"

"The obvious. It would kill the sport."

"What do you mean?"

"They know that so many of their athletes are on the juice, that it would completely decimate track and field. You'd see most of the guys on top retire. And the ones who continued to compete would have their choice. Of getting off the stuff and having their performances slip to nothing. Or chance staying on the juice and getting busted."

"If what you're saying's true, there must be a lot of external pressure on the track federation to adopt blood testing. Surely others are privy to what you're telling me."

"Who's going to pressure them? Besides, even if someone did, they'd come up with a million excuses. They'd say the athletes hate it. Getting stuck with needles. They'd tell you that blood spoils. That the containers break. That blood clots during shipping if it gets warm. That some athletes pass out when they get stuck with needles. And then there's always the religious argument. That having blood drawn is against some people's religious beliefs. Hey, the truth is that the International Track Federation is scared shitless about blood testing. They depend on sponsorship money from big corporations to keep their water flowing. If the Olympic athletes taking roids got nailed, two things would happen. First, all the big names would be history. And second, the big sponsors. I'm talking the real players. The Coca-Cola's, the McDonald's, the telephone companies. They'd shut off the faucet. Cut their sponsorship, so they wouldn't have their name commingled with drug users. That happens, and the Olympics are toast. In a New York fucking minute."

"Haven't they caught athletes in the past?"

Pesko sneered. "You know how many athletes got busted in the '96 games in Atlanta?"

"No."

"Two. Out of 11,000 athletes, the ITF sanctioned two positive drug tests." Pesko chewed quickly. Then he leaned forward in his chair and pointed his stubby index finger at Frost. "And you know what? That was down from five positives at the 1992 Olympics in Barcelona. And an all time high of 12 positive at the '84 games in L.A. I've heard assholes say that it just proves that the '96 Olympics were the cleanest games they've ever had. Since they began testing at the '72 games in Munich. You know what I tell those turkeys? I tell them that when their i.q. hits 37, to sell. And it's not just track and field that's involved with cover-ups. Hey, you know what goes on in the NBA? Did you read the investigative piece they did in the *New York Times*? They interviewed a ton of NBA players anonymously. They say that at least 70 per cent of them smoke pot. You think the league wants to test for that? You know what that would do to their marketability? Hey, the drug stuff goes on in every sport. But the difference, the way I see it, is that track and field athletes aren't into drugs to get high. Their agenda is performance enhancement. Nothing else."

"Surely track and field athletes have to be aware of the long term effects of taking steroids."

"You've got to understand the mentality of these kids. Basically they've got a choice. Stay clean in their sport and never go past a local level. Or get on the juice and have a shot at making it big time. You couldn't find a sprinter or field event guy with an Olympic medal who's been clean a whole career. I'd bet the ranch on that. My money against their lie detector test. You know how many takers I'd get? Zippo."

"How about the long term effects on their health? Aren't they concerned?"

"Let me tell you this. A couple of years ago a poll was put out. Over 500 sprinters, field men, swimmers, and other athletes were questioned. The poll asked if they were offered steroids and were guaranteed that they wouldn't be caught and that they'd win, would they take them? There were six no's out of 500 questioned. Then they were asked if they were guaranteed they wouldn't be caught, and would win every competition they entered for the next four years, and then they would die from the side effects of the juice, would they still take it? More than half answered yes. Does that answer your question about the mentality of these kids?"

"I see your point."

"Hey, to a man and woman, almost every one of these kids that have been under my care tell me the same thing. They say they don't want to do drugs. But unless they come up with a testing method that will keep their competitors from using them, they've got no choice."

"You agree with that?"

"Sure. They play it clean and go nowhere. While athletes from Asia, Africa, and Europe who are on the juice, mop up on the medals. It's a no-brainer, man. When you reach the level of these kids, you're no longer talking about amateurs. That notion's been dead forever. The amount of time and dough that these kids and their families have invested gives them no other choice. They either play the game to win, or they lose. No different than business or politics. Strictly Machiavellian. Do whatever it takes."

"I can see the advantage of steroids in the power events. Sprinting, throwing, weight lifting. Even swimming. But I don't see where how it would benefit a middle or long distance runner. Wouldn't added muscle mass there be a hindrance?"

"What you're saying is right on. And as a group, middle and long distance runners are a hell of a lot cleaner than sprinters. But it still goes on."

"What's the advantage?"

"First of all, female distance runners benefit from the juice a lot more than men. Why, no one is sure. But it's been pretty well documented. Look at the Chinese women who set all those distance running records before the Atlanta Olympics. Everyone knows they were on the juice. They ran times that no women have been able to come anywhere near to since. The Chinese brought over East German chemists. The same ones who'd pumped up their swimmers back when they were setting all those records. And bingo, almost overnight, same thing happened. China went from a nothing, to overnight having the greatest female distance running times ever."

"But how about the male distance runners?"

"They're into EPO."

"What's that?"

"Genetically engineered erythropoietin. Basically it's a natural hormone which physicians prescribe for kidney disease, anemia, and other disorders. The stuff stimulates the formation of red blood cells that carry oxygen to the muscles. That helps build endurance. The stuff showed up in Europe in the late eighties. And it caught on quick with cyclists. A bunch of Dutch cyclists died from taking it. But the drug's still popular. Guys want to win at any cost. Right now the Italians are the masters of EPO. There's no definitive tests for EPO or blood doping, so they get away with it. Any of the foreign runners who are spending time in Italy training—including the Africans— are there for a reason. And I can tell you it's not the climate or the food. Almost all the middle and long distance records are coming from the athletes who are training in Italy."

"Do distance men use other steroids?"

"I haven't personally witnessed it. But I hear it's done."

"What would the advantage be? What good would it do? I thought building muscle mass for distance runners would be undesirable."

"The bump a distance runner gets on the juice is being able to get in more quality workouts."

"I don't understand."

"It's not that difficult. Suppose you're a distance runner. You train hard on Monday, and Tuesday you're tired. So you back off. That goes on the rest of the week. One day you whack it, the next day you back off. Now let's say you're on the juice. After Monday's workout you still feel good on Tuesday, so you come right back with another hard workout. That goes on for the time you're on the course of the juice, maybe six to eight weeks. Who do you think is going to have the most advanced cardiovascular system at the time of the race? The distance runner whose had three to four quality days a week? Or the one that's running full throttle seven days a week?"

"I hear you. What are we talking cost wise? To get this stuff?"

"Depends. I've had sprinters dish out up to four grand a month. That may sound like a lot, but when you're making seven figures a year, through competitions and endorsements, it's just a drop in the bucket."

"So only the top athletes can afford steroids?"

"No. The guys who are forking out that kind of dough are paying for designer steroids."

"What are they?"

"Basically, steroids that have been chemically altered to modify them to an athlete's personal specs and made almost impossible for testers to identify. You see counselor, every steroid has its own unique signature that shows up in the urine of the guy using it. But the catch is the track federation only tests for the signatures of steroids that are commercially available. Once I've done my tweaking, they'll never detect it."

"How about the athlete on limited funds?"

"Kind of like your racquet. Lots of attorneys out there. Maybe you can find a cheap one to get the job done. But if you had your choice, who'd you rather go with? See, the trick is knowing how much to give and when. Timing is everything."

"So which steroid was biggest at the Atlanta Games?"

"Wasn't a steroid at all. And it wasn't illegal."

"Oh?"

"Stuff called hGH. Human growth hormone. Doesn't show up in the urine. Helps you recover quickly from workouts. Hell, there were so many athletes on that shit in Atlanta, that in the trade they were calling Atlanta the Growth Hormone Games."

"If what you're saying is true, the Track Federations have done a pretty good job of misleading the public."

"Biggest snow job in history. I'm telling you, they're all smoke and mirrors. They've been an active party in suppressing what they know goes on. You know anything about testosterone levels?"

"Not much."

"I'll try and simplify. Most men have a testosterone/epitestosterone ratio of 1.3 to 1 or lower. About one guy in a thousand has a t/e ratio of more than 5 to 1. So the Track Federations made 6 to 1 as their acceptable level which you could get under the wire with when testing for steroids. So let's say that you come to me, and you've got a normal t/e level of one to one. I put you on the juice, about 200 milligrams of testosterone three times a week, and I bring up your levels to where they're just under 6 to 1. Know what that means?....Means that along with the hGH that I put you on, you're athletic performance is going to improve 10 to 20 per cent. And I know you're a smart man, Mr. Frost. I know that you can figure what that comes to in a track race or a throwing event. And you know, I can always spot athletes who have been taking hGH on a long term basis."

"How's that?"

"I just look at their jaws. They've got GH jaws."

"What's that?"

"From taking the growth hormone, their jaws start to grow. You'll see a lot of those guys getting braces and retainers. Throws everything out of kilter. Sometimes the bones start growing so long—not just in the jaws but also in the hands and feet—that they start pushing through the skin. I know one guy who had to have skin grafts."

"Whole different world."

"Hey. Every world-class athlete needs three things. A world-class coach, a world-class attorney, and a world-class biochemist. I am numero trois." He grinned as he opened a new package of Juicy Fruit. He began stripping down the gum.

"What you've told me today will be invaluable for my client's defense."

"Glad I could help. Whenever I'm brought cash, I get real helpful."

"You've earned your fee."

"Mind if I ask you a question, counselor?"

"Go right ahead."

"Obviously, somebody didn't like your boy. Doesn't take a rocket scientist to figure that out. He was singled out. He must have pissed off some heavy hitters."

"I suspect you're right."

"Your client's Jesse Sanchez, isn't it?"

Frost nodded.

"That explains. The track federations are all afraid of McClanahan. He's an honest guy. Guy's like that are danger-ous."

Frost just nodded.

When Frost drove home that evening he thought of his own son, Josh. In a way it was a blessing that Josh was only a moderately talented runner. He'd never be faced with the nagging dilemma that haunted his world-class peers.

The next day, Frost sent Jesse to a private lab in the Houston Medical Center for blood and urine samples. He arranged for a hematologist, a renowned physician considered an authority on steroids, to witness the tests as a disinterested third party. When the test results came back, he contacted Janicke and Hartwick, the legal firm representing the Track Federation. He told them where and how Jesse had been tested and offered them to designate a lab, for follow up tests. The Federation's attorneys declined Frost's offer. They stated that Jesse's original test results, from Eugene, Oregon, were effica-cious. And that subsequent tests were not in order.

Chapter 14

On a Sunday evening, Sanchez, McClanahan, and Frost flew to Indianapolis. Monday morning they waited in the reception room of the NATF. At a few minutes past 9 a.m., they were led into an oak-paneled conference room. Sitting on the far side of a rectangular glass-topped table, were three men in dark business suits. One appeared to be in his mid-forties, the other two in their mid-to-late fifties.

"Please have a seat."

The spokesman was heavy-set. He had closely cropped salt and pepper hair and a mean looking mouth. Jesse sat facing him. Frost was on his right and McClanahan to the left.

After icy introductions, the NATF official said, "We have no hard and fast rules here as far as legal procedure. Our main concern is that we conduct a fair hearing. One where you're able to present your side fairly. With as few encumbrances as possible. Naturally, we'd like this inquest to remain as civil as possible. If you have no objections, Mr. Frost, why don't you and your client make your presentation. If you have any questions, we'll try and answer them. Though I feel that we've provided you with more than adequate data on how we arrived at our findings. At the conclusion of your presentation, we'll have a question and answer session."

Bullshit, McClanahan thought. They didn't give a damn about fairness. They'd already deemed Jesse guilty. It was their burden to prove Jesse innocent. About as likely as a West Bank love-in.

Frost took his time as he spelled out the evidence supporting Jesse's case. He harped on Sanchez's blood tests, independent lab results confirming that Slinger was clean.

The blood tests showed that Jesse's testosterone/epitestosterone ratio was 1 to 1, a fraction infinitesimally smaller than the legal limit of 6 to 1 set for Olympic athletes. It was a level far removed from the 20 to 1 measure at which Jesse had tested.

Frost presented a profusion of documents. Findings by experts in the drug-testing field that corroborated his contentions. It was data that unequivocally demonstrated that Jesse's Olympic drug test results could not have been accurate. He showed how it would have been impossible to reduce Sanchez's alleged elevated testosterone levels so dramatically, in such a short time frame. The findings further substantiated Frost's contention that blood testing, not urine testing, was decidedly more accurate in determining an athlete's blood composition.

Jesse and McClanahan remained silent as Frost presented his documents. His testimony took over an hour to deliver. When he finished, the man with the salt and pepper hair said, "Why don't we take a ten minute break, and then return."

Ten minutes later the moderator said, "Thank you Mr. Frost for your presentation. If you have no further findings to present to this committee, we'd like to ask your client some questions."

"Go ahead."

"Fine." He turned to a swarthy complexioned man on his left. "Michael, would you like to begin?"

"That was a very impressive run at the U.S. Olympic Trials, Jesse. Quite a surprise. I'm curious. How does a man come to run a time like that?"

"I train hard."

"Indeed. No doubt very hard. But can you imagine how an outsider would find it a bit suspicious, for a young man with a background like yours, to run a world record?"

"A background like mine? What's wrong with my background?"

"I wasn't inferring there was anything wrong with your background. It's just the fact that outside of your coach, and perhaps some of the people who may train with you, that coming into the U.S. Olympic Trials, you were a virtual unknown."

"How many Africans do you know? You know how many runners they have over there who are capable of running world records, but never get a chance to compete on the international circuit?"

"Certainly but..."

"You know what it's like at all-comers meets in Kenya? They have barefoot runners who show up who range from grade school age children, to grandmothers and grandfathers. You have any idea how many of those people are capable of running world records? Unknowns?"

"Mr. Sanchez. I think..."

"How many people had heard of Miruts Yifter before he emerged from Ethiopia? You know how old he was when he took the gold at Montreal? He wasn't even sure himself. A lot of people swear he was pushing fifty. The world's full of talent. Most of it not known."

"Passionate answer. However, I'm not certain I understand your point."

"Point's simple," McClanahan broke in. "Just 'cause ya' ain't heard of a guy don't mean he can't run. Lots of talent out there."

"Are you comparing your runner to an African?" the official with thinning sandy hair on the far right of McClanahan asked.

"I ain't comparin' Jesse to no one. Cause no one compares to him. Africans included. He can kick the ass of any half miler in the world. And in the next four years of any runner at any distance up to five thousand meters."

"That's a very lofty goal." It was the moderator who answered. He had a sardonic grin.

"It ain't lofty. It's the truth. He's already proved he's the fastest 800-meter runner to ever lace up a pair of spikes. And he's got the endurance base to take all the other records. The other ones will fall easier than the 800. It's just a question of when we decide to take 'em."

"So Jesse," the balding man said. "Are you telling us you weren't even a little surprised that you won the trials?"

"I was happy to win the trials."

"How about running a world record?"

"Kevin and I knew I was capable of running that kind of time. It was just a question of when. We happened to have peaked just right. As far as the other runners in the field, I wasn't sure what they could do. Judging by times they'd run in the past, I thought I could handle them. But you never know what another runner's doing. Sometimes guys hold back. Like poker players, they don't show their hands."

"Is that how you'd characterize yourself?" the sandy-haired man asked. "A poker player?"

"I'm just a runner. Nothing else. Nothing more."

"Mr. McClanahan," the moderator asked. "I'm still having trouble with this concept of Jesse coming out of the woodwork, so to speak, and running such a spectacular time. Why on earth did you wait until the last moment to have him qualify? And why was he hidden for all these years?"

"Answer to both question's simple. I didn't want no pressure on him. I knew what he could do. The last thing Slinger needed was the press breathin' down his neck. Look at the bullshit that he's gone through since the trials. He's had agents houndin' him. And he's had to get an unlisted telephone number to keep the press from buggin' him."

127

"Jesse, you must admit that it's difficult to imagine that a young man could come out of nowhere and run a world record time," the baldheaded man said.

"Is Houston more of a nowhere than some remote village in Kenya?"

"I'm not so sure it's fair to compare yourself to a Kenyan."

"Why? Do you have some cultural bias that elevates those guys to superman status? Is it impossible to believe that a guy whose mother's side of the family is Mexican, and father's side is European, could have produced a world record holder?"

A nasty rictus followed on the official's puffy lips. "I have no racial bias. Only a deep commitment to ferret out the truth."

"Jesse," the moderator asked. "What is your feeling about drugs?"

"I don't even take aspirin. I hate drugs."

"But you are aware that there are athletes who abuse drugs."

"I'm not an idiot."

"Your testosterone levels were well above the maximum level approved by the Olympic Committee. How can you explain that?"

"I don't know. Maybe you can tell me."

Jesse's eyes were firing darts. The moderator searched the eyes of his panel. Then he looked at Jesse." Do you have any further statements, Mr. Sanchez?"

Jesse shook his head.

He looked at McClanahan and Frost. "And you gentlemen?"

Frost made eye contact with McClanahan. He motioned him to speak.

"I got somethin'. I been coachin' Jesse since he's fourteen. And what he's tellin' you is the truth. He hates drugs. I

128

can't even get him to take nuthin' when he gets sick. And as far as what he's been charged with, it's total bullshit. You guys know as well as I do what it costs for an athlete to get some asshole to keep him on the juice and keep him from gettin' caught. We're talkin' upwards of three grand a month. Jesse ain't got that kind of dough. He works as a roofer, for Crissakes. All the dough he makes goes back to his mother, so she can take care of him and her other son. And I sure as hell ain't got that kind of bread. I work for the city in the water department. You think I got a spare three grand a month to pay some asshole for juice? " McClanahan stroked his beard. Then he pointed his finger. "Yooo guys and me know what this is all about. It's about payback. Yer coming back at me for all the shit that's gone down in the past. Yooo got us by the balls. But for Crissakes don't take it out on this kid," he said pointing at Jesse. "Why destroy his life because yer pissed off at me?"

None of the three men answered.

It was a silent plane ride back from Indianapolis, as Sanchez, McClanahan, and Frost pondered the committee's outcome. There was nothing left to say.

A week later, after Monday evening's track workout, Jesse drove back to his apartment in Southwest Houston. Less than fifteen minutes later he climbed the two flights of stairs leading to his apartment. As he entered he smelled the fragrant scent of sizzling onions and frying chili peppers.

They were the sounds and smells that normally stoked a voracious appetite after a tough workout. But Jesse had little appetite for food. Since returning from Indianapolis his zest for the most basic of pleasures had evaporated. He was emotionally and physically drained, the stress of the committee's pending verdict having consumed him.

His nights were long and difficult, fitful segments of troubled sleep punctuated by vivid nightmares. The nightmares were unresolved demons from his past, horrors of a troubled childhood that would always haunt him. The past, coupled with the pending charges leveled against him, had coalesced into a terror that had paralyzed him with fear. Whatever vestiges of rage had driven him in the past were no longer motivators. He felt as if his life had fragmented. The pending decision had rendered him quiet. An eerie gloom that was infectious to those who were close to him.

Carmen Sanchez watched her son with worried eyes as he withdrew into himself. It was as if he had left his body to live in his troubled mind. He had isolated himself from her, McClanahan, and all his friends. Shauna Arnold had continued to call and leave messages for Jesse. But he had ignored her calls. Carmen Sanchez was frightened by her son's behavior. She wondered what the ultimate effect of a guilty verdict would have on Jesse. A broken heart could be mended. But a shattered spirit was not so easily knitted. Each night before Carmen Sanchez went to sleep, she prayed for a miracle to end her son's nightmare. Anything less could have an ending too horrible for her to imagine. As Jesse walked into the kitchen he saw the registered letter sitting on the counter top.

Jesse picked up the letter, and walked over to his mother. He kissed her cheek. "Hi Mama."

"How are you, Jesse?"

"I'll let you know when I finish reading this." As Jesse spoke he held up the letter. He turned and headed toward his bedroom, clutching the letter in his right hand. As he sat on his bed he opened it.

> Mr. Sanchez:
> After careful deliberation of your case, the NATF regrets to inform you that our committee's original findings remain intact. Your appeal has been denied, and you are of this date banned from all competitions sanctioned by the NATF and the ITF. This ban will remain in effect for a period of two years from the date of this letter.

At that time you may apply for reinstatement under the guidelines and procedures set forth by the NATF and ITF. Upon written request, this office will supply you with those documents at that time.

Subsequent to this notice you are formally banned from any and all competitions in track and field. Failure to comply with this edict may result in a lifetime ban from both the NATF and ITF, and all sanctioned competitions.

Furthermore, it is at the discretion of our committee to test you randomly for drug usage, at any time, unannounced, during the two-year period subsequent to this letter's date. Failure to submit to this random testing, or resultant future positive tests, may also result in lifetime bans.

Once again, this committee urges you to employ prudence and restraint when discussing this matter in public. Castigation of this committee's findings, or condemnation of either the NATF or ITF, will only weaken your case in any future attempt at reinstatement.

For further correspondence concerning your case, please contact the legal offices of:

Janicke & Hartwick
117 State Street
Indianapolis, Indiana 10076

It is our sincere desire that you will take the appropriate measures necessary, to be considered for reinstatement to our organization.

Respectfully,
Joseph Nixon
NATF Director

Jesse felt numb. He folded the single page and fitted it back in the envelope. Then he put it in the athletic bag near his dresser.

He walked back into the kitchen and smiled broadly at his mother. As Carmen Sanchez searched Jesse's face he said, "Everything's okay mamma. It all worked out."

Carmen Sanchez lifted a black frying skillet off the flame and onto a cool element. She moved to Jesse, smoothed back his thick dark hair, and smothered him in a bear hug. "Thank God. My prayers were answered."

Jesse felt his mother's hot tears of joy stream down his neck. "I told you not to worry mamma. Things always work out for the best."

Late that night as Carmen Sanchez and her son Jose slept, Jesse dressed and packed his belongings. He gently pushed open the door of his mother's room, his breathing measured as he watched her sleep. His eyes filled with tears as he watched her. Then he shut it and walked down the foyer. Moments later he pulled out of the parking lot and drove toward the freeway. Soon he was on Interstate 45 heading north to Dallas. He felt anesthetized as he drove. His over loaded brain unable to process more.

Chapter 15

The velveteen blackness of a silent Texas night shrouded the barren landscape as Jesse drove north on the interstate. He felt as if he were in a dark pocket. A lonely pebble in an endless sea of tar and cement. The prairie flanking the asphalt was a blur. A flat-faced vista rendered shapeless by the ink black sky. Texas passed by with monotonous sameness. At Raton, New Mexico, the landscape changed. The first vestiges of immense peaks loomed hauntingly beyond the mesa. The mountains came alive the next day in Colorado. But in eastern Wyoming the landscape once again turned bleak. It was a desolate prairie. As lonely as a foreign planet. Mile after mile he drove, across Wyoming, then Montana. Endless miles of ubiquitous plains. A wasteland which offered no vestiges of hope. As scenes of the last few months flashed in his mind, his emotions shifted. At times he felt himself gripping his steering wheel with vise-like intensity, full of anger. He'd ball his fist and slam it against the window. And then he'd think of what might have been, and what he was leaving behind. His eyes would fill with tears. But mostly he felt a sense of hopelessness. As if his life had ended.

The bleakness of the landscape heightened his sense of desperation and futility. And he imagined that if there was such a thing as hell, that this was it. A never ending journey on a God forsaken road.

As Jesse crossed the barren landscape, he drove until the weight of sleep sealed his eyes. As his head slumped forward, an electric jolt righted him. He gripped the steering wheel. He could feel his heart pounding as he straightened his truck. He was on the wrong side of the road. He drove less than a mile before pulling off the shoulder of the two-lane highway and into a rest area. A fitful sleep of almost six hours followed. Blaring horns shook him awake.

He drove for almost two and a half days without eating a hot meal. He lived on coffee and cokes and crackers, before pulling into the parking lot of a McDonald's in Selby, Montana. He was less than two hundred miles from the Canadian border, and his destination of Glacier National Park.

The Rocky Mountains had come into view earlier. It was a landscape where great natural forces had collided over sixty million years before. From his vantage to the east, the mountain front loomed like a towering barrier reef of limestone cliffs, their serrated peaks reaching toward the sunset. It was a vista shaped by a titanic pileup of rock layers deep beneath the earth's surface. A place where the Great Plains collide with the broad shoulders of the mighty Rockies and slams to a standstill.

The convergence of mountain and prairie produced a wildlife region so rich, that the front is often referred to as America's Serengeti. The reference pays homage to the herds of elk, bighorn sheep, and grizzly bears which still roam the paradise. Much the same as they did when Lewis and Clark forged up the Missouri River almost two hundred years earlier. The mountains marked the end of the first phase of Jesse's journey, an odyssey whose endpoint he'd not yet formulated.

He parked his pickup, got out, stretched, and walked inside the restaurant. He ordered breakfast. Then he walked to a table on the west wall of the McDonald's. He sat across from two Indians, facing the parking lot and his truck. The men were in their sixties, both with shoulder length silver hair. The taller one had his hair tethered in a ponytail like Jesse's. They watched as Jesse ate ravenously. As he drained a container of orange juice, he saw a Montana police car pull into the parking lot. It eased beside his pickup. Jesse watched as a middle-aged policeman emerged from the squad car. He was a wiry man, about 5'6", with shortly cropped white hair, dark aviator glasses and black boots. The trooper took his time, peering into Jesse's truck. Satisfied, he hitched up his trousers and walked slowly toward the McDonald's entrance. He stopped at the only other occupied booth in the restaurant, a table near the door. "Is that your pickup? Texas plates?" He was questioning a ginger-haired man in his early thirties.

"No sir."

"Pickup's mine." Jesse lifted a Styrofoam cup of coffee and sipped slowly. The coffee was still hot. He blew on the lid to cool it.

The trooper stared at Jesse through his dark glasses. "Mind stepping outside?"

Jesse noticed the cop's right hand, fingertips brushing the handle of his holstered revolver.

"Okay."

Sanchez's tone was polite. Jesse had encountered several run-ins with cops in the small towns of Bellaire, West University and Southside Place. They were cottage communities, incorporated cities within the city of Houston. Places whose main source of income were traffic tickets. Jesse had been stopped in the past, as were most of the blue-collar construction workers with whom he worked. He'd learned to remain cool. Authority figures generally responded positively to politeness and cooperation. Sometimes it was just a matter of playing their game and they'd let you go.

But Jesse was perplexed about this cop. He hadn't been in town for more than a few minutes. It was unlikely he had been followed in from the highway. There were no vehicles behind or in front of him. Besides, Montana's highways had no registered speed limits. Theoretically he could travel as fast as he wanted. As long as he wasn't endangering other vehicles.

As Sanchez followed the policeman to his squad car, the Indians watched the unfolding scene with wide eyes. Again he noticed the cop's fingertips as they nervously grazed the handle of his revolver.

"From Texas?"

"Yes sir. Houston."

"Long way from home."

"Right." Jesse furtively fingered his earring.

"What brings you up here?"

"Heading to Glacier National Park."

"Vacation?"

"Kind of. I needed to get away. Have some time to myself. To think."

"Makes sense. So what do you do in Houston?"

"I'm a student. And I work as a roofer."

"Long way to come to clear your head."

"I suppose. But I hear that park's special."

"Yup. Real nice place."

"Can I ask what this is about?"

"Seems there's been a complaint filed against you." Jesse noticed the cop's hand. It continually returned to his gun, grazing the handle. Jesse just grinned.

"Think that's funny?"

"Kind of."

"Really? Why's that?"

"I just got off the highway, drove a few blocks into your town, and pulled into this McDonald's. I don't think I've been here more than five minutes. How could anybody have filed a complaint that quickly?"

"People in this town are real sensitive to lawbreakers. Probably a lot different than where you come from in Houston."

"I don't break the law. I'm a law abiding citizen."

"Not according to the complainant."

"What kind of complaint was filed against me?" Jesse smoothed his ponytail.

"Seems you whipped around a man in the middle of town, and passed him on a solid yellow line."

"That's absurd. The speed limit in your town is 25 miles an hour. And I was going even slower than that. I was looking for a place to pull over and have some breakfast. I'm telling you, I couldn't have been here for more than five minutes. How could anybody file a complaint against me that quickly?"

"There's a complaint being filed against you. And you have to answer it." The cop hitched up his trousers, adjusted his sunglasses. And then his right hand grazed over his gun handle.

"I don't understand." Jesse's neck flushed hot with anger.

"What don't you understand?"

"How could someone file a traffic complaint against me? I've never heard of anything like that."

"That's our law here in Montana. If a resident files a complaint, the case has to be heard."

Jesse's mouth went dry. "What if I filed a complaint against someone for the same thing? Would they have to answer that?"

The cop shook his head. "Nope. You're from out of state. The law only applies to Montana residents."

"I've never heard of a law like that."

"Now you have."

"I'm a citizen of the United States. I thought that everybody in this country got equal treatment under the law."

"I don't make the laws. Just enforce them. A complainant has filed charges against you. And you have to answer."

Jesse held his hands at his side, his fists clenched. "What are my options?"

"You can either come with me on your own volition, or I'll have to arrest you."

"That doesn't sound like an option."

"Your choice."

Jesse fingered his earring. His teeth were gritted and his eyes had narrowed. He realized he had no choice. He would play along. "Alright. I'll come in with you."

"If you're found guilty of this crime, you'll need cash to make bail. We don't take anything else."

'Crime,' Sanchez thought? The little son of a bitch had already elevated an alleged traffic violation, supposedly filed by some town citizen, to a crime? His mind raced ahead. He only had a few credit cards and less than two hundred dollars cash. He wondered if he could make bail. His inclination was to explode. But he fought to retain his composure.

"Whatever. Want me to drive with you in your squad car, or want me to follow you?"

"You can follow me to the station. But I'd advise you not to try and pull anything smart. There's only one road going in and out of town. And there's no way you can make a break out of here."

"I hadn't intended to. I haven't done anything wrong."

"Okay. Just follow me to the station."

As Jesse walked to his truck and the trooper to his squad car, the two Indians inside the restaurant watched. The one with the ponytail broke the silence.

"What do you think?"

"Goerring's found himself a live one."

"Looks that way."

"One of these days Carl's going to make a mistake."

"Hope so. Want to be there when he does."

"Me too."

As the policeman pulled out into the intersection, with the Indians watching, Jesse followed. The cop drove several blocks before turning right. And Jesse followed him down a quiet, tree-lined side street. The trooper parked parallel to a white building, a flat-faced one-story structure.

Jesse pulled up behind him and shut off his ignition. He got out of his truck and followed the trooper to the front door of the building. On the door was a sign that read SELBY COURT-HOUSE AND POLICE STATION.

He trailed the patrolman inside. They continued down a narrow foyer. The policeman held the door for him at a room at the end of the hall. A rectangular pine table sat in the middle of the room, flanked by hard back metal chairs. Resting on the tabletop was a tape recorder and a microphone. "Have a seat." As he spoke he lifted off his sunglasses, and Jesse saw the cop's eyes. They were small eyes, hard, and blue.

As Jesse sat, the patrolman said, "I'm going to go get the judge."

Jesse waited for almost ten minutes before the police-man, Carl Goerring, returned. He entered the room with Judge Harold Ketchum, who appeared to be in his early seventies, an individual with deeply wrinkled skin and cold hazel eyes. The corners of the Ketchum's mouth turned downward, a perma-nent scowl etched in weathered leather. "You the fellow from Houston?" Ketchum asked. It was a gravelly voice, void of emotion.

"That's right."

"Complainant hasn't finished filling out his complaint. As soon as he finishes we'll come back."

"Okay."

Jesse waited for almost fifteen minutes before Ketchum and Goerring reappeared. They were with a man who appeared to be in his early thirties, sporting a thick head of dark scraggly hair and beard to match. He looked unkempt, clad in an olive green fatigue shirt, grimy blue jeans, and mud-caked brown boots. He was carrying a clipboard with a yellow legal pad attached. The exposed top page of the narrow lined pad was filled. Every line was covered in black ink. It was scratchy looking cursive script that painted the page. Without paragraph breaks. What the hell had this guy filed, Jesse thought? Traffic complaint? What he was carrying looked more like the body of the Magna Carta.

Ketchum motioned for the bearded man to have a seat. As he did, Goerring and Ketchum sat flanking him, directly across from Jesse. Sanchez's stomach quaked. He realized that this scene was a replay, a carefully choreographed repeat performance that would play for seasons to come.

"Would you like to tell the court what you witnessed, Charles?" Ketchum said.

"Yes sir. That man there broke the law." He pointed a crooked forefinger at Jesse, the nail encrusted with blue-black crud. "I was driving through town off Main Street when he came out of nowhere at a high rate of speed and passed me on my left. It was a good thing I was going slow your honor, or he probably would have killed me. When he went around me on the inside, and crossed a solid yellow line, I slammed on my brakes. I just barely missed hitting a car, which was coming the other way. It made me really mad when he did that. And I knew what I had to do.

"You called Officer Goerring?"

"Yes sir. Got him on his police radio, and told him what happened. He chased this man down to a McDonald's. You know what's happened since then."

"You're sure this man broke the law?"

"Yes sir, your honor. This one's no different than the other ones. And you've always found them guilty."

Jesse felt his neck heat. Son of a bitch, he thought. He was screwed. He fingered his earring and stroked his ponytail.

Ketchum nodded. "How's that sweet little wife of yours doing, Charles?"

"Catherine's back in Missoula with her parents."

"Problems?"

"We had a fight last night. She left this morning." Charles dropped his head and wiggled his feet. He massaged the bridge of his nose and his eyes.

"Hope everything works out, Charles."

"Thank you, your honor."

"And you sir?" As Ketchum spoke his eyes were glued to the complaint form. "Mr. Sanchez?"

Jesse nodded.

"You a Spanish fellow?"

Jesse felt his fists tighten. "I'm American."

"Of course you are. I'm referring to your ethnic background. I assume Sanchez is Spanish. Or Mexican....Whatever. You know what I mean."

"I was born in the United States. And I'm American. I don't understand why you're asking me that question. What does my ethnic background have to do with anything? Is that germane?"

"My, my. An educated one. That's a fifty dollar word, son."

Jesse's fists were clenched so tight that his knuckles looked like white stones. "So, Mister SAN-CHEZZZ. What brings you all the way up here to Montana?"

"I already explained that to the officer. I came here to visit Glacier National Park."

"According to this complaint, sounds like you must have been in a real hurry to get there."

"That complaint's bullshit. There's not a word of truth in it."

"You'll refrain from using that kind of language in my courtroom!"

"What is this any way? How the hell can you hold me for an alleged traffic violation that no authority witnessed? I've never heard of anything like this in my life."

"I told you to watch your mouth!" Ketchum pointed his bony index finger at Jesse. "I don't need any Goddamn, foul-mouthed, long-haired, earring-wearing, greasy Spic soiling my courtroom."

"You have no grounds to hold me. I demand the right to speak to an attorney."

Jesse got up from his chair. As Jesse rose, Goerring popped up from his seat and headed to the other end of the table. He was clutching a wooden baton.

"I demand an attorney!"

"Restrain him Carl!"

Before Jesse could turn his head, he felt the weight of Goerring's wooden baton as it crashed against the side of his head. As he struck the ground, a high pitch ringing filled his ears. A second blow to the back of his skull was followed by darkness.

Chapter 16

As Jesse opened his eyes, he stared up into the dark orbs of a thick-shouldered German Shepherd. From his prone position on the hardwood floor, the Shepherd's face looked as large as a horse's head. A deep, menacing growl followed. It began with the rhythm of a well-tuned motor and built slowly, like a rumbling volcano on an isolated cay. Jesse could feel the warped planks of the gnarled pine floor vibrate beneath him.

As Sanchez stared into the animal's threatening eyes, the dog bared matching rows of gleaming white fangs. That was followed by thunderous barks. Jesse could feel the floor vibrate. As the crazed animal barked, the bellows roaring like gun blasts in Sanchez's throbbing skull, he tried to inch backward. But the movement was awkward, his hands cuffed behind his back.

"He's come to!"

Jesse continued worming his way backward, the dog woofing with bone shaking intensity. The Shepherd strained to get at Jesse, but a thick leather leash restrained it.

"Stay still, you son of a bitch," Goerring shouted.

The restrained Shepherd lunged forward, baring its teeth like pearl stilettos. Its barks echoed like gun blasts. As Jesse watched the dog straining to break its leash, the sharp toe of a heavy black boot found the side of his ribcage. A cracking sound followed, and he made a high pitch gasping noise. A sharp, excruciating pain shot through him. His whole body throbbed. Reflexively he moved toward his other side.

"I told you to stay still," Goerring said. That was followed by a second kick, which found its target on his other side. Racked by pain, a surge of adrenaline flooded his system as he focused on the boot. Jesse lunged forward. With his shoulder he was able to knock the jack-booted cop off his feet. Goerring went down in a thud, and as Jesse tried to right himself, Goerring yelled, "Let Rommel loose!"

A split second later the freed shepherd leapt forward. It's teeth found the back of Jesse's thigh, and chomped down with vise-like pressure. The dog twisted its head. As it ripped out denim and tissue, a geyser of blood ejaculated from a gaping wound. As the Shepherd clung to the mass of quivering flesh, Jesse rolled and kicked upwards. His foot found the animal's testicles. The dog howled and squealed. Then it bolted across the interrogation room and down the foyer.

"Stun him," Goerring shouted. Jesse turned. Then a pain that was too immense to cope with racked his body. He felt like a lineman who had just struck a live wire. The stun gun jolted Jesse's thin frame. His torso leapt from the floor. He lay without movement, his bladder emptying in his jeans.

Goerring righted himself. He stared down at Jesse. "Drag the son of a bitch to the isolation cell in the basement."

When Jesse awoke his mattress was coated with crimson. The wound on the back of his leg had darkened, the blood and jeans having coagulated in a thick black crust. As he lay he felt the throbbing of his ribs. The dungeon had a dank smell, and it was cold and dark. As his body throbbed he pictured Goerring's face. Then he replayed the sequence of events since being arrested at the McDonald's. Goerring would pay, Jesse thought. It may take time. But some day he'd get even with the little jack-booted son of a bitch.

The next morning Dr. Michael Earnhardt and his wife Clair woke up at a few minutes past seven.

"I was freezing last night," Clair said. She nuzzled against her husband, her sleeping bag pressed against his. "I should have brought my down bag."

"Me too. I woke up in the middle of the night shivering. I went out to the car and got a pair of wool socks and wool Pendleton shirt. I still felt cold. A hard front blew through."

Clair nudged Michael with her elbow. "How come you didn't tell me you were going to the car? I'd have died for some warm clothing."

"You were sleeping so soundly I didn't want to waken you. I figured you were okay."

"You figured wrong, Dr. Earnhardt." She unzipped her sleeping bag. "Unforgivable misdiagnosis."

She stood up, her legs bare, clad in an oversize long sleeve T-shirt, with 'FBI' emblazoned on the left breast pocket. "Move over."

As she knelt, Michael scooted over to the far-left side of his sleeping bag. Clair crawled in next to him. "Your feet are cold, Michael." As she spoke, she spooned up against him. Her fingers made their way inside his shirt and feathered his chest. "So are your hands."

She wriggled and groped in the tight bag until she had climbed up on top of him, straddling his hips with her bare legs. "I think we...."

As he spoke, she covered his mouth with her palm. "Shut up and kiss me."

Michael gazed into Clair's liquid eyes. Understanding the wisdom of listening to his wife, he pulled her down toward him. A soft, long kiss was followed by languorous lovemaking. Though the lovemaking was familiar, it was still satisfying to each. Twenty-three years of marriage may have blunted the fervor of youthful lust, but time had only strengthened their mutual affection. The two genuinely liked each other. Kindred spirits who had never strayed outside the bounds of marriage, and likely never would.

Later, as the two lay side by side, Clair said, "How come you never traded me in for a new model? Almost every one of your med-school buddies did."

"I was waiting for the twenty five year mark. I hear that's when used wives command the highest trade-in value."

As Michael spoke he hugged her, and she kissed him softly on the lips. "You'd never find another woman who'd spend her vacations camping," Clair said. "Especially once she saw your 1040."

"I wouldn't show her my 1040. Besides. This isn't a vacation. You're here investigating those jerks in Selby."

"This is a vacation combined with business. And as far as not showing her the 1040, you wouldn't have to worry. I would."

"I wonder what my take home pay after alimony payments would be?"

"More than you could afford. I'd take you to the cleaners. And then I'd make sure that no young sweet thing could ever enjoy your services." She made a scissoring motion with her fingers to illustrate her point.

"You wouldn't do that..... Would you?"

She nodded "Yes darling."

"They'd suspend you from the force."

"Don't bet on it, Michael. The FBI takes care of its' own."

"They'd have a hard time justifying that kind of behavior."

"They'd come up with something plausible. Probably make it look like self defense."

"That would be no small task."

"We have ways." As she spoke her fingertips brushed across his thigh. As they came to a halt she said, "Dr. Earnhardt, unless I've misplaced my sense of touch, it appears you're on the cusp of setting a record. According to Guinness, you have a chance to set the standard for 45-year-old men camping at altitude."

"I've always fantasized a world record. What are the chances of us putting the current mark out of reach?"

"You know how I feel about competition."

It was a few minutes past eight when Dr. Michael Earnhardt finally unzipped the flaps of the two-person dome tent. As he stepped outside a fresh mountain breeze whipped across the Rockies. He breathed deeply, and his body felt cleansed as it filled with crisp, mountain air. He and Clair were camping at Rising Sun Campground, a site about six miles from the eastern entrance to Waterton/Glacier National Park. They had camped at every major National Park in the continental U.S. But Waterton/Glacier was their favorite.

Bridging Canada and the United States, the park encompasses over a million acres of perhaps the most spectacular mountain scenery in North America. Located in northwestern Montana and southern Alberta, it is a land of soaring mountain ranges, sugared by snow-capped peaks, and sculptured glacial valleys. It's a guarded vista of clean, ice cold lakes, of deep shocking blue. A land where fields of brilliant wild flowers dapple an immense pallet. A panorama where emerald alpine meadows spill into flowing fields of amber prairie.

As Michael exhaled, he felt at peace, wondering why he had been rewarded with such a charmed life.

Almost everything had gone according to plan in his first 45 years, the speed bumps along the way few and far between. He'd graduated near the top of his class at UCLA before enrolling in Harvard Medical School. He took a residency in Internal Medicine at the University of Virginia. It was in Virginia that he met Clair. She was enrolled at the FBI Academy in Quantico, having graduated law school at Duke University.

Upon Clair's graduation from the Academy, the two left for Salt Lake City, Utah where Michael took a second residency

147

in respiratory medicine. Both fell in love with Utah, and following their daughter Casey's birth, decided to make Salt Lake City their permanent home. It was a decision the two never regretted. Michael took a staff position at the University of Utah, where he became an associate professor of Medicine, Division of Respiratory, Critical Care and Occupational Medicine.

Clair was in her twentieth year with the FBI. She'd spent the last four years investigating credit card fraud, tracking down sophisticated international crime rings. It was an industry that each year bilked the American public out of billions of dollars.

Clair loved her job with the bureau. She found her work interesting and challenging. She was captivated by the intricacies of the criminal mind. She'd confided to Michael, that the best criminal minds often possessed intelligence that was difficult to measure. Though twisted they were brilliant. Always at least one step ahead of the most sophisticated law enforcement agencies.

As Michael Earnhardt stretched, he looked upward. There was good reason why he and Clair had been so cold the previous night, he thought. The mountains were frosted with a fresh layer of clean white powder. Though early August, snow in northern Montana was not that uncommon. Sometimes it happened even earlier. As Michael drank in the dramatic landscape, the western sky a shocking blue, a gentle breeze whistled through the trees. He felt as if he were in paradise, a place that whispered of sacred creation.

As he stood, Clair emerged from the tent. As she zipped her chinos she focused on the mountains. "My God! Isn't it breathtaking?" she said. She took Michael's arm. The two stood transfixed, speechless. The stenciling from no template could have formed such a scene. The etching was done free hand, from an artist far too complex to understand.

Several minutes later the two got inside their Four-Runner, and as Michael started the engine, Clair turned on the radio. She pressed the 'seek' button, and a male voice followed. "This is Jimmy Nichols reporting from Selby, Montana. Yesterday we had a total of nine complaints filed in Selby. The first one involved a suspicious looking man who was walking on the eastern side of town. The complaint was followed up on him, and the man was brought in for questioning."

Michael pulled out of the campsite parking spot. He eased out on to the gravel road which looped the campground, heading toward the Going to the Sun Highway. He drove at a snail's pace through the campground, watching campers as they folded their tents and packed gear.

Clair turned up the volume. "We're currently holding this man for further questioning until we can determine what he was doing in Selby."

"A complaint was also filed against a stranger whose vehicle was packed with meat. We have reason to believe he was intending to sell the meat here in Selby without a license. He's been booked. He was unable to make bail and is being held until a trial date is set."

The announcer reading the police report continued, carefully detailing each complaint that had been filed the previous day, and its ensuing action. The complaints were filed by Selby's citizens, alleged infractions which ranged from barking dogs and jay walking, to traffic violations and 'suspicious looking' individuals. The reporter ended his narrative by stating that the Selby jail was at capacity, and that a second facility, a warehouse that the city had rented, would be put into use to handle the overflow.

"They're still at it. What do you think Clair?"

"Going Strong."

"How long is it going to take you guys to nail them?"

"I'm not sure. Probably within the next few weeks. The logistics are in place. Now it's just timing."

"Do you have anything that will stick on them?"

"I think so. There's an Indian boy who died in their jail. Hopefully what we have on them will hold up in court. But you know how that goes. Lately, the F.B.I. hasn't been a big hit with juries and judges."

"I know an agent who would."

Clair smiled. She leaned over and kissed her husband softly on the lips. And then she ruffled his hair. It was a nasty world, she thought. And it kept getting nastier.

Chapter 17

Two weeks later, Harold Ketchum, mayor, judge, and for all practical purposes, king of Selby, Montana, called Officer Carl Goerring into his private chambers. Goerring knew right away that something was wrong. Ketchum was puffing on a filtered cigarette, a habit that he'd forsaken almost five years ago to the day. The lifestyle change had come after a heart attack. It was a near fatal coronary, suffered on an elk-hunting trip just outside the Lewis and Clark Forest.

The cardiologist who worked on Ketchum had scared the beejesus out of the old geezer. Selby's potentate listened with open ears as his physician offered two choices. A change of lifestyle, or quick death. Ketchum exercised the first. He gave up smoking, modified his diet, and cut back on his drinking.

As Ketchum smoked, he motioned for Goerring to have a seat. The ferret-eyed cop took his cue. He sat in a deep leather chair fronting the old leather neck's glass-topped desk. Goerring took off his black aviator glasses. He massaged the bridge of his sharp nose with his index finger and thumb. He was fatigued, his blue eyes mapped with blood red lines, after a sleepless night. Goerring's sixteen-year-old daughter Holly had run away from home less than forty-eight hours earlier. But Goerring's fear was not for the girl's safety. His terror was that she would be found.

He had been sexually abusing the youngster for more than eight years. The assaults began after the child's mother died of breast cancer, on a chill fall day in October. If the teen-ager was found and talked, Goerring faced life in a Montana prison. It was a prospect he viewed as worse than death.

He had spent the last two nights weighing his options, and had formulated a plan. He would make a new beginning south of the border, a move that would carry few regrets. He was sick of Montana's long, cold winters, and the police work too. Given carte blanche to crack heads at will, with no one to answer to, no longer gave him the satisfaction it once did. That, and Selby's top cop, was no longer hungry. With his pension, savings, and unreported cash, a safe deposit box jammed with blood money he had split with Ketchum, Goerring would be set for life. South of the border he could live like a king.

"Goddamnit," Ketchum said. He took a long drag on his cigarette. A thick cloud of chalky smoke followed. "Goddamn fucking Commie sons of bitches in Washington. They've dumped us in shit creek without a paddle. If we don't move quickly, we're fucked."

"What are you talking about?"

Ketchum puffed nervously on his cigarette. Then he began coughing uncontrollably, fitfully hacking, as his face reddened like a beefsteak tomato. It had been a long time since Goerring had seen Ketchum cough like that. Not since he had been smoking upwards of two packs a day, more than five years ago.

When Ketchum finally caught his breath, his forehead was beaded with sweat. "I got a call from a contact in Missoula. A guy whose wife has a secretarial job with the FBI tipped me. Appears that they're moving to bust us.

Goerring's eyes narrowed. He massaged the corners of his mouth with his thumb and forefinger.

"What do we do?"

"Cover our asses. Pronto."

"Shit."

"We need to do two things. First, we shred every file in this fucking building. Then we empty the jails. I want every son of a bitch that's locked up out of here, and as far away as we can get them." Ketchum puffed on his cigarette. More fitful coughing followed. When he caught his breath he eyed Goerring. "What's up with that slime ball Spic? The one from Houston?"

"He's trouble. He's been on a hunger strike."

"I knew that son of a bitch was dangerous. First time he opened his mouth. He's too Goddamn smart for his own Mexican good. We need to get rid of him. He's not like the rest of the shit we've got locked up."

"What do you suggest?"

"I believe Mr. Sanchez is about to run into some more hard luck, Carl. I foresee a fatal traffic accident in his near future. The result of an over indulgence in alcohol. Are we on the same page with my vision?"

"I've got the picture."

"Good. Take Fricker and Hardy with you. And get far out of town. Have one of them drive the Spic's truck, and the other a squad car. Then send Fricker and Hardy back here. I don't want any witnesses when that taco vender has his accident."

"No problem."

"Don't fuck this up, Goerring. Our asses are both on the line if you do."

Goerring just nodded.

Late that night, deputies Hardy and Fricker dragged Jesse Sanchez out of his cell. His hands were cuffed behind his back, and his mouth gagged, as he was thrown into the back seat of a caged squad car.

Less than thirty minutes later Fricker pulled off an isolated mountain road, followed by Goerring and Hardy. Goerring was driving his squad car, Hardy in Jesse's truck. The three vehicles eased off the side of the road and on to the shoulder. The night was dead silent, not another vehicle in sight. The cops got out of their vehicles as Jesse sat handcuffed in the back of the squad car.

"Get him out." Goerring's blue eyes were narrow and hard.

The two young cops walked to Fricker's car, and yanked Jesse out. His hands were cuffed behind him. Goerring took out his pistol. He gripped the gun with both hands. "Pull out his gag, and open his cuffs."

Hardy did the work. As he lifted off the cuffs, Jesse rubbed his wrists. He looked sick to Goerring. The kid's weight had dropped to a shocking low since they incarcerated him, and his face was sunken. His eyes had a jaundiced cast, and his hair was matted. He was stooped over and look wizened. Goerring knew why. Sanchez had spent ten days in a dank basement jail cell. His hands were cuffed and he had refused food. And he'd had the shit kicked out of him. Goerring felt certain he'd broken some of Sanchez's ribs.

"I won't need you guys any more. I'll see you in the morning."

"Leave the keys in his truck, Carl?"

"Right."

"Sure you don't need us?"

"I'm fine, Fricker."

"Okay. We'll see you tomorrow."

The two cops walked back to Fricker's squad car. Then they drove down the steep hill, their taillights fading in the darkness.

"Looks like your lucky night, Sanchez. We're going to party."

"What are you going to do to me?"

"Not a thing. We're going to party, and then I'm going to let you go. You've done your time. Just be sociable, and you'll be fine."

As Goerring spoke he kept his pistol pointed at Jesse. He moved slowly to his squad car. With his left hand he reached inside. When it came out, it was clutching a bottle of Jack Daniels. Goerring motioned with the gun. "Let's go party."

Jesse walked off the side of the road, Goerring trailing. The two continued deep into the scrub until the road was no longer visible. Jesse could hear Goerring's labored breathing as they walked. Far from the road, Goerring said, "That's good enough. You can turn around now."

Jesse did. He watched as Goerring unscrewed the lid of the liquor bottle. He took a small swig. Then he extended the bottle toward Jesse. "No hard feelings, son. First we're going to do a little partying. And then you can just get in your pickup truck, and drive down that mountain, right out of here."

As he held forth the bottle, a ray of light blinded Sanchez's eyes. The pumping sound of shotguns followed. "Drop the piece."

The voice stunned Goerring. Jesse's eyes focused on Goerring's right hand, holding the gun. It was shaking. "Drop it, Goerring. Or I stop your clock."

Goerring dropped the handgun. "Now turn around Carl."

Goerring turned, still clutching the liquor bottle with his left hand. The light that had blinded Jesse was now focused on Goerring. Facing the cop were two men. Jesse judged them to be in their early sixties, both native Americans, each clad in faded blue jeans and coarse wool jackets. Both men had full heads of shoulder length white hair. The taller one had his hair tethered in a ponytail. Each was brandishing a twelve-gauge shotgun. They looked familiar to Jesse. He was certain that he had seen them before, but he was unable to place them.

"Partying Carl?" the one with the ponytail asked.

"You can have him. Just let me go, and you can have him."

"Doesn't look like he has much," the second Indian said.

The Indian with the ponytail made eye contact with Jesse. "That your pickup on the road, son?"

"Yes."

"What happened?"

Jesse told the Indians his story. As he finished, the Indian with the ponytail said, "Where's his wallet and I.D., Carl?"

"In the glove compartment of his truck."

"Bet there's cash in it, too."

"His things are intact."

"So when he has his accident, and they find his body, it won't look suspicious."

"I was just trying to scare him. That's all."

"You believe that son?"

Jesse rubbed his wrists as he shook his head. "No. He was planning exactly what you're thinking. Getting me drunk until I passed out. And then sticking me in my pickup truck, and sending me down that mountain."

"Think you're right, son." He walked over to Jesse and lay his hand on his shoulder. "Son, I'd advise you to walk back to your pickup truck, and drive as far away from here as you can. Just forget about what happened to you these last ten days, and chalk it up as bad luck. If you do that, you have my word that justice will be served."

Jesse stared at Goerring. The trooper's eyes were electric with fear. Then he turned back to the Indian.

"Okay. Thanks."

"No need for thanks, son. Just be on your way."

Jesse took two steps forward, and stopped in front of Goerring. He stared silently at the cop." He pulled back his fist. Then he held it. "No, that would look suspicious in the coroners report. The punch would indicate more than an accident. You know Goerring, I've got a gut feeling that even God can't help you now."

156

Sanchez turned and walked back toward the road. Minutes later he was in his pickup driving west. The Indians were kindred spirits, Jesse thought as he drove. He wondered if it was more than fate that had brought them together.

As Jesse drove, Henry Broadfoot and Thomas Laughingbrook kept their shotguns leveled on Goerring. As Goerring drank whiskey Broadfoot asked, "Know what it's like to lose a son, Carl?"

"I didn't kill your son." His tongue was thick, his words slurred.

"Right. Died of a fall in his jail cell. Isn't that what the coroner's report said? Fell and cracked his skull?"

"That's what happened. That's the truth."

"Just another drunken Indian," Broadfoot muttered.

Goerring's forehead had beaded with sweat. There was a noticeable tremor in his right hand that was clutching the fifth of whiskey. Broadfoot looked at Laughingbrook. "Think that's what happened, Thomas?"

"Nope. Your son didn't drink."

"Thomas doesn't believe you, Goerring."

"He fell. I swear to God."

"Strong words." As Goerring lowered the whiskey bottle, Broadfoot stepped forward and planted the barrel of his shotgun against Goerring's forehead. "Drain the whiskey, Goerring. Or I paint the prairie with your brains."

Goerring's hand shook fitfully as he gulped whiskey. He continued drinking until the bottle was almost empty. With less than a finger of whiskey left, Goerring passed out.

Less than fifteen minutes later, when Laughingbrook pulled back up to the shoulder of the road in Goerring's squad car, he got out and left the motor running.

"Set the cruise control, Thomas?"

"At 90."

Broadfoot nodded.

The Indians loaded Goerring's flaccid body into the driver's side of his squad car and shut the door. Goerring was slumped behind the wheel, drunk, and passed out. Broadfoot reached across the steering column, pressed the resume button on the cruise control, and put the car in drive.

The Indians watched in silence as the squad car took off down the hill. It gained speed quickly, roaring to ninety miles an hour as it flew down the steep slope. They stood without speaking, the mountain night eerily silent, when the sound of smashing steel striking concrete shattered the calm. A series of crashes followed, each subsequent crash diminishing in intensity. The final crash was followed by an eerie quiet.

The two men stood frozen, just staring emptily down the dark road. Broadfoot turned to Laughingbrook. "Bad to drink and drive."

Laughingbrook just nodded.

Chapter 18

It was late Thursday evening when Jesse rolled into the ski basin, just above Santa Fe, New Mexico. He was exhausted, having traveled almost non-stop from northern Montana. And he was in pain, his ribs and back aching. Adrenaline had driven him, the horror of Montana still fresh in his mind.

He pulled into a parking lot fronting a campground, eased into a space, and turned off the engine. Then he reached onto the floor of the passenger side of the truck. He grabbed a tightly rolled sleeping bag, and continued outside. As he shut the door, a cool mountain breeze whistled through the trees. It was a clear evening, and the temperature was rapidly dropping. He walked to the back of his truck, opened the sleeping bag, and lay it on the floor of the flat bed. As dusk became darkness, Jesse crawled inside. Sleep came quickly.

The mountain sky was like black velvet, a profusion of shimmering stars lighting the backdrop like white diamonds. As Jesse slept, the temperature dipped into the high 30's.But he was unaware of the change. He slept like an infant, feeling a sense of peace, delivered from a horror whose ending would have been final. He felt as if another force had been at work, an energy that had protected him with the ghosts of kindred spirits. He felt a link to the Indians who had freed him, men who had a special connection to the land of their ancestors.

He slept until noon the next day. When he got up his ribs were sore. He was certain that some had been broken. But bones healed, he reasoned. And it was unlikely that other internal damage had been done. He had coughed up no blood, and none had been passed. The ringing in his ears from the club strikes had subsided. And he'd experienced no memory loss or headaches. His body was mending, he thought. Soon he would be whole.

After rolling up his sleeping bag, Jesse got back into his pickup truck and headed down the mountain. Minutes later he pulled into the parking lot of the Fort Marcy Fitness Center, a community facility near the foot of the mountain. He took his time there, as he showered and changed into fresh clothes. The hot water pelted his bruised flesh, and the feel of ridding himself of almost two weeks of grime was a heavenly sensation. At a few minutes before one p.m. he drove to town. He stopped at a Food Mart not far from the interstate, purchased a sack of groceries, and drove back up to the ski basin. There he ate ravenously, stuffing himself with sandwiches and chips. It was the first full meal he'd consumed in weeks. When he finished eating, he felt both full and fatigued. He grabbed his sleeping bag, rolled it out in the flat bed of his pickup, and slipped inside. He closed his eyes and fell back in a deep sleep. He slept straight through the afternoon and night, and didn't awaken until the next morning.

When he got up he felt rested, the first time he'd had that sensation since receiving his fateful letter. He drove back down the mountain to the Fort Marcy Community Center, showered, changed, and drove into town. He ate a leisurely breakfast at a Mexican restaurant near the square. There he killed more than an hour, sipping coffee and reading the morning paper, before walking to the town-square.

The square was crowded with tourists, eager shoppers searching the craft-laden sidewalks for bargains. They moved slowly, necks craned downward, studying jewelry, leather goods, and paintings. It was a potpourri of hand-made offerings from local artisans.

At half past three Jesse returned to the campsite at the ski basin. He felt rested and itchy. He knew what he had to do.

A few minutes later he was outside his pickup truck, clad in running shorts and racing flats. He remained motionless, contemplating the task to come, and then he moved forward. He moved slowly at first, aware of his aching ribs as he headed down the mountain. He jogged for almost fifteen minutes before stopping. The pain in his ribs was still present as he stopped, but the intensity was not as bad as when he had begun. He had learned it was often like that with pain and running. Once his body warmed, and the combination of adrenaline and endorphins kicked in, pain usually diminished. He changed his chronograph to timer mode. Then he took a deep breath, pushed off on his left foot, and punched the start button. He moved on the balls of his feet as he ran down the steep descent, quickly lengthening to the powerful full stride that was uniquely his.

He ran for sixty seconds until his beeper sounded. It was a distance that he estimated about a quarter of a mile. He took a thirty-second rest, and repeated the first effort. He ran a total of forty sprints before stopping. He was drenched in sweat, his heart thumping madly.

He stood for a long time as he recovered from the effort. A myriad of disconnected thoughts raced through his mind. As his pulse rate fell, he gazed back up the mountain. He'd run at least ten miles, he thought. Going back to the campsite would be less stressful, even though he was heading up hill. There would be no time strictures on his return trip, just a relaxing easy jog.

As he pushed off his left foot to head back up the mountain, a sharp pain in his Achilles stopped him in his tracks. He rested for almost a minute, denying the obvious, before moving forward again. The second attempt mirrored the first. The pain in his Achilles tendon was as if he'd been stabbed with a hot knife. It was a crippling sensation, unlike any he'd experienced in the past.

He limped toward the shoulder of the road and sat. He took his time as he unlaced his shoe. He lifted off the left racing-flat, peeled back his sock, and examined the back of his heel. The sight confronting him sent a chill down his spine. The tendon was bulging, puffed like a red balloon. Jesse gently pincered it with his middle finger and thumb. The onset of pain that followed was excruciating. Maybe it was ruptured, he thought, the tendon sheath split. Or maybe even worse, he'd ripped it clean of the bone.

Jesse struggled to get back on his feet. As he headed up the mountain he was reduced to a hobble, crippled by the pain of the throbbing Achilles. It was almost four hours later when he finally limped up to his truck in the campground parking lot. He hobbled to the cab of his truck, and lifted out his nylon running bag. He unzipped it, reached inside, and took out his spikes. Then he staggered to a metal trashcan anchored to a concrete base. He stopped when he reached the trashcan and dropped the spikes inside. His eyes were full of tears as he limped back to his truck. His life as a runner had come to an end.

The next morning he drove down the mountain and through town, before heading out on the interstate going west. It was on a Friday afternoon that he reached the city limits of Las Vegas, Nevada. There was plenty of work in the building trade in Vegas, Jesse had heard. And he was ready to get back to work. His mother and brother needed his help, and he was determined not to let them down.

It was time to carve out a new life without running. He'd chased a dream for years, and now the dream was over. His new focus was to succeed in his professional life, to provide financial security for his mother and brother. And more importantly, to make up for the pain and embarrassment he had caused her. There was no time to cry about the past, he thought.

It was dead and buried. Now it was time to grow up. Grow up and become a man.

"Hello."

"Carmen?"

"Yes."

"This is Margaret."

"Hello Margaret. How are you?"

"I'm fine. I have some good news for you."

"You do?"

"We heard from Jesse. And he's okay."

"Mother of God." Margaret paused. Carmen Sanchez wept loudly. It had been over a year since Jesse had disappeared. "Where is he?"

"We don't know. He contacted Kevin on his computer by electronic mail."

"Isn't there a return address?"

"Yes. We can contact him. But there's no way we can find out where he's living."

"I don't understand."

"That's how electronic mail works. We have his electronic mail address, but not his actual address. The Internet companies do that to protect the sender."

"So you have no idea where he is?"

"Unfortunately, no. But he says he's okay. Working and in good health." Margaret paused. "Would you like to come over and read his letter? Jesse said he wanted you to read what he had to say. And if you want to, you can answer him back."

"Yes! How soon can I come?"

"Right now if you want."

"Are you sure I won't be disturbing you and Kevin? It's late."

"We're up. Come on over."

"Thank you!" Carmen blurted. " I'll be right there."

At 10:30 p.m. Carmen Sanchez sat in front of Kevin McClanahan's computer monitor. On the screen was the e-mail that Jesse had sent to McClanahan.

> Dear Mama,
> I just wanted to let you know that I'm okay. I'm sorry about everything. You don't know how sorry. I know that I've caused you terrible embarrassment and pain, especially when all that drug stuff about me came out in the press. I don't know how I can ever make it up to you. But mama, it's not true. I never took any drugs then, and I wouldn't now. I think you know me well enough that I wouldn't lie to you about something like that. It's just something that I wouldn't do.
> I know that Kevin blames himself for what happened to me, but it's not his fault. His only crime was speaking out against injustice and evil. If that's a crime, I hope I'm found guilty some day of the same.
> If I've learned anything in this lifetime, it's that sometimes bad things happen to good people for no reason at all. Just look at yourself mama. And all the bad things that have happened to you. A better person than you couldn't have been created. You deserved a good husband. Look what you got. And then all the problems with Jose. And now me.
> I know I have to be your biggest disappointment. I wanted to make you proud of me. And I wanted to make the rest of your life easy. I was right on the verge of that. And then it was all taken away.
> I've experienced a lot of life since those Olympic Trials, mama. And I've come to understand that there are good people out there. But not everyone is. There are those out there who would hurt you for no good reason. And this has nothing to do with me getting in fights or my temper. It's about evil people. Those who aren't happy unless they can ruin someone else's life. I had a wonderful opportunity just waiting for me. Now it's gone. But I can't dwell on the past. It's dead, and I have to look toward the future. I wanted to be the greatest runner in the world. But that didn't happen. I can't change the past, only look to the future. I just hope, that more than anything mama, I haven't caused you too much pain. I'm sorry for all the shame that I've brought upon you. You must believe me though, that I never took drugs. I would never do such a thing, regardless of how I was judged.

Since I have left home I have tried to better myself. I've been working in the building trade and have made good money. I hope you've been getting the deposits I put into your checking account each month. I am living in a nice clean place, and I eat well. And I've continued my college studies. Since I'm not running I have a lot more time, and I'm taking more classes in school. If things continue as they have, I should earn a Bachelor's degree within the next year.

When I come back home, you will be proud of me. I will never bring you any more shame.

I hope that I've sent you and Jose enough money. If you need more, please have Kevin e-mail me. I'll do whatever I can.

I love you mama. When I come back to Houston some day you will be proud of me.

Jesse

Carmen Sanchez read the letter. As she finished she broke down in tears. She wept fitfully as Margaret went to the washroom for a box of tissues. As she disappeared down a narrow foyer, the sound of a teakettle screamed in the background. "Tea's ready," McClanahan called from the kitchen. "Get your asses back here."

Carmen Sanchez got up from the computer table and shuffled into the kitchen. As she wiped her eyes, she felt sad but hopeful. Her son was alive. As always, he had made her proud. Jesse had never had the luxury of experiencing a childhood, she thought. From the time he was a small boy he was like a little man, doing whatever he could to take care of her and Jose. She missed him desperately, but realized the time away had made him even stronger. Life was like that, she thought. When an individual survived bad things, it often made him stronger. When Jesse returned home he would be a much stronger man. He would return home, she thought. It was just a question of when.

When Carmen Sanchez finished her tea, she returned to the computer with Margaret. She dictated a letter as Margaret typed.

My dear son Jesse,

How good it was to hear from you. Thank God you are all right. I have prayed every day since you left that you were all right. God has answered my prayers.

I am doing fine, as is your brother. Jose misses you also, and if he were with me right now, I know he'd want to say hello.

I have been receiving the money you deposit in my account every two weeks. Jesse, it is so much that you send. We have more than enough to live on. I only hope that you're not depriving yourself. I know how you are. Please live well yourself. You must take care of yourself first.

You are a very proud man, Jesse, and I feel your pride has caused you much unnecessary pain. Of course I know you never took no drugs. I understand what happened to you. I want you to know you have brought no shame on me. You are my son, I love you, and I know that you are innocent of the charges leveled against you.

Everyone who knows you, and loves you, understands that. I can understand how you must feel, but you are wrong to think you have brought any of us shame. Anyone who believes you were guilty doesn't know you. If they knew you as I do, and Kevin and Margaret, and all your friends, they would understand how you were wrongfully judged. But you must not let them defeat you, my son. My home is your home, and you will always be welcome and loved here. I pray for you Jesse, and the day you return.

Please come back Jesse. You must swallow your pride and come back. I love you and will pray for your return.

Late that night, after Carmen Sanchez left and Margaret had gone to bed, Kevin McClanahan sat in front of his computer terminal. He was online, his modem whirring as he composed an e-mail:

Slinger:
Lick your wounds and come back.
McClanahan

McClanahan clicked the send button on the e-mail, waited until the message was confirmed sent, and powered down.

He missed the kid desperately. He couldn't put it into words. That was his way. It was always difficult for him to verbalize emotion. Slinger would understand, McClanahan thought. The kid understood him.

Chapter 19

Monday morning, a few minutes past ten, two years and three days past the date that Jesse Sanchez was formally banned from track and field, Kevin McClanahan got a call at work.

"Yeah?"

McClanahan was perched in front of his computer terminal, watching city council in action on the municipal channel. Idiots, he thought. The year two thousand had been a disaster for the city. They had refused to heed his warnings about the millennia crisis facing software programs. It had completely disrupted the billing systems. The mess still was not straight. And now they were heading down the same road, ignoring hardware systems that he told them needed replacing.

"What are you doing?" The voice on the other end of the line was Murray's.

"Practicin' my puttin'." He spoke with his eyes glued to his computer screen.

"Figures. Our tax dollars hard at work."

"What do ya' want?"

"Can't you ask any nicer than that?"

"What do ya' want, ass-hole?"

"That's much nicer. Spoken with sincerity, and in a much more pleasing tone."

"I'm busy, Murray. What the fuck do ya' want?"

"Are you on line?"

"We're never off."

"You have the web site for 'Elite Runner' book-marked?"

"Uh huh."

"Call it up."

"I'm busy."

"Call it up, right now."

"What the f...."

"Call it up!"

Murray's bark startled McClanahan. It was out of character for him to be demanding like that. Something had to be up or he wouldn't be bothering him at work.

"Yooo better not be wasting my time." As he spoke he clicked on to his web browser. Then he clicked 'Bookmarks.' He scrolled down to Elite Runner and clicked again. Then he waited as the site's home page appeared.

"You in?"

"Uh huh."

'Click Breaking News.'

McClanahan pulled the mouse down to 'Breaking News' and clicked. Murray waited as the story filled McClanahan's screen.

Eugene, Oregon

Almost exactly two years from the date of half miler Jesse Sanchez's expulsion from competition by the NATF and ITF, a woman has stepped forward to clear his name. Bonnie Callaway, a former employee of Evergreen Labs, a defunct drug testing lab employed at the 2000 trials in Eugene, Oregon, said at a press conference this morning, that Jesse Sanchez's positive drug tests were bogus.

Speaking at a press conference with her attorney at side, Callaway said that Sanchez had been framed for taking anabolic steroids, and that his test results were intentionally altered. The following is a transcript of her remarks:

"In August of 2000 I was employed at Evergreen Laboratories as a specimen analyst. Evergreen was chosen as the drug-testing laboratory for the Olympic trials track and field athletes, which were held in Eugene that summer.

During that time I analyzed the samples of a number of athletes, among them the specimen of Jesse Sanchez. I remember testing his specimen specifically, because of events leading up to that moment. My ex-husband, who was a former track runner at the University of Texas at El Paso, was very excited when Jesse Sanchez broke the world record with his finals race. I remember specifically checking Mr. Sanchez's sample, and that it was negative. If it had been positive, I definitely would not have forgotten.

Several weeks later, when it was released to the press that Mr. Sanchez's specimen had tested positive, I asked for a meeting with my supervisor. I explained to him that I had remembered testing Jesse Sanchez's specimen, and that it had been negative.

My supervisor told me that I was mistaken, that his specimen had tested positive. I insisted that I had tested Mr. Sanchez's specimen, and remembered clearly what the test results were. Again, he told me that I was mistaken, and it would be wise to drop the matter and discuss it no further.

Unsatisfied by that explanation, I went a step further and spoke with the owner of the lab. He also assured me that I was mistaken. And then he told me that Jesse Sanchez was a known cheater, and that this was the first of many tests that had been run on him. All had yielded the same positive results, he told me. He emphasized to me that it was imperative, that I drop whatever misguided notion I had. And not to repeat my mistaken findings in public. He said that doing so would result in my termination at Evergreen Labs.

At the time of this incident, my ex-husband and I were having financial problems. I explained the incident to my ex-husband, and he told me to keep what I knew to myself. He said that if I spoke out, it would mean nothing but trouble for the two of us. With my husband out of work at the time, and the two of us living on my sole income at Evergreen, I took his advice. I did not speak out. Since the Olympic Trials in Eugene, Evergreen has gone out of business. And I have lived a life filled with guilt. My deception has made my life hell. I have not been able to sleep well at night. Nor does a moment go by when the thought of that young man is not on my mind.

I feel a large degree of personal responsibility for his dilemma. I had neither the courage nor conviction to speak out against that which I knew was wrong. I realize that whatever damage has been done to his life cannot be undone. But I hope that by this admission, he will at least be able to salvage the shattered pieces of his broken past with a cleared name.

I cannot tell you why this injustice was committed against him, though my suspicions point to the heavy hand of author-ity. I am talking of the organizations who gave us the contract

*for drug testing, specifically the NATF and ITF. I would like
to ask for Mr. Sanchez's forgiveness. I will be available for him
to take whatever action is necessary to help clear his name.*

As McClanahan finished reading, his mouth was dry.

"Wrecked his life." McClanahan spoke in almost a
whisper. He stroked his beard, staring idly at the screen.

"Jesse's got a potential multimillion dollar lawsuit."
Murray's tone was excited.

"Can't bring back what they took from him."

"Maybe not. But it can ease the pain."

As Murray got off the wire, McClanahan clicked open
his e-mail. Then he brought in the woman's statement from the
net. He sent it to Jesse as an attached file. At the end of her
statement he wrote:

'Get your ass back here, Slinger. Now!'

Two weeks later, Jesse, McClanahan, and James Frost
met with Joseph Nixon in his Indianapolis office.

Frost's eyes burned hot as he reprimanded Nixon, his
finger pointing as he spoke in damning tones.

As Frost finished his diatribe, he reached into a leather
portfolio case and pulled out a folder of documents. He tossed
the documents on the desk and said, "I've had two independent
accounting firms compile a projected earnings statement of
Jesse Sanchez's missed income since the Olympic games in
Sydney. With product endorsements, shoe contracts, appearance
fees, and prize winnings, a figure of five million dollars is at the
low end of the spectrum. Especially in light of the fact he was
going into the games as the world record holder in the 800
meters. A gold medal at the Sydney games would have significantly increased that amount. This does not take into account
the damage to his name. Or the suffering and disgrace which
this affair has brought upon him and his family. This young

man has been wronged. And you and your organization are going to pay for that wrong."

Nixon sat with his hands folded. He tightened the knot on his tie. His beady brown eyes narrowed. "Whatever insidious plot you and Mr. McClanahan believe has been perpetrated against this young man is ridiculous. There were no plots. There was no conspiracy. And as far as trying to resurrect your original pleas with the threat of a lawsuit, may I tell you that you are wasting your time." Nixon pointed his finger at Frost and shook it. "The NATF has absolutely no intention of retracting its original position, Mr. Frost. You are wasting my time and trying my patience!"

Nixon wiped the sweat off his forehead. "A lab of unimpeachable integrity checked Mr. Sanchez's urine specimen. Now a disgruntled former employee, a woman whose irrational behavior is well documented, is questioning that integrity. This is a woman who's obviously trying for her fifteen minutes of fame. No doubt there's a book deal and talk show appearances already in the works."

"But may I remind you gentleman, that her word in this matter has absolutely no significance. The position our organization takes on this matter is that her statement to the press is a total fabrication. An abominable lie, with not a single shred of truth or evidence attached."

Nixon pointed his index finger at Frost. "You will not threaten us with lawsuits, Mr. Frost. May I remind you that Mr. Sanchez's expulsion has just expired. Any threats coming from his side will only further damage his already tenuous position. A continuation down that road will most certainly preclude him from ever competing again. With that in mind, proceed as you wish. But be forewarned that any fantasies you may have of punishing this organization will not come to fruition. The words of a troubled, and hysterical, woman will mean nothing in a court of law."

Frost grinned. "You know, I've locked horns with some arrogant sons of bitches in my time, Nixon. You take the cake. Your arrogance won't get you through this. The worm has turned. And we've got you by the short hairs. You're going to pay for this one. And you're going to pay dearly."

Nixon rocked back in his chair and folded his hands. "I trust you've had your say, Mr. Frost?"

"For today. The next time will be in court."

"I suggest you polish your aphorisms, Mr. Frost. I'm not so certain that a judge and jury will find your pithy little rejoinders nearly as amusing as you do."

"You're going to pay."

Nixon made eye contact with Jesse. He tightened the knot of his tie. "Mr. Sanchez, it has been more than two years since your ban from competition. Currently you are free to reapply for reinstatement into our organization. May I encourage you to drop this matter. And do so immediately. Otherwise you will never run a step in competition again. On that, you have my word."

"Yer word's not worth shit, Nixon. He'll compete again."

"Really? What makes you think so, Mr. McClanahan?"

"'Cause this ain't about runnin' no more. It's about price."

"This has nothing to do with money or negotiation."

"Awww, you know better than that. See, we already know yer a fuckin' whore. Now all we're doin' is dickerin' over price."

Nixon's face turned red. "You cannot speak to me like that.

McClanahan shrugged his shoulders. "Why ya' gettin' so upset? Ya' are what ya' are. Why get pissy over the truth?"

"You're from the gutter!" Nixon wiped his sweat soaked forehead.

"Lower than that. I'm a Scot. But that don't mean shit about nuthin'. Way I see it, yooo got one of two choices. Either ya' cut a deal with Jesse now, or he'll see yer ass in court."

Nixon eyed Jesse. "I can assure you Mr. Sanchez, that if you pursue this matter in court, you will not receive one dime. And you will never run again."

"Maybe. But so what? That wouldn't be any different from where I am right now."

"If you're interested in competing again, you'll drop this matter." Nixon's forehead had beaded with sweat. His heavy beard looked like it had grown from the time they came in.

Jesse shook his head. "No. Can't do that."

"Then this meeting is finished."

Jesse nodded. "You're the man." He made eye contact with McClanahan. The two laughed loudly, like two bad kids. They got up and slapped high fives. Frost had a grin on his face too.

"Shouldn't threaten a man with nuthin' to lose. We'll see yer ass in court, sweetie." McClanahan blew a kiss to Nixon, and turned toward the door. The three walked out of Nixon's office, laughing and carrying on, as if they'd just stumbled out of the neighborhood pub

The next Saturday, Jesse, McClanahan, and Frost met at the Village Brewery, a restaurant-bar located off Kirby, not far from the Rice Track. Overhead wall-mounted televisions blared, as a soccer match between Argentina and Ireland heated. Over the din of drinking patrons, clinking glasses, and blaring televisions, Jesse eyed McClanahan and Frost. "Bassler said he can't guarantee anything. But he thinks he can fix my Achilles. It all depends on how much damage has been done. And that's impossible to know until he goes inside. I want him to cut. If he can fix it, I'm going to give the running another shot. My goal is to be competing within twelve months."

"What about the lawsuit?" Frost's forehead wrinkled as he spoke. "You know this case won't be settled over night. It'll take a lot longer than a year. By the time this thing hits court, even if we win, we're looking at a lengthy series of appeals. We're talking about a situation that could easily run two years. Probably more."

"I know that. That's why I don't want to go that route."

"What do you mean?"

"I'm saying, I'd like you to make a settlement with them. I want to get cut on and run again. That's my priority. Not wasting my life screwing with a lawsuit."

McClanahan's brow raised as he rocked his glass. His eyes widened and shined. He stroked his beard. As he did, his hand covered his mouth, masking a barely perceptible smile.

"That's crazy, Jesse." Frost shook his head as he spoke. "We've got the upper hand on them, and they know it. I feel good about this case. I can tell you truthfully that a seven-figure award is not an unreasonable amount to anticipate. But you have to be patient. You have to be willing to go through the process."

"What do I get if we win?"

"The obvious. If you win, you're rewarded money. In a case like this, seven figures is not unrealistic."

"Alright. Suppose I'm patient. We sue. And eventually we get some money. What then? Like you say, by the time this thing plays out, we're talking years. I don't have years, Mr. Frost. I'm almost twenty-five. If I'm going to have a shot at a comeback, I need to get started right away. The longer I wait, the less chance I have."

"Why would you want to attempt a comeback? Why go through all that torture? Surgery? And then rehab? And then the brutal training you'd have to go through? All for the remote chance of regaining your old form? For what? None of that's necessary. If you're patient, and ride this lawsuit through, you won't have to worry about a comeback. You'll be set for life. You'll never have to work again."

"I want to run. I'm not sure you can understand. But that's what I want."

"There's more to life than just running, Jesse."

"I know that. In these last two years I figured that out."

"So do the smart thing."

"I don't care about smart. I had a dream to become the greatest runner in the world. If I don't give that an honest shot, I'm going to end up bitter."

"Jesse, I can understand where you're coming from. But you've got to think about your future. I'm not trying to be negative, but even if your surgery were to go perfectly, what would be the chances of you gaining your prior form?"

"There are no guarantees. But there's no guarantees attached to this case, either. I listened carefully to what Nixon said to me at our meeting. I know he was trying to intimidate me. But there was also a lot of truth to what he said. No one knows how a judge or jury would react to this case if it went to court."

"It's a calculated risk. But it's one you should take."

"I'm not so sure. If a slick lawyer cross-examines that lady in court, who knows what a jury will think? He'll fill their minds with doubt. Probably paint her as being mentally un-stable. Bring in ex-coworkers and her ex-husband to back up that claim."

"Sounds like ya' been doin' a lotta readin' since ya' left town. Ya' plannin' on going to law school, Slinger?"

Frost shook his head. "You're not looking at the big picture, Jesse."

"Yes I am. What if that attorney's convincing, and she comes off as some hysterical, raging fool? Then what? When it comes right down to it, if this case went to court, it would be her word against everyone else's. Who'd side with her?"

"Never fuckin' know." McClanahan drained his beer as the waitress put down a filled glass.

"I'd bet no one who worked in that drug company." Jeese's eyes narrowed and his face grew taut. "Not her ex-husband. And would they believe me? I doubt it. The press already judged me guilty before I ever ran the 800 finals in Eugene. A jury's not likely to buy that I could have broken a world record without the help of drugs. Why should they? No one else did?"

"The woman's testimony is strong, Jesse. A jury will understand she had no motive, other than a selfless one to come forward."

"I'm not so sure. I don't think there's anything cut and dried about this case. Nothing. If it goes to court it's a crapshoot. But that's not the real issue here. Now, all I want to do is have surgery and start training again. I want get back what they took from me. I want to prove to myself, and the world, that I can toe the line with any man."

"You're being a romantic, Jesse. You really need to consider your future at this point."

"You know Mr. Frost, this may sound hokey, but something I read as a kid stuck to me all these years. Something I never let go of. Carlos Lopes, the great Portuguese distance runner, had suffered for years with a really bad Achilles. He tried everything, and nothing worked. Then, at age 37, after years of frustration and misery, things finally turned around for him. He came back and won the gold medal in the marathon at the 1984 Los Angeles Games. And then at age 38, he set a world record in the marathon at Rotterdam. The words he said right after those victories, I'll never forget. That in all those years, when he was hobbled with injury, when nothing went right, when no doctor or therapist was able to help him, that he never lost hope. Lopes had been written off as way beyond his prime.

It had been twelve years since he had competed in the 1972 Olympic games at Munich. Twelve years of training and running with a near crippling injury. But in all that time, he never lost hope. Those words had a powerful impact on me as a youngster."

"You're clinging to a slender thread, Jesse. I still don't feel you've weighed this thing out carefully."

"Yes I have. I've had a lot of time to think these past two years. When I got that registered letter saying I'd been banned from competition, I thought that I'd lost hope. But now I realize I hadn't. The hope was there all along. I'd never lost it, just misplaced it. You see, in the back of my mind, I knew that I had to give the running another shot. I tried to rationalize myself out of it, but the hunger never left.

"If I don't play out this dream, I'll always regret what might have been. I don't want to be some middle-aged guy, looking back at life, and wondering what might have been. To me, the only failure worse than not making it is not trying. I hope you can understand that."

McClanahan sat numb, stone-faced, glowing inside. It was exactly how he felt, but never would have told the kid. After what Jesse had gone through, how could he have? Sure, running and runners were McClanahan's life. But how could he in good conscience have advised Jesse to attempt what he was now suggesting? The odds of an involved Achilles surgery ending in an unqualified success were extremely long. And even longer were the chances of Jesse regaining his prior form. They were immense long shots, the type of hopes that a caring coach would never falsely encourage.

"Okay, Jesse. What kind of deal do you have in mind?"

"I drop this suit against them, and in return they clear my name. They reinstate me to run, and pay for my surgery and rehabilitation. That, and two years living expenses."

"What dollar figure are we talking about?"

"I'd like what I was making as a roofer. Enough so I can continue helping out my mother while I train." Jesse fingered his earring. He smoothed his hair.

"We're talking very small dollars here. My inclination would be to press for a great deal more."

"I can live with what I just told you. Surgery, rehab, and two years' funds to train on. After that, I'm not concerned. If I can get what I've just told you, everything else will work out."

Frost turned to McClanahan. "What do you think, Kevin?"

"His life."

Frost took a sip of beer. As he put down the mug he studied Jesse's dark eyes which held steady. A small smile parted Frost's lips. "Okay. My guess is, that what you're asking for can be easily arranged. I think they'll jump on a settlement offer like that."

"Good." Jesse turned to McClanahan. "Coaching fees still ten bucks a month?"

"Yup."

"You've got your choice. Ten bucks a month now, or fifteen per cent of my future winnings."

"Both."

"You're a hard ass."

McClanahan grinned devilishly as he drained his beer. "Yu'll see how fuckin' hard once yer well."

"That's okay. I'll handle whatever you throw at me. If I'm training full time, I'll be able to get a lot more sleep."

"Won't make no difference how much sleep ya get. 'Cause the kind of work yer gonna' do, yu'll still be buggered."

Jesse grinned. He turned to Frost. "Sounds like fun, doesn't it? You think I'm crazy?"

Frost just nodded. But the tension had melted off his face. Big heart, he thought. His elbow bent as he drained his mug.

Chapter 20

As Frost anticipated, the track and field federation quickly approved the terms of Jesse's settlement. Accepting no blame for his predicament, the federation reinstated him without public statement. Sanchez agreed not to discuss the terms of the agreement. It included payment for his Achilles surgery, rehabilitation, and two years stipend for training.

On a Monday morning, Jesse went in to the hospital for his surgery. Bassler performed the procedure, and came in to visit Sanchez in recovery. He told Jesse that he had found the tendon intact, still adhered to the bone. But he explained that the tendon sheath had been torn, and the area surrounding it was knotted by scar tissue. The surgery involved scraping the scar tissue, repairing the torn tendon sheath, and the bursa sack at the bottom of the heel.

That afternoon Jesse left the hospital on crutches. He was wearing a hard cast, a plaster boot that covered his foot and left leg all the way up to his knee. A week later the hard cast was removed and replaced with a walking cast that could be taken off at night. Two weeks later the stitches were removed. That was followed by running in place in a swimming pool with a floating belt strapped around his waist.

Soon he progressed to a stationary bicycle, along with stretching and foot exercises. They ranged from picking up tissues with his toes, to walking on his toes and heels. It was a painful part of the process, an attempt to break up post-surgical adhesions. As he progressed, walking was added to his routine.

He continued the rehabilitation process for more than nine months before Bassler gave him the okay to begin easy jogging. On July fifth, Jesse parked his car parallel to the hike and bike trail on Allen Parkway. It was a five-mile asphalt loop that mirrored Buffalo Bayou from the underpass at Shepherd, to the Sabine Street exit in downtown Houston. Just off the trail were the steep hills that McClanahan's runners would begin training on the second week of September. But there would be none of that today. Nothing that would put undue stress on an Achilles that had been recently cut.

McClanahan's workout had Jesse walking for eight minutes, followed by a two-minute jog. The set of walk-jogs was to be repeated a total of five more times, a time passage of one hour. McClanahan had warned Sanchez not to attempt more, that taking on too much, too soon, could be disastrous.

As Jesse finished his first eight-minute walk he felt anxious, much like he felt during the week of the Olympic Trials. This would be his first time back running in almost three years. It was the moment he had dreamt of, ever since he'd received the e-mail from McClanahan with the attached file of a press release. When Jesse read the release, that a former employee of a drug-testing laboratory was attempting to clear his name, he thought one thing. That some day, some how, he would compete again. The prospect of filing a lawsuit never entered his mind.

More than three years had past since that fateful day he'd been banned. Nothing seemed the same. His body, the instrument he'd always taken for granted, had failed him. Going into the trials he'd thought of it as bulletproof. But the Achilles had changed all that. He'd come to realize the tenuous nature of a strong body and good health. Both were gifts, he thought. And the ability to run, an offering without measure. Never again would he take either for granted.

As he pushed off his foot to jog, he felt stiffness and pain in his left heel. Each subsequent foot strike produced a like result. When the two minutes were up, he was sweating profusely. The sweat was not from the July heat and humidity, but from the effort. His first steps back were worse than he had imagined.

And it wasn't only the Achilles that bothered him. Nothing else felt right either. Jesse's former running motion, a gazelle-like stride that was as smooth as silk, had been reduced to a painful shuffle. As he walked his recovery, he felt as if his bones and joints had been rattled. Everything felt wrong, his legs included. The walking had gone well for him, but the jogging was a different story. He was shocked that an action that had once come so naturally to him was now so painful and foreign.

The eight-minute walk that followed his jog went by quickly. It was like an interval shorter than he had bargained for. The next two minutes of jogging went no better than the first. By the time Jesse finished the hour set he was exhausted and hurting. He labored back to his truck, toweled off, and slipped into a pair of walking shorts and a fresh T-shirt. As he changed, thoughts of doubt flooded his mind. He wondered if his days as a competitive runner were finished. Was he just kidding himself?

But as he drove toward Shepherd, events of the past three years played out in his mind. His name had been cleared. He was back home. And back on his feet. One day at a time, he repeated silently. It would take time. It would be painful, but he would come back.

Less than five minutes later Jesse pulled into the 'Hot Bagel Shop', a hole in the wall bakery in a dilapidated strip center off Shepherd. He sat outside the shop, munching on a turkey sandwich on a sesame bagel. The establishment's front door opened. A portly man with curly hair, and a cherubic looking face, emerged. A wide grin separated the face, a smile that could light a cavern. He pulled up a white plastic chair and sat down beside Jesse. Pigeons pecked for crumbs at the two men's feet as Jesse ate.

"I can't get rid of these damn pigeons. Whatever I do, they keep coming back."

"How's business?"

"Great."

"Don't mess with the pigeons then."

Danny grinned. "You superstitious, Jesse?"

"Yup."

Danny studied Jesse's face. "You know Sanchez, you've aged a lot since you took off for Vegas."

"Think so?" Jesse's mouth was full, chewing on his sandwich as he spoke.

"Definitely."

Jesse shrugged his shoulders. "No one gets younger."

"Went through some tough times, didn't you?"

"Everybody does."

Danny nodded as he shooed away pigeons with his feet. The birds flew a few feet back. Then began their return march. "Damn birds." He got up kicked at the birds, and Jesse laughed. It was a futile action, he thought. He'd never get rid of them. Danny sat back down and stared at Jesse. "You run today?"

"If you can call it that. More like a shuffle."

"I figured."

"How did you know?"

"I'm not sure. Probably all the times you came in here before you left. I could always tell when you'd just run. Something about you."

"You're a good detective."

"Are you planning on competing again?"

"Not planning. I'm going to."

Danny nodded. "You know Jesse, I never took down the picture of you from the shop wall inside. The one of you setting that world record in Eugene. I never believed any of that bullshit that you used drugs."

Jesse grinned. "Thanks."

"Next time you set a world record, you come to the shop for a day to sign autographs."

"Do I get a dozen bagels of my choice?"

Danny's cherubic face glowed. "I'll even throw in some marinated pigeon breasts."

"Forget that. I don't want those PETA people breathing down my neck."

Danny laughed loudly. "How about some cream cheese?"

"Throw in a pound of lox, and you've got a deal."

"You know lox?"

"Sure. Have you ever met a Mexican that didn't like lox and cream cheese?"

"You're crazy, Sanchez. A certified nut."

"No lox, no deal."

"That stuff's thirty bucks a pound."

"No lox, no deal."

"Okay. But you sign autographs here from opening time until closing."

"Deal."

He extended his hand and Danny took it. It would happen, Jesse thought. Just a question of when.

Chapter 21

The recovery process went a lot slower for Sanchez than he anticipated. Through June and July his days were spent aqua jogging, riding on a stationary bicycle, stretching, walking, and jogging. Twice a week he received physical therapy from an Italian woman, a lady with dark shining eyes and a wicked sense of humor. McClanahan recommended her. And she and Jesse had clicked immediately.

Unlike massage therapists whom Jesse had visited in the past, Rita Ferraro was a woman who knew and loved her craft. A former dancer, she had spent years working with professional dancers in Europe. Artists who suffered from many of the same type of chronic injuries that plagued serious runners.

Her therapy combined massage and stretching, and a series of exercises that Jesse dreaded. She worked on Sanchez in an upstairs garage apartment, a place that Sanchez labeled 'the house of pain.' It was therapy which required a discipline every bit as demanding as a hard running session.

Jesse had never stretched nor done body maintenance in the past. They were exercises that countered the compressing and tightening effects of running. The drills would have kept his calf and hamstring muscles supple, ultra-tight areas that contributed to his torn Achilles.

As Rita worked with Jesse, patiently toiling to return him to his prior form, he learned things about himself he'd never known. He came to understand that succeeding an injury, the body tries to compensate by changing its biomechanics. But Sanchez had learned that the inclination to give in to that dictate, the path of least pain, was a choice that had to be fought. That failure to do so would end in permanent restrictive motion. That in running, as in dance, biomechanics were of utmost importance. And that the most graceful movers attained the highest levels. And that when injured, the elite performers had the patience and tolerance to do the proper rehabilitation. No matter how tedious and painful.

As Rita kneaded Jesse's hamstrings she said, "How's your love life, sweetie?"

"What love life?"

"I dunno. You tell me.'"

"Ooooh. Don't go so deep. That hurts."

A sardonic, husky laugh followed. "For such a big strong man who runs world records, you have very low pain threshold."

He has a high pain threshold, she thought as she worked. But she would not tell him. She had her reasons. Like McClanahan, her praise was sparing. And like McClanahan, she understood the mentality of driven athletes. She had learned to be a button pusher. Experience and intuition had taught her when to be tough, and when to coddle. The latter was a rare occurrence.

Jesse gritted his teeth. He held on tightly to the end of the massage table. "I can accept plenty of running pain. But this stuff is different. I wasn't wired to be a yoga master." As he spoke her fingers dug into his flesh like pistons.

"You don't answer me. Why you have no love life?"

Jesse winced. "What are you? A massage therapist or a shrink?"

"Whichever you prefer sweetie." She dug in deeper into his hamstrings. Jesse gripped the massage table with vise-like intensity. He felt like crying the pain was so intense.

"I think you're the Marquis de Sade reincarnated." Sanchez's eyes were squeezed shut and his teeth were gritted.

"No sweetie. The Marquis was French. Me, ee-tal—ee—ahhnah."

"You cruel—ee—ahhnah." Jesse spoke in measured gasps as her stone-like fingers ripped loose thickened scar tissue.

"So why you have no love life?"

"Maybe no one will have me."

"This is not what I hear."

"OOOOhhh! "Easy!" She eased back the pressure and Jesse relaxed. "Believe nothing you hear, and half of what you see."

"I'm like good journalist." Rita reapplied pressure as she spoke. "I got good source."

"I can imagine."

"So! You call me liar?"

"You've been known to stretch the truth."

Rita grinned devilishly. Then she dug her elbow deep into Jesse's hamstring. "Easy!!!!"

"Shame on to you. Saying bad things about me."

"What did this so called 'source' tell you?" Jesse spoke between deep breaths.

"That there's a woman out there who think you very special, but you never call her back."

"I was doing her a favor."

"Why's that?" She had finished his hamstrings, and was prepping his calves with oil.

"Because it wouldn't have worked."

"How do you know, sweetie?"

"Maybe it would have worked if things had gone as planned. If I'd run at the Olympics and gotten that gold medal, and gone on from there. I'd have had money, and it would have put us on a more equal footing. But after what happened, how could I possibly have dragged her along with what I went through? The woman is going to be a physician. And she's already set herself up financially with her modeling career. I had nothing to offer her."

"What about you?" As Rita spoke she kneaded his left calf.

"No. It wouldn't have been right. Sure, I've dreamt of her every night since we met. And sometimes I still fantasize that we can have a future together. But it could never work with her. Not where I'm at now. She deserves something better than me. I'm in no position to be chasing a lady like her. Right now, I'm a nobody."

"Sounds like your father speaking." It was another woman's voice that came from the hallway. Jesse's head craned to the right. He watched the doorknob turn. As the door opened his pulse quickened. Shauna Arnold entered, looking just like he remembered her. She was wearing jeans and a cream-colored blouse, her hair knotted in the back and held by a claret-colored clip.

"What the hell! Rita! Cover me!" He was lying on his stomach, buck-naked.

"She's almost doctor. Besides, she thinks you have cute butt."

"You've crossed the line, Rita! You could get sued for pulling a stunt like this."

"No way. Rita's within her legal rights. This is merely a case of a concerned massage therapist, bringing in a physician for a second opinion."

Jesse reached for the side of the table and pulled up the sheet. He did the same thing on the other side, and then he wrapped the sheet around him. Then he sat up, and stared at the two women who were at the foot of the table. The two eyed him with moon pie sized grins pasted on their faces.

Jesse pointed his finger at Rita. "You're in big trouble."

Rita grinned. "I already know you're chicken. McClanahan told me you don't sue nobody."

"You two get out of here while I get dressed!"

188

The two women stood their ground, amused grins on their faces, their arms crossed as Jesse wormed off the massage table. He was holding the ill-fitted sheet around him with one hand, and with the other picking up clothes that were lying on a cloth couch. As he slithered out of the room the sheet opened, exposing him from behind. Ferraro and Arnold giggled like two little girls.

That evening Jesse waited for Arnold in the lobby of the Warwick Hotel, an old but elegant Houston landmark which overlooked Hermann Park, the Medical Center, and Rice University. His pulse quickened as she headed out of the elevator and walked across the lobby toward him. She was wearing a black, silk-charmeuse mini skirt, and a pearl chiffon blouse. Her hair was pulled back in a twist, held fast by a cappuccino-colored comb. As she approached he caught the scent of her perfume. His head felt light, as if intoxicated by the nectar.

She came forward, got up on her toes, and gently kissed his cheek. "Nice place, Shauna."

"I know what you're thinking."

"Which is?"

"That this place is expensive."

He nodded.

"You're right. But I'm not paying."

"Really? Who's your sugar daddy?"

She gently punched his arm. "'Women's Health Magazine' you geek. The hotel's part of the deal my agent arranged for the photo session."

"Good agent."

"First class. I've also got a two hundred dollar a day per diem for meals."

"Two hundred dollars? I could eat for a month on that."

"Not where I'm taking you."

"Where are we going?"

"To a place I guarantee you'll like."

"Do I have any say so here?"

"No."

"Do you always get your way?"

"Always."

"That, and you never give up."

"Rarely."

"That leaves me with few alternatives."

"None."

"Then I guess we should leave here and drive to dinner."

"Immediately." She took Jeese's arm. "Let's go before I get surly. I am starving."

Less than fifteen minutes later they pulled into the parking lot of 'Ruth Chris', a steakhouse off Westheimer. After cocktails and dinner, they sipped Brandy Alexander's.

"I had you figured all wrong, Arnold. I labeled you the tofu and bean sprout type."

"When this body craves red meat, nothing else will do. Besides, ever since I went through that bout with anemia, I've been extra careful to get my iron."

"That could get expensive. Ever considered hamburgers?"

"This tab's being picked up."

"Good thing. Because coming here probably cost you as much as going to the doctor who diagnosed you anemic."

"I resent that. I'm almost a physician."

"I'm not. That's why I don't eat at places like this."

"You're really hung up on money. Aren't you?"

"I'm just a realist. I know my standing."

"What are you really talking about, Jesse?"

"You and me. We're poles apart."

"Because of money?"

"That's right."

"I don't understand you."

"It's not that hard. I grew up dirt poor. And worked my way through school as a roofer. Now I've got a bachelor's degree that qualifies me to teach children. Have any idea what the earning potential of a school teacher is?"

"I don't really care. What difference does that make?"

"None. Except that you and I are from different planets. Our earning potentials are so far out of balance, it's not even close."

"What if it were the other way around?"

"You mean if I was the doctor, and you were the school teacher?"

"Uh huh."

"That would be different."

"Why would that be any different?" Arnold rocked her crystal glass. "Because I'm a woman and you're a man?"

"Probably."

"That's sexist."

"Call it what you want. It's the truth."

"Where are you going with this?"

"You live in Boston. And you commute to New York. Big cities. Just like Houston. People of every color and ethnicity live there. But the one constant is money. Men want it. And so do women. It's always the men with the most coins who get the most beautiful women. Isn't it amazing how ordinary men become so handsome and sexy when they've got deep pockets?"

"Not to me."

"I find that hard to believe."

"Believe it."

"You must get chased ragged by wealthy guys who tell you you're beautiful."

"What do you think?"

"It's a given."

"No. That's not what I mean." Arnold's eyes opened wide. "I mean, what do you think? Do you think that they're on the right track?"

Jesse laughed. "Are you asking me if I think you're beautiful?"

"I was fishing for that. Yes."

"You know that."

"No I don't!" The intensity of her words startled Sanchez.

"Give me a break, Shauna."

"I'll give you nothing! Why should I take that for granted? I thought you'd rejected me."

A faint smile curled on Jesse's lips. "Are you serious?"

"Dead serious. You never returned any of my calls. I assumed you had another woman. Or women. I figured you had all the women you wanted."

"I didn't want anyone else. Just you." Jesse spoke quietly, his eyes lowered.

Arnold picked up her brandy. She rocked it gently in her hand, and then she took a sip. "Why don't you rob a bank? Or kidnap some oil man's wife and hold her as ransom?"

"What are you talking about?"

"Well unless you hit the lottery, I can't think of a quicker way to bring you up to speed. I want you. And since you need money as a pre-condition to be with me, I thought I'd help you out. Give you a few options to speed up the process."

Jesse gazed at Arnold with doleful eyes. "You know, if we were together, at first it would probably be fun. But after awhile, you'd probably have second thoughts."

"What are you saying, Jesse?"

"Listen. You're headstrong. And so am I. You'll be making so much more than me. We'll probably end up fighting over money."

"The problem the way I see it is purely sexist. You're just not willing to surrender your chauvinism."

"That's not it. I turned down an offer by an agent right after the Olympic Trials that could have brought me a pile of dough. Right on the spot. Same thing if I'd pursued the lawsuit with the track and field federations."

"Where are you going with this, Jesse?"

" I want money. But I don't ever want to feel that I'm being controlled. Or that I'm getting something I haven't earned."

"You see me as controlling?"Arnold's dark eyes pierced into Jesse's.

"No. Just as a woman who has her life together. And seems intent on resurrecting a guy whose life has gone all wrong."

"Where's the problem, Sanchez? Isn't that what love is supposed to be all about?"

Jesse searched her dark eyes. They didn't waver. "I think you're more of a romantic than I am. I don't think you've given this as much thought as you should have. Maybe you're putting me on a pedestal, when I should be under one."

She slammed down her brandy glass. "You think I'm bright?"

"Obviously."

"But not bright enough to make my own decisions."

"I didn't say that. "I just….."

"Exactly what you implied. Bright woman. But the bottom-line, still a broad. Irrational."

"I didn't say that."

"Sure you did. Maybe not directly. But that's exactly what I'm hearing from you. I'm a romantic. I haven't really thought this thing out. And if I had, I'd be rolling in the hay with an Arab Sheik or a Kennedy."

"More likely A Bill Gates type. Lower maintenance. And a lot less chance of him fooling around on you. I'll bet he likes the feel of fiber optics better than lingerie."

"You know, you think because you've had a few rough times, that you've become wise beyond your years, Mr. Sanchez. Well, let me tell you something. My childhood was not a piece of cake either."

"I didn't say that."

"Let me finish! Sure, since I got a break in modeling I've become financially secure. And the medicine will make me even more secure. But that security hasn't rendered me brain dead. I've met a lot of men. And I've been pursued by a lot of men. But when I saw you, I knew exactly what I wanted. Now do you have the nerve of sitting here and telling me that unless all your asinine pre-conditions are met, that you're not going to give us a chance together?"

Arnold picked up the napkin off her lap and threw it at Jesse. She got up from her chair, her eyes blazing. "I'm out of here."

Jesse got up, reached over and grabbed her arm. "Don't leave. I want you. I just have trouble accepting the fact you want me."

She wrested loose her arm. Her eyes were blazing. She stared at Jesse, for what seemed to him an eternity, before she sat. He followed suit, and then he signaled the waiter for more drinks.

On the way back to the hotel, the two drove in silence. They passed the Mecom Fountain, the cascading waters sparkling like crystals under the starlit sky. Jesse pulled Arnold's rent car up to the hotel's entrance. The concierge took the keys. As the two walked into the lobby Arnold gently touched Jesse's shoulder. "Come up. I've got something for you. I've been saving it since the Olympics."

Jesse followed her across the lobby, and the two rode the elevator up to her room without speaking. The room had a large bay window and the faille drapes were open. Hermann Park and the glittering lights of the Houston Medical Center provided the backdrop. "Don't go anywhere, Jesse." She walked to the washroom and shut the door.

As Jesse stood by the window, he gazed out over the park and the Medical Center. The complex had evolved into one of the most renowned health centers in the world. It was the home of DeBakey and Cooley, pioneers who had blazed a trail in open-heart surgery. And now it was at the vanguard of biotechnology, cutting edge science that was redefining the boundaries of health care and ethics. A life flight helicopter hovered overhead, descending slowly as it headed across the emerald greenbelt of Hermann Park down to Hermann Hospital.

As Sanchez stood, mesmerized by the Medical Center's bright lights, his mind wandered. He thought about Shauna Arnold and himself. How would he fit into her world? Would she truly be happy living with a man whose passion was running? And would likely end up a schoolteacher, destined to a life of paltry paychecks. How would that play out in the future?"

"Jesse."

Sanchez turned around. Arnold was facing him, wearing a tattered, over-sized gray sweatshirt. Her feet were bare and her hose were gone. She unclipped her hair and it tumbled down her back. "You were robbed Jesse. So was I. They took away what was ours."

She hiked the sweatshirt over her head and dropped it on the floor. As Jesse's eyes passed over her naked body, he felt the blood rush from his head.

"I waited for you. There hasn't been anyone else." She moved slowly toward Jesse as his pulse quickened. As she reached him he drank in her jasmine scent. She got up on her toes. "You're not going to turn me down are you?"

Her lips were moist and warm as she kissed him, and Jesse felt lightheaded, his body on fire. He lifted her, and she sat cradled in his arms as he carried her across the room. As he lay her on the bed, she reached up and pulled him toward her.

As the lovers struggled, years of wanting turned night into dawn. Sunday passed quickly, and the two never saw the light of day until Monday morning.

Jesse drove Arnold to the airport, and at a few minutes before noon, she boarded her plane. He felt a sense of emptiness as she disappeared into the plane, as if a part of him had been taken. As he walked back to his car he tried to steady himself.

As he thought of her, he imagined the telephone call or letter that would signal her change of heart. The fatal fantasy was his way of preparing himself for failure. He'd had his share of heartbreaks, and now he was erecting a wall to blunt the pain of others. Besides, he'd never had a woman like Shauna Arnold. If she broke his heart, it could be more than he could bear.

Chapter 22

The second week of September, on a Monday evening at half past five, Jesse Sanchez pulled into the parking lot of American General Insurance Company. The building was located directly across the street from the hike and bike trail that mirrored Allen Parkway.

Rush hour traffic was heavy as Sanchez jogged across the street. He moved toward a group of runners who had congregated on the asphalt hike and bike trail. They were young, lean, hollow-cheeked athletes, flat-bellied males with hungry looking eyes.

"Come on Sling-ah," a blonde, curly-haired runner with a New Zealand accent yelled. "Get the lead out."

Sanchez grinned as he advanced toward the group. "Jeeezus," The New Zealander taunted, "I've seen bloody turds move quicker."

As Jesse reached the runners, he put up his fists, and threw a mock punch that stopped well short of the New Zealander. "Don't press your luck Waitts." Jesse said. "I may be slow, but I can still kick your ass."

"Awww, you never could kick my ass, Sling-ah. You're a bloody wanker."

"Sean's been a bit testy lately. Badly misses his sheep." The runner speaking had a British accent. He was tall, dark, and had Patrician features. He had a regal air, an upbringing that echoed of gentry's privilege.

"Yeahh, you'd know about that, Justin. The bloody prince of buggery from the house of Chalmers."

Sanchez grinned. "I see nothing's changed since I left. Same old group."

Waitts bent over and touched his toes. "Just that they're all gettin' slower. Bunch of lazy buggers."

"What the fuck is this? A hill session or a sewin' circle?" The Scottish accent was unmistakable.

Waitts rose from his stretch. "More like a damn circle jerk."

McClanahan tromped up to the group holding a clipboard with running schedules in one hand, and a water bottle in the other. He was wearing a half T-shirt, mid-section exposed, with the message 'Will Work For Sex' inscribed across the chest, floral printed radish-red splits, taxi-yellow running shoes with small rubber cleats, and coarse black socks with white swooshes.

As McClanahan spoke, Danny Murray pulled up along the parkway in a dark green Ford Explorer. He rolled down the passenger window and yelled, "Coolers are in the back. Take them out."

Waitts screwed up his face. "What do we look like? Bloody servants?"

Murray put on his blinking lights to warn approaching motorists. "Your choice. You want beer after the workout, take out the coolers. If not, go get your own."

Waitts grinned as the men moved to the rear of Murray's Explorer. "What'd you bring, Murray?"

"What do you care, Steinie? If it's got alcohol, you'll drink it."

"Got that right." Waitts and Chalmers dragged out a cooler and lay it on the grass by the curb. Waitts opened the cooler and peeked inside. "MGD. Good on ya' Murray. At least you didn't bring fucking Budweiser. I can't stand that shit."

Murray parked his Explorer. As he ambled toward McClanahan he said, "Nice socks Kevin. What did you do? Mug that poor homeless guy who lives under the Sabine Street Bridge?"

McClanahan grinned. "Only free thing I ever got from Nike."

"Yeah, that's because they were thrown out. Nobody else would take them." The voice was female. McClanahan's wife Margaret approached. She was wearing baggy running shorts, an oversize man's singlet, a pair of dark, wraparound sunglasses, and a billed cap. Like every item of clothing on her, it was a good two sizes too large. It accented her gaunt face, making her look even thinner.

"They weren't thrown out." McClanahan's tone sounded hurt.

"Well excuse me," Margaret hissed. "I guess technically the socks weren't thrown out. They only made it as far as the dumpster. Not to the landfill."

"That ain't true. I had a friend who worked for Nike."

"Yeah. He befriended the janitor."

"Got me fifty pair of free socks. Never have to buy another pair."

Murray stared in disbelief at McClanahan's socks. "I'll bet you could work out a deal with Nike where they'd pay you not to wear them. It doesn't take a rocket scientist to figure out why those were thrown out."

Waitts cuffed Chalmers on the back of head with an open palm. "Are we gonna' stand around here and shoot the shit, or are we gonna' run?" Let's warm-up."

Waitts took off, and the group of elite runners followed, except for Jesse who remained behind. As they ran on the parkway toward town, Waitts turned his head. "What's the matter, Sling-ah? Can't run now that you're off the juice?"

Jesse grinned broadly and pointed at Waitts as if firing a pistol. "You're number one on my hit list, Steinie."

Waitts laughed loudly as the group loped along the parkway toward downtown.

Jesse struggled as he warmed up with McClanahan's group, a circle of master's runners that included Margaret. The banter was light and the pace was easy, but Jesse was struggling. It was the second week in September, but summer was still in full session. The temperature was in the 90's with matching humidity and no breeze. As the group completed their warm-up, Jesse was coated with sweat.

Less than ten minutes later a group of about forty runners congregated in a grassy area adjoining the bayou. They stood silently as McClanahan gave them the night's workout. It was ten times a short hill, followed by a four-minute break. Then a cross-country route, a circuit that included two very steep hills, one that was almost straight up. The second route was to be covered a total of four times, with a two-minute rest between efforts. Then a four-minute rest after the set, before repeating the first set of ten hills. Another four-minute rest was to follow. And then a series of hundred meter strides on the grass flats. A two-mile cool down would end the workout.

It was the first and easiest session of the new season. Each week the workouts would become progressively tougher.

As Jesse struggled up the short hill for the first effort, he could feel his Achilles stretch. He walk-jogged gingerly down the hill, and repeated the set nine more times. As he ran the workout, faster runners flew past him. It was a humbling experience. Like nothing he'd encountered in the past. For years Jesse had led the pack, the strongest and fastest runner in the group.

But as he ran that day, surrounded by people he sincerely liked, he felt his confidence soaring. He was back into it, and the Achilles was holding up. The heel was still painful, but it was apparent to Jesse that it was intact.

The hill work would help break up scar tissue from the surgery, he thought. And that's what he was after. With a clean heel everything else would fall into place. It was a long road back, a process where taking one step at a time was more than a worn out cliche.

After the workout, the runners congregated at the top of a hill just off the parkway, directly across the street from American General. Some drank beer, others soft drinks, munching on pretzels and chips as they unwound.

Dusk slid into darkness. The weary runners felt refreshed as a welcome breeze wafted across the parkway. And the whirring of cicadas filled the airwaves. As the air cooled, Jesse gazed out over the city's skyline. It was a clear night, a star studded-sky lit by a full pearl moon. The skyscrapers, like gleaming monoliths of glass and steel that seemed to erupt from the prairie in daylight, had a magical cast at night. The pastiche of lights and shapes shimmered in the darkness, mystical images that both mesmerized and bewitched.

As his gaze lowered, two weathered looking men approached. They were clad in worn jeans and soiled T-shirts, their leathery faces erupting cobalt. Jesse recognized the men, newspaper vendors who hawked *Chronicle*s on intersections connecting the loop.

Three leashed dogs trailed the men, thick chested, shiny-coated black labs, contented looking creatures with rhythmic wagging tails. The men sat off by themselves, on the far end of the same raised cement block where the runners were perched. As they sat their dogs settled next to them.

The vendors sat in silence, stroking their dogs, sipping bottled beer, sheathed in brown paper sacks. As Jesse watched them, he wondered where they would stay that night. Did they have shelter, or would they be sleeping along the parkway? Maybe just below where they were sitting? The dogs appeared to have been cared for better than the men, Sanchez thought. It was something he'd noticed a lot, street people putting their pets ahead of themselves. Love was a powerful emotion, Jesse thought. An attachment whose depth was immeasurable.

As the running group thinned out, men and women returning to their families and single homes, Jesse and Sean Waitts remained. As they drank beer, Waits said, "No more marathons for me. For at least a year."

"You've done your share."

"I'm buggered. I'm twenty-eight, and I feel like I'm fifty. Too many bloody fucking miles."

"You've got a lot of good running years left. If you want."

"Yeah. But it's a hell of a price to pay. I can't do this forever."

"What do you plan on doing when you hang them up?"

"Awww, if I ever save up enough dough, I'll probably move down to Mexico. Get me a boat and take tourists fishing. Just enough to get by. I don't need much."

"Think you'll save up enough?"

"Yeah. As long as I don't get involved with a designing broad. Jesus Christ, these American chicks are high maintenance." Waitts drained his beer, tossed it into a garbage can, and opened the cooler. He lifted out another can and popped the top. Then he took a long sip.

"You need to find the right one, Steinie."

"I find all the wrong ones. I'd like to hook up with just one good one."

"I never thought I'd hear that coming from you. I can't imagine you settling down with one woman."

"I'm just tired of all the bullshit. I just want to meet one broad, who likes me for me."

"You attract enough women."

"Yeah. All the loonies."

Jesse grinned."Birds of a feather, Steinie."

"How about you, Sling-ah?"

202

"What about me?"

"Running? Women? You know what I mean."

"I'm going to give the running another shot. Take care of some unfinished business."

"If I'd have been in your shoes, I'd have sued those motherfuckers. There's no way I'd be busting my ass making a comeback after what you've been through."

"I've still got some things to prove to myself."

"Who cares about proving anything? Only proof I need is a fat bank account. Give me a sub 2:07 marathon and I'm set for life. Once I got the dough from that, I'd never run another bloody step."

"Yeah you would. I know you too well."

"Bullshit."

"I know you, Steinie. If you ran a 2:06, you'd want a 2:05. You didn't go in this just for the money."

"You know nothing, Sling-ah. And I think you're fucking crazy. Busting your ass trying to prove something stupid. If I'd of been you, I'd of had that lawyer kick their asses."

"I don't believe you for a second. I know what drives you. And it isn't the money."

"You've done your thing. You ran a bloody world record." Waitts drained more beer. His voice was beginning to thicken.

"That was thrown out."

"You mean they won't reinstate it?"

"That was part of the agreement. That I wouldn't protest that."

"That's bullshit. Motherfuckers."

Jesse nodded.

"Okay. So you're a dumb fuck. And you're going to try and run again. How about the second part of my question. The broads?"

"Same as you. Settle down. If the right one came along."

"How about that broad that was sweet on you? The chick with the long legs and the big....."

"Shauna Arnold."

"Yeah. The model chick. What's up with her?"

"I like her."

"I hear she's still carrying a torch for you."

"Who told you that? McClanahan?"

"I'm not saying, butthead."

"If it's McClanahan, don't believe him. What does he know?"

Waitts laughed. "Got that right. Jesus Christ he's getting old. That bird's got to be on the back end of fifty. He could croak on us any minute."

"Hope not."

"Yeah. Me too. I'd miss him." He eyed Jesse. "Don't tell the old bastard I said that." His tone was deep and serious. "I don't want him to think I've gone gooey."

Jesse grinned. "I wouldn't. He wouldn't believe it any way."

"Old bugger kind of grows on you."

"Closest thing to a father I ever had."

"Life's a crock of piss." Waitts drained more beer. He wiped his mouth. "You live, you die, and then they shovel dirt in your face."

"You should write poetry, Steinie. You've got a great way with words."

Waitts tossed the empty beer can in the trash. Then he reached into the cooler and pulled out another one. He popped the top and took a sip.

"That was a first class chick that was on your case. If she's still got a torch for you, go for it! Hell, I'd drill her in a second."

Jesse just grinned. He knew Steinie was all talk when it came to women. The two sat without speaking as they finished their beers.

As Jesse drove home that evening he thought about McClanahan, Steinie, and himself. They were all running bums, he thought. None of them cared much for things or status. It was a love for their sport that drove them. Love, Jesse thought. That's exactly what it was all about. Love.

Chapter 23

For the next six weeks Jesse struggled through Monday night hill workouts, and a Wednesday night 'fartlek' session. 'Fartlek' was the Swedish term for speed play. It was a continuous run employing varying paces. Sanchez's session started with a two-mile warm-up, followed by two miles of running at his current ten-kilometer race pace. Then two faster miles at five-kilometer pace, another mile at ten-kilometer pace. And finally a mile at five-kilometer pace, followed by a two-mile cool down.

His workout times were slow. So bad compared to what he'd done in the past, that self-doubt continued to rear its ugly head. His Achilles was also an issue. There was still pain, and his movement was restricted. But his support team, especially those who had gone through similar surgeries, urged him to be patient. Recovery was a slow process, they reminded him, one which took time.

The second week of October, on a Monday evening, Jesse arrived at the Rice Track. It was the first time he had stepped foot on a track since his ill-fated Olympic Trials 800 meter final in Eugene. That was over three years ago. It felt to Jesse like an eternity. Subsequent to his warm-up, a three-mile jog around the perimeter of the campus, he waited anxiously as McClanahan laid out the evening's workout. The sheet was clipped in a rubberized folder, placed on a wooden stand to the left of the scorer's scaffold.

Jesse waited for the huddled runners to clear before he shuffled to the stand. Pencilled in at the top of the page was (8x800—2-min-r). It translated to eight times eight hundred meters, with a two-minute recovery between efforts. After reading the workout, he searched the list for his name. He found it typed near the bottom of the page, his times printed on the far right hand side. His eight hundreds were scheduled for three minutes.

Three minutes, he thought. It was a pace that would have been a comfortable run when he was in world-class form. But that past was far removed. The thought of running just a half-mile at that speed was now daunting.

As Jesse's head came up from the workout sheet, McClanahan approached. "How's the Achilles?"

"Not bad. A little tender, but okay."

"Wear yar' training shoes. Give that bugger some time 'till ya' go to flats."

"I thought I'd wear spikes." Jesse's tone was sardonic.

"Ya' can. In the bedroom."

"You're not well."

McClanahan grinned. "Just run three minutes. Don't go no faster."

"That won't be a problem."

It was a clear October night, and a front had blown through clearing the air. Jesse paused, focusing his mind, before punching his chronograph. He pushed forward, running up on the balls of his feet as he went through the first hundred meters. He glanced at his watch. Twenty seconds. Too fast, he thought. He consciously slowed his pace. At two hundred meters he checked his chronograph again. Forty-five seconds. Right on pace. He continued through the quarter mile in eighty-nine seconds, finishing the eight hundred just a shade under three minutes. He stood on an outside lane, leaning forward, his hands on his thighs, as he recovered.

He was running at a six minute a mile pace. It was a tempo that had been pedestrian for him prior to his ill-fated Olympic Trials. But the once gentle pace was now taxing. As he recovered, thinking how difficult it had been to make the slow times, he walked a few steps. Then it dawned on him. His

Achilles was still stiff. But there was no sharp pain. He felt a rush of adrenaline as his emotions soared. Then he calmed himself. Don't get carried away, he repeated silently.

The second eight hundred mirrored the first, as did the remaining six. All were within a second or two of his projected time. The workout had gone without a hitch. And he realized that through all the time off, he had still retained his sense of pace.   As a youngster, when McClanahan had first introduced him to the track, he had learned the importance of pace. That great runners learned to run with metronome-like consistency. And that through years of disciplined track work, they could often hit times without the use of a watch. Like a great pianist or dancer, a flawless sense of tempo was critical to a great runner. Without it he went nowhere.

Sanchez understood that pace was currently more critical than speed. That his focus was to regain his feel for the track, to slowly work back into speed. He would do that through patient work, at tempo speeds that were light years removed from his final goal. He had learned that it was the mark of a savvy coach who understood the process of building endurance and speed. The art of gently guiding runners over extended periods of time. It took years to build a great distance runner, Jesse had learned. But misguided coaching was not a concern of Sanchez's. He trusted McClanahan's judgment, discretion that would guide him as his conditioning improved.

As Jesse finished his last effort, the Scotsman punched his chronograph. Sanchez continued to the infield. He sat on the grass and stretched. Then he and McClanahan jogged out of the track complex. As they began their two-mile cool down, McClanahan turned to Jesse. "How'd it go?"

"Better than I expected. I didn't have any trouble hitting the times."

McClanahan nodded. "Keep goin' to Rita and doin' the rehab. Every week the workout's are gonna' get tougher."

"I'm ready."

McClanahan didn't answer. The two men ran stride for stride in silence. Slinger's stride looked okay, McClanahan thought. Not like it had when he was in top form, but getting there. Not bad at all for a guy who was coming off Achilles surgery, and hadn't stepped on a track for over three years. He'd be patient with Jesse as he brought him back, he thought. But he wouldn't coddle him.

McClanahan knew that there would come a time when the tendon had to be tested. To see how much stress it could take. That was always the toughest judgment call for a coach to make, he thought. Knowing exactly the right time to apply pressure, and precisely how much. If he was too cautious, Jesse could sense that fear, and never make the necessary break. But if he were foolhardy, he could ruin the surgery. The Scotsman had been there himself, and knew what it took. That only a special runner could reach the top of his craft. And an even more unique one, who could come back after a major injury. Only time would tell how Jesse would do. Time. The only measure in a sport where everything else was window dressing.

From October until January, Jesse's conditioning steadily improved. McClanahan's Monday and Wednesday track workouts had lengthened, interval sessions that progressed to six miles in duration. He ran the track workouts in heavy training shoes. But in spite of the added weight, his times continued to fall. His repeat miles had plummeted to a 5:30 pace, his shorter distances even quicker.

Like all great distance runners coming back from a layoff, Jesse's cardiovascular system quickly outpaced his body. It was both a blessing and curse of the highly talented, he realized. A double-edged sword whose cut was seldom a cure. Sanchez was aware that runners with the biggest 'engines', advanced cardiovascular systems that rapidly regain their former brilliance, frequently become re-injured. Like spirited thoroughbreds, he knew the heart of a world-class runner instructs the body to fly. But that the body, when not properly mended, cannot accept the stresses sent by way of healthy heart and lungs.

That predicament fit Sanchez to a 'T'. And McClanahan fully understood the ramifications of his runner's dilemma. He knew that when Jesse's body was sound, everything else would fall into place. The powerful engine was still intact. Only the wheels needed changing.

The changing of seasons had always been a welcomed break for Jesse. Especially after having struggled through six long months of oppressive heat and humidity. But this time, the onset of fall and winter had brought him little relief. The cold, coupled with dampness, exacerbated his post surgical pain. His Achilles was stiff and ached. His discomfort levels mirrored the daily shifts in temperature and humidity. But it had gotten better since the surgery, improvement that his therapist Rita Ferraro could see more readily than he had.

Since his return to running, Sanchez was spending an hour in rehab for every one he ran. Gym work, physical therapy, and yoga consumed an equal share of time with his running. It was a routine that was diametrically opposed to his past, a time when he ran, and that was all.

The rehabilitation program was the most painful regime he'd ever undertaken. Unlike the running, nothing in rehab felt natural. As he isolated and stressed a myriad of opposing body parts, pieces that he'd never considered in the past, he experienced pain and discomfort. But with them he came to understand another truth. That a balanced body was essential in his quest for healing and renewal. And that prior form could no longer be recaptured through running alone. And probably even more significantly, he realized that the skill that he had taken for granted in his past, was in fact a rare gift. Early in his career the running had come too easily for him, he thought. Perhaps his benefactor had been too generous. He came to understand the uniqueness of his talent. A genetic endowment that was a one in a billion offering. But he also realized that the gift had come with a statement, a debt that demanded repayment.

Chapter 24

On a blustery Sunday morning, the third week in January, Jesse Sanchez slipped into a pair of black lycra tights, and a white cotton turtleneck. In an hour he would meet Murray and McClanahan in downtown Houston, a few blocks from the Houston Convention Center. The three would run half the Houston Marathon as a workout, before being driven back downtown by Kevin's wife Margaret to watch the finish.

Sanchez laced up his training shoes and zipped his windbreaker. He grabbed a pair of thin gloves and a wool cap, and headed out the door. At a few minutes past seven, he parked his pickup in a lot several blocks north of the Convention Center. He drained the remainder of a cup of coffee he'd purchased from a Starbucks off West Gray and Shepherd, before killing his engine. As he stepped outside his pickup, he could see his breath in the early morning light. Good day for a marathon, he thought. But not a good day for him.

The cold, clear weather would be a blessing for the elite runners, serious marathoners attempting fast times. Sure, most novice runners would complain about the cold, he thought. But they were neophytes. Runners with little understanding of the deadly effects of heat and humidity. Jesse had witnessed running deaths on sultry Houston days, the type that sometimes happened in the heart of winter.

The city's winters were little more than a series of fronts, evanescent puffs of Canadian air that seldom lasted. A hard norther sometimes dropped the mercury into the 30's, seldom below. The timely front would be a blessing for the fast runners, he realized. But not for him. Cold weather now played havoc with his Achilles, causing the reconfigured tendon to stiffen and ache. As Jesse stretched, he saw Danny Murray's dark green Explorer pull into the lot.

Murray was the kind of guy you either loved or hated, Jesse thought. For every one of the former, there were legions of the latter. He was like McClanahan in that respect. And like the Scotsman, Jesse Sanchez had an affinity for the Irishman that ran blood deep.

Murray had always been there for him when he needed help, personal or monetary. It was sub-rosa assistance, a confidence that the Irishman demanded that Sanchez never make public. Giving and anonymity were traits that Danny had inherited from his deceased father, Patrick. Danny Murray was unconsciously mirroring him, as his own life's second half sped toward conclusion.

McClanahan had told Jesse that Murray had been a hot head as a kid. A youngster who threw punches first and asked questions later. He was a golden gloves champ. A lightweight who'd fought at a hundred and thirty five pounds. He told him that Danny had experienced his share of scrapes outside of the ring, since then. Jesse knew that the Irishman still worked out regularly at the Heights Gym. But since the death of Murray's first wife, Sanchez had noticed a change in him. There wasn't much fight left in him, Jesse thought. With the death of his wife, so seemed to go Danny's fire.

Eileen O'Connor was the only real love of his life, Murray had confessed to McClanahan at her wake. The breast cancer had spread through her body with lightning speed. It ravaged an extraordinary woman. A ginger-haired beauty with skin like cream. And a radiant smile. The cancer had devastated her once robust body. It reduced her to little more than a specter.

After Eileen died, Jesse remembered Danny hastily remarrying. But it was an error, one that Murray realized soon after the wedding. The woman was mean-spirited, a far cry from his beloved Eileen, he'd told McClanahan. Danny tried to make the best of the marriage. But it was a union that wasn't to be. A bitter battle followed. When the lawyers had left and the divorce was final, Murray confessed to the Scotsman that he was broke.

Murray pulled his Explorer next to Jesse's pickup, shut off the engine, and got out. He looked up at the sky as he zipped his windbreaker. "They should pop one today."

"Good conditions." As Sanchez spoke, his hands were pressed against his pickup, one leg straight, the other extended back. His weight was on his back leg, as he stretched out his calf muscle and Achilles.

"What are you going to try and run, Jesse?"

"I don't know. I'll probably start out running sixes and play it by ear. If the Achilles loosens up, then I'll pick it up. If not, I'll just hold it at six minutes."

Murray nodded. "I guess you've got a race number." His tone was sardonic.

Jesse grinned. "Riiiight. The race director gave me an invited runner's packet. Just like he did you and McClanahan."

"I've got a number." Murray lifted his T-shirt and exposed a race number that was pinned to his singlet.

"That's not a Houston Marathon number. That's from our beer drinking relay."

"So what? It's a number."

"You're crazy, Murray."

"Talking about crazy." Their eyes shifted as the roar of a dysfunctional engine puttered into the parking lot. McClanahan parked his battered MG next to Murray's Explorer. The two men watched as the tall Scotsman eased his gnarled frame, piece by piece, out of the tiny sportster.

"At least it's not bloody hoot." McClanahan righted himself from the small car.

"The word's hot. Not hoot. Hot. Rhymes with lot, not, and pot." Murray's tone was disgusted.

"If ya' got laid once in awhile, ya' wouldn't be such a nasty little shite."

"If you got laid, we'd have to call 911 to get you out of bed. I've seen pretzels that look straighter than your back." Jesse laughed loudly at Murray's quip. McClanahan extended his middle finger.

McClanahan then started doing some type of movement that remotely emulated a stretch, twisting his contorted back from side to side. "Back gets buggered in the cold."

Murray made eye contact with Jesse. "Listen to him. All summer long he pisses and moans about the heat. And now that we get a perfect day, he bitches about the cold. Why does he even run any more?"

"Because if he didn't, what would he have to complain about?"

The trio took off in a slow jog, and eased in toward the back of the pack of marathoners. As the three bandits waited, the smell of liniment was strong. Anxious runners leaned forward, most with their right forefingers lightly grazing the start button of their chronographs. It was an action in anticipation of the starter's gun. There were runners in all sizes and shapes surrounding them, a far cry from the lean and mean elite runners, men and women who would comprise the race's front rows.

The elite crew was bone-thin, runners with body fat as low as three per cent. It was the figure at which Jesse had been measured just prior to the Olympic Trials. With three per cent adipose sheathing their frames, world class runners have virtually no excess to keep them warm. They are like fine-tuned machines, living on the edge, always just a heartbeat away from injury or sickness.

Since the trials Jesse had put on twelve pounds, and at six feet two, and a hundred and sixty, still looked painfully thin. But the extra poundage would have to be shed for any chance to regain his former brilliance, he realized. The weight would come off as his conditioning improved, McClanahan had told him. As his mileage increased, along with the speed and intensity of his workouts, the extra poundage would melt off. Diet was not the key, Jesse understood. Like former marathon great Derek Clayton, the first marathoner to break 2:09 for the 26.2-mile race, McClanahan also scoffed at the barrage of 'miracle' diets that nutritionists touted for runners. After his record-breaking race, when asked what he ate, Clayton replied, "Whatever I want. When the furnace is hot enough, it'll consume anything."

Jesse had come to learn that the weird eating habits of elite distance runners was legion. Bill Rodgers, the great marathon runner, was known to keep an industrial size vat of mayonnaise in his refrigerator. When hunger roused him in the middle of the night, he'd amble into the kitchen. He'd open his pantry and extract a two-pound bag of chocolate chip cookies. Then he'd go to the refrigerator to retrieve the Mayonnaise. He'd dip the cookies into the Mayonnaise, devouring gargantuan sums of fat and sugar that defied all rules of nutritional prudence. It was a stunning feat of consumption for a wisp of a man with a bird-like frame.

And Jesse had heard about Alberto Salazar, former American record holder at ten thousand meters and the marathon. Salazar had set back the clock of health-Nazis, as onlookers watched him eviscerate heaping plates of greasy ribs the night before a major competition. And of Olympic marathoner Don Kardong, who when asked what had propelled him to greatness, replied his diet of Fruit Loops and beer. The revelations were anathema to the growing wave of health food evangelists. Men and women who spoke of fiber and roughage in whispered breaths of reverence.

As the starter's hand went up, Jesse felt a rush. The pistol cracked, and a puff of white smoke wafted from the barrel. The back runners jogged in place, and Jesse did the same. He felt the hands of a runner in back of him on his waist. Runners all around were doing the same, a protective practice to keep from falling. It was a new experience for Sanchez, never having run from the back. Soon the human wave was shuffling slowly, plowing forward, as they advanced toward the start line.

The first mile, the crush of runners leading up to the Elysian Street Bridge was so thick, that he eked through in 8:30. The second mile he continued weaving in and out of runners, and managed a seven-minute mile. By the third mile he was able to break relatively free, and ran a few seconds over six minutes. As he calculated his three-mile split, he took stock of his body. His Achilles had loosened, and he was breathing easily. He moved forward on the balls of his feet and his stride opened. As the four-mile mark approached, he checked his watch. He'd run a 5:30 mile, and it felt relaxed.

He consciously held that rhythm, clicking off consecutive 5:30 miles, before reaching the ten-mile mark. As he passed ten miles, he spotted a cluster of runners from his training group. As they urged him forward, Jesse realized he had five thousand meters to go before reaching Margaret at the Marathon's halfway point. The Achilles felt fine, he thought. So did everything else. Go for it, he thought. Run the final five kilometers of his training effort hard. His turnover quickened. He moved from his forefoot to his toes as his feet lightly kissed the pavement.

At mile 11 he checked his split. 4:58. He was still well under control, he thought. At 12 he looked again. 4:52. 'Hammer', he thought. He opened up, his stride lengthening. At mile 13 he checked his watch again. 4:38. He felt a rush of adrenaline. He hadn't run a mile that had even approached that speed in over three years. As he took the split, he pushed forward. He ran smoothly until reaching the race's halfway point at the Weslayan overpass.

As he reached 13.1 miles, the race's halfway point, he punched the stop button on his chronograph. Then he totaled up his splits from the ten-mile mark. He'd run the last 5K in 14:56. It was a time that was more than two minutes slower than his five-K projected time, just prior to the Olympic Trials. But it was an effort much quicker than what he and McClanahan had planned for that day.

As Jesse jogged forward he spotted Margaret. She was clutching three sets of warm-ups. Sanchez jogged up to her, and as he stopped she said, "How'd it go?" As she spoke she handed Jesse his warm-ups.

"Not bad." The warm-up top went on easily, but the bottoms took more work. His lower body was stiff and sore from the pounding on the hard, cold pavement.

Margaret studied Jesse. Her eyes narrowed. "You ran faster than you were supposed to. Didn't you?"

Jesse placed his forefinger to his lips, signaling her to speak in hushed tones. "Don't tell Kevin."

"What did you do?"

Jesse replayed his run, from its gentle beginning until its hard five-K finish.

"You try and come back too fast, you're going to re-injure yourself." Margaret shook her finger at him as she spoke.

Jesse nodded. "I need to cool down, Margaret. I'll be back."

Sanchez took off. He jogged down the road and returned almost ten minutes later. Margaret was still holding two sets of warm ups as Sanchez moved back toward her.

Less than five minutes later McClanahan and Murray came trudging down the hill. Kevin looked terrible to Margaret, his chronic bad back exacerbated by the bone chilling cold, and the thirteen plus miles of pounding on hard pavement.

Minutes later the foursome walked back toward McClanahan's work-vehicle, a Mazda Protégé. Standing across the road was a blocky looking, dark-haired character, with thick chest and wide shoulders. "The prick, the Mick, and the juiced up Spic," he barked. Then he grabbed his crotch, hunched his shoulders and stooped, and made some ape like sounds.

Murray froze. His eyes focused and narrowed as they zoomed in on the taunting fool. Murray had a crazed look, unlike any Jesse had previously witnessed. Sanchez had heard stories about Murray. But in the years he'd known him, he'd never witnessed an incident. The stories were from Murray's past, when he threw punches first and asked questions later.

Margaret put her hand on Murray's shoulder "Forget him, Danny. Let's go."

Murray held his stare, oblivious to Margaret's warning. He lifted Margaret's hand from his shoulder, and walked toward the man. Jesse and McClanahan followed. As Murray approached the man he said, "Surely you're not addressing us?"

"Who are you, asshole? The group spokesman?"

"No. I speak for myself."

Murray continued walking and stopped less than an arm's length from the man. Jesse moved forward but McClanahan caught him by the neck of his warm-up. Sanchez turned around. He stared incredulously at McClanahan. "What are you doing? I'm going to give Murray some backup."

"He don't need no backup. Leave him be."

Murray sized up the situation. The asshole was large. Very large. "You've made a grievous error. You've insulted my friends."

The man grinned. "And what do you plan on doing about it, you skinny little, red-haired, piece of shit?" Murray didn't flinch. His gaze stayed steady as he stared into the menacing hazel eyes of the man towering over him.

"Depends on your response. Apologize and I leave. Don't and I lose my sense of humor."

As Jesse and McClanahan watched the two men, Jesse's fists doubled. He knew that Murray was in good shape. And his past boxing skills. But it had been over thirty years since the wiry Irishman was a lightweight golden gloves champion. And now he was on the back end of forty. Though he worked out regularly with boxers at a downtown gym near the Convention Center, he was still no youngster. He was in a stare-down with a man who was at least twenty years his junior, and who towered over him. And who outweighed him by a good fifty pounds. Murray had bitten off more than he could chew, Jesse thought. He would end up getting murdered.

The man reared back and threw a roundhouse right. Murray moved his head and slipped the punch. "Bad response. Try that again and I'll dent your face."

The man lunged forward and swung again. But Murray had already anticipated the punch. His quick movement slipped another wild right. Murray backpedaled and unzipped his warm-up jacket. He tossed it to McClanahan.

"One more chance. Apologize, or I take your right eye."

The man charged, throwing a barrage of wild punches. The punches touched nothing but air. Murray moved underneath, and followed with a lightning fast, left-right combination. Popping sounds followed as Murray's hard hands connected squarely with the man's right eye socket. Murray was up on his forefeet as Jesse watched, dancing lightly.

The man staggered back, and reflexively touched his eye. He had a stunned look on his face. Then he put his head down and charged. He threw three more wild punches, and Murray followed with a left hook. A crimson gusher followed a thwap sound, as the punch again found the man's right eye. Blood squirted from a wound at the bottom of the eye, and Murray bobbed and weaved. He moved to his left, and right, and then forward. His hands were like pistons as he continued peppering the eye with a series of stiletto-like jabs. Then he got all his shoulder behind a hard left. Crack! The big guy's head shot back. The eye had puffed and closed like a red ball. Blood gushed down his face, staining his white shirt.

Jesse made eye contact with McClanahan "Jesus Christ, Mac. Danny's going to kill him."

McClanahan just nodded.

As the man staggered, his right eye shut and weeping blood, Murray moved lightly, his fists held high. "You've got an option. Apologize, and I leave. Don't, and I take your left eye too."

The big guy lunged forward, wildly punching, touching nothing but air. Murray unleashed a roundhouse right hook. As his knuckles found the clean left eye socket, Jesse cringed. The sound of fist striking bone was like a ripe melon splitting on a concrete slab. Murray danced to the side, and then he moved forward. He moved nimbly as he pelted the second eye with a series of short right jabs. Then he followed with another right hook. The punch sounded like a pistol crack as it struck the eyesocket. As the punch made contact, the man's knees buckled. He fell to the pavement, his body jolting as he sat. Both eyes were shut, swollen and bleeding. They looked to Sanchez like shattered tomatoes. The man's palms moved up to his eyes. As he covered them he sat motionless.

McClanahan moved forward and placed his large hand on Murray's shoulder. "Let's get out of here Murray. Yooo don't need no fuckin' lawsuits."

Jesse watched Murray. The wiry Irishman still had the crazed look in his eyes as he focused on his fallen victim. The man was sitting perfectly still, his palms shielding his eyes. Murray turned toward McClanahan. Jesse could see the Irishman's eyes as they connected with the Scotsman's. They still looked crazed. The stare down seemed to last for an eternity to Jesse. Finally, Murray nodded. The threesome wasted no time as they walked briskly toward Margaret and then to McClanahan's car.

Chapter 25

"Hey, haven't I met you somewhere before?"

A trim but shapely woman froze in her tracks. She was wearing a white lab coat and a stethoscope around her neck. She turned around. "Jesse!"

She ran forward, her arms wrapping around him with vise-like force. The two clung together tightly for a long time, until she gently pushed him back. She gazed into his dark eyes. Then she reached up and pulled his head forward. They drank each other in, Shauna Arnold and Jesse Sanchez oblivious to the sea of hospital staff and patients moving in the hallway.

"What are you doing here, Jesse?"

"I'm stalking you."

"Should I call the police?"

"If you feel threatened."

"I'm petrified."

"Then I'll stay."

"Where are your things?"

"In a locker at the bus station."

"Bus station?"

"That's right."

"You came up by bus?"

"You know the price of a plane ticket from Houston to Boston?"

"I don't even know where the bus station is."

"Not far from here. I jogged over."

"I'm off shift in a half hour. Will that give you enough time to get your things, and meet me back here in front of the hospital?"

"Plenty."

"Good. Go get them."

"Then what?"

"Then I take you back to my apartment, and make sure you never leave here."

"How can you do that?"

"I have my ways."

"This sounds like the beginning of a Stephen King novel."

"What I had in mind wasn't nearly as sinister." She leaned forward and kissed him again.

"I'll go."

"Hurry."

As Jesse moved back down the hall, two nurses who had been watching the scene smiled at each other mischievously. As they headed in the other direction, Arnold tapped a string of numbers on her cellular phone. A long conversation followed. She glanced at her watch. "I had no idea my mother was coming in. It was a total surprise.....I'll give you a call as soon as she leaves.....Me too....See you soon."

She pressed a button ending the call, and fitted the phone back into her lab coat pocket.

The two had barely gotten inside Arnold's apartment before she was yanking Jesse's arm. As she led him into the washroom, her hands were everywhere, undressing Jesse and herself. She led him into the shower, and turned on the water. As cascading needles of spray pelted them, her arms encircled his neck. Jesse gently lifted her from underneath, and she wrapped her legs around his back. She cupped his face with her hands as they drank each other in. As the kiss ended she stared deep into Jesse's big black eyes, his pupils fully dilated. He touched her cheek. "Glad you put such a premium on cleanliness."

"An extension of my medical training. I always scrub down before examining a patient."

"Been awhile since I've had a physical. Everything look okay?"

She hiked herself up on Jesse's torso, reached below, and took him in her hand. Then she moved down slowly. She shut her eyes and moaned softly as she settled. She didn't answer.

Later that night the two ate dinner at a neighborhood Italian restaurant, just blocks from Arnold's apartment.

"I can't believe you took a bus from Houston, Sanchez. That must have been murder."

"It wasn't that bad."

"Why a bus?"

"Money."

"Trying to save money for Europe?"

Jesse just nodded. His mouth was full of pasta shells.

"How long are you planning on staying?" As she spoke, she twirled spaghetti in red sauce around a silver-plated fork.

"About four months. From now until the end of August, or the beginning of September. I'll run as many Grand Prix meets as I can."

"What kind of shape are you in?"

"Probably in the mid to high 1:40's. But I've got a great base behind me. The best buildup I've ever done. I've had almost five months of hundred mile plus weeks. Right before I left, McClanahan had Steinie and me run two times a two mile, with a three-minute break, on the Rice Track. We averaged 8:55. Kevin figures I'm in sub 13:30 shape for five thousand. And that means I'm strong. But I haven't done any intensive speed work. Once I cut back on my mileage and start doing intensive speed work and racing, the 800 times should fall dramatically. "

She nodded and took a sip of wine. "Can you make any money running that kind of time?"

"No. Probably not. I'll need to be back down in the low 1:40's to make any money."

"Do you think you can get there?"

"Definitely. If I stay healthy and go through the season injury free, there's no reason why I can't run what I did at the trials. Kevin figures it'll take a good three months of track work and racing to get me back in top form. The plan is to be peaking at the end of the summer. That by running the Grand Prix Circuit, I'll be racing my way back in shape."

She rocked her wineglass. "Did you get an agent?"

"I had to. Everyone I talked to said I had to. Dealing with meet directors. Setting an itinerary. All the things I couldn't have done on my own. I was against it, but once I realized what was involved, I had to get one."

"Who?"

"A guy from England. Ian James. He ran the 5,000 for Great Britain in the 80's. Kevin said he's pretty straight up."

"So he's already gotten you in some meets?"

"Yeah. I was surprised how quickly he was able to confirm. Evidently there's still interest in me in Europe. A lot of hard core track addicts in that country. And they're still curious about what I can do. You know my 800 record's still intact. Well... Unofficially... Since it was disallowed. But still, nobody's touched that time."

"I know that. What a bummer you can't get it reinstated."

"I can't look back. The focus now is to take it to another level."

"You're going to be a marked man. But meet directors will welcome you. You're controversial. And controversy sells."

"You think so?"

"Sure. But you can bet your butt that the NATF and the ITF would like nothing better than to bust you again. There's no love lost between them and Kevin. Especially when that lady from the drug company came forward to clear you. That made them look bad. They're going to be out to get you."

"I know that. But there's nothing I can do about that. I'm clean. Just as I've always been. When you run, you're always subject to random drug testing. I doubt if they'd try to pull what they did before. Too risky." Jesse picked up a chunk of bread, and dipped it in the spaghetti sauce of his cleaned platter. He was famished, Arnold thought. Probably hadn't eaten since yesterday.

"Jesse, I wouldn't put anything past them."

"Maybe, but I've got to put that out of my mind. My thing is to go to Europe. Stay healthy and train. And by the end of the season kick ass and take names. That's all."

Arnold nodded. With her thumb and middle finger, she fondled a pearl on a thin gold chain. She was wearing a low cut silk blouse. As she let the pearl go, it settled between her cleavage. She leaned forward, aware that she was revealing more, and Jesse's eyes followed the pearl downward. He felt a stirring, and then he lifted his gaze. His eyes met Arnold's. "You know the training I did in Boulder before I got here was really great. The best early spring I ever had. I wish you could have been there. It was beautiful."

"If things work out, I'd like to move to a place like Boulder. I love the mountains."

"Ditto."

"Wouldn't it be a great place to raise a family?"

Jesse's lips tightened. He nervously fingered his earring. He sipped wine.

"Did I say something wrong?"

"No."

"Then why the silence?"

"I've been doing some thinking."

"About what?"

"You. Me. That kind of thing."

Arnold nodded. "And?"

Jesse's head dropped. He picked up his knife and tapped it. Then he made eye contact with Arnold. He felt tongue-tied as he fumbled for words. "I've got enough dough to get me by until the end of the summer. After that, I'll have to go back to work. I'm not going to do construction any more. I'm going to teach."

"Sounds good to me."

"School teachers make even less money than roofers."

"And much less than physicians."

A faint smile parted Jesse's lips. "You're giving me a hard time. Aren't you?"

"You deserve it. We've had this conversation before. You know how I feel."

"Not completely."

"What do you mean?"

"I mean, how you feel. Not completely."

"Do I have to spell it out?"

"No. Just a one word answer. Yes or no."

He reached under the seat, pulled out a book size package that was wrapped in brown paper, and handed it to Arnold. His eyes appeared to her like saucers. She detected a tremor in his hand as he held forth the package.

She looked at Jesse quizzically. He didn't answer. She shook the package. Then she held it to her ear and shook it again. "Open it."

She ripped off the brown wrapping paper, exposing a white box. She opened it. Inside was a smaller package, also wrapped in brown paper. She tore the paper off the second offering, and exposed a third package. It was a palm-sized box, also sheathed in brown paper. As she shed the final wrapper, another white box was exposed. She opened the white box, and she paused. Inside was another box, this one made of black velvet. She looked across at Jesse. His dark eyes were liquid.

She lifted back the top of the velvet box and Jesse watched her eyes widen. Her chest rose and fell rapidly as she stared at the offering. Sparkling in the velvet box was a round diamond solitaire. She stared at the ring, and then at Jesse. Then she reached down, pincered the ring, and fitted it on the forefinger of her left hand. "It's beautiful. I'm stunned."

Jesse moved forward and knelt beneath her. "Will you marry me?"

She looked at Jesse, and then at the ring. Her lips pursed. "You've caught me totally by surprise. You know this is what I've always dreamt of."

Jesse got up, leaned over, and kissed her. It was a long, soft kiss, one that he wished would never end. She stroked the back of his head as he kissed her, her hand running down his silky ponytail. When he sat back down he watched her. Her eyes were shining, her face radiant, as she gazed at the diamond.

Following dinner they walked along city streets, the summer night clear and warm. They held hands as they moved, their words sparing. As they wove their way through the fabric of the historic town, time lost its meaning to Jesse. They walked until the wee hours of the morning, a circuitous route before ending back at Arnold's apartment.

Two days later Arnold drove Jesse to New York, and he caught a British Airways flight to London. Sanchez felt like a different man as he left her behind, one whose life had taken on a whole new meaning.

As Arnold drove back from the airport her cell phone rang. She picked it up and answered.

"Hello?...Right.....Just dropped her off at the airport.....Okay. See you tonight....Ciao."

She hung up and checked her ring. It must have been hell for him to scrape up the money to purchase a diamond, she thought. At a stoplight she took it off and examined it more carefully. Then she reached for her purse and dropped it inside.

Chapter 26

The third week in May, on a sun-drenched Monday, Jesse Sanchez strolled along the Rio Gaudalquivir River. The river flowed from north to south, and he followed its movement as he walked.

He had spent the last week in Seville and he felt at home. Possibly more at ease than in any place he'd ever been. Perhaps it made sense that he felt that way, he thought. For Spanish was his mother's native tongue. Though Carmen Sanchez's ancestors were from Mexico, the language touched a nerve chord of familiarity for Jesse. It was a feeling that was unlike anything he had sensed in the states.

But along with the familiarity there was a sense of strangeness. The peculiar feeling of being in a land where Spanish, not English, was the mother tongue. The romance language had a musical sound to his ear. Unlike the harsh, metallic sounds of English. Here that tongue was more than accepted. It was favored.

The exploding Latin population in the states had made bilingualism a hot button topic. Jesse had heard endless debates over the pros and cons of a two-language education system. But he realized it was talk, nothing more. He understood that the vast majority of Americans, felt scorn toward those who communicated in their native tongue. It was a disapproval that was sometimes tacit, but more often open. For many U.S. citizens were diametrically opposed to any changes they perceived as threats to their society. They viewed Latinos who clung to Spanish as foreigners, outsiders who refused to assimilate. They saw them as lazy and undependable. Aliens who had infected an English speaking culture. They were diminished to vermin status. And though technically they enjoyed all the rights of citizenship, they were viewed by many of their fellow Americans as foreign interlopers.

Jesse knew that Spanish speaking Americans frequently faced the indignity of proving their citizenship. They were forced to show documentation in a land whose laws specifically forbade that type of action. He had witnessed it with his mother. And when he read in school that all U.S. citizens were immune from all types of government sponsored harassment, the words rang hollow.

But even in Seville, Jesse still felt himself an outsider. It was still not possible for him to go unnoticed when he spoke Spanish. His speech patterns echoed the inflections of his mother's Spanish. That which was spoken in her birthplace of Cuernavaca. It was unlike the pulsing Castillian rhythms that flowed from the lyrical tongues of Seville's natives.

Still, he adored Seville, almost everything about it. After his morning run he would stop at the Mercado del Arenal, a market near the bullring on C. Pastor y Leandro, between C. Almansa and C. Arenal. From the market he purchased fresh fruit from screaming vendors. He would then return to his hostel for a breakfast of fruit, fresh rolls, and steaming coffee. After breakfast he would take long strolls through the historic city.

He learned that Seville was the seat of Moorish culture, the site of a small Roman acropolis founded by Julius Caesar. That the Spanish Renaissance had flowered there, and it was the capital of Andalusian culture. And that Jean Cocteau had bundled it with Venice and Peking as his trio of magical cities. While Mozart, Rossini, and Bizet wrote operas inspired by that magic. Jesse had come across the 16th century maxim "Aui non ha visto Sevilla non has visto maravilla" when reading about the city. It roughly translated as, 'one who has not seen Seville, has not seen a marvel.' Sanchez came to embrace that idea.

In the daytime he'd visit the cathedrals, from the Barrio de Santa Cruz, which marks Seville's center, and outward. And Seville's shopping district, which lies north of the cathedral where Av. Constitucion fades into Plaza Nueva.

He learned that Christians razed an Almohad mosque to clear space for Seville's cathedral in 1401, leaving only the famed La Giralda minaret. And that along with the tower's twins in Marrakech and Rabat was the oldest and largest surviving Almohad minaret.

Jesse found the cathedral, which took over a century to complete and stands as the largest Gothic edifice in the world, Seville's most impressive sight. He wondered about religious fervor, and the type of mentality that had spurred conquerors to construct a church so great, an edifice that in their own words would make "those who come after us, take us as madmen." Near the entrance he saw the black and gold coffin-bearers that guarded the Tumba de Cristobal Colon (Tomb of Columbus). And outside the cathedral on the northeast end, he saw the patio de los Naranjos (orange trees). It was one of the few areas preserved that brought back the past of the Arab Caliphate.

He visited the site of the Alcazar Palace, finished by the Moors in 1181, where only the Patio del Yeso remains. The 9th century walls of the Alcazar—the oldest palace still used by European royalty—face the south side of the cathedral. Within them he saw the exquisitely carved Patio de las Munecas (Courtyard of the Dolls). And later Christian additions to the palace, the stunning Patio de Las Doncellas (Maid's Court), resplendent with foliated archways, glistening tile work, and a central fountain. And he toured the golden-domed Salon de los Embajadores, a site where Fernando and Isabel welcomed Columbus upon his return from America.

He loved the city's neighborhoods, or barrios, which he explored while walking. In the Macarena district in the north, he saw the remains of Roman walls and an Arab gate, the San

Bernardo with its Alameda de Hercules, a parkway with two Roman columns, and the Calle de la Feria, a bustling area with a Thursday morning flea market.

He explored the Santa Clara and San Vincente neighborhoods, places where aristocratic homes, housing ensconced medieval contents, stood steadfast against the ravages of 'progress.' And most of all he loved the Barrio de Santa Cruz, a labyrinth of alleys and balconied houses, a place where winsome streets and vibrant plazas teemed with life.

He sampled the jams, pastry, and candy, sold in Plaza del Cabildo near the cathedral. And went bar hopping (tapeo), in Barrio Triana after his evening meal. Sangria and tinto verano was the local favorite, a cold blend of red wine and Casera (sweetened, citrus flavored tonic water).

In his walks he traversed the alleyways of the old Bario de Santa Cruz along the east bank. And as the Spanish sun set, he'd head to the west bank. There he ate cheaply, a place where nightlife turned electric in the Barrios de Triana and de los Remedios.

It was still warm at night when the sun went down, and he walked among crowds of locals and tourists. Sangria flowed freely in crowded bares, terrazzo, and chiringuitos, as partygoers reveled through the night.

The chiringuitos, outdoor bars that pulsate to bacalao (techno dance music), cluster on the riverside along Paseo de Cristobal Colon, between Puente del Generalissimo and Puente de Isabel II. Jesse would sometimes get caught in the crush, a place so packed that it would overflow into nearby streets and parking lots. But the bars' proximity to the water gave them a serene tropical feeling that was irresistible.

He had come to love Seville, a place where Don Juan romanced and Figaro barbered. It was a place where gypsies still sang ballads, flamenco dancers still reeled, and matadors still taunted raging bulls.

That Friday morning, after checking out from his hostel, Jesse walked with his backpack and athletic bag to the bus station. That evening he lay in his hotel room, the designated housing for the first stop on the ITF European Track Grand Prix. As he lay he read <u>One Hundred Years of Solitude</u>, a novel by Gabriela Garcia Marquez. It was a haunting work that he found both mysterious and beautiful. He read in Spanish, the mother tongue of the Nobel Prize winning author, who lived in Mexico City.

The book was helping to take his mind off the next evening. When he would run 800 meters, his first sanctioned race in almost four years. He was a different man than the naive youth who had lined up at U.S. Olympic Trials in Eugene, Oregon. He had become hardened, but not cynical. He still clung to his dream. That some day he would become the world's greatest runner.

He was rooming with an Englishman, a stiff-lipped 1,500-meter runner named Colin Bond. Bond seemed snobbish to Jesse. He had disappeared after dinner with two other English athletes, the three men searching for a pub. Sanchez went back to his room on his own. It was just as well, he thought. It was the night before his race. For the next twenty-four hours he would not stray far from his room. It was a time to try and relax, to rest up for the coming night's effort.

The hotel the ITF had booked for the athletes was five star. It was a surprise for Jesse, whose sleeping bag was rolled in his backpack. The plush accommodations were unexpected, and so was the food. A sumptuous buffet had been laid out for the evening meal, a feast unlike any he'd experienced. He fought the urge to overeat, but his focus kept him in line. He was still more than ten pounds over his target racing weight of 148.

He learned from fellow athletes at the buffet table, that the lavish feeds were standard for ITF events. Sit-down meals for track and field athletes were unfeasible. Especially for a group of competitors whose weight ranges were so vast. Female long distance runners sometimes weighed under a hundred pounds, while male shot putters often eclipsed 300. The buffets satisfied the dilemma. There was an abundance of food, copious spreads that encompassed a variety of choices. Every athlete took whatever, and as much, as he needed.

With housing and meals taken care of, Jesse could relax until the next night. There would be three heats of the 800 in the season's first Grand Prix event. Sanchez would be running in the third, a 'B' event.

The only payment for his effort would be five hundred dollars, regardless of how he fared in the race. It was the minimum appearance money doled out to all competitors. Fifteen percent of that five hundred would go to his agent. He would keep the rest. It was money that would allow him to scrape by from meet to meet. By camping out, rooming at youth hostels, and eating from markets, he could make it through the summer. But it would be a no frills, shoestring existence. Europe was expensive, especially compared to the states.

The race's only carrot was small but coveted. A stellar showing in a 'B' race guaranteed a spot in an 'A' race at a future meet. And along with that, the chance to win prize money for a top three finish.

Jesse's appearance fee was a pittance compared to the sums that star athletes received. Marquis performers commanded anywhere from twenty, to a hundred thousand dollars per meet. And that was for appearance money alone. Add on winnings and shoe contracts, and some of the top performers eclipsed seven figure yearly incomes. It was the type of money that Sanchez would have made if he had not been wrongfully denied. From the day he was falsely accused, until the time he was cleared, he had been bitter. But the source of his bitterness was not so much from the money or fame that had been denied him. Rather, the rancor's provenance was shame. The degradation that he, his family, and his friends had endured from the denigration of his name and character.

He had never lusted for personal wealth. Not for flashy cars or expensive homes. Nor any of the accompanying accoutrements that frequently followed newfound wealth. His longing for money was tied to a striving for security. That, and a means to repay his mother. To give her all the things that a lifetime of struggle had denied her. He dreamt of buying her a small house, freeing her permanently from the backbreaking work that had aged her prematurely. And he wanted to repay McClanahan. To give him the percentage of his earnings that loyal athletes gave to their coaches.

Jesse had come to learn that money in track and field was very large for only a handful of competitors. The vast majority made little or nothing. In many ways it was unfair, Jesse thought. But it was the big name athletes who packed the stadiums. Track and field fanatics scrambled for tickets, regardless of the price, when a world record attempt was imminent.

Money drove track and field, Sanchez understood. Just like it did every other business. And money put blinders on the powerful. They plugged their ears, blindfolded their eyes, and clamped their tongues. They bent the rules however they found fit, to preserve their progeny's commercial viability. The monkey troika feigned ignorance. A charade that reached epic heights with their drug enforcement policy. They knew that blood testing, a simple procedure that could be administered as easily as urine testing, would cause the sport to collapse overnight. And that if the procedure was initiated, a profusion of stars would quit. They understood that 'clean' performances, would fall far short of their substance-aided records. That the fans would follow the stars' exodus, as angry track and field fanatics, hell-bent on witnessing records, would no longer pay big bucks for ticket prices. The power brokers understood that Track and Field, as is any spectator sport, is driven by performance. They realized that fans continually demanded more. And as long as the bar was raised, they were happy. They further understood that few cared whether athletes were on drugs or clean. Fans wanted excitement for their entertainment dollar. Ethics be damned! It was a vicious cycle. One that Jesse had learned would probably never change. It sickened him.

Only two athletes had tested positive at the Atlanta games, he remembered. And that was out of eleven thousand participants. Anyone that believed only two athletes were using performance-enhancing substances was one step beneath troglodyte, he thought. But Jesse was resigned to remain clean. If the other athletes were on the juice, so be it, he reasoned. He would beat them drug-free.

The past had wrongfully convicted him. But the past was dead. Now he had another chance. An opportunity to prove to the world that he could run with anyone. It would be a slow process, but one he was determined to complete.

He closed his book and turned off the lamp. As he lay in the dark room his thoughts turned to his loved ones. It was a time to be strong, he thought. His thoughts turned to his mother, brother, McClanahan, and his training buddies in Houston. But most of all he thought of Shauna Arnold, his bride to be. She meant the most. As he pictured her in the dark, he imagined her beside him. Failure was out of the question, he thought. He had to succeed this summer. The stakes were too high for anything else.

The next evening as Jesse lined up in lane six for his 800-meter heat, he felt nervous. It was the same type of angst that had followed him throughout the Olympic Trials. He tried to assuage his tenseness, telling himself that the anxiety was a precursor to a fast race. His adrenaline was pumping, and his body was ready for flight. But as he stood on the tartan surface, the track seemed to have doubled in size. The distance around was daunting, unlike the 400 meter stretch that he rationalized had not changed. That, and the din of the crowd. The resonating thunder did nothing to mitigate his discomfort.

He felt like his whole body was shaking as he watched the starter's hand go up. And he could feel his heart thump in his chest as he waited. A crack was followed by a puff of smoke, and he sprinted.

As he broke toward lane one at the hundred-meter mark, he felt the sting of an elbow as it struck his ribs. The action slowed him, and he was boxed in at the back of the pack. Rage consumed him as the leaders crossed 200 meters in 24 seconds.

As he ran around the 200-meter curve, he was bumped again. He fought to keep from stumbling as the spikes from a runner behind him struck his right calf, and then his heel. A Czech runner shouted an angry epithet at Jesse as the clip propelled him forward, into the Czech's back. As Sanchez passed 300 meters, he was still boxed in at the back of the throng. He swung wide and sprinted down the straight, running wide in lane four as he attempted to improve his position.

As he fought his way toward the inside lane, a hard elbow found his solar plexus. Almost instantly his breath left him. A split second later he stumbled and went down. Flying spikes gnashed overhead as he lay, some of them finding flesh. Vitriolic curses of foreign tongues echoed in his ears as runners leaped over him. By the time he righted himself he was far behind the field. The digital clock turned sixty-four seconds as he completed his first lap. He struggled to make up ground on the field, but his efforts were in vain. He finished in 1:59, far back from the winning time of 1:47.

As he came across the finish line he bent over at the waist to catch his breath. His fists were clenched as the nightmare replayed on his screen. He slammed his fist on the track. Then he got up and jogged back under the stands.

As he dressed he took stock of his wounds. Both the fronts and backs of his legs were sliced with angry spike marks, as was the back of his right shoulder. Some were still bleeding, but he didn't care. He was furious. But it wasn't the pain of the cuts that had stoked his fury. It was his stupidity.

He had been warned about the mano-mano tactics that characterized European track. But he hadn't listened well enough.

In the states, track running was a gentlemanly endeavor compared to Europe. Runners could be disqualified for any type of touch that was considered flagrant. But in Europe, almost anything was allowed. Physical contact was an integral part of international track. You either accepted the fact, or didn't run, he had been told. Runners pushed, shoved, elbowed, spiked and punched. They grabbed the back of jerseys and shorts. Almost anything to improve their position.

As Jesse sat, his fist doubled. He was enraged at the error of his ways. He punched his locker, and the sound of fist striking metal reverberated loudly.

"Not in Kansas anymore. Are ya' mate?" The accent was Aussie, the tone sardonic. Though the man was bearded, it provided inadequate cover for his pitted skin.

Jesse glared angrily. "Piss off!"

The Aussie back-pedaled until he reached the door. "Little testy. Aren't we mate? Go dip your eye in shit." Then he flew out the door.

Jesse got up, walked out the tunnel, and caught the shuttle back to the hotel. On the ride back he remained locked in his own world, oblivious to everything. He had screwed up big time in his first race back, he thought. It was hardly the type of beginning he had envisioned.

That night he e-mailed McClanahan, on the laptop he had loaned him for the summer. He told him about his race. The next morning he received his reply:

Be patient. It's going to take you a good three months before you're racing like your old self. You better learn how to defend yourself. Those buggers will murder you if they get the chance. Forget about your times. Just do the workouts and keep racing. The times will come. See ya'.
McClanahan

Sanchez grinned as he read the words. He knew that patience wasn't one of his greatest virtues. Nor his ability to accept defeat. And that he would never grow accustomed to getting his butt stomped.

Chapter 27

Kip Korir watched from the stands, undetected, as Jesse Sanchez hit the split button on his chronograph. The Kenyan runner studied the tall American's form as he cruised around the 400-meter Rome oval. They both had a lot in common, Korir thought. Each had endured their share of agony in track and field, and each had been the target of controversy. But the American's plight had been worse, a lot more trying than what he had endured.

Korir had emerged from the Nandi Hills region of Kenya. He was just one more of a profusion of young Kenyan runners with the promise of setting world records. A Dutch coach, Peter Burger, first spotted the youngster at a Kenyan All-Comers' meet. He was running in an event that almost every Kenyan competitor has tried. The race was the steeplechase, the most revered athletic contest in the East African nation.

Burger had watched the high-hipped youngster cruise over the hurdles. And then fly when he hit the flats. It was apparent to him that the Masai had extraordinarily quick leg turnover. By his naked eye, more so than any of the Kenyan runners whom he'd witnessed. And that included Kenyans in their 20's and 30's who were at their physical peaks.

Burger met Korir later that summer. On a 400-meter strip of red dirt road that the Dutchman had wheeled, he measured the teenager's speed. As he suspected, the African youth had blazing short quickness. Under Burger's tutelage, he weaned the youngster from the steeplechase, bringing him down in distance to 1,500 and 800 meters. Korir progressed steadily for the next four years as he attended school with future Kenyan stars Joseph Rono and Henry Nyariki. He paid for his tuition painting school buildings during holidays.

He was poised to run for the Kenyan Olympic team as an 18-year-old, after winning the World Juniors in both the 800 and 1,500 events. But he fell prey to the politics rife in the Kenyan hierarchy.

Unwilling to comply with their strictures, he moved to Holland. In doing so he passed up scholarship offers from American colleges and universities in which he had no interest. In Amsterdam he began training full time under his Dutch coach, Peter Burger. At first, Korir didn't like Amsterdam, the climate and terrain so radically different from his native Kenya. But within time, he came to love the city and the country. More so than he had ever anticipated.

Like Jesse Sanchez, Kip Korir's training sessions were kept secret. And like Jesse, the clandestine nature of his running set rumor mongers gossiping. Four years later Korir was denied another Olympic berth, this time on the Dutch team. Politics again reared its ugly head. The current controversy concerned his Dutch citizenship, the timing of which failed to satisfy ITF rules.

The denial was a blow to Korir but he persisted. Another four years passed before his Olympic dreams finally coalesced with twin gold medals in the 800 and 1,500 meters. He had become a wealthy man by running Grand Prix events. Combined with his shoe contracts, he had made more money than he'd ever dreamt possible. In addition to his Olympic gold medals, the gifted East African held the recognized world records in the 800 meters, the 1,500, and the mile. But his 800 meter record was over a second slower than Jesse Sanchez's personal best. The time the American ran in his fated 800 final at the U.S. Olympic Trials. It was a fact that haunted Korir.

The Kenyan felt that his half-mile record was tainted. He had never said anything publicly, but the reality gnawed at his viscera. He knew that Jesse Sanchez had run over a second faster. It was a measure of time that seemed infinitesimal to the unenlightened. But those who understood the nuances of track and field realized that a second was an eternity in a two-lap race. That knowledge brought deep angst for Korir. Accompanied by the consciousness that Jesse Sanchez had been deprived of what was rightfully his. The American had been asphyxiated by politics. It was the same fetid stench that had suffocated the Kenyan's early career. The effluence had spewed from open sewers, communal cesspools shared by global autocracies. He viewed their power as all consumptive, cold-blooded cartels that systematically destroyed hope and life.

When Korir learned that Sanchez had been cleared of drug charges and the circumstances involving his acquittal, he felt a deep sense of guilt. It was a guilt born from the fact that he had never toed the line in an 800 with a runner who should have been his master. And an even worse sense of guilt plagued him, that the man who should have been king would probably never regain his old form. Jesse Sanchez, subsequent to his Achilles surgery, would likely be no more than a shadow of his old self. He would never again run the times he was once capable of running. And he'd never be accorded the respect he was due. Fate, Korir reasoned. It was fate that had afforded one runner a life of wealth and fame, while another struggled to survive.

Track and field was full of inequities, Korir thought. And he had survived more than his share. He'd been omitted from a race in Hengelo, Holland, a contest that was billed locally as "The Duel." It was an event set up to lower the two-mile record, under eight minutes.

Korir had already run a world record time for three thousand meters, a time that was much faster than the equivalent two-mile mark that he also held. But he was denied a spot in the race, an event that was sponsored by a company whose shoes he did not wear.

Instead the duel was set up between Ethiopia's Mohammed Hussein, and Algeria's Chadli Zerhouni. A million-dollar incentive was offered for a sub-eight minute time.

Both runners appeared relaxed as they sat on the shoulders of rabbits who took them through 1,200 meters in 3:02.04, and the 1,600 mark in 4:00.77. It was the equivalent of a 4:02 mile. But within meters of finishing four laps, Zerhouni took off on his own as Hussein faltered. Hussein continued to fade as runner after runner passed him. Zerhouni was able to muster three sub 60 second splits in the next four laps, reaching 2km in 5:00, and 3km in 7:29. 31. The 3k split was almost nine seconds slower than what Korir had run previously for the same distance.

Twenty thousand spectators in Fanny Blankers Koen Stadium watched as Zerhouni struggled over the remaining 218.7 meters, before finishing in 8:01.08. It was a great effort. But Korir felt certain that if he had been there, the outcome would have been different.

As Korir watched Jesse Sanchez glide down the track for the final straight of his four hundred, he was impressed by the long, fluid stride that the American still possessed. There was no trace of a hitch. Nothing in his stroke to call attention to an Achilles that had been shredded and remade. Other than the fact that Sanchez appeared a bit heavier, maybe ten pounds more than in the films that Korir had watched of Jesse running at the Eugene Trials, he looked good. He appeared strong and supple, like a force to be reckoned with.

Maybe a miracle was possible, Korir thought. Maybe Jesse Sanchez could race himself back into his old form. And if so, then perhaps the two could meet some day. Korir longed for the opportunity. It would give him peace of mind. A satisfaction that no amount of money, or fame, could ever replace. He needed that peace of mind. And as he watched Sanchez, he fantasized the contest that he'd dreamt of for years. He longed to run against the American, when Jesse Sanchez was once again at the top of his game. Anything less would be meaningless.

Two nights later Jesse Sanchez watched from the side, as Kip Korir lined up in lane five. It was the feature heat of the men's 800 meters. Sanchez's earlier race had gone better than his run in Seville. But anything short of total disaster would have bettered his Spanish debacle. He'd barely broken 1:49 in the Roman affair, having finished a distant eighth in a field of eight. He'd gone out hard, positioned on the outside of lane one, just behind the leaders. They had cruised through the first two hundred meters in twenty-five seconds. He hung on for a first quarter split of 52.1. Shortly after he went into oxygen debt. He struggled home the final lap in 57.5. A chorus line of runners blew by him.

His finishing time was 1:49.6, light years from his vision. But at least it was a start, he rationalized, a benchmark defining his current condition. Like a sculptor with a hammer and chisel, he'd chip away at the granite block. Whittling away at the barrier as the season progressed.

If there was any redemptive value of his last place finish, it was the way he had raced. He had run assertively, establishing position and returning flying elbows with those of his own. In the time between Seville and Rome, Jesse had spoken with many seasoned runners. Their words had a common thread. That European and American track were light years removed. They verbalized what McClanahan had told him repeatedly. That international runners would jump right in front of him and cut him off. That his singlet and shorts would be grabbed. That he would be intentionally trapped and cut off. And that he'd be elbowed and punched. They repeated the Scotsman's warning. That it was common practice to nudge and elbow when passing. There was no sense to get upset by it, they explained. It was just the way things were. Expect it to happen, they warned him.

And when it did, retain his cool and refrain from overreacting. To retaliate in anger was a mistake, they explained. Any actions, defensive or offensive, must have a tactical basis. It was always critical to keep thinking. To anticipate what would happen next. Because the emotional runner was doomed for failure.

They told Jesse that runners often got disqualified for bumping or shoving at NATF events. But not so in Europe. And that as physical as European 800 meter races got, things were even more physical in the 1,500 and the mile. In those events runners fanned out behind a circular line, sometimes as many as 20 runners in a race. It was a dogfight they told him. As anxious runners lined up on a semi-circle battled for a position in lane one. Besides the dangers of being pushed, shoved, and spiked, the miler had to be wary of too quick a start. With a herd of nervous runners roaring toward the first two hundred, 25 second opening splits were not uncommon. They spelled almost certain death. As Sanchez watched Korir, he studied the Kenyan's face. The visage showed no signs of stress, nor did the eyes. He looked peaceful but focused. It was a look that spoke of an inner peace and quiet confidence, one that transcended arrogance. Korir was special, Jesse thought. As were the other Kenyan runners he'd met. They were gifted runners and fearless warriors. Men and women who didn't seem to know the meaning of setting self-limitations.

Jesse had learned that the confidence was a by-product of their culture, a society whose people had few physical possessions. But a federation where family and community were unbending. The sense of belonging provided a background that few American runners had. Though invested with a myriad of material goods that the Africans would never know, the Americans were largely bereft of the Kenyan's most highly cherished holding. Most had never known the type of rock solid support that nurtured their Kenyan counterparts, a critical element in their development. It was a confidence that fostered faith. The conviction that physical limitations were set by the mind. In a word it was love, a deep-seated affection that nourished and sustained them. It was the same love that had rescued Jesse Sanchez when all else had failed.

As Jesse studied Korir, the gun went off. American Mark Pratt sprinted into the lead. Pratt, who had finished behind Jesse at Eugene, had made steady progress since those trials. Eliminated in the semi-finals 800-meter event in Sydney, Pratt had become toughened on the European circuit. He was the leader of a new breed of American 800-meter runners, a cadre of former 400-meter men. They were all black, speed merchants who had moved up in distance. As Jesse watched, Pratt blazed through the opening 200 in 24 seconds, Korir right on his shoulder. The American roared through the opening quarter in 50 flat. Korir was right with him, on the outside of lane one. As Moroccan Hicham El Kouzekanah moved quickly to the outside of Korir, along with Kenyan Moses Konchella, Korir accelerated. Quickly it became a two-man race, as Konchella and Korir traded strides. The Kenyans flew around the 600-meter curve as they headed for home. Kouzekana, and the Italian Giuseppe Delarosa, were left in their wake.

As they sprinted around the final curve, Jesse focused on Korir. The Kenyan opened his stride, and magically, in a split second, the race was over. The Olympic champion put twenty meters on his fellow Kenyan, powering to victory in 1:43.2. As Jesse watched, he was impressed with the ease that Korir had won. He had put away the field when he wanted.

Korir was a great runner, Jesse thought. And was an almost a certain pick for two more gold medals at the coming Athens Olympics. The Games were to be staged that September, another Olympics that Jesse Sanchez would not race. But as Sanchez viewed the Kenyan's race, he couldn't help but make the inevitable comparison. Sanchez remembered when he was in top form. When he could turn a 200 in 21.1 and a quarter in

43.9. They were times that Korir could not touch. Nor could any other half miler on the international circuit. The question he posed was, what type of speed, if any, did he still have? Were his 200 and 400-meter times gone, or merely misplaced?

He'd laid a great strength foundation. A critical element for every middle and long distance runner who competed on a world class level. But it was throw-down speed, the ability to churn out a blazing finishing kick that separated the good runners from the great ones. Jesse wondered if he still possessed that kind of speed. The worn cliche still had meaning. Only time would tell.

Chapter 28

The sun had not yet risen on Lake Lucerne as Jesse Sanchez jogged on the deserted street. The mountain air was fresh and clean, and the town was peacefully quiet. It was a welcome respite from Paris, a place of perpetual motion and sound.

Though Lucerne was more to his liking, Paris had been a good experience. It was a city unlike any he had encountered. The greenery of the French gem was not what he had expected. Paris was resplendent with parks and gardens. Each day, after his workout, he'd get on the subway, getting off at stops unknown. With no prior planning he'd walk and explore, experiencing the city in a primal, but immediate, fashion. He was never disappointed at his stops. The endless parks, botanical gardens, and architectural wonders, he came upon at each new locale. It was a city that was unmatched in symmetry and style. Hemingway's description of the French gem stuck in Jesse's mind. Paris was a moveable feast, a place he'd always take with him.

But like all feasts, it was a meal he was thankful had come to an end. Paris was teeming with people, the greater metropolitan area in excess of ten million. It was a place where every inch of space was precious, not the type of locale where he would choose to live.

Since arriving on the continent, Sanchez had developed an affinity for small towns, places where people and attitudes seemed more human. Lucerne, with a population over sixty thousand, was a far cry from the hustle and bustle of Paris. The pace was slow, to his liking, unlike the megalopolis where everything was frenetic. Sanchez was quickly getting his fill of big cities, places where the ITF tour made most of its stops.

Since Rome, the tour had gone through Moscow, Bratislava, Turku, Nuremberg, Helsinki, Budapest, Paris, and Turin.

Jesse had run (Nuremberg, June 13), (Budapest, June 21), and (Paris, June 23). His subsequent times were 1:47.3, 1:47.9, and 1:47.5 respectively. In Nuremberg and Paris he finished sixth out of a field of eight, while at Budapest he was last. The past month of training, racing, and travel around the continent had hardened him. He felt himself slowly becoming racing fit. He had shed an additional four pounds, his weight having dropped to a hundred and fifty four. The weight drop left him only six pounds over his target goal of 148, a standard he'd set for summer's end.

Europe had changed Jesse Sanchez in ways he'd never imagined. Since coming to the continent, he'd adapted to a culture that was starkly different from U.S. society. Most apparent to him was the size of automobiles. The big sport utility vehicles that had swept the American market were almost non-existent. A profusion of small cars dominated the Continent's roadways, vehicles with small engines and light chassis. Efficient machines that could run endlessly on drops of petrol. With gasoline prices so high, many times the price of American fuel, small cars were the norm.

Houses were generally smaller also. Water and electrical usage was lower. And large appliances were more expensive, and less prevalent, than in American homes. It became apparent to Sanchez that most Europeans possessed a fraction of the material accoutrements of their American counterparts. And they paid higher taxes for social systems that Americans did not subsidize.

In many ways the Continent was backward, set in its ways, Jesse thought. But in others it was advanced. Europeans had addressed, and dealt with, issues that Americans had delayed for future generations. It took little time for Jesse to realize that Europe was safer than the states. With handguns almost non-existent, and gun ownership of any type made difficult by strictly enforced laws, the murder rate was low.

By the time Jesse finished his morning run, the sun had risen. He went back to his pensione and showered. Then he walked toward a small cafe for a light breakfast. Above Mount Pilatus the clean blue sky was a shocking shade of cerulean blue. He felt alive in the mountain majesty, his body and spirit re-energized by the pristine air. There was a sense of freedom escaping the city. The noise, the congestion, and the pollution. It was as if a weight had been lifted from his shoulders, his lungs filled with fresh air. His legs felt light as he walked. The best he had felt since coming to Europe. He was anxious to race the next night.

After breakfast he checked out of his pensione, and walked to the ITF designated hotel. He checked in and met his roommate, a Belgian steeplechaser. Then he went to lunch, before going back upstairs for a nap. Upon waking he got into his running clothes, walked downstairs, and caught a shuttle bus to the track stadium.

After a lengthy warm-up that consisted of jogging and stretching, Sanchez slipped into spikes. Soon his workout began. It was a sharpening affair, 8x200 meters, with a minute rest between efforts. As he began his first effort, Kip Korir, clad in a blue Adidas warmup suit with a red, white and blue Dutch flag sewn on his right sleeve, walked across the track toward the starting line.

As Korir walked, his dark eyes focused on Jesse. The American was moving well, he thought. Even better than he had just days before in Paris.

Sanchez hadn't spotted Korir as he crossed the two-hundred-meter mark. He punched his chronograph and a high pitch beep followed. Jesse gazed down at the watch crystal, his heart beating rapidly. He'd turned the 200 in just under twenty-five seconds. And it felt easy.

The next six efforts went equally well, chipping off tenths of seconds on each interval. As he pressed the start button on his chronograph for his final effort, Korir did the same. The angular American seemed to float around the curve, and then he thundered down the straight toward home. As Jesse breezed across the finish line, he hit his chronograph. It made a high pitch squealing sound, coinciding almost precisely with Korir's timepiece. Sanchez studied his digital read out. 23.1. The Kenyan eyed his crystal, and the same numbers displayed. Sanchez jogged and walked a lap. Then he sat on the infield. As he slipped out of his spikes and pulled on his warmups, Korir approached him.

"You look like you are coming into form, Jesse."

"Slowly."

"Keep your faith. It will come."

Jesse got up and extended his hand. The Kenyan took it. "Thanks. It's a pleasure meeting you."

"The pleasure's mine." The Kenyan smiled, displaying a gap-toothed grin, the trademark of Nandi tribesmen. He took off his warmups, and slipped into his spikes. "See you later, Jesse." He jogged to an outside lane, circling the track in deliberate strides as he got ready for his workout.

Korir's gesture heartened Jesse. It was an action that Sanchez never would have initiated. Part of his reluctance stemmed from shyness, part from respect. In Jesse's mind, to approach Korir would have been presumptuous. Korir was universally considered the greatest middle distance runner of his time. Jesse was unproven. If he would win Korir's respect it would come through racing, Sanchez reasoned.

The next night Sanchez drew lane 2 for his 800-meter heat. As the gun went off he ran quickly but controlled, careful not to go out at a break neck pace. As he cut over into lane one, he was positioned on the inside of the lane, just behind the two leaders. As he moved, the runner to his right, the Spaniard

Ernesto Gomez stumbled. Gomez's left foot struck Jesse's right calf. As the Spaniard teetered, Robin Hughes, the Australian runner behind Sanchez, tried to move up through the space created. Hughes was the bearded runner who had confronted Jesse in Seville.

As Hughes tried to shove and elbow his way through the opening, he jolted Sanchez. But Jesse was prepared. Sanchez fired a quick, short, right elbow that struck the Aussie squarely in the chest.

"Bleeding, fucking, bloody asshole." Hughes fell back after bellowing. Then he surged forward. Jesse heard the Aussie's locomotive-like breathing as he approached. Then he felt Hughes' fist as it struck him near his kidney. But the punch lacked force, the Australian winded by a pace he couldn't handle. Jesse kept running, never looking back.

As Sanchez went through the first 400 in 53 seconds, Hughes fell further back. Sanchez held his position behind the leaders. With two hundred meters to go, Jesse went wide and sprinted for home. As he caught the leaders going around the curve, he felt himself tying up. He struggled to hold on but could not, rigging up down the final straight. But even with the shaky ending, he still managed to hang on for fourth. He ran 1:46.4, a season best.

Less than a minute later the angry Aussie approached. He pointed and shook the extended forefinger of his right hand at Jesse. "You ever pull any shit like that again, and I'll tear you a new asshole." Jesse was overcome by the stench of the man's body odor.

Jesse just grinned. "Why don't you save some of that venom for your next race?"

"I'm warning you. I'll rip your lips."

The smile left Jesse's face. He moved forward and stopped just inches from the Aussie's face. "You want a piece of me, go for it right now, track trash. I'll take you apart."

254

The Aussie's eyes darted fitfully as he watched Jesse. He moved back two steps, shocked at the force of Sanchez's resolve.

"Don't ever try that shit again." The Aussie shook his finger as he spoke. But his voice cracked as he backpedaled, its tone tinged in fear. He continued moving back.

Jesse said, "Why don't you take a bath, you fucking wanker. You're in a civilized country now."

Hughes hands were noticeably shaking as he turned and jogged back under the stands.

As Jesse watched Hughes jog off, he spotted a figure approaching from the corner of his eye. He turned his head. It was Korir. The Kenyan jogged up and stopped, just short of Sanchez. "I watched the race, Jesse. You did the right thing. That man has a history of initiating contact and making trouble. No one likes him. He is a gutless bully."

"Sometimes it gets a little rough out there."

"Yes. And one must react swiftly. You did."

"I'm slowly learning. Good luck in your race, Kip."

"Thanks. I will need it."

Instead of catching the shuttle back to the hotel, Jesse stayed to watch Korir. The former Kenyan obliterated the field with a sizzling 3:30.4 fifteen hundred. When he made his move, it was like all the other runners in the race were standing still.

It had been a good night, Jesse thought. He was becoming race hardened and his conditioning was continuing to improve. Things were finally starting to feel right.

Chapter 29

Dear Shauna,

Sorry I haven't e-mailed you since Lucerne, but I wasn't able to. (Modem problems). It is 10:30 a.m., and I am in Oslo, Norway, getting ready for the Mobil Bislett Games. A Norwegian fellow, a high jumper named Olaf Gerhardsen, took the laptop that McClanahan loaned me and gave it to a friend of his. (A guy living here in Oslo, who's a computer wizard). He made the repair right on the spot.

I miss you so badly, Shauna. You're always on my mind. Sometimes it's hard to stay focused on the running, I think about you so much. You know I'd rather be back home with you. But we both know this is something I have to do.

I hope you're doing fine, and also hope that you think of me a fraction as often as I think of you.

Since Lucerne my running schedule has been really frantic. I ran three meets in seven days, and right now I'm feeling a little fatigued. That's why I'm resting, trying not to get run down and end up getting sick.

Since Lucerne, the tour has made stops in:

June 27   Turin, Italy
June 29   Madrid, Spain
June 30   Sheffield, Great Britain
July 2   Lausanne, Switzerland

I skipped Sheffield, mainly because I didn't feel like flying back to England. But in the three meets I ran, my times held steady. I feel like I'm right on the edge of making a break-through. In Turin I ran 1:46.8 (4th place), Madrid 1:46.9 (5th place), and Lausanne, 1:46.2 (4th place.)

I'm still stuck in the secondary heats, and I'm sure I'll have to go under 1:45 before they let me in a championship heat. I guess I have to be patient, though you know that's not one of my strong points. I've got a good feeling about tomorrow night's race. Yesterday's meet in Lausanne went well. If I run a little smarter, I know I can cut at least another second. I went out too hard, (a mistake I continue to make), going through the first two hundred in 24.

I've dropped a few more pounds, and am currently at 152. That's only four pounds more than what I weighed in Eugene.

I have a good feeling that I'll be racing fit, and ready to kick ass and take names within another month.

This is the first time I've been out of Houston on the Fourth of July since I was a kid. It's funny how, when you're out of the country, things like national holidays take on a different meaning. Mom and Jose will probably go to Miller Theater to hear the concert and watch the fireworks display. I'm sure I'll miss that. How about you? What do you have planned?

I can't even begin to tell you how much I miss you. Just knowing that you're back in Boston waiting for me gives me the strength and incentive to make this dream happen. The fact that you're a runner truly helps, since you understand what I'm going through. I think if you weren't, it would be a pretty hard thing to try and explain and justify.

Europe has been great, but all the travel wears me out. Sometimes I wake up in the middle of the night, in a strange hotel room and I can't remember what country I'm in. It's crazy. All this travel. Everything seems to blend together.

Unfortunately, there's not a lot of time for sight-seeing either. When I ran my first meet in Seville, I got there early. I was able to spend some quality time exploring the city. But since then it's been harder. There really isn't much time. We fly into a place, go to a hotel, and in between training and racing, basically eat and sleep. It's hardly a glamorous life. And it's not the way I'd choose to see Europe if I had the time. I guess in that way I was a bit naive. I thought I'd have more time to visit different places and see different things. But that's just not possible. At least not for me. The training, racing and travelling takes its toll. I'm trying to get as much rest as I can. Doing what I can to keep from breaking down and getting sick. I know you've experienced that same cycle and can understand where I'm coming from.

I hate to repeat myself about how much I miss you. But I can't help it. You're so beautiful. At times I think that every-thing that's happened between us has been a dream. And that I'll wake up one morning with reality slapping me in the face. You'll be gone. Just a dream that was all in my head. I've never had anything as good as you happen to me. Sometimes I dream about you at night, and the family we will make. I know you said you wanted a big family. And I look forward to the day of being the father of your children. I just hope that I don't screw things up the way our fathers did.

I wish you were here with me. But it's actually better for us both that you're not. This wouldn't be a holiday for you at all. And I'd be miserable knowing that I couldn't go to all the places, and do all the things I'd like to, with you. Some day in the future we will. I promise.

I love you more than anything in the world, and I count the days until we're together.

Jesse

The next morning after breakfast, Jesse plugged into a phone line and turned on his computer. He got on line, and went straight to his e-mails. His heart beat quickly as he read the fist message:

Dear Jesse,

I was going crazy not having heard from you for a week. I figured that you'd left me for some flaxen-haired beauty. And then I thought, no, some raven-haired beauty. And then I thought no, some stunning redhead. And then I went through all the different sizes and shapes of women who you'd left me for. Statuesque women. Petite women. Bone thin women. Buxom bombshells. Believe me, I've pictured the whole gamut of continental beauties crooked to your elbow. The thoughts have given me no peace. During the day, when I'm imagining all these nightmares, I am a raging bitch. I'm surly with hospital staff, doctors, and the patients. All the time I'm thinking about my former fiancée, who's dumped me for some gorgeous European broad. Don't even think of it Mr. Sanchez! If you were to leave me, I would undoubtedly commit a dastardly act. One too horrible to describe in words.

Meanwhile, I find some solace in the fact that you are exhausted. That's good, since it will undoubtedly limit your social life. Hopefully you don't have enough strength to go out at night. Bar hopping through European bistros and cafes, all those trendy European hot spots where Continental women would undoubtedly thrust themselves at you. I could just imagine them tearing at your clothes, in public, with everyone watching. Naturally that is what I would do! If I had the opportunity! But instead I am mired here in Boston, sur-rounded by pasty-faced interns and residents. Nerdy looking geeks with all the sex appeal of Beavis and Butthead. Jesse, if you even look at another woman I will be devastated. This is a

*mature, twenty-six-year-old, non-possessive, non-jealous
woman speaking to you. Bullshit! I want you right now! And
I am pissed because I can't have you!*

*My running has been relegated to whenever I can get in a
few miles. But my heart's not in it. I don't have that burning
desire that you do. I think that my best days as a runner are
probably past. Maybe I'll think about it in the future. But
right now it has no appeal to me. What's most important to me
is that I don't lose focus and get through medical school!*

*Don't worry Jesse. The reason I say that is because I know
you. I know you're worrying about how you're going to do.
The future. Money. All the things you don't need to be worrying about. If the running works, fine. If not, it isn't the end of
the world. It's just running.*

*You better not have anything planned when you get back
to the states. Because when I pick you up at JFK in New York,
I will drive you straight to the nearest hotel. And take advantage of your body in ways that you could not even begin to
imagine.*

*You are an incredible lover! And I want you right now! I
can't wait until you're back in my bed!*

Shauna

Jesse read Arnold's letter four more times before clicking
it off. Though he was glad to hear from her, he felt unsettled
that there had been no mention of their future. Only that she
couldn't wait to get him back in bed. He wondered if he was
being paranoid. He fingered his earring, anxious thoughts
racing through his mind, before opening his second e-mail:

Slinger:

Where the fuck have you been?

Got the results of your races over the net. Not bad.

*Don't do anything else stupid, (like you did in Boston),
and you should be kicking ass by the middle of August.*

*If you want to run decent, get the pussy off your mind.
It's not going nowhere. It's always around. You're a dumb
fuck for getting engaged that quick. You don't even know her.
But that's your business. My business is to keep you focused.
You got a whole lifetime to be dealing with women. But not so
long as a runner.*

Stay focused man. Take a lot of cold showers.
McClanahan

After reading McClanahan's e-mail, he e-mailed him right back:

Kevin,
   Sorry I didn't get back to you. My modem wasn't working. All's well.
   I'm going to pop one tonight.
Jesse
P.S. Don't be so suspicious. Shauna's a good lady.

As Jesse powered down, he thought about the cryptic one line prediction he'd just sent to McClanahan. It wasn't like him to say things like that. To make brash predictions about fast races. It was dangerous to let emotions run away, he thought. That kind of behavior could get him in a lot of trouble. Especially in big races. But he was feeling it, the strongest gut feeling that he was on the verge of a major breakthrough since coming back. Maybe his words would come back to haunt him. And maybe he'd make an ass out of himself tonight, he thought. But whatever happened, it was comforting knowing that he had a woman back in the states who was crazy for him.

As he thought about his coming race that night, he tried to calm himself. Emotional roller coasters came down a lot quicker than they went up. It was important to maintain his composure.

That evening Jesse drew lane eight for his event. It was the first 800 in a card of three. As he watched the starter's hand go up, he felt remarkably composed. It was unlike any race that he had experienced that summer.

A puff of white smoke was followed by a crack. Jesse took off. His legs felt light and fresh as his spikes kissed the tartan. He was high on his toes as he crossed the hundred-meter mark. He broke toward lane one in a deliberate fashion, assertive but under control. The movement positioned him in the middle of a large pack, running outside in lane three.

His two-hundred-meter split was twenty-six seconds, and he felt relaxed. His breathing was easy and his legs felt light as he turned the curve. The sounds of furtive breathing, and flashing spikes glancing off the fast tartan, were not discomforting to his ears. As the hungry pack pulled him along, his confidence grew. It was the first race of the season where he felt in control. As if the pack was doing the work. It felt as if he was sitting in a sleek wagon, a team of powerful horses pulling him along. Sanchez held his position through the third curve. He remained on the outside of lane two as he went through three hundred meters in 39.3 seconds. As he ran he stayed focused on his tempo. He concentrated on keeping his stride length and turnover ratio constant. The focus paid off in another metronome like 13 second split. He reached the 400 meter mark in 52.3. He had run all four hundred splits in almost precisely thirteen seconds. It was a consistency that he'd been unable to duplicate in prior Grand Prix races. His splits had been up and down coming into the night's contest. It was an action that had culminated in poor and mediocre times. Now he was running the kind of race that he had trained for, an even paced affair that maximized efficiency and effort.

As Jesse reached the quarter split he held his sixth position, tucked in behind a group of runners. He maintained his spot through 500 meters in 1:05.4. It was another 13-second split. Sanchez maintained his pace as he moved down the straight. At six hundred meters he was positioned on the outside of lane one. He ran next to a Frenchman, on the shoulders of a Moroccan and a Kenyan. His six hundred-meter-split was 1:18.6, another thirteen second hundred. As he rounded the curve with two hundred meters to go he fought the temptation to surge. Be paient, he cautioned himself.

He held his position on the outside of lane one as runners circled the curve. He maintained his post, cruising at precisely the same pace for the next hundred meters. He passed 700 meters in 1:31.6

With precisely 100 meters remaining, Jesse's torso seemed to elevate as he toe-danced down the straight. He pumped his arms, went wide, and flew by the Moroccan and the Kenyan. Sanchez never looked back as he felt his calves and arms burning. As he sprinted for home he ran wide open, his long, powerful stride, eating up huge chunks of tartan. Kip Korir watched with wide eyes as Sanchez extended his lead. The American was leaving behind the field as if they were encased in cement. He flew to the finish, a clear winner by what Korir judged as almost fifteen meters. The Kenyan glanced at the digital clock as Jesse hit the finish line in 1:43.7. He'd blazed the final hundred meters in 12.1. The lightning finish gave him a second four-hundred-meter split of 51.4. He'd run negative splits. From Korir's viewpoint, it appeared that Jesse had relaxed. He sensed that the American was every bit as talented as he had suspected. And more so. There was not even the slightest of hints that Sanchez's Achilles was anything less than perfect. Another month of racing, and Sanchez could be right back to where he was four years ago, Korir thought. All it would take was good health and a little luck. Every world-class runner needed a little luck. For world class runners were always no more than a heartbeat away from injury or sickness.

As Jesse passed the finish line he closed his hand and pumped his fist. He was back, he thought! Now it was just a matter of being smart and staying healthy. It was happening! He felt an adrenaline surge pump through his veins, while endorphins flooded his brain. They were naturally produced opiates, chemicals that erased all sense of fatigue and pain from his magnificent effort.

There was a buzzing in the crowd as Sanchez finished. It was the din of a shocked crowd. It was like a communal trauma. The staggering disbelief that the American who had fallen from grace, the man who had run such pedestrian times in events leading up to Bislett, could have made such a dramatic turnaround. And even more shocking, in a 'B' race. It was a stunning occurrence. A happening like his Olympic Trials performance, that would surely spark controversy.

As Jesse finished, a race official, with silver hair and a neatly trimmed salt and pepper beard took his arm. "You've been selected for drug testing."

Sanchez just nodded and smiled still elated from his victory. As he walked with the official to the drug testing area, Kip Korir approached. "Next race, you and I." The Kenyan had a wide grin on his hollow-cheeked face. He shook Jesse's hand heartily and patted him on the back.

"Think they'll let me in to the 'A' race at Stockholm?"

"No doubt, Jesse."

"That would be great."

"You ran a smart race tonight. You're learning."

"My confidence is coming back."

"Nothing breeds confidence like success."

"We need to proceed to the drug testing facility, Mr. Sanchez."

"Okay. See you later Kip. Good luck."

"Stockholm. You and me." Korir was still grinning broadly. There was no malice in his tone. It was apparent to Jesse that the Kenyan wanted him to succeed.

As Korir jogged off, Jesse followed the official to the drug testing area.

Chapter 30

It was a relief to Jesse when his drug test results from Bislett came back negative. Though the conclusions were as they should have been, he had fretted. The source of his angst was his troubled past, the disaster in Eugene a recurrent nightmare that constantly plagued him. He realized that athletes on the ITF tour never know when they are going to be tested. Participants are selected randomly with no pre-warning. At least that was the official line of the federation. It seemed ironic to him that he was selected for random testing in the only meet he had placed. Were they still out to get him, he wondered? Why had he been passed over for testing in all the other meets, races in which he wasn't a factor? What was the message? That he'd be left alone as long as he wasn't in the money? What were their motives, he thought? Were they still vindictive? Wasn't the incident that had almost ruined his life enough? Or was he just being paranoid?

None of his questions would be definitively answered, he thought. But after careful deliberation, he ruled out paranoia. He rationalized that his skepticism had just cause. How could he develop trust for an organization that had proven untrustworthy? Even a fool would be suspicious after the ordeal that he'd been through.

Drugs had once again reared their ugly head on the ITF tour. Rumors were rife that EPO and blood doping was at an all-time high. And that record setting middle and long distance runners were the major culprits. The buzz in running circles linked the Italians, in particular the group coached by Donatella Groza, as the most brazen offenders. Along with his Italian troops, Groza counted a profusion of African runners who employed his services. Groza vehemently denied that his runners were involved with drugs. And specifically, EPO and blood doping. They were tandem procedures that state of the art Italian labs had taken to new heights.

Groza's denials came amidst a firestorm of international finger pointing and accusations. But the Italian was adamant in his denials, insisting that his athletes' stellar performances were the result of his perseverance and genius. He maintained that he had trained the same stable of runners for years, "big talents whose results were clear."

"I don't understand the mentality of the finger point-ers," Groza was quoted, concerning the accusations leveled at him by other runners and coaches. "Why can they not accept that my training methods and my athletes are superior? It is always like that when you are at the top. Their jealousy is not my problem."

Jesse wondered about the accusations himself. Especially after what he'd been through. But it was clear that the African runners who 'trained' under the Italian, especially the Kenyans, had performed much better than their Kenyan counterparts who lived and trained elsewhere. The most glaring exception was Kip Korir, who lived and trained in Holland. He never touched foot on Italian soil except when competing. There was no question in Jesse's mind that Korir was clean. As Olympic champion and world record holder, the press tracked his every movement. For him to step out of line would have been diffi-cult, if not impossible.

The ease that Jesse had felt leading up to the Bislett race was no longer with him. Tomorrow night he'd compete in the 'A' division of the Stockholm DN Galan race. He'd be going head to head with Korir, and a profusion of the world's top 800-meter runners. Other than the Olympic Trials, it was the biggest race of his life.

Subsequent to his evening session, a series of controlled 150's, Jesse went back to his hotel and ate a light supper. He went back to his room and tried to read. But he could not keep

265

his mind on his novel. Finally, in frustration, he turned out the lights. He closed his eyes, trying to will a sleep that wouldn't come.

Jesse's roommate, a 200-meter specialist from Namibia, came in later that evening. The two chatted for almost an hour before turning in. It was past midnight before Sanchez finally fell asleep. When he awoke several hours later, his sheets were soaking wet and his stomach was pitching. He stumbled into the bathroom and started vomiting violently. By the time he made it back to his bed, he was drained and still nauseous. Less than fifteen minutes later he was back in the bathroom heaving. That was followed by diarrhea.

The cycle continued throughout the night. The next morning the Namibian hailed a cab. He escorted Jesse to the hospital. There, a Swedish emergency team hooked him up intravenously. They told the Namibian that Sanchez was in guarded condition, his system severely dehydrated.

Jesse remained in the hospital for the next three days, the victim of what had been diagnosed as a severe viral infection. When he was released he was extremely weak. It was a struggle for him to walk.

Korir had visited Jesse in the hospital after his own 800. The Kenyan had once again won easily, taking the Swedish race in a time of 1:42.1 He offered to let Jesse stay at his home in Amsterdam to recover. But Sanchez declined, opting for a rain check later that summer.

The day after his release from the hospital, Jesse flew back to London. At Victoria Station he caught a bus for Glasgow, and slept the entire seven-hour trip. McClanahan's brother Iaian, picked him up at the station. It was a damp and cold evening, the type of weather that did little for Sanchez's weakened spirit.

It took ten days before Jesse regained his strength and was able to resume training. The sickness had sapped him of almost ten pounds, bringing his weight down to a hundred and forty. The weight loss had come from the severe dehydration suffered from his sickness. But a steady dose of Iaian's cooking, a diet heavy in fats, and potatoes of every conceivable kind, brought his weight back up to 148 pounds. It was the target he'd set for summer's end. It was a far cry from how he'd intended to lose the weight. But now that he was there, it would be easier to maintain.

With Stockholm and Nice missed opportunities, Jesse picked a 'B' meet in Hamburg, Germany, to make his return. The German race was run the same day as a major meet in Helsinki, Finland. Jesse's agent had e-mailed him that the Helsinki group would not grant him a spot in their field. He suspected it was a reaction to his Stockholm no-show. It was apparent to him that he would have to prove himself all over again. He would need another Bislett-like performance to get back in the 'A' field.

At Hamburg Jesse was out-kicked, finishing second in 1:45.3. After the race he caught a train to Linz, Austria. Three nights later he won his second 'B' meet of the summer, this time in a world class effort of 1:43.2.

The Linz victory, and the accompanying fast time, secured Sanchez a slot at Zurich, August 17. He was scheduled to run in the main heat of the 800, one of the summer's showcase events. The Swiss meet was scheduled one week subsequent to the Olympics, slated for Athens.

The same day that Jesse received news of his Zurich acceptance, he received e-mail from Korir. The former Kenyan again extended his offer to him to come to Amsterdam. The Kenyan wrote that he was skipping the remaining tour events leading up to the Olympics in Athens, to focus on the Games.

Jesse wasted no time. He e-mailed Korir back and accepted his offer. That afternoon Sanchez boarded a train in Linz. It sped him across the continent toward Amsterdam.

Five days before Korir's scheduled departure for the Olympics in Athens, Jesse Sanchez and Kip Korir shed their warmups. They sat in silence as they slipped on their spikes. Moments later they stepped onto the tartan track. The two ran in tandem as they did the first of a series of 150-meter strides. It was the final warmup preceding their workout. The session would be over quickly, one of short duration and no complexity. It was an 800-meter time trial, an all-out effort, race simulation. As the two men did their strides, Korir's coach Peter Burger studied the two runners intently. He stood on the infield, watch in hand, nervously awaiting the time trial.

The fair-skinned, sandy-haired Dutchman had put on almost fifty pounds since his days as a Dutch ten-thousand-meter champion. That was more than three decades ago. The face was lined. And coupled with his pear-shaped torso, did little to belie his fifty-three years. But his eyes were liquid and clear, shockingly blue. They belonged to a younger man.

Since Jesse Sanchez had come to stay with Korir, Burger had felt uneasy. It was a nervousness he had not relayed to his Kenyan star. Though Sanchez had run track workouts separate from Korir's, it quickly became apparent to Burger that Sanchez was a talent of unprecedented measure. That his invalidated world record had legitimacy, an effort he had previously discounted as drug-aided. As Burger watched Jesse complete McClanahan's workouts, he witnessed Sanchez's raw speed. It was throw-down speed, unmatched by any middle distance runner he'd ever seen.

Coming to Amsterdam and staying with Korir had been a blessing for Sanchez. Jesse had developed an affinity for the city and its people. An air of tolerance permeated the Dutch landscape. It was something that was indefinable, yet unquestionably there. Korir was married to a flaxen-haired Dutch woman. Their union had produced two small children. No eyebrows were raised when the family of mixed skin, strolled

Amsterdam's streets. The Dutch city was unlike most places that Jesse had been. Locales where race was still a pronounced issue. He liked the tolerance of the Dutch. And the country's climate. Holland had mild weather, the type that was ideal for running. The interlude with Korir had boosted his spirits.

Korir was planning on doubling again at the Athens Olympics. He would run both the 800 and 1,500. The same as he'd done at the Sydney Games four years earlier. Korir and Sanchez had done all their road training together, runs where strength was of essence as opposed to speed. But the workout the two were about to attempt was an 800 meter time trial. It would be an all out test of endurance and speed. It was a session that Korir had insisted upon, one that Burger had been reluctant to accept. Korir wondered why his coach was so opposed to the time trial. Did he fear injury? Or was there another reason? It was a workout that Kevin McClanahan had quickly acquiesced to, when Jesse e-mailed for his approval.

The stadium was empty except for the three men. One more that Burger normally permitted for Korir's workouts. It was a luxury afforded him by a grateful country. One that was happy to have an Olympic, and world champion, as a native son.

As the two men completed their final stride, Korir approached Sanchez. "How do you feel, Jesse?"

"Fine."

"If you could take me through the first 400 in 50 seconds, I'd be grateful."

"No problem. But I can't guarantee anything after that. I'm not certain of my fitness level."

"You are in fine condition. Let's go through the four hundred in 50, and see where it takes us."

"Okay."

Korir looked over at Burger. "Are you ready Peter?"

"Yes. Do you want me to signal a start, or do you want to start on your own?"

Korir turned to Jesse for an answer. "I don't care, Kip. Either way."

"Why don't we just start on our own."

Jesse nodded.

The two men lined up in lane one, Korir on the inside of the lane, Jesse to his right. As they leaned forward, Korir said, "Let's go." Sanchez punched his chronograph, but Korir didn't. He ran without a watch, relying on Burger for his splits.

The runners ran stride for stride, hitting the first hundred-meter curve in precisely 12.5. As they moved down the straight Burger felt his pulse beat rapidly as Jesse glided beside the Kenyan. They were poetry in motion, liquid dancers black and brown, skimming over the tartan like sleek gazelles. At two hundred meters Burger checked his watch again. "Twenty five."

Sanchez had an impeccable sense of pace, Burger thought. The American had regained his old sense of metronome like consistency. Running unencumbered, without the worry of shoving and elbowing competitors, the two men were engaged in a match race. Jesse sensed it was the way that running races were surely intended. At three hundred meters Burger glanced at his chronograph. 37.6. Another hundred effort almost exactly. The runners matched each other stride for stride. As they passed four hundred meters, Burger shouted "Forty nine point nine."

As Jesse passed the quarter mark he felt relaxed but anxious. His pace was quicker than what he should be logically running. But he felt good. Too fast, he thought. He would pay big time within the next two hundred meters. He saw Korir from the corner of his eye. The Kenyan appeared to be running smoothly, his breathing not labored. Jesse consciously tried to relax his arms and shoulders as the two men crossed five hundred meters in 1:02.4. He focused straight ahead as they honed in on six hundred meters.

Burger glanced at his watch again at 600 meters. He was about to shout 1:14.5, but held his tongue. "Scheist." He mumbled imperceptibly as he watched the two runners. Jesse, feeling that something was wrong, resisted the temptation to look at his watch. It was movement he knew would cost him valuable time. Instead he drove with his arms. He quickly put a meter, and then five on Korir, as the two men motored around the final curve. At seven hundred meters Burger again glanced at his watch. 1:26.5. Sanchez was lengthening his stride. Korir was tightening and falling further behind. The American looked like a thoroughbred racehorse as he sped down the final straight, Burger thought. He had never seen an 800-meter runner with the type of speed that Sanchez was displaying. Perhaps even a quarter miler, Burger thought. Sanchez could probably run a world class four hundred meter effort as well. He reminded the Dutch coach of the great Cuban, Alberto Juantorena. Except more fluid and graceful.

Jesse felt that he had slowed. Everything was going too easily. He continued, flowing like silk, and punching his chronograph as he hit the finish line. Burger glanced at his watch, his teeth clamped tightly in disgust. Korir followed several seconds later, and the Dutch coach cleared his watch. Both Sanchez and Korir bent over double trying to catch their breath.

Korir looked over at Burger. "What were our times?"

"My watch malfunctioned. I didn't get them."

Korir stared at his coach in disbelief. "How is that possible? You gave us all our splits up to six hundred meters.

"I don't know! But it happened."

Korir turned to Jesse who was still doubled over. "Did you get our times?"

"Just mine." Jesse's voice was soft, almost a whisper.

"What was it?"

Jesse turned his wrist, displaying the crystal for Korir to see. The digits read 1:38.1 A moon-sized pie grin broke on Korir's face. "You have just run the fastest unofficial 800 meters of all time, Jesse Sanchez!"

"Hand held's usually quicker than Accutrack."

"Yes. But we're talking tenths of seconds. You have run more than two seconds faster than what you ran in Eugene. You have regained all your former brilliance and more! You have done today what no other man has even dreamt of doing! You are truly spectacular!"

As Korir turned, he watched Burger who was walking out of the stadium.

"Peter! Do you know what Jesse just did?"

The Dutchman never turned around. He continued out of the stadium to his car. Korir made eye contact with Jesse. "Peter doesn't handle defeat well. I apologize for his bad behavior."

"No need to apologize This wasn't a race. Just a workout. It's one thing to do it here, another in competition."

Korir studied Jesse's face. He looked embarrassed. "There is no reason why you can't own every world record from 800 meters to the five k. With your speed and endurance, it's just a matter of time before they're all yours."

"Just a workout, Kip."

"Jesse, this is no time for humility. I'm sure I ran a PR today, also. But I know I don't have your speed. I could never run 800 meters anywhere close to what you have just done. Right now I may have more endurance than you. But speed? No way! There is no middle distance runner in the world that can match your speed. No one even close."

Jesse just nodded. Then he sat down to remove his spikes. The scary part of the time trial was the ease with which it had gone, he thought. He felt that he could have gone faster if he'd been pushed. He'd unofficially shattered his former world record by over two seconds. And it felt easy. But he knew that a race and a time trial were not the same. But then again, hadn't he run his previous fastest 800 in race conditions? Maybe he could go even faster in a race. If he stayed healthy and the right race came, who knew? Maybe Zurich would be the coronation of a new master. Maybe his day wasn't far off.

That evening Jesse e-mailed McClanahan:

> Kevin,
> Time trial with Korir went better than expected. Ran hand held time of 1:38.1. Splits were even until the last two hundred. I put down the hammer and had something left. Burger's no big fan of mine. Korir's a prince. What do I do now?
> Jesse

The next morning Jesse got McClanahan's return message:

> Lay low between now and Zurich. You got some ball buster workouts coming. Be ready.
> McClanahan

Jesse and Korir went for a long easy run that morning. Conversation was limited. But the message that Sanchez received was clear. Korir wanted him to have his day in the sun, Jesse thought. There was no uneasy sense of jealousy or envy that so often divides competitors.

As the Kenyan ran beside Sanchez he thought of the American's troubled past. It was a career that had gone wrong. By things that were out of Jesse's control. To keep a talent like Jesse Sanchez buried would be a tragic loss, Korir thought. Not only for him, but also for the world of track and field. Stunning genius was rare. Often no more than a once in a lifetime occurrence.

After the televised final of Korir's Olympic victory in the 1,500 meters, Jesse left the Kenyan's wife and her two children, and went for a run. As he ran, he thought of Korir and his stunning accomplishment. He had become the first man in history to double at the two middle distance events in consecutive Games.

Sanchez felt peculiar as he ran. He had done a grueling workout the previous evening, a series of lightning-fast thousand-meter repeats, with a two-minute interval. His stomach had been acting up since the workout. As it had frequently since his bout with the strange virus that had landed him in a Swedish hospital. The recurrent stomach bouts were troubling him. And he'd been struggling with his workouts ever since his 800-time trial with Korir. Through the years of running he'd come to accept fatigue. The kind that a distance runner copes with daily, from the time he awakens in the morning, until he falls asleep at night. But the fatigue he'd been experiencing since the time trial was of a different nature. He felt himself on the cusp of exhaustion.

As he returned from his run, he felt as if his bloated stomach was about to burst. He rushed into the bathroom. As he sat down to eliminate, diarrhea and blood came gushing out of him.

When he emerged from the bathroom he said nothing to Irene. But she noticed that his skin had a wan, pallid pallor. The diarrhea and bleeding continued throughout the afternoon. Jesse told Irene that he was going out for another run, and would be back later. Instead he took a bus to a local hospital, and walked into the emergency room. There he told a resident what he had experienced. Then he fainted. When he woke up he was in a ward with other patients. Needles and tubes snaked in and out of his body, as intravenous fluids fed his veins.

A subsequent consultation with the attending Dutch physician revealed that he had a bleeding ulcer. Whether he had been misdiagnosed in Sweden was hard to determine, the doctor said. Perhaps a viral infection had accompanied the ulcer. But there was one thing that was clear. Jesse had lost a tremendous amount of blood through his stool. And the blood loss via the ulcer had rendered him badly anemic. It was essential for him to continue on a heavy dose of antibiotics after being released from the hospital, the physician explained. And to get as much rest as he possibly could for the next few weeks. Any type of strenuous physical exercise would be dangerous and foolish, the physician explained. Running was not an option. And when he did resume, it was essential that he start back slowly.

The news was devastating to Sanchez, as he lay in his hospital bed. The hard reality struck home that his run in Zurich would never materialize. And that he would return to the states, without having made a dime, the whole summer. And even more crushing was the realization that the world record time trial that he'd run with Korir was nothing more than spit in the wind.

Upon being discharged from the hospital, he returned to Korir's home. That evening he e-mailed Arnold and told her what had happened. The next morning he got up, connected his modem to a phone line in his room, and powered on. He went into mail where there was a new message from Arnold:

Dear Jesse,

I'm so sorry to hear what's happened to you. I really don't know what to tell you. Other than I'm sorry. I think it would be wise of you to listen to the Dutch physician who attended to you. A bleeding ulcer is nothing to fool around with. You need to address it and get well.

You mentioned in your e-mail that you were considering giving up competitive running, and getting on with your life. I can understand your sentiments. Basically, I've done the same thing. Running is not life, Jesse. And romance and dreams do not pay the bills.

Jesse, I have some bad news for you. I'm sorry, because I know that this couldn't have come at a worse time. But for your sake and mine, I have to tell you. I feel that our relation-ship was rooted in romance, not reality. I think a lot of the issues that you brought up to me in the past are true. And that I was in denial at the time. You were right. There is definitely a huge imbalance between us. Educationally, and in other ways too. In the time we spent together, you continually harped on money. How the potential-gap in our earning power would eventually lead to problems. I denied everything you said. I'm sorry for that. Like you, I'm a romantic. I got swept away by a dream. One whose consequences I didn't properly consider. I think—no, I mean I know—that you were right! The discrepancy in our incomes, and earning potentials, would eventually cause nothing but conflict between us. All the issues that you mentioned, concerning choices, and control, would come into play. And I know the way you are, and the way I am. It would not be healthy.

I've met another man, Jesse. One who I realize now, is better suited to my needs. I never intended it to be. It just happened. I can't tell you how sorry I am. But I know this is the right thing for me. In the end, I'm certain it will be better for us both. He's also a physician, Jesse. And it's apparent that the two of us have many things in common. Things that you and I just didn't.

Again, I'm so sorry for any pain that I have caused you. I never intended to hurt you. There will always be a place in my heart for you. But now it's time that both of us face up to reality, and move on with our lives.

Teaching is a noble profession. And hopefully you'll realize all the professional goals that you fell short of in your run-ning.

Wishing you only the best,
Shauna.

Jesse reread the note, his mouth as dry as cotton. He powered down his computer and crawled back in bed. Tears streamed down his cheeks as he lay. He didn't emerge from his room until the next afternoon, when Korir returned from the Olympics. That evening he received another e-mail, this one from his agent. The terse message informed him that their relationship had been terminated.

Three days later Jesse caught a plane back to Houston. He changed his ticket from the original return to New York. Before he left Europe, he e-mailed McClanahan:

Kevin,

I got a 'Dear John' from Shauna. Evidently she's found another guy. She repeated in her e-mail a lot of the things I'd told her before. She's realized that there's more to life than just running. She's right. I gave running all there was to give. It just wasn't in the cards. At this point, the smartest thing for me to do is what I should have done, a long time ago. Just get on with my life. And leave the competitive running behind.

I appreciate everything you've ever done for me. You can't imagine how much. But what Shauna said to me is right. It's time for me to get on with my life. I had my shot as a runner, and it didn't happen. It's not the end of life.

I hope you're not angry with me. You've been the closest thing to a real father I've ever had. I hope we can remain close friends.

Jesse

Chapter 31

On a Sunday night, back in Houston, Jesse was lying in his bedroom. Thunderous banging vibrated the apartment's front door. He heard his mother go to the door. Then he heard muffled voices. Seconds later his bedroom door flew open. McClanahan stormed in. He slammed the door behind him, continued to Jesse's bed, reached down, and grabbed him by the collar. His right hand was doubled in a fist, a paw that looked to Jesse like a Virginia ham. The Scotsman's dark brown eyes spit an ugly venomous rancor.

"Who da ya' think ya' are? Ya' little shite!" As he spoke he yanked Jesse to his feet. He reared back his fist, aimed at Jesse's face. Jesse stood limply, his hands by his side, waiting to be struck. Getting hit by McClanahan wouldn't be nearly as painful as taking a brow beating, he thought. If the Scotsman were going to slug him so be it. He'd put up no resistance. McClanahan just stood like that, holding Jesse by the collar, his fist drawn back, neither man moving. Then he pushed Jesse backwards. Sanchez bounced on the bed. "Ya' ain't even worth hittin', ya' gutless little motherfucker."

As McClanahan bellowed, the front door opened and shut. Carmen Sanchez had taken Jose and left the apartment.

"I know how you must feel, but...."

"Don't ya' tell me how I feel, ya' little shite! Cause ya' got no idea how I feel!"

Jesse's neck heated. He got up from the bed. He pointed his finger back at McClanahan. "It's over Kevin. Let it rest!"

"Don't ya' tell me what's over, ya little fucker! Ya' get dumped by some worthless wooman, and ya' tell me it's over? Do ya' think you're the first motherfucker that ever got dumped on?"

"All you think about is yourself. I've got feelings too. There's more to life than just running."

"Because she said so? That fuckin', back stabber. Who the fuck is she?"

"An honest woman."

"Honest? Ya' stupid, pecker blind little fucker. That son of a bitch don't know the fuckin' meanin' of honest. I was on to her right from the get-go. She saw you as a meal ticket, ya' stupid little shite. When ya' won the trials, she had her sights honed in on yer ass. I never had the balls to tell ya' what was goin' on. From the time ya' got banned, until now. She had more motherfuckin' affairs with world class athletes, than ya' could count with a calculator.

"I...."

"Let me finish! I never thought you'd be stupid enough to buy her a ring. When ya' did, I kept my mouth shut. Thought that maybe gettin' that ring would straighten her ass out. But I shoulda' listened to my gut. Fuckin' leopard never changes its spots. I shoulda' warned ya.'"

"Okay. So I was wrong about her. You want an award because you saw through her? I'll tell you one thing, Kevin. She's right about the running part. I've had my shot. And I've blown it repeatedly. I'm sick of this shit. I'm finished. Go find yourself a new horse to whip."

"Don't ya' tell me when yar day is over!" The Scotsman pointed his long index finger at Sanchez. "I'll tell yar' ass when it's over. Ya' run a fuckin' world record in a time trial, and ya' tell me it's over? Ya' stupid little shite. I thought ya' were smarter than I gave ya' credit for. What kind of mother fuckin' drugs did them assholes put ya' on in that hospital over there? Ya' brainless little shite."

McClanahan was ranting. Jesse had never heard him so upset. The Scotsman's face was dark crimson. And his normally thick Scottish brogue had worsened to an almost undecipherable garble.

"What do you want, Kevin?"

"What do I want? What the fuck do yooo want? After all the shite ya' been through? Ya' gonna quit now?"

"That's right. I'm going to get on with my life."

McClanahan stroked his beard. He just stood staring silently at Jesse. The two stared each other down for what seemed an eternity to Jesse before Mcclanahan finally said, "When ya' get yar head out of yar ass, let me know. Cause in the condition yar in now, ya' ain't worth fuckin' with."

At that the Scotsman turned, and walked out of the room. Jesse heard the front door slam as McClanahan left. When Carmen Sanchez returned later that evening, she never said a word to Jesse. Sanchez knew that his mother was a co-conspirator with the Scot's visit. But neither his mother, nor the Scotsman, had any idea of the kind of pain he was feeling, he reasoned. They didn't understand. That there was only so much pain a man could take.

Chapter 32

"I want Jesse Sanchez to rabbit me the through the first half mile. Tell the DigiNet people I insist."

Peter Burger's face turned a ghostly shade of gray. "That's not possible, Kip. The rabbits in that race have already been selected. Besides, there is no love lost for Jesse Sanchez or his coach in Eugene, Oregon. Both are pariahs in that town."

"Peter, I am the world record holder in the 800 meters, the 1,500 meters, and the mile. The DigiNet people know that. That's why they are offering a multi-million dollar purse. Without my presence, their meet has no marquis value." The Kenyan's tone was soft and matter of fact.

Burger reached into his pants and extracted a pair of silver nail clippers. He opened them and began to trim the nails on his left hand. "It's not wise to issue ultimatums, Kip. Especially for a man whose at the point of his career that you are. You can potentially win two million dollars in this meet. A million dollars for winning and another million for setting a world record. Do you really feel it's worth risking all that for some suspect American? A man who, undoubtedly, would not do the same for you, if he were in a similar position?"

"First of all, Peter, I do not share your pessimism concerning Jesse Sanchez's character. The man was wrongfully convicted of drug charges. Solely because of the unpopularity of his coach. A man whom I have come to respect. And secondly, I'm certain that Jesse would do the same thing for me, if he were in my position. Like me, he loves this sport. And like me, he values fair play."

"I refuse to exert any kind of pressure on the DigiNet people. Especially not to include Jesse Sanchez as a rabbit in their mile." Burger closed the nail clippers and slipped them back into his pocket.

"Peter, you have profited richly from my running."

"I have been your coach. Who has made you?"

"I am grateful for all you efforts. But I've been at least an equal partner in this relationship. Now I'm asking for a favor. Something that comes from my heart."

"I will do nothing to encourage Jesse Sanchez's acceptance as a rabbit in the DigiNet mile. That is final."

"I understand Peter. And I accept your decision. But if that's your final word, from this day on, we are divested of any business relationship. You have a potential to collect three hundred thousand dollars in the DigiNet mile. That is, if I were to win the race, and set a world record. That's your fifteen per cent fee of a two million dollar purse."

"If you persist with your nonsense, there will be no DigiNet mile. And you will become the same pariah that is Jesse Sanchez. Of that fact, I guarantee."

"That's a chance I'll just have to take."

The Dutchman's cheeks flushed-red. He pointed his finger at the Kenyan and shook it menacingly. "You will regret this. You are making the most grievous error of your life if you continue down this road. Your loss in future earnings is more than your narrow focus is capable of seeing."

"I have nothing to lose. Only my self-dignity, if I fail to do what I know is right. I have all the money I will ever need. At this point, money is secondary."

"You are a fool."

The gentle look left Korir's face. "I would appreciate if you would leave my house now, Peter. Perhaps in the future we can speak again. When cooler heads prevail."

"You will become a pariah, just like Jesse Sanchez and his coach." Burger's neck had reddened like a tomato.

"Perhaps. But that's a risk I choose to take."

Burger got up and stormed out of Korir's home.

Two days later Korir e-mailed Jesse:

"Dear Jesse,

I hope your health is returning, and that the disappointment of your broken engagement is healing. I don't envy you. I'm certain your spirit must still be deeply wounded.

Fortunately, I have some urgent news for you that is very positive. As you know, DigiNet is sponsoring a mile October 15, Hayward Field, Eugene, Oregon. There is a million-dollar prize being offered for the winner. Plus an additional million-dollar bonus, for a world record. That, and a million-dollars for a new American record.

I know that your health has been frail, and this leaves you little time for training. But I have made arrangements through meet directors, to include you, as one of the two rabbits in the field. Your only task is to take me through the half mile in 1:50. For that you will be guaranteed $10,000. I am certain you are capable of that, even if you're not in top form.

Peter and I no longer have an association. So, like you, I will be going to this meet without an agent. I know that ten thousand dollars is not a large sum of money, but it is the most I could bargain for. In addition to your fee, I've arranged for meet directors to send you two round-trip airline tickets, and a room for lodging.

Good luck in your training. Looking forward to seeing you in Eugene.

Please advise.

Sincerely,

Kip

Jesse's pulse quickened as he read the e-mail. He wasted no time as he phoned McClanahan. The flare up between the two was quickly buried as Jesse told the Scotsman the news. Following their conversation, he sent a return e-mail to Korir:

Kip,

Can't thank you enough. I'll be there.

Jesse

Chapter 33

"It's deja vu all over again," Mickey Landis said to Chip Martin. The two were sitting in the broadcast booth of ESPN 2 as the runner's stretched and warmed up on Hayward Field.

"That's right," Landis said. "This is a race steeped in controversy, not unlike a similar race that was held right here in Hayward Field."

"And the race that Mickey's talking about was the Olympic Trials final, for the 2000 games in Sydney. That's the race where Jesse Sanchez, a virtual unknown in track and field, shocked the world with a stunning 1:40.5, 800 meter. He ran that time in the Trials final, a world record. But it was a short-lived world record. A record that was stripped from him when he tested positive for anabolic steroids."

"That's right, Chip. But a conviction that was ultimately challenged and overturned. A former employee of the now defunct drug testing company that released Jesse Sanchez's fated results, came forward and cleared his name. What could have been a long, protracted legal battle was settled quickly. Jesse Sanchez's name was cleared. And in return he agreed to pursue no further claims against the ITF."

"It's a decision that still breeds heated controversy in track and field circles. There are still more than a fair share of cynics who insist that Jesse Sanchez's record run, a record which was not allowed to stand, was drug-aided."

"And throwing even more fuel on that controversy is his being chosen as one of the two rabbits in this field," Landis said. "World 800, 1,500, and mile record-holder Kip Korir, according to reliable sources, was said to have pressured meet directors to include Sanchez as this race's rabbit. It was either that, or hold this contest without Korir. And a world class mile race today without Kip Korir would be no contest at all. It would have no meaning, and no drawing power."

"That's right," Martin said. "And the controversy continues to roil. Korir is said to have split all ties with his former coach-agent, Peter Burger, the Dutchman who played such a major role in Kip Korir's running career. The imbroglio surfaced when Burger failed to honor Korir's request of including Jesse Sanchez as a rabbit in this field."

"Why Jesse Sanchez?" Martin asked Landis. "Why would the Kenyan have been so insistent to include the American?"

"I can only tell you what I've heard through the grapevine. And that is a two-fold answer. First of all, Jesse Sanchez and the former Kenyan, became close friends this summer. As Sanchez struggled along in 'B' meets on the ITF tour, he and the former Kenyan cemented a strong friendship. And secondly, sources tell me that Korir was carrying an innate sense of guilt. Ever since Jesse Sanchez's ill-fated effort, right here, on this same Hayward Field Track a little over four years ago. Insiders claim that Korir never felt secure about his own record. That Jesse Sanchez had been wrongly stripped of what was rightfully his."

"How about the time trial rumor that's spread like wildfire throughout the track and field world?"

"Apparently Korir has told close friends that Jesse Sanchez ran a 1:38.1, 800. That supposedly took place in a private time trial, that the two men ran just before Korir left to Athens for the Olympics. Korir's former coach-agent, Peter Burger, who was allegedly present at that workout, denies the claim. But Korir doesn't. When pressed if Sanchez had run that kind of time, Korir only told me that Jesse Sanchez had not lost a step since his world record 800. And was as fit as ever. And that's coming after Achilles surgery. And a host of other problems the American has endured since that fateful day. If there's any truth to the alleged time trial, Jesse Sanchez, prior to his bout with a bleeding ulcer, had regained all his former brilliance. And more! His rumored 800-meter time trial far exceeds the bounds of what any living runner could touch. If he's pushed the envelope that far, he's in a class by himself for 800-meter runners."

"So in a sense, what you're saying is that Jesse Sanchez was hand-picked, by Korir, to rabbit this race. As a form of reparation?" Martin said.

"That's exactly right. A ten thousand dollar fee for taking him through the half in 1:50."

"A pittance compared to the kind of pay day that Kip Korir is facing," Martin said.

"Right. Ten thousand dollars is a long way from the seven-figure purse that Kip Korir stands to make. But for Jesse Sanchez, a man who has barely made bus money in track and field, ten thousand dollars will at least buy some groceries."

"Okay. So now that we've discussed the Jesse Sanchez controversy, let's get to the real heart of this race. Kip Korir is obviously the favorite. Who else in this field can give him a run for his money?"

"There are three other men who have a legitimate chance of upending Korir, and taking a shot at his world record mile best of 3:42.1." Landis said. "There's fellow Kenyan Joseph Barmasai, a man who was out kicked by Korir in the final fifty meters of the Olympics in Athens. There's Moroccan Mohammed Hissou, who next to Korir has run the fastest 1,500 meters this year. And finally, there's British star Graham Kent, a young man who is being hailed as the greatest middle distance runner from Great Britain, since the Sebastian Coe and Steve Ovett era."

"And there's two Americans in the field who have good chances of breaking the existing American mile record of Jim Ballard. Ballard, you'll remember, was the man who seemed destined to be America's greatest miler ever. That coming after his stunning bronze medal performance at Sydney. But a tragic automobile crash, just six weeks later, snuffed out his life. With his death, America's return in the mile appeared to have been cut cruelly short. But since then, two more American milers have emerged. Young men who are eager to grab the torch that Ballard left behind. I'm speaking, first of all, of Todd Earnhardt, from Spokane, Washington a 3:47.2 miler. And secondly, Floridian Steve Anderson, a man who ran a 3:47.8 this past summer at Zurich. A million dollars for an American record as well," Landis said. "That's 3:46.3, that they need to better the American record."

"Both records definitely ready to go," said Landis. "Especially in light of Korir's lightning fast 1:41.2, 800, a time that he popped just weeks ago at the Olympics. He's fit and healthy. Look for some excitement out there and a real burner."

"Any other possible surprises?"

"Unlikely," Landis said. "Look for the winner, and best American, to come out of one of the men I've just mentioned. No dark horses in this one."

"Okay Mickey. Let's go down on the track as the runners get ready for, the largest paying mile ever staged on American soil."

As milers strode down the straight-aways, Korir approached Jesse.

"How do you feel, Jesse?"

"Not as fit as when we ran our time trial. But a lot better than when I landed in the hospital."

"All I need are a pair of back to back 55 quarters, Jesse. Then you can step off the track."

"I'll give it my best."

"Just relax." The Kenyan's voice was steady. "It's twelve seconds slower than your time trial in Amsterdam. You could come off your death bed and run a 1:50 half."

"Here's hoping this won't put me there."

"You'll be fine. Just run tempo."

Jesse nodded and took off for his final hundred-meter stride down the Hayward Field Track. As he glanced at the stands, a packed house of over fourteen thousand Oregonians, he remembered the fateful night in June over four years ago. It was a night when he'd run 800 meters. Faster than any human had ever gone before. It was a record that was wrongfully thrown out. A mark that still had not been equaled.

As Jesse searched the stands, he spotted NATF President, Joseph Nixon, sitting in a special box. Next to him was ITF President, Primo Magiano. As Sanchez watched the pair, he felt his fists tighten. It was difficult for him to separate which one he loathed more. Though neither had been caught, rumors were rife that both were thieves. That each had tapped corporate giants for millions of dollars in under the table payments. The money had allegedly been hidden in numbered accounts, in offshore havens.

Both Nixon and Magiano were lowlifes, Jesse thought. Men who had sold their souls. And were universally despised by those who knew the truth. Jesse made eye contact with Magiano. The Italian was clad in a fashionable gray silk suit, a perfectly trimmed pencil white mustache, covering a thin upper lip. Nixon's suit was dark, a color like the cobalt beard erupting from his creased skin. Sanchez made eye contact with them. He smiled sardonically, and waved with his fingers. Just like McClanahan had done in Indianapolis. First the Italian turned away, then Nixon. Jesse turned around, and jogged back to the starting line.

Sanchez took his place on the inside of a semi-circle, the starting line for the race's 15 competitors. Directly to his right was the great Spanish runner Fernando Pena, a fellow half miler, the race's other rabbit. Pena had an 800-meter p.r. of

1:42.3. Along with Jesse he would share the first two laps before dropping out.

On the outside of Pena was Korir. And to his right the challengers. They were men all anxious to take a shot at the multi-million dollar jackpot. It was the largest amount of money ever put up for grabs on American soil, for a single race. As Jesse stood, watching the starter's pistol rise in the air, he felt remarkably at ease. Calmer than he'd ever felt before a big race. There was little pressure on him. Just run a half-mile at the pedestrian pace of 1:50 and step off the track. Do that and ten thousand dollars would be his. It would be the first payday of his career, a circuit that had gone nowhere.

As the gun popped, Jesse and the Spaniard, Pena, took command of lane one. At the hundred-meter mark, the field filed behind them content to let the rabbits do their work. As Jesse and Pena went through 220 yards in 27.5 seconds, exactly on the pace that Korir had requested, Sanchez felt as if he were jogging. At the quarter mark he saw the digital read out on the clock light at 55.1. He felt awkward, abbreviating his stride. It was a pace that felt much slower than what he had anticipated. It felt so deceptively easy, that he wondered if was he deluding himself? Surely the time he had been forced to take off, and the limited speed training that he'd done since his 800-meter time trial in Amsterdam, would take its toll. Just keep you mind on the pace, Jesse muttered silently. One more lap at a 55 second pace, and he'd be ten thousand dollars richer.

It was money that would be sorely needed at home. Stay focused, Jesse, thought. Do the job and stay focused.

In the broadcast booth Landis and Martin chattered rapidly. "So far the rabbits are doing their jobs perfectly," Landis said. "They've gone through the quarter in fifty five seconds, a pace that will take the runners through a 1:50 half mile."

"Good rabbiting," Martin said. "Pena looks relaxed running this pace. But not so Jesse Sanchez. His stride appears chopped, like he's laboring."

"Either that, or he's not accustomed to running this slowly. You've got to remember, that this is a young man who once possessed 21 second, two-hundred meter speed. Of course that was before his Achilles tendon was cut on. And that could be bothering him too."

"Regardless of that, the rabbits are doing their jobs. And Kip Korir, who's definitely the man, laying just in back of Jesse Sanchez, looks like he's going for a stroll in the park."

"Kip Korir is the current world-record holder, with a personal best of 3:42.1. With a win today, and anything faster than that, he will be worth over two million dollars. Next to Korir is fellow Kenyan Joseph Barmasai, a man who finished just a hair behind Korir at last month's final in Athens. And on the outside of him is British star Graham Kent, a young Englishman whom I mentioned earlier in the broadcast. Bunched behind the three are the Moroccan Mohammed Hissou, and Americans Todd Earnhardt and Steve Anderson. New Zealander Ron Green. Australian Pat Edwards. And Kenyans, Henry Keter and Moses Boit."

At 660 yards there were few changes in the tightly bunched field. Jesse and the Spaniard danced around the curve in 1:22.5, precisely on 1:50 half mile pace. As Sanchez and the Spaniard powered around the curve, Jesse heard the sound of scraping spikes. Then he felt the sharp sting of a spiked shoe strike his right calf. And then a hard hand, as it struck the small of his lower back. The force of the hand pushed him forward. It jolted him, but he did not lose his balance. He continued running, more surprised than shaken.

"Oh my God," Landis blurted. "This is truly tragic. World record holder Kip Korir has just been kicked by American Todd Earnhardt. The naturalized Kenyan who is now a

Dutch citizen, along with Earnhardt and fellow American Steve Anderson, have all gone down. Runners are hurdling the fallen trio as if this were a steeplechase. And the pack is quickly pulling away from the fallen athletes. Kip Korir is sitting on the infield grass, not moving. The world record holder is out of this field!"

As Jesse glanced back he realized what had happened. Korir was gone. And other runners were too. As he and the Spaniard approached the half-mile mark, Jesse's addled mind struggled to assess his next move.

"What a horrid turn of events," Martin said. "Kip Korir, the man who holds the world record in the mile, is gone. And with his departure the luster of this race. Plus both Americans are out of it. So any chance for a new American mile record is gone too."

As Jesse hit the half-mile mark, out of the corner of his eye, he saw the Spaniard pull wide. As Pena walked toward the stands, Sanchez glanced at the clock. 1:50. He had done his job. Ten thousand dollars was his. But it was a bittersweet victory. Korir, the man who had made the evening possible for him, was gone. And worse than that, he was possibly injured.

"The rabbits have done their jobs," Landis said. "But again, in case you've just tuned in, a tragic set of events has unfolded. From the best that we could see, Kip Korir appeared to have been accidentally tripped by Todd Earnhardt. A crash followed, bringing down Earnhardt, Korir, and American Steve Anderson. Korir is lying on the infield near the two hundred-meter curve. Anderson is standing with his hands on his hips, his race over. And the other American, Todd Earnhardt, the man who apparently spiked Korir, has dropped out too."

"Tragic," Martin repeated. "Absolutely tragic."

As Jesse saw the digital readout, he remembered a scene from his past. Hayward Field, over four years ago, the Olympic Trials. He remembered lunging for the finish line. And then lying on the track, the sounds of thundering spikes flying over and around him, certain that he had lost. He remembered the elation of learning that he had won. And then the hostile press who attacked him afterwards. As he recalled the event, a myriad of images flashed on his screen. Positive drug test. Appeal. Loss. Flight. Achilles rupture. Vindication. Rehabilitation. Pain. Sickness. Desertion. Heartbreak.

And then images of his mother and brother shot by. And then of McClanahan, and the many friends in Houston who had supported him. The vision of Korir flashed. And as he imagined him lying on the infield, McClanahan's thick Scottish brogue echoed in his brain. He heard split times from past workouts being yelled out. And the gentle taunts and the teases, words that always made him try harder. As the images and words flashed in Jesse's brain, he moved forward, his arms and legs pulling him toward nine hundred meters. As he ran he glanced to his right. The figure of Joseph Barmasai had pulled next to him. Jesse retained his rhythm. He and the second Kenyan ran stride for stride as the eleven hundred-yard-mark approached.

"Pena has pulled out on cue, but Jesse Sanchez continues," Landis said. "Chip, is there a bonus for him if he takes the field through three quarters?"

"I'm not sure. I apologize to our viewers for my ignorance. But that's information which I haven't received. To the best of my knowledge, Sanchez and Pena were 800-meter rabbits. And after that, the field was on its' own. But it is very possible there may be additional bonus money for Jesse Sanchez, to take this field through three quarters."

As Martin spoke, Sanchez, Barmasai, and the Moroccan Mohammed Hissou, began pulling away from the field. As they approached the bell lap, they were fifteen yards ahead of Englishman Graham Kent. He was followed by a tightly bunched pack another ten meters back.

As the bell for the final lap rang, he felt Barmasai surging. Sanchez went with him, and there was a thunderous roar from the crowd. The two men went through three quarters in 2:47.

"That was a relatively slow third quarter," Landis said. "Fifty seven seconds. But they're still on world record pace!"

As Barmasai moved, Jesse matched strides with the Kenyan.

"This is bizarre!" Landis shouted. "Jesse Sanchez, the man who was hand picked to rabbit the first half mile of this race for Kip Korir, is still in this contest, with one lap to go."

"And he looks good," Martin said. "So far he's not showing any signs of tying up."

"This is a mile, though" Landis said loudly. "And as far as I know, Jesse Sanchez has never run a competitive mile. My guess is he doesn't have the endurance to pull off something like this. Especially in light of his latest health problem. A bleeding ulcer that cut his European tour short in early September."

"We've got less than a quarter of a mile to find out," Martin returned. "We'll see if Jesse Sanchez had something up his sleeve that none of us were aware of."

The thunder of the Hayward Field stands was deafening as Sanchez, Barmasai, and Hissou roared toward the final two twenty. As Jesse approached the final curve, Kip Korir got up from the track. He watched with wide eyes as the drama unfolded.

As Sanchez moved, he never saw the Moroccan who stumbled and lunged behind him. The Moroccans spike caught the back of Jesse's heel. A wave of panic flooded Jesse's thoughts as his right shoe came off. The Moroccan fell, and then it was just Jesse Sanchez and Joseph Barmasai. The two men hit the final 220 in 3:14. They had covered the last two twenty in 27 seconds.

As Jesse ran, the sharpness of the stinging spike wound fresh on the back of his naked heel, he felt panicked. The imbalance of running with just one shoe sent strange sensations throughout his body, every time his socked foot hit the tartan. As he moved he could hear the heavy breathing of the Kenyan beside him. And the heavy footsteps of what appeared to be a laboring runner. Stay focused, he repeated silently to himself. Don't panic.

Two twenty left, Jesse, thought. It had been more than four years since he had run twenty-one seconds for two hundred meters. And that had come in a workout on the Rice Track. Two of the best runs in workouts. One in Houston, and another in Amsterdam. The only great race of his ill fated-career—his 800 trials run— had been thrown out.

He was still a nothing runner, he thought. A nobody who had done nothing and proved nothing. Suddenly he was the focal point of a bizarre race. A foolish clown running with one shoe. The runner who belonged in his place was gone. Korir had pressured race directors into making Jesse a rabbit. And now he was finished. He had been knocked down, possibly injured. Sanchez had no idea.

As that horror flooded his brain, his thoughts turned toward the Scotsman. Gut wrenching workouts flew through his mind. Interval sessions through heat, cold, sleet and rain. McClanahan always there timing him. It wasn't worth it, he thought. Not what he'd gone through. All that work with nothing to show. And then it became clear. Everything crystallized in that split second. He knew exactly what he had to do.

"Jesse Sanchez is opening up!" Landis yelled. "What a tremendous stride! Just like that, he's opened up a huge gap on Joseph Barmasai. And unless he's hit by a freight train, this race is Slinger Sanchez's for the taking!"

As Jesse pumped his arms for the final hundred meters, it seemed as if every muscle in his body was screaming. But the pain was not unwelcome. Intuitively he knew he was flying. Sprinting at a breakneck speed. His body reverberated from the thunder in the stands as he sprinted toward the finish.

"Unreal!" Landis screamed. "Unreal! Unreal! Unreal! Jesse 'Slinger' Sanchez has obliterated this world class field in the unbelievable world record time of 3:39.6! The first man under 3:40! A new world-record! A new American-record! A purse of three million dollars for a rabbit who was scheduled to drop out at the half mile point! I can't believe this!"

"I've seen two races in this stadium that I'll never forget as long as I live," Martin chimed in. "And they've both been run by this man."

"Ladies and gentleman, you have just witnessed the fastest mile ever run. By a man who may ultimately go down as the greatest middle distance runner ever to lace up a pair of spikes. Jesse 'Slinger' Sanchez from Houston, Texas. Oh my God! What a performance!"

As Jesse finished, he bent over double. After catching his breath he jogged across the infield toward Korir, who was jogging toward him.

"How are you, Kip?"

"Fine. Only my pride was wounded."

"This victory is half yours. I want you to split the pot with me."

The Kenyan shook his head, his eyes hot. "No way! This day is yours. I couldn't have run what you did today. I know my fitness level. You were almost two seconds quicker than what I could have possibly run."

Jesse was dumbfounded at the Kenyan's words.

"How can I ever repay you?"

"You just have. You've lifted a burden off my shoulders that I've been carrying for over four years. Ever since you were wrongfully convicted. This is not just compensation for what you've gone through. Nor is it justice. But for me, it's some relief. It is proof to the world of your true greatness. My only regret, is that I couldn't have been on the track with you. I would have loved to have felt you move, and then watched you kick down that final straight away."

As the crowd roared, Sanchez led Korir out on the track. The two men then took a victory lap together. As they finished, Jesse spotted McClanahan on the far side of the track. He shook hands with Korir. Then he jogged toward the Scotsman. He reached McClanahan and stopped directly in front of him. With a dour look on his face, Jesse said, "How much is fifteen per cent of three million dollars?"

The Scotsman's face lost its color. "Whadda ya' mean?"

"Just that. What's fifteen percent of three million dollars."

Sanchez waited. The Scotsman had a peculiar look in his eyes. As if he'd seen a ghost. "$450,000 grand?"

"Think you can retire on that?"

"Ya' shittin' me?"

"Does it sound like I'm shittin' ya'?" As Sanchez studied McClanahan's face, he saw something he'd never seen before. A glistening pearl slid from the corner of the Scotsman's right eye painting his cheek.

"This time piss in front of the whole stadium if they want ya' to."

Jesse just nodded. For three million bucks, he probably would.

The drug tests were administered immediately after his run. And the results were done that night. Jesse tested negative. The next day, Jesse and McClanahan boarded a flight back to Houston. Three million dollars has been deposited in Sanchez's account. As they flew across Oregon heading east, McClanahan reached into his satchel. He lifted out a Guinness and opened it. Five beers later his eyes were closed, and he was sleeping soundly. A funny little smile was pasted on his face, a grin that was unlike any Jesse had ever seen.

As McClanahan slept, Sanchez reached into his nylon jacket. He pulled out a package. It was a box wrapped in newspaper that Korir had given him right before he boarded his plane. Jesse shook it. Then he took his time as he tore off the wrapping paper. Inside was a white-velvet box. He opened it slowly. His eyes widened. Staring up at him were a pair of gleaming gold medals. They were affixed to silk ribbons, a note stuffed underneath. The medals had a trance-like effect on him. Finally he reached for the note:

Dear Jesse,
  These are the 800-meter gold medals from Sydney and Athens. I know what you are thinking. That Kip Korir is giving you a gift, a gratuitous offering, like Emil Zatopek gave to Ron Clarke. In fact, this is not so. For this is not a gift. I am merely returning to you, what was rightfully yours all along.
  The 1,500 gold medals I will keep for myself. Perhaps that will provide incentive for you to continue in this sport, and bring home that gold at the next Olympics. If not, it is of no consequence. No one can diminish what you have accomplished. You know what you have done, as do those who know and love you. What the rest of the world thinks is of no value.
  Your friend,
  Kip Korir

Jesse gazed at the medals for several minutes, before shutting the case.

A tailwind pushed the jet as the craft hurtled through the universe. It was the kind of wind that runners pray for.

Here's a peek at Bruce Glikin's next novel, <u>SLUMMING</u>
<u>ANGELS</u>. You'll want to read all of it from Amber Fields
Publishing.

Internet address: www.amberfields.com
Phone: 1-877-RUN-GUNS

*Private eye Johnny Dakota finds himself entangled with a well en-
dowed blonde whose m.o. redefines nymphomania. The case involves a
Texas oil tycoon, three potentially deadly women, a life insurance
scam, blackmail, and of course, murder.*

That afternoon when I awoke I felt rested. The room
was quiet and I was alone. As I got out of bed I saw a sheet of
powder blue hotel stationery lying on top of the dresser. I went
over and picked it up.

"I'll never forget you. Kristine."

The note was scrawled in the center of the sheet in
peacock blue ink. I stared emptily at the message, thinking of
the previous night, before laying it back on the dresser.

After a shower and a shave I slipped on a pair of light
tan Chinos, a grape colored polo shirt, and White Nike
Cerrone's with blue and red leather stitching on the sides.

I left the room, went downstairs, and continued out to
the patio. I sat on a white plastic chair at a matching table. A
brown wooden pole was stuck in the middle of the table and a
saffron umbrella flowered at the top. An ocean breeze swept
across the beach. It had a fresh tangy scent.

I ordered Huevos Rancheros with a side of bacon, fresh
orange juice, boleros, and a pot of black coffee. I finished and
went back upstairs to my room and opened my suitcase. I got
out my holstered Smith and Wesson, fitted it behind my right
hip, and slipped into a thin powder blue nylon shell before
heading out the door.

At the edge of town I spotted a green and white diamond sign, pulled into the Pemex station and filled up. The Dodge took close to forty liters of gas.

I paid for the gas, tipped the attendant, and headed out to the foothills to the address Kristy had given me. The house was about a quarter mile off the main highway sitting on the edge of a cliff. It was a split level ranch job with a red tile roof.

I pulled up on a crushed stone driveway behind a British racing green Ford Explorer, an Eddie Bauer model that looked brand new.

I killed the engine, got out of the Dodge and walked to the front door. The door was chocolate colored oak with thick pebbled glass panes on the top. I rang the doorbell, waited, and rang again. Then I banged on the door with my fist. I continued the ringing and banging drill for several minutes with no response before reaching into my jacket and pulling out a thin metal pick. A few deft pokes and the tumbler released. I slipped the pick back inside my jacket. Then I reached for my gun. I pushed open the front door and made my way inside. I was gripping the Smith and Wesson with both hands as I made my way down a corridor of slate gray stone tile.

"Harrington?"

No answer.

I walked slowly down the corridor until I came to a dining room. A sprawling rectangular glass table set on a chrome base filled most of it. In the center of the table sat a tall crystal vase holding an arrangement of silk flowers. The table was surrounded by chrome chairs with tan leather seats and backs. A crystal chandelier hung suspended from the ceiling. I was facing a mirrored wall and I saw my reflection.

I moved slowly through the dining room and into the kitchen. The kitchen floor was covered in reddish brown Mexican tile. The counters were blond butcher block and everything stood at attention.

I paused for a moment. And then I continued into the den. At the far end of the den were glass sliding doors that looked out onto a patio and a heart shaped swimming pool. The pool was surrounded by a lush tropical garden. On the wall to my right were ceiling to floor bookcases packed with tomes. On the wall to my left was a tan leather couch. A matching love seat was wedged up to the left of the couch.

Fronting the couch and the love seat was a large Oriental rug done in earth tones with a navy blue border. The ends of the rug were fringed in white lace.

Sitting on the couch in a peach colored sundress with matching sandals was Jennifer Robindale. She was wearing dangling silver earrings with turquoise stones and a matching silver and turquoise necklace. Her hair was pulled back by a fire engine red comb. Her lips and nails were painted a like hue.

She was holding a small black gun in her hands. From where I stood it looked like a .22 Biretta. The blush on her face was a soft peach flame mirroring her dress. But her skin had an unhealthy looking pasty pallor.

Lying about a yard from Jennifer's feet on his back on the Oriental rug was Carter Harrington. He was wearing an egg shell white tennis shirt with a green alligator on the pocket, navy walking shorts, and tan Sperry Topsiders without socks. His hard blue eyes were open but the intensity wasn't there.

Harrington's left temple looked like a dartboard. The holes were small and neat, purplish fissures uniform in size. Streaks of clotted plum colored blood painted his ear and the side of his face. A pool of thick red soup had soaked the Oriental. A fly buzzed around his ear as he lay. Harrington didn't seem to mind.

ORDER FORM

Qty.	Title	Amount
	Slinger Sanchez Running Gun @ $15.95 ea	

Florida & Ohio residents, add 7% sales tax	
Houston residents, add 8.25% sales tax	
Standard Shipping - $3.00, first book	
+$.50 for each additional book	
Call the 1-877 number below if special shipping arrangements are desired.	
TOTAL ENCLOSED	

NAME _____

ADDRESS _____

CITY _____ STATE _____ ZIP _____

DAYTIME PHONE NO. _____
Please provide a daytime phone no. in case there are any questions
regarding your order.

❑ Check or money order
❑ VISA or MasterCard
❑ American Express

Card No. _____
Expiration Date _____

Signature _____

To order by mail, fill out the above order form and send check, money order or credit card authorization to: Amber Fields Publishing Co., P.O. Box 35746, Houston, TX 77235-5746.

To order by phone, fill out the above order form, call 1-877-RUN-GUNS and be ready to supply the operator with ordering details.

Orders can also be taken via e-mail or Internet — contact Bruce Glikin at bglikin@msn.com or visit the web site: www.amberfields. com